RETURN OF THE SHADE

RETURN OF THE SHADE

Bevis Longstreth

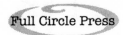

Return of the Shade
Bevis Longstreth

Copyright 2009 by Bevis Longstreth

Published September 2009 by Full Circle Press LLC

Interior and cover illustrations © 2009 by Ben Potter

Cover and interior design © 2009 by Full Circle Press LLC

Map on page 9 from *Forgotten Empire: The World of Ancient Persia*, edited by J.E. Curtis and Nigel Tallis. © 2006 The Trustees of the British Museum. Published jointly by the University of California Press and the British Museum. Used by permission.

Full Circle Press LLC
PO Box 71
West Hartford, Vermont 05084
www.FullCirclePress.com

ISBN: 978-0-9790046-2-9

Library of Congress Cataloging-in-Publication data
Longstreth, Bevis.
  Return of the shade / Bevis Longstreth.
    p. cm.
  ISBN 978-0-9790046-2-9 (pbk.)
 1. Parysatis, Queen of Persia—Fiction. 2. Achaemenid
dynasty, 559-330 B.C.—Fiction. 3. Queens—Iran--Fiction.
4. Iran—Kings and rulers--Fiction. 5. Iran—History—To
640--Fiction. I. Title.
  PS3612.O545P37 2008
  813'.6--dc22
                                    2008029033

❧ ACKNOWLEDGEMENTS

I AM GRATEFUL to those who undertook to read and advise on the manuscript at early stages in its development. They include Judy Amory, Susan Heath, Allan Miller, Franny Taliaferro, Amy White, and Marie Winn. Their comments provided much needed encouragement while enlarging my vision and improving my approach to the subject matter.

To my wife, Clara, I am grateful for her enthusiastic support for this project, her close reading of various drafts, and her helpful responses to my questions, large and small.

Again, as in *Spindle & Bow*, I enjoyed the good fortune of having as an editor, Karen Shepard, Lecturer in English at Williams College and distinguished novelist. Her wise suggestions and frequent challenges contributed in many dimensions to the ultimate shape, style, and content of the manuscript.

The sketches atop each chapter are the work of Ben Potter, a compelling artist and teacher living in Maine. They derive from bas reliefs found in the Persian palaces at Persepolis and Susa. I feel lucky in having his willing and timely help. And thanks to John Duncan, a busy design professional from New York City, for making it possible to include the map of the Persian Empire.

This project would not have been attempted without the ancient yet sturdy guideposts furnished by Herodotus and the other Greek historians who recorded the rise and fall of the Persian Empire. To them, my debt is large.

RETURN OF THE SHADE

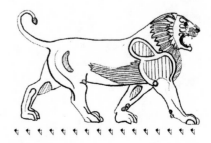

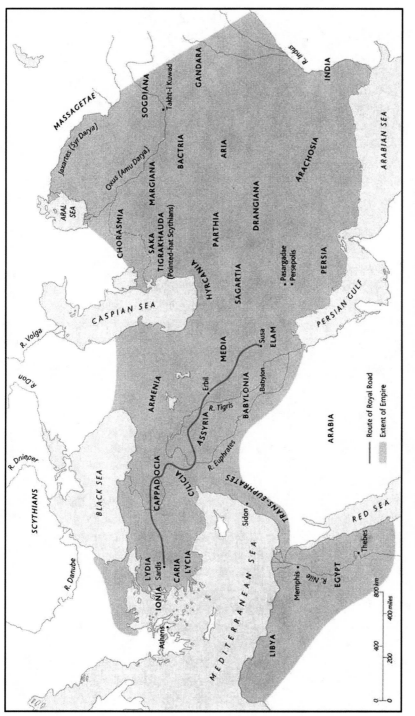

Map of Persian Empire at its greatest extent. Used by permission.

❧ PROLOGUE:

THE SHADE

 I AM PARYSATIS, an Achaemenid. My lineage reaches the founding of this Empire, 106 years before my birth. I am the wife of Darius II, daughter of Artaxerxes I, granddaughter of Xerxes I, great-granddaughter of Darius I and great-great-granddaughter of Cyrus, each a Great King, King of Kings, an Achaemenid.

With pallid face, I come from the region of the Shades. Through the Stygian marsh and its great forest. Across the River Styx, despite Charon's reluctance to pole me against the normal flow of his cargo.

To speak, at last, of myself, of a life spent in the Achaemenid Empire, land of the two rivers. In its day the greatest empire known to history, it extended from the Indus River to North Africa, from the Aral Sea to the Persian Gulf, all told some one million square miles. Founded by Cyrus the Great upon his conquest of the Median Empire, it was to last forever. In fact, it survived for only 220 years, brought down by Alexander, the Macedonian.

I will give brief account. Enough, I pray, to correct the calumnies of the Greeks, whose inked plumes spilled oceans of falsehood across the pages of history.

I mean you, Dinon, and you, Aelian, Xenophon, and Diodorus Siculus. Even you, Ctesias, our family's physician, whom we welcomed in the palace and embraced with love and trust.

11

To listen to these vilifiers is to believe I wallowed in cruelty, took delight in revenge, and was consumed by feverish lust for power, which I pursued with ruthless and bloodthirsty devotion to myself alone.

And what of Plutarch? Plutarch the palimpsest. This celebrated historian accepted the Greek impostors without a glimmer of skepticism. His was a feat of alchemy. Tracing their claims he wrote with eloquence, transmuting falsehood into truth.

There is more at stake here than retrieving a single life from the muck of falsity. The Greeks were able to use their fantasies about my life to smear the entire Achaemenid Empire. I know as well as others who think clearly, and with honesty, that no history can embrace the whole truth. Homer's *Iliad* tells only the Greek side of that conflict. It took the Roman Virgil to imagine a Trojan hero and recount his harrowing tale of love, war, and the founding of the Roman Empire.

I was independently rich. The only fact the Greeks got right. They suggest I was the guiding force behind the mysterious deaths, on the same day, of my father and his wife. And of their only legitimate son, assassinated 45 days after his accession. They claim I guided my husband's hand in overthrowing his half-brother, who had assumed the mantle of Great King only to be murdered after a reign of 6 months and 15 days. And that my husband, when seated on the throne, followed my commands in putting to death his brother and other nobles. Thus was the Great King Darius II reduced to a willing tool in the hands of his cunning wife.

There's more. After our daughter, Amestris, married Teritushmes, he fell in love with his sister and murdered Amestris. I am charged with causing the torture and death of Teritushmes and most of his family. And, after my husband died, with summoning my favorite son, Cyrus, from Sardis to assassinate his brother during his investiture as Great King Artaxerxes II. When that failed, they claim I directed Cyrus to raise an army to strike down the Great King, all the while deceiving Artaxerxes II with my feigned love. Upon the death of Cyrus on the field of battle at Cunaxa, they assert that for each Persian who claimed a hand in Cyrus' demise, and there were many, I contrived a hideous torture. And that, like a puppeteer, I toyed with my son, the Great King, first by eliminating his wife, Stateira, with poison, and then by causing him to marry his two daughters. All of these things, they allege, I did in pursuit of self-aggrandizement and power.

To be honest, the Greeks got more than my wealth right. But how power was used is worthless without understanding why. Didn't Parysatis have a childhood?

With youth, friends, the triumphs and tragedies of growing up? Didn't she love and grieve? Do the Greek tales account for the fifteen children I bore, eleven of whom died before reaching their third birthday? And what of an Achaemenid's duty to her people? Was there nothing other than torture and killing worth noting in my long tenure as Queen to one Great King and Queen Mother to another? The worm casts deeper shadows. The wolf's motive for the kill is more layered. For the Greek charlatans, nothing else mattered. In their story, I emerged fully grown from the rotten ooze of Achaemenid culture, dripping with more than enough hatred to carry out pitiless acts of depravity.

There is urgency to what I have to say. Much more is at stake than proving Plutarch and the others wrong. In truth, the Greek historians concern me less than it might appear. Not enough, certainly, to hazard the return voyage.

I was driven back by Hades, Lord of the lower world, and his circle of Gods, whose laughter still echoes in my ears, whose derision and contempt humiliated me, bringing such pain, suffering and sense of failure as I had never experienced or even imagined through a lifetime.

You see, as regards the Achaemenid Empire, I had much to boast about. I left the Empire in good hands, for Achaemenids to pass from generation to generation and rule forever. So I thought, and so I boasted upon reaching the region of Shades. My arrogant ways irritated Hades, who kept his annoyance to himself, allowing it to fester as I set myself up for the fall.

When Alexander destroyed my Empire, ravaging my people, pillaging our treasures, and burning to the ground my home, the great palace of Persepolis, the news hit me as storm-tossed waves beat upon the same bit of shore, over and over again. Then, at the nadir of my despair, Hades let me know that it was my insufferable arrogance that caused the Gods to favor the Macedonian. Death's sting was nothing to the pain and anguish that afflicted me. If any relief could be found, it would be through a return to tell my story. I knew, of course, that the destruction of my Empire and the suffering of my people rested, irreversibly, on my shoulders. I could keen day and night; nothing would change. Nor would my story consist of an Aristotelian "good life," like the one this tutor of Alexander taught the great conqueror to live. Moderation in all things? Happiness the ultimate good? By Aristotle's measure, Alexander failed and so, decisively, did I.

In returning, I have no illusion that I can capture your love. No. Not even sympathy have I the ambition to expect. I know, in the telling, I risk having you find me hateful, as did the Greeks. It is a risk I am driven to take.

I had a full life, although, at the end, I felt cheated because it seemed to have passed me by, like a black kite far above that one sees for a moment and then, in the blink of an eye, cannot see. I invite you to judge, as I have tried to judge from a goodly distance in time and space, whether mine was a life worthy of my effort to explain and of yours to comprehend; whether, in the end, it was a life important enough to be remembered.

It is time to tell my story.

1

IN THE BEEYARD

"NOAH THE PRIZE."

"Noah the wise."

We pranced like wild colts, exchanging quips in front of a distinctly tall and lean man whose age was past the point where we could conceive of him having ever been a child. We sought to provoke. The bright spring day, which had begun briskly, was, at last, turning warm. Noah had removed his thick leather workcoat, protection from the most rambunctious honeybee. He pushed the sleeves of his linen shirt above the elbow. An outdoorsman of dark complexion, he was made more so by constant exposure to the sun. His long, curly black hair, now matted thick on his forearms, glistened with perspiration. The wind had risen with the temperature, making music in the tall cedars that surrounded the royal beeyard at Persepolis, located outside the palace gates but within the three protective rings of its fortification wall.

"Noah's no wizard, Noah's no miss." Udusana fairly shouted the words in rhythmic pattern, her eyes a challenge to me.

"Noah's a lover, come give us a kiss," I responded, arms extended, fingers at first pointing to the most important man in our young lives, then playfully curling to beckon him to me. Dismissively, Noah stood his ground.

With peals of glee, we grabbed for Noah, seizing any part of him we could hold onto, offering our cheeks for attention. We knew our man. Slowly bending

15

low in the ancient manner of one born to tenderness, he bestowed two kisses as directed.

I was born on March 21. Daughter of Macrochir, an Achaemenid who changed his name to Artaxerxes upon ascending the throne of Persia, and Andia, a Babylonian concubine, whose authority within the harem, I'm told, was unrivaled. They named me Parysatis, a word neither beautiful nor easy to pronounce (Pah-rih-sa-tihs). At ten, I wished for something better. Of royal stock, I seldom saw the male part of the root from which I sprang. I knew my father no better than those to whom he presented himself with formality, intoning in public: "I am Artaxerxes the Great King, King of Kings, son of Xerxes the King, grandson of Darius, an Achaemenid." He inscribed this title at the entrance to his tomb on the cliff at Naqsh-I Rustam. As others before him, he claimed God-like attributes, a man above men.

My best friend Udusana told me I had a large opinion of myself, and I won't deny it. Consider this: My birthday was the vernal equinox, beginning of a new year, a fecund moment when the desert blooms, when nature's rebirth is celebrated. Persians consider this day the point of balance, the most propitious time of the year, when almost any human drama would be favored by the Gods. It is the day on which our vassal states pay homage, led by a parade of dignitaries bearing gifts. Elamites, Parthians, Egyptians, Babylonians. No Greeks.

Noah claimed we knew little of the world outside the gates of Persepolis, where we had been cosseted for the whole of our short lives. Nothing Noah said did we doubt. We came to believe the wisdom of the ages had funneled into his brain, a library open to us on demand. To us alone.

In turn, Noah came to trust us with the truth. He was incapable of speaking falsely. He wanted, indeed, needed to share. At the time we didn't appreciate the risks he took. Looking back, I see how naïve and reckless he was. Despite his grasp of nature's resolute ways, he was a dreamer, longing for change, oblivious to danger.

A ring of grownups encircled me from birth. Not my parents, you understand. Magi and other paid guardians of one kind or another. They never tired of making Noah's point, particularly when I misbehaved. Lacking his caring attitude, their posturing became hateful to me, unreachable nettles against soft skin.

"The special blessings of your birth date impose special duties," one particularly obnoxious Magus assigned to my education would chant. He tried to dazzle the royal children with dream interpretation, prophecy, herbal lore, and remedies, all the things adults believed gave Magi their place in the sun. Too young to be impressed, we angered him. Lessons in discipline and respect often involved the cane, administered with vigor and the full support of my parents, who turned a deaf ear to my cries of injustice.

My advance through the odyssey of childhood afforded ever expanding opportunities for mischief, both within the huge terrace on which the palace rested and beyond, when escape permitted. Custom among royals supported my tendencies, as it offered their children plenty of time for unsupervised play. To the dismay of my handlers, I exploited those opportunities when the spirit moved me. Unlike dogs and horses, I grew less tame with handling, more immune to punishment.

Having been born on the first day of a new year, I thought it natural to see myself, even before my tenth year, as the center of things, a very important person who became more so with each passing day. I know it's common for children of apparent talent to form these opinions, warranted or not. I had formed a high opinion of myself despite exhibiting a talent for nothing in particular. But why not? Wasn't I daughter to the King of Kings? He who had recently completed, in my home, an amazing hall with 100 columns of white stone. They were sixty feet high, topped with capitals of fantastic animals in pairs, facing away from each other. They cradled cedar beams cut from trees too massive to imagine. The hall was used for what the adults called receptions. Sometimes, 10,000 and more were in attendance, not counting the Immortals. When allowed to attend, I made sure to be noticed. I had a long white neck. From earliest days, I was aware but not able to take its measure. I developed a slow, deliberate way of turning my neck when glancing this way or that. One day someone commented favorably, and I refined the technique, alert to its impression on others. Those oblivious to this charming effect I considered insensitive to beauty.

At ten, I stopped wishing I were a boy. With the Great King for a father, I had come to believe, from the time I started to see the space around me as bigger than myself alone, that there was advantage in being a prince. Power, with all its trappings, seemed to cluster around the royal males, like a swarm of bees to their leader, iron filings to a magnet. I blamed my mother for tipping the balance the other way.

By the time I reached the end of my first decade, my father's concubines had produced a disproportionate number of sons, a trend that continued. At his death in the Empire's 126th year, when I was 20, his male offspring numbered 17. By ten I had developed a more nuanced sense of a royal woman's power. I was content with my lot.

My mother had been a slave. It was a point of pride that she repeated more than once. She never forgot nor ceased to be grateful for the bit of good fortune that saw her plucked from a Babylonian crowd by Artaxerxes, whose eye caught a glimmer of something even Andia had failed to notice about herself. She was thrust into the King's harem, where eunuchs and senior concubines wielded nearly absolute power in ways ingenious, arbitrary, cruel, and capricious. She was grateful, for whatever strange force made her the subject of praise rather than punishment by the monarchs of the harem.

As a child, feelings of gratitude were as foreign to me as sandstorms to Susa. In my teenage years, I arrived at opinions swiftly and was seldom in doubt. I often accused my mother of retaining the mental state of a slave. Her humbleness pricked my skin. I would remind her that she was a Queen. As such, she must assume a Queen's stature. The ending was always the same. I would say, "You mortify me," my right index finger jabbing the air.

I can now trace the slow migration of my feelings for Andia from love to sympathy and thence to contempt, where they stuck, beyond my power to change or control, even when in later years sporadic spasms of remorse drove me to try. It was especially hard to be accepting of those within my immediate family, forgiving of their foibles and other short-comings. I suspect this is true of most families, at least to some degree. But intolerance grew to become a prominent feature of my palace reputation as a teenager. In youth I possessed no instinct for kindness and, with one exception, was taught nothing of its value by those around me. That exception, which I now recall with the remorse of one who failed the lesson, was Noah. He shocked me one day by observing that I lacked kindness. He urged me to practice being kind to others as one might practice other acquired skills, like the art of weaving. My humiliation was short-lived. I thought Noah's advice unworthy of an Achaemenid.

Only as an adult did I take note enough to try by force of will to cultivate what Noah had said I lacked, an effort that I pursued erratically and never with noticeable success.

As a child I was easily embarrassed. Even by the little things others did around me, when they didn't measure up to conduct I expected to see. I chose to be dressed in pastels, which, looking back, was odd considering my habit of judging others in the bold colors of black and white.

Well before reaching the end of my first decade, I had learned to lie. I told myself it was a woman's art to be mastered, as sword play or riding was to men. It became a contest in which I pitted myself against the world. As a baby, I must have feigned hurt or hunger when all I wanted was to be held. But the first outright lie I recall occurred when I was nine. I had taken one of the palace cats to the balcony of the Harem to test a claim made by Noah the day before. He said a cat, no matter what, would always land on its feet.

My first cat was named Cyrus. Short-haired and tawny, with complex tipping in various shades of blue and black, he was large, lean, and lazy. I loved him, despite his self absorption and independence. My earliest experience with love unrequited. My interest in cats never grew stale. I saw them as exemplars of the feminine. What started out as love migrated with maturity to admiration. I'm still amazed at the detachment, even indifference, of a cat to those on whom its welfare depends. It's the mark of their greatness. How different the dog, whose loyalty and devotion to its master are valued as strengths.

To use Cyrus in the experiment was out of the question. There were many palace felines towards whom I felt a catlike indifference. It was a matter of minutes to find one and, feigning an offering of food, bring it close enough to be swept up in tight embrace. I swiftly carried my charge to a balcony overlooking an interior courtyard. Panting from the ascent, I held the cat upside down with arms outstretched over the railing, far above the stone floor below. I checked to be sure no one was looking, then released the animal. Immediately it twisted, bringing its body around, with legs and feet extended to meet the stone first. Noah was right. The cat had landed on its feet. But it wasn't moving.

One of the newer eunuchs from the Harem had arrived on the scene just before I dropped the cat. I saw him staring at the motionless beast. He caught me staring at him before he hurried away. I knew he would tell Andia. With eunuch in tow, she found me in the playroom. Accused of deliberately dropping a cat to its death, I told her the eunuch lied, that the cat, which was evading my efforts to pet it, had jumped over the railing, confused as to direction. I had tried to catch it before it fell, but was a split second too slow.

At first, my mother didn't accept this story. "Mother," I screamed, "one of us is lying. You must choose: your daughter or this eunuch, princess or slave." As she retreated, I pressed the attack. "He should be put to the whip."

I had learned the value of lying. And the dangers of over-shooting. Guilt gripped me when I heard the eunuch had been beaten. Often I replayed that incident throughout the night, helpless to stop the cycle of recall and remorse. One morning, after a sleepless episode, I went alone to the beeyard. When Noah commented on my sallow look, I confessed. In fact, I must have gone there for the purpose, because tearfully I welcomed his sympathy. As for my wayward mind, he claimed that gaining better control was part of growing up; that guilt over the pains one inflicts on others tends to erode as one matures, especially among royals; that, for example, the powers of statecraft exercised by my father often cause immense suffering and, yet, through training and practice, he sleeps, guiltless, through the night.

"There's another way," he added, "and that is to shun the power to cause pain in others, practicing kindness instead. Such has been my choice. It is not the choice of many. I am certain it will not be yours."

Years later, I modified my childhood belief that lying was practiced mainly by women. I formed a granite-hard conviction that everyone lies when it serves their purposes and they think they can escape discovery. Some do it better than others, some do it more often than others, some suffer more guilt than others, and some treat it as a form of art. But all humans lie. As I began to savor life's ironies, I would smile at the pretentious goals of a Persian education for royal males, captured by our famous motto "To ride, to draw the bow, to tell the truth."

❧ ❧ ❧ ❧ ❧ ❧

Growing up, Udusana was my constant companion. She was two years older. We met when she was ten. She had the emotional temperament of an April day, one moment sunny all over with laughter, the next crying as though her heart would break.

Udusana was daughter to the Royal Groundskeeper. As the one who always seemed to get things done, he was a man of large, albeit opaque, power within the Kingdom. It was Udusana who introduced me to Noah, the Royal Beekeeper. He lived alone, but those who knew him could plainly see that he was neither alone nor lonely, although he wore a melancholy look. That is, until he spoke, when his face assumed a capacious smile, the promise of ready good humor. "I have a multitude of friends," he was fond of saying. "A tiny race, some seven million of them. We understand each other."

Noah became a special destination, an escape from the confines of the palace. His kingdom was the beeyard, where he presided over 300 hives, each occupied by 25,000 or more honeybees. Whether it was his unaffected kindness, his choice of companions, his sapient grasp of all things natural or the iconic mystery of his solitude, he became my only source of enthrallment, a divine who, I believed, had descended into the beeyard expressly to amuse and beguile me.

Formal instruction came from one of several Magi who surrounded my father. Where Noah had a prodigious nose, a marvel to which my eyes lovingly were drawn, my Magus had a lean, pale and consumptive face that my eyes sought regularly to avoid. Where Noah's hands were oxhide tough, with fingers gnarled and nails permanently soiled and scratched, the Magus' hands were feather-soft and manicured. Where Noah was gentle, the Magus was harsh. Where Noah taught kindness, the Magus advanced the cause of cruelty. Where Noah cared for me, asking nothing in return, the Magus cared only for the Great King's opinion of him, asking much in return for trying to educate me. Where Noah was my mentor by choice, the Magus was thrust upon me, against my will. I detested him. Indeed, these feelings still inhabit my memory, although I now realize this childish picture, product of my infatuation with Noah, a mentor of my own choosing, without adult guidance, distorts the truth.

When Udusana first took me to the beeyard, Noah was opening hives.

"Noah, I've brought the King's daughter to meet you. Her name's Parysatis. She's eight and very smart."

Noah ignored our presence for what, to me, seemed far too long. Was he being disrespectful before royalty? Or just graceless? I was at a loss. Should I speak sharply, as I did with servants inside the palace? I watched as Noah pried loose the round plug in the tightly woven reed hive. Beside him was a clay pot with a spout in its carefully fitted cap, out of which flowed pine-scented smoke. I was on the verge of attack when he gently removed the plug. Immediately, bees began to fly out. Noah showed no sign of concern. With a coolness that astonished me, he gently moved the pot to the opening and blew smoke into the hive. I would grant him time to finish before acknowledging my presence.

When he had subdued the bees with smoke, he turned the hive towards the sun, inviting me to peer inside. "I don't allow Udusana to get this close. She was bitten once. Went pale and cold. Almost fainted. I've never seen such a reaction. Possibly something she ate, but I blame the bees. It mustn't happen again."

I tried to look inside the hive but could only make out blurred motion. I felt as excited as a butterfly, my mind filling with questions. "Can you tell them apart? Where do bees come from? How do they make honey? How many in the hive?"

Moving back to Udusana, we sat with our knees touching, backs to the sun, enraptured by the soothing bass of the beekeeper, as he answered these questions and many more, until the sun had reached its zenith, a sign to Noah that it was past our mealtime.

By the time I was ten, I was spending more time with Noah than any other human being except, perhaps, Udusana. My obsession with life in the hive began with that first encounter and waxed with the passage of time, as he drew from a deep reservoir of knowledge to respond to my interest. Noah was brimming with beelore, a sponge that, unconsciously, I sought to squeeze dry. At first it was slow going. Noah was as cautious in explaining the life of the bee as he was deliberate in handling the hive. It took me a long time to understand why. Noah's knowledge and the theories he had developed from all that he observed were in important details unknown to others, even experienced beekeepers. If disclosed, they would be thought heretical. To such an extent, Noah believed, as to endanger his position and, quite possibly, his life.

My curiosity, expressed with persistence and passion, wore him down. That and both his trust in us and the natural desire of this solitary man to share the mysterious ways of the honeybee that he had deciphered.

Until one late fall day overcast and blustery with the threat of winter, I had never gotten a clear message from Noah about the three castes of bee found in the hives. He was precise in all matters save this. It was puzzling. That day we were watching the opening of one of his most active hives. On the ground below were countless corpses, their wings torn, antennae broken, legs parted. We saw a continuous flow of bees falling from the opening, dead or dying, each being pushed by several of their brethren.

"Noah! They're killing each other."

Noah sat mute in front of the hive, eyes darting this way and that. Much later I realized that, whether out of loneliness, an unfulfilled need for an offspring or simple attraction, Noah had become as addicted to mentoring me as I was to being nourished by him.

Waiting, I tried to be analytical, precisely what Noah would expect of me. Moving in for a closer look, I realized that the bees being tossed from the hive were slightly different in shape and size from those pushing them out. Once detected, these differences seemed to enlarge, soon becoming impossible to miss.

"Noah, I think the dead ones are not the same as those in the hive."

"How so?"

"Bigger. And shaped more like a box."

"Bravo, my royal friend. Nothing amiss here. It happens at the end of every summer. In every hive, almost at the same time, as if from a signal. It's a massacre, the massacre of the 'drones,' for that's what we call this caste of bee, because they sit around all day, doing nothing useful."

"What about those doing the killing? The little active ones. I mean, what's going on? Where's the King? He's lost control of the hive, obviously."

"The lean ones we call 'worker bees.' They do the work of the hive, from bringing in the nectar to feeding the larvae, from cleaning the hive to killing the drones. But no one's lost control."

"So the massacre's directed by the King. I should have guessed. Remember the way you've described him to us? Long-bodied, always attended by others, the small ones—those you just called worker bees—who surround him, never turning their backs to him, backing up to make way as he moves forward. That's the way people behave in front of my father." I laughed.

Noah smiled, looking distracted. He grew quiet. Reaching out, he took my hand and held it in his. Looking down into my eyes, he whispered. "I'm now going to tell you something I've told no one before. You've promised to keep all that I've taught you about the bee to yourself, and I believe ..."

I was in thrall to Noah's secrets. Breaking in, I exclaimed "I have, I have, and I will. What...?"

"What I'm about to say is the most dangerous theory of all, and so, if you care for me, you must hold it all tight in your head, disclosing to no one."

I remember how hard he squeezed my hand at the word "tight." As he released his grip, I slipped my hand from his and then raised it, palm open. I was nodding vigorously.

"The 'King' is a female. A Queen. She spends all her days, save one each year, in the dark hive, laying eggs. She is, in fact, the mother of her city."

"How do you know that?" I stared at him.

"Long hours of observation. Watching her every movement. Actually, it's not so subtle. And I'm not as clever as you think." He looked at me with those gentle, lamb's eyes that, from our first meeting, made me want to curl up in his arms. He flashed me the sly smile of a conspirator, about to reveal the plan.

"Close observers see exactly what I see. The trick is to be open-minded about the possibilities, willing, that is, to put aside one's assumptions ..."

"...that it's a King?"

"It's not an easy thing to do. We see what we want to see. Believing in miracles enables one to see them. Mind over matter, as the Magi inform us."

"Constantly," I added, too excited to remain just a listener.

"And, yet," he continued, "looking without preconceived notions one observes that this 'King' spends the day entering empty cells and depositing an egg in each—eggs that grow into bees. Now, among the birds, beasts, and fish you know, how many males lay eggs?"

I shook my head. "But Noah, I don't know much about birds and those other things. Perhaps, in the case of bees ..." Feeling beyond my depth, I broke off the thought, wishing we hadn't started down this road. But there was no stopping Noah, who didn't seem to notice my growing discomfort.

"Why, I asked myself, would the honeybee be different? Why, if this ruler is a male, does he never mate with those who attend him, who I believe are females? And, why, if he's a male, doesn't he look like the other male bees, the drones?"

"But if the 'King' is really the 'Queen,' then who is the King? There must be one somewhere."

"I know it's confusing. There is no King. The only male is the drone. There are many of them, a fact I can't explain. Their only contribution to the life of the hive, at least the only one I know of, is to fertilize the Queen during her flight from the hive, which occurs but once a year, at the beginning of spring."

"On my birthday?"

Noah paused to pass me his kind smile. "When a new Queen is hatched from a cell, the female attendants brush, caress and clean her, and then stand aside to watch an extraordinary event. This new-born Queen sets about the hive, opening each cell she comes upon that contains a future queen. Don't ask me how she knows which they are. A mystery. Stripping off the wax cover, she tears away the cocoon to reveal a rival. Turning, she places her sting in the capsule and repeatedly stabs the victim with this venomous weapon. She continues, cell after cell, until all her rivals have been eliminated. What appears as maddened hate could be pure instinct. But I prefer to imagine it's the Queen's painful duty, knowingly rendered in service to the hive, which can flourish with only one leader."

Noah was staring at me. I felt the heat of embarrassment and turned away.

❧ ❧ ❧ ❧ ❧ ❧

As the days lengthened, spring turned to face summer. Dusk came well after my supper. One hot night Udusana joined me to walk beside the palace wall in search of cooling breezes. Under towering palms whose deeply cleft fronds high above quivered with promise of a waxing wind, we threw ourselves to the ground, stretching out beside one another to stare up at the darkening sky and the stars that began to appear as if some lamplighter were hard at work.

"Are they there all day, even though we can't see them?" I asked, as much to myself as to my companion.

"Or do they come each night from far away, just to please us?" Udusana replied, anticipating as usual her friend's next question.

"Hush! It's coming. Listen!"

"The zephyr. Feel it, rippling. Delightful." Inspired by the moment, she removed her garments to rest naked on the still-warm sand. "My breasts and stomach are cool, my bottom's hot. Try it."

There was ample evidence that I trailed Udusana in the race to puberty, source of fickle turns from hate to love, love to hate, the oscillating engine of my attraction to her. Stripping off my clothes, I edged an inch closer to my friend, bringing our bodies into contact at various points from shoulder to foot. I felt coolness as a shiver descended the length of me. Was it the breeze that made me shiver, or something under my skin?

Udusana's breasts were almost fully developed. Mine had not begun. At these moments I hated Udusana for being ahead, for being born two years earlier, for her child-like wonder at outgrowing childhood. But that night, beyond the Palace walls, I would play the eager explorer, finding Udusana's physical progress immensely attractive.

We were still, ears tuned. Among the fronds far above a gentle swishing sound could be heard, overlaid periodically by the distant trill of a nightingale. The sky beyond, now dark, revealed the immensity of starlight, pale white dots that seemed to blink, too numerous to count. I numbered the tactile pleasures of the moment: the heat of sand on my backside, the coolness of breezes across my chest, the soft warmth of skin against skin, the silence that makes intimacy palpable.

Her hand was the first to begin. Mine swiftly followed. Neither excuse nor explanation proved necessary. My hand acted as if disengaged from the mind that guided it. This would be an exploration unseen and unspoken.

A palace guard approached, lamp swinging at his side. Gathering our clothes, we stood and moved behind the smooth trunk of a lofty palm, the sole witness of our journey. By the time he was gone, the spell we had cast for each other had vanished. In silence, we retreated to the palace. Udusana took my arm in hers. Instead of shame, I felt a thrill that lingered into the next day and beyond. Later, trying to sleep, I marveled at our ability to communicate without speaking a word.

Even now, the memory of that evening remains sweet, as it always did through my years as a grown-up. What is it about sensual pleasures that make us recall those that came first as the best. Is it a trick of memory? Must pleasures repeated always turn stale?

❧ ❧ ❧ ❧ ❧ ❧

It was June. Our keeper of bees was also a tender of flowers. By noon the beeyard was perfumed with the wind-borne blending of spring's gifts. In bloom were chestnut, oleander, and pomegranate trees, whose fragrances met those ascending from well-tended patches of rosemary, lavender, saffron, and frankincense. The glory of the day made me giddy.

"Noah's gleeful," I shouted, giving Udusana an easy response.

"Ever beeful," came the reply.

He strained to ignore our rhyming banter, intent on showing us how to deal with a crowded hive prone to swarm.

"Noah's warm," I cried.

"He won't swarm," replied Udusana.

"His shirt's torn." I answered.

"That doesn't rhyme," Udusana said. We turned to Noah.

"Let me tell you about the 'spirit of the hive.' Until you understand it, nothing about the honeybee will make much sense. Of all sentient beings, and not just butterflies, but dogs, cats, cattle, whatever, honeybees have the highest intellect after us. Why? Because of their guiding spirit. To an almost unimaginable extent, life in the hive involves individual sacrifice for general welfare."

Noah must have caught the doubt underlying my condescending smile.

"You both look skeptical. You know many examples already: the fighting spirit of the workers, their willingness to die to defend the hive, as they must die whenever they use their stinger; the Queen's consuming ..." I let out a cry, casting my arms upward as if to catch Noah's words before they reached Udusana's ears.

"She knows about the Queen," Noah said, his voice dropping to a whisper.

"No," I shouted. "That's my secret." Hurt hung about my eyes, which burned as I stared at him.

"I know. I just told her yesterday. You two are much too close for me to expect secrets to be kept. Now, the swarm."

Hurt turned to anger. I tried not to listen to Noah's story, but the sound of the hive's inhabitants suddenly grew loud, silencing Noah and distracting me. The number of bees exiting and re-entering the hive increased to a dense cluster. Randomness of motion overcame purposefulness, as if the workers were bewitched.

"It's close. Listen. Here, in this well stocked hive, where some 90,000 bees have attained the heights of prosperity, over half are about to abandon their home to face unknown risks. Led by the Queen, they will sally forth in what I believe is a well-considered sacrifice by the present generation in favor of the one to come."

Udusana was quick to realize how intensely serious Noah had become, how passionate. She asked, "If that's the key to the 'spirit of the hive,' why don't we make it our own?"

"Yes," I chimed in, "why not a 'spirit of the palace?' In place of all these ministers of this and that, buzzing around the Great King in search of honey instead of making it.

"I'm told father calls the palace a battlefield where people gather to kill or be killed in pursuit of power. For themselves, I mean. I've heard he thinks the harem eunuchs dreadful, constantly fighting each other to gain position. You know something: if you're right, bees are smarter than adults. I have an idea." To insist upon their attention, I put up my hand in the manner of one accustomed to command.

"Noah will instruct the Great King and his ministers about the honeybee. Udusana and I will arrange it. The 'spirit of the hive' will launch a new beginning for the Achaemenids." I had that gleam in my eye, the one Noah had seen before, the one he said meant trouble.

Noah was laughing. "You carry my point too far. You can't transfer the work-ings of the hive to the palace. I'm flattered that you think I could do that. But putting me in the palace to teach can result, most certainly, in loss of my job and, perhaps, something worse.

"Now, be quiet. It's the song of the hive: a tumultuous beating of 30,000 pairs of wings. The swarm is close. When this happens, the bees exult, riding a mad impulse. As if possessed, they suddenly revel not in the ecstasy of work, but in joy, even folly. Instead of making honey, they partake of it, as much as they can hold. They fly aimlessly, allowing themselves to be gathered by hand like a bunch of grapes. Watch." His hand swept across the mouth of the hive, gathering up as many of these newly irresolute worker bees as he could hold without harming them.

"What can you do to stop it?" we asked, almost in unison.

"The only thing is to open the hive, find the old Queen and kill her before she splits the colony. Sometimes it's too late. They reach a state of enthusiasm for a new home that won't be stopped. I'm afraid we're at that stage here."

Opening the hive, Noah brushed off those still clinging to his hand, then tried to smoke the bees into submission. They were too aroused. When he found the old Queen, she was surrounded by workers dancing with excitement. Before he could collect her, she led her large escort out of the hive. They were followed by a stream of bees, pouring forth. Thousands, I guessed, quivering with life, throbbing with sound. They flew low to the ground at first and were easy to see. Noah ducked away from the open hive, put down the smoker and told us as he did so that, now, all that could be done was to follow the swarm and try to capture it, kill the Queen and then combine it with another colony. Dashing off in pursuit, Noah yelled back instructions. "Smoke the hive. Then close it. I won't be back for a while. Parysatis, you might try to find the new Queen."

Udusana stood a good distance away from the hive when the swarm began. Her fear of being bitten put me in charge. Picking up the smoker, I blew pitch-scented smoke into the hive until the remaining bees were subdued. Then I plugged the opening and joined Udusana in the perfumed glen of the beeyard.

The air was still, the temperature sizzling. Udusana had opened her shirt, exposing her breasts and cleavage, glistening with sweat. I felt coerced to look.

Since our night of exploration, I had kept my distance, rebuffing her overtures to revisit our feelings. I don't know exactly why I recoiled. Part instinct, part fear. Despite her openness, I had even begun to imagine that she found me wanting. Of course, it's now easy for me to see that this was my route around feelings of self-hate.

"I hate you. You can't imagine how much I hate you."

"We are what we are. That can't be changed."

I sulked. That she spoke wisely made me, at that moment, hate her even more. I wanted to retaliate, to inflict pain, but words failed me. We sat in the glen, silent and apart, waiting for Noah's return. Minutes passed. I rose. Sweat fell away from my face as I turned from my friend and descended to the hive. There I resuscitated the smoker with a handful of pine needles and removed the plug. I pointed the smoker at the bees gathering at the opening and forced them back into the hive with puffs of smoke. Then, looking in the hive, I searched for the Queen.

"What are you doing?" Udusana said.

"Looking for the new Queen." Bees were still trying to emerge from the opening. I applied the smoker again, forcing them back. I could see the bees receding into the comb to take their fill of honey, just as Noah had said they did upon being smoked. A survival instinct, he said, triggered by an unseen enemy. To safeguard the colony, they submit rather than fight.

The haze had dissipated. I dragged the hive around so that the sun, now high in the sky, could shine directly into the opening. Searching for the distinct shape of a Queen, when one had never seen it except in the mind's eye, was hard. I felt unsure of myself even though I was pretty confident in distinguishing worker from drone.

"Yell out if you find her," Udusana said. "I want to have a look."

Again a few worker bees began to emerge from the opening. Still subdued by the smoke, they were crawling. Using the smoker, I forced a retreat. When the smoke cleared, I looked inside, trying not to block out the sunlight.

"Hey, I think I've found her. Big. She glistens. Raven-black face. She's surrounded by attendants. Oh, you'll want to see this."

Buttoning up her shirt, Udusana ran the short distance to the hive, happy to be friends again. "Show me where to look," she said.

"Wait till I smoke them once more. Then look straight down. She's in the center, ringed by workers. You can't miss her." I picked up the smoker and aimed it at the already subdued bees. I moved aside, signaling for Udusana that the moment for her to spot the Queen had come. She moved swiftly, bringing her face to the opening to look inside. Neither of us was aware that the lid to the smoker had opened, allowing the hot, smoldering pine needles to fall into the hive. It took only seconds before anger over the presence of burning needles in the hive became coherent and directed. For the bee, smoke and the material that creates it are two very different threats. Burning pine needles dumped inside a hive will invariably turn docile bees into crazed soldiers ready to die for revenge.

Udusana must have heard them an instant before they hit. Watching, I could see bees stinging her above and below her eyes, in the softness of her cheeks, then on her neck and below, crawling inside her shirt.

She fell hard to the ground. Her face emptied of color, becoming dull and pale. I knelt beside her, not knowing what to do. Touching her face, I felt moist skin, cold despite the heat.

"Udusana," I cried. She was panting, unable to speak, right up to the moment she lost consciousness.

I had been bitten too. Enraged bees were still coming at us. I reached for the smoker, only to remember that it had lost its tinder to the hive. Grabbing the plug, I closed the opening. Then with stones I tried as best I could to cover the small holes in the hive that permitted bees to come and go. I brushed away the attackers that were still on my friend's face and clothes. The sound of one remained, somewhere inside her shirt. I tried to crush it, guessing where it was by the buzz and pushing down hard. I must have missed, since the bee's sound continued. Udusana was growing paler by the second, her breathing forced and faint. I felt desperate, the buzzing in her blouse like a fire alarm pulsating in my head. I tore open her front, found the bee near the nipple and crushed it with my open palm.

Noah returned to find me clutching Udusana's face, repeatedly ordering her to awaken, as if the cry of a princess, invoked enough, could restore a life as suddenly as it had been lost.

Noah's grief and anguish turned to astonishment as I tried to describe what had happened. Only the bees were witness to these events. Were they capable of speaking, they might have given a different account, one no less self-interested than mine.

Noah remained silent for what seemed minutes after I finished my story, his eyes black dots probing every detail of the scene around me, then coming to rest on my own, red from tears.

"I know you didn't expect her to die. The whole thing's an accident. Tinder fell in the hive. It can easily happen. You mustn't blame yourself. Nothing you could have done to save her. She came too close."

Sitting on the ground beside Udusana, I could not look at Noah as he stood above me or even when he sat down to face me across the front of the hive. Worker bees came and went as my tale unfolded, seemingly as oblivious to the swarm that had carried more than half their family away as Noah and I were to their presence. My sobbing ceased. I caught his eye with mine and held it.

"She humiliated me." My face was dry, salt streaks the only evidence of recent tears.

"How so?"

I looked away, unable to answer.

❧ ❧ ❧ ❧ ❧

Of the 15 children I brought to term and delivered 11 died before reaching three. What is it about the loss of an infant that's so profoundly disturbing? Here, although my expeience runs deep, I have no clear answer. A winter's bud swelling from the warmth of springtime, dressed in the pale green of promise at the moment it is cut off; a perfectly formed unripe apple, sparkling in the sun of summer, tinged with streaks of red and gold as it falls to rot on the ground. A fledgling falling like a stone from the nest as it prepares to fly. While helping to understand, metaphors fail to ease the pain.

Words, however true, are flimsy platforms for the grief of those who know the loss of a child. Human feelings at their most acute are beyond measurement or vicarious experience.

Udusana's funeral service was well attended, stretching the capacity of the palace room. All those who felt the hurt of her sudden and needless death were present, joined for an hour in shared grief.

Her father was beloved throughout the palace. And Udusana, age 12, was a palace favorite. Chief among her endearing traits was an irrepressible enthusiasm for life, which she expressed in the music she chose to play, the poems she wrote and the ebullient spirit she applied to all she undertook, infectious to those around her.

Of the Achaemenid dynasty, only two were present, my mother, Andia, and I. We were offered seats in the front row. Declining, we tried to move to the back of the room. Ushers blocked our way, gently urging us to take the seats up front. Andia swept around them, leading me back. I had never seen my mother looking so defiant. I suddenly realized she wanted to see rather than be seen.

The Great King, my father, rejected my entreaties to attend. Nor would he allow me an audience to beg, receiving my message and responding through staff with neither explanation nor apology. That the Great King sets his own schedule, ordered by his priorities alone is known throughout the palace.

Noah reported Udusana's death as an accident. Many times by Noah, and through him by her parents, she had been cautioned about the unique danger bees posed. Her mother received word of her death with resignation, convinced that our great God, Ahura-Mazda, had willed it in retribution for something they had done. Immediately, she sought through prayers to identify their wrong-doings and correct them. Her father took the news cautiously, uncertain as to cause.

The service was brief. The palace priest spoke of Udusana in ways that brought tears to all eyes. To be sure, those eyes were prone to weep. But the eloquence of the priest, and his apparent knowledge of his subject's life, made the grieving more focused, poignant, and painful.

Her father was the only other speaker. He refreshed the weeping brought finally under control after the priest concluded his homily. There was something in his manner that scared me. Not for my safety but for his. As the Royal Groundskeeper, he was beholden for his job, indeed for his life, to the good will of the royals. Yet, in speaking of his daughter's death there was ambiguity. Was anger woven into his remarks? Even blame? A collective murmur, a shifting of position, bespeaking anxiety, coursed through the room. Given my own tortured feelings, I couldn't begin to pin down the attitude of this grief-stricken father.

When he finished, the priest rose to conclude the service. Before releasing the attendants, he followed the customary practice of inviting anyone wishing to speak to come forward. Some had already risen from their seats to leave, and many had begun talking, when I rose and walked swiftly down the central aisle to the front of the room. I caught the alarmed sound of my mother's voice and the word "What …" I began to speak. The stir was such that few realized what was happening. The priest restored order by announcing in a loud voice that there was, indeed, one more speaker. "It is Parysatis, daughter of the Great King; Udusana's playmate. Her height makes it hard for some of you to see her. Please be seated. And Parysatis, please speak loudly, so that all may know your words."

Looking out at the audience, I saw no one in particular. All was a blur as I concentrated on words I had rehearsed.

"Udusana was my closest friend. She taught me many things, like make-believe. We had fun together. Sometimes we pretended to be grown-ups. But neither of us really was. At times we were sad. Mostly we were happy and I loved her. Sometimes I hated her, like just before she was bitten. I was feeling sad and angry because she had hurt my feelings. Hating her then makes me feel guilty now. It doesn't go away. There is blood on my hands because I wanted to hurt her at that moment, as she had hurt me. Now, I want to confess, to ask her forgiveness."

I was preternaturally alert, vividly aware of how I appeared to the audience, how they were reacting to me. I stood upright, feet solidly planted. My dress was floor-length, made of black linen with blue embroidery on the sleeves and across the chest. The room was bathed in candlelight and silence. I waited a few seconds and then, with head erect, moved swiftly down the aisle to my seat.

As many were quick to note on leaving the room, I had delivered these brief remarks with a poise that belied my years, and, despite my words, the look of neither self-consciousness nor guilt.

In youth, emotions are skin deep. Easily removed with hardly a blemish. They come and go with the speed of mountain weather. With age, emotions penetrate to the bone, deepened by pain and long memories. They ebb and flow gradually, modulated by experience and the complexity of relationships. I had my full share of each.

◁ 2

A PRINCESS IN THE PALACE

UDUSANA WAS BURIED in the beeyard, under the cypress tree that anchored its southwest corner. Her father had sought permission from the Great King, through one of the King's Eyes who was known for his soft heart. There were 20 of these men serving as general inspectors and surrogates for the Great King. They were spread across the Empire, in constant motion. Out of respect for Noah's dominion, her father had first confirmed that the Royal Beekeeper would not object. Noah was pleased, as I knew he would be.

On my trips to the beeyard after her burial, I would first visit the slight mound of sod under the cypress, in which violets competed with creeping thyme and rosemary for attention through three seasons and more of the year. Recalling our friendship filled me with gladness. So, too, did my confession at her funeral, which I recalled with perhaps too much pride.

It shocks me, now, to realize the uniqueness of my friendship with Udusana. Friendship unstained by other motives. Growing up a royal in the palace meant outgrowing purity of feeling; surviving meant accepting a multitude of motives to explain your actions and understanding those behind the actions of others.

I was good at ridding myself of guilt. In regard to Udusana's death, I just scraped it away, like soot from a sauce pan. Yet, after hearing what I said at the service, adult concern for my well being grew within the palace. From chefs to chamberlains, from cupbearers to captains, and throughout the palace chambers, large and small, the doleful refrain was the same: "Beware, lest self-blame and pity scar her for life."

Noah was consulted. Despite his assurance that I would feel no lasting guilt, indeed, that I had already left it behind, concern grew.

Sympathy and understanding flowed from every human tributary within the palace, seeking to lift me up. I felt embarrassment at being so undeserving of the attention, which even came from the Great King, who, for the first and only time, summoned me to the throne for what became more than the brief private audience his attendant told me to expect.

Except for this servant, who stood behind the throne with the ever-ready fly-whisk, we were alone. My father sat in regal splendor beneath the large canopy, a box-like crown perched above his coiffed hair. He held a staff in his left hand and a white flower in his right. In front of the canopy, extending almost to the door through which I appeared, was a sheared pile runner fifty feet in length. It was dazzling in color and design.

I fell to the stone floor just in front of the runner, first to my knees, then back on my haunches, finally bending at the waist with arms outstretched till my nose touched the cool slab. He left me there long enough to catalog my feelings: pride in being his daughter pushing against awe at the vast power the Great King wielded over his subjects, and especially over me; hope at having been told, by my mother, that I was his favorite, warring against the absence of any sign in support and the painful remembrance of his refusal to attend Udusana's service; fear that, regardless, he was known as an unkind man who changed favorites within the palace as the wind changed direction, and not just among concubines and eunuchs.

I was too young, then, to notice the void between us that grew as I matured, causing me to erect a wall of indifference to what I saw as royal abandonment.

When he said "Advance and be recognized," in tones pitiless to my ear, I forgot the guard's careful, insistent instruction. Rising, I began to walk towards my father. I had not advanced two steps when a thunderous cry filled the audience room. "Off the royal carpet! Now." Trembling, I moved aside and froze. Of course. Only the Great King had the right to tread on this royal textile. And I was only his daughter. Now, he invited me forward, beckoning with arms outstretched.

Anxiety melted away, as it always did in those early years, before I caught on. I saw too little of him, and so too did the multitudes, to notice the mask. It seldom remained in place for long.

Approaching in gladness, I wondered at the need for a fly-whisk. Wouldn't it take a bold and reckless insect to light on the Great King's skin? And, yet, as I neared the throne, a large black fly settled on his forehead. The royal fly-whisk couldn't see it. The King's hands were engaged with custom. I could see that he was trying to remove the beast by wrinkling his forehead.

Sensing that the throne's dignity was at risk, I saw an opportunity to redeem myself, a chance to prove my resourcefulness, to show that I could do for the King of Kings what a mere attendant could not. It would take all the boldness I could summon. I moved swiftly forward. "There's an impudent insect on the Great King's forehead. If the Great King holds perfectly still I will catch it in my hand." Without waiting for permission, I stepped on the throne stool, then onto my father's sandaled feet and, holding his shoulder with my left hand, reached high with my right and palmed the fly with a quick sweep across his forehead.

"Bravo!" he roared, face beaming with surprise. "Now, will you see that it won't bother us again?" his voice rising not to question but to command.

"I have already attended to that, Great King." Opening my hand, I lifted it to my face and blew the crushed annoyance off to the side.

Playfulness lasted but an instant. "Why did I summon you? Not to be the royal fly-swatter. Your mother pesters me about your feelings. Udusana's death was no accident. That I know. The blame rests with Anahita, voracious mother-goddess. A deliberate killing."

I was astounded. So much for the Great King's claim to Zoroastrianism.

"You're growing up, Parysatis, and it makes you fearless. What do you want to become?"

I knew then I wanted to be Queen. I also knew I should keep that ambition to myself. "I don't know. Am I not too young for those decisions?"

"Step back, child, from under the canopy, and look up. What do you see?"

I had seen the embroidered sides of the canopy many times, but never close enough to examine. Now I identified two winged disks, one above the other flanked by two types of animal facing the disks from either side. The top row were bulls, the bottom lions. When I answered the Great King, he asked, "Which would you like to be?"

"That's easy. The winged disks. I'd like to be Ahura-Mazda."

I could see from father's expression that he hadn't meant to include among the choices Persia's greatest God. "More than the bull or lion? How so?" His voice rose in anger, which at the time I missed.

"I'd rather control the bulls and lions than be one of them."

❧ ❧ ❧ ❧ ❧

Life in the hive was simple, compared to what I saw in the palace. My father had many concubines, in addition to my mother, Andia. There was Cosmartidene, a Babylonian, who had given birth to my half-brother, Ochus, and Alogune, also a Babylonian, who had given birth to another half-brother, Sogdianus. And there was his latest wife, Damaspia, who had given birth to a boy named Xerxes. I thought 'Xerxes' an absurd name for this child. I had good reason for my opinion, having played with him from nursery days on. He wasn't anything like his famous namesake, at least as I had been taught to believe, for Xerxes lived on in legend that few among the young would dare call myth.

Competition was the dominant theme of palace life. By ten, I had been exposed long enough to accept its presence in all that I did as unconsciously as the intake of air that I breathed. The Great King stood between the Gods and humankind. Around him, like an onion sliced across the grain, were rings of influence oozing with life, the zealous pursuits of actors competing for attention.

I was not yet aware of the darker competition that swirled about the Achaemenid dynasty itself. I remember the day, shortly after turning ten, when Andia escorted me to her room. "Now you're old enough to learn of the events that put your father on the throne. You may hear many wild stories. I want you anchored by the truth."

I looked at her quizzically.

"Xerxes, your grandfather, was a Great King. He was assassinated in his bedroom at night by his chief bodyguard, a giant of a man, and two other conspirators, the eunuch chamberman, and your father's oldest brother, Darius. No one saw the act, which wasn't discovered until morning. Such was the body-guard's authority in the palace, that he was able to convince your father it was Darius, alone, who committed patricide. Assembling a guard, your father had Darius put to death. He then became King."

"Amazing. Who chose him?"

My mother furled her brow, a sure sign that she was losing patience.

"What about father's other brother?"

"He was away in Bactria at the time. Its Satrap. But, in fact, your father was chosen because, within the family, he was the most qualified for the throne. But questions later. Be still or you'll be late for dinner. There's more."

I searched her face for signs, any sign that might add or subtract to this strange story. It was not that I found the tale unbelievable. At least not any more unbelievable than other palace tales. For they all had the capacity, upon first hearing, to make one gasp. Rather, it was my well developed instinct, as more generally it was the instinct of all sensitive occupants of the palace, to question anything that could not personally be verified by taste, sight, sound, or smell.

From my days in the Achaemenid palace, I learned that survival beyond childhood depended on this instinct. As it did in other palaces. As it always will.

I knew my father's nickname was "the Long-Handed," a name Andia claimed he received because his power was so vast, stretching almost to the outer boundaries of the known world. Of course, no one ever used that term in front of him, or for that matter, within earshot of others inside the palace walls. Even I could not refer to my father as anything other than "Great King" or "King of Kings" when in the presence of others.

Later I heard a different story from Noah, that father's nickname came from a mundane anomaly: his right hand was much longer than his left. He wasn't contradicting my mother's account, which he claimed he'd never heard.

Andia also claimed that, of all the kings of Persia, my father was the most beloved for his gentle and noble spirit.

"Remarkable," I said, keeping my churning thoughts to myself. Over the first decade of my life, I saw little of my father. What I remembered during those years was always the same: reports from Andia or the Magi or others among the King's retinue as to his impatience, which I was told was ripening into disappointment, anger, even rejection, over his unrepentant daughter's misbehavior, real or imagined.

Mother resumed her story. "The giant bodyguard continued his plot to seize the throne. He tried to enlist your uncle to his cause. That was a mistake, for this loyal man told your father. In the presence of his army, your father drew his sword and killed the bodyguard, ending the plot."

"Did they fight each other?"

"It was fair, if that's what you mean. His armor was taken away. They fought with swords. You know how good your father could be, even with a trained giant."

Outside Andia's window, I saw half an orange orb, beaming its ebbing light from its momentary perch atop the west wall of the palace. An emptiness filled my stomach.

"Soon after your father broke open the plot, his brother…"

"My uncle."

39

"Yes, your uncle. The Satrap of Bactria. He tried to secede. Your father led the army against him. Of course, he was victorious. He put this rebel to the sword, restoring order to the land."

"His own brother."

"That's right. This is the story I want you to remember. You'll be told others. Abide by mine. It's the truth. I know you have questions. You always do. Later. You'll miss dinner."

Andia rose, took my hands and lifted me up for a hug, which I returned. She looked relieved. We moved to the door, arm in arm.

"You should feel very proud of your father, the Achaemenid," Andia whispered. Feeling a gentle push, I walked swiftly down the long hall toward the children's dining quarters.

How was it possible, I remember thinking at the time, for one as gentle and noble as my mother claimed he was, to slay his two brothers, even in service to the kingdom?

Did love or hate play a role? Ambition? Or was it just a matter of duty, as in the beeyard? Given that the queen bee kills without having grown up with her rivals, I thought it far less of a challenge. For humans, it should be harder. But, then, perhaps for the first time, I realized that for humans, it can go either way.

❧ ❧ ❧ ❧ ❧ ❧

Amestris, the Queen Mother, lived in the third house of the harem. Andia went there regularly. For me, however, it was foreign territory, a mysterious place to which I was denied access and from which unchallenged orders for swift execution seemed to flow both day and night. More often than not, the bearer of these orders was Artoxares, the Queen Mother's favorite eunuch.

I was too young to have mastered the technicalities of becoming a eunuch, or its possible variations. I had eyes sufficient to see that Artoxares was a youth of great beauty, marred only by a scar extending on the right side of his face from just below the ear down the length of his neck. Deep red, it couldn't be missed. Artoxares' opinion of himself even exceeded the Queen Mother's praise. He loved to banter and flirt, the one easily migrating into the other with both male and female.

On occasion, even I attracted his attentions and would, as often, fall victim to his unflagging effulgence. But not without cost. His gaze made me painfully aware of my lack of physical development, a condition that seemed out of joint with my galloping mental advances. I felt wronged but wasn't sure on whose head to place the blame. Sometimes I wondered if Ahura-Mazda was punishing me for Udusana's death. Sometimes, just before falling asleep, I would repeat the same little prayer to Cebele, goddess of fertility, invoking her help that very night so that I would awake a woman in full.

Surely, I reasoned, my father, the Great King Artaxerxes, must be aware, indeed, must have ordered, or at least condoned, the many actions being initiated by the Queen Mother. After all, they concerned the administration of the Empire. And he was the King of Kings, as was Xerxes before him. And yet, I had doubts. I heard that the Queen Mother used spies of her own. I began to consider it possible that Amestris wielded power over the Empire separate and apart from that of her son. Slowly this wonder migrated toward belief and, in time, arrived at conviction. Amestris had vast influence within the palace. There was nothing remarkable about her. The source of her power, quite simply, was the position of Queen Mother. Here was a point I would never forget.

↰ 3

GROWING UP:
THE EARLY YEARS

BY TWELVE, I dominated the children's table. My step-brother, Sogdianus, whom we called 'moon-face', had gradu-ated to the adults' dining room, leaving as my sole companions my older brother, Bagopaios, a quiet, slow thinker as plain as unleav-ened bread, and my half-brothers, Ochus, then eleven, and Arsites, eight. Ochus was fair with a face empty of distinct promise. He had long curly hair of subtle shades of sand. Aware of its value, he resisted having it cut. First with one hand and then with the other, he was constantly at work weaving and teasing each curl of his lengthy locks into place. His eyebrows were bushy and brown, matching eyes of deeper shade and long lashes that curled naturally. His hair was the envy of females large and small. Arsites, in contrast, had a dark Babylonian complexion and an already chiseled face with high potential for future elegance.

It was the curiosity of Ochus that brought the table to a discussion of poison. He was obsessed with the Achaemenid dynasty.

"Again and again, I pressed my mother about our family's history, from Artaxerxes I, my father, to Xerxes, my grandfather, to Darius I, my great-grand-father, and even to Cyrus, founder of our dynasty. I had overheard her ask Artoxares, the scarred eunuch, about a rumor to the effect that Cambyses, son of Cyrus the Great and successor to the throne, had not died of a self-inflicted wound from his spear while in Egypt, as we've been taught, but had been murdered by someone who had dipped that spear in poison. Have any of you heard such a thing?"

All heads shook.

"Then what did you do, Ochus?" I asked.

"I begged her. Was the story true? What kind of poison? As an Achaemenid, didn't I have a right? She refused, saying I was too young for such matters."

I believe she wouldn't respond because she couldn't. Because she didn't know. Hardly anyone in the palace did. The subject was dangerous. Its pursuit by the young Ochus, however innocent, caused those with awareness of the conflicting accounts to recoil from the boy in fear.

Oddly enough, fear was not in our vocabulary. As children of royals, we glided through youth with what, in our ignorance, we took to be an assured right of safe passage. The topic of poison carried no link to our personal safety. Excitement, yes, a sense of mystery and danger, of course, but a personal threat, not at all. Danger only entered our heads at the threshold of maturity.

◀ ◀ ◀ ◀ ◀ ◀

Although I didn't know it then, I discovered soon enough that regicide ran in our family. Patricide too. Despite my mother's story, in fact, my father, Artaxerxes, killed his father, Great King Xerxes, to gain the throne. In so doing, he was following his mother's plan. The distaff side could handle power as well as their mates. We Persians believe that a family that commits regicide is cursed for breaking the most sacred of laws. Born innocent, I too was supposed to be cursed, and not just for the acts of my father and grandmother. They too had been born innocent, yet cursed by the acts of Achaemenids who came before. The cycle repeated itself, both before my time and after. What this curse meant to me, however, I could never resolve. If its power ever imposed on my free will, I was unaware. I never wanted to blame this family curse for things I did that turned out badly, as many did. I resisted because I didn't want to credit some unseen force, even in the slightest, for the things I did that turned out well. In searching for answers to human outcomes, I remain steadfast, as I slowly became through life, in looking only to the thoughts, beliefs, and emotions of human actors.

It all started with Cyrus the Great's progeny. Atossa was his most famous daughter. Those who knew her report a graceful presence in the palace. Unreported, although well known to close observers, was the power of her presence, a fact that attracted me greatly. She was married to her brother, Cambyses, the first to succeed Cyrus, and then, upon Cambyses' death, to her brother Bardiya, the second successor, and finally, to Darius, the third to succeed Cyrus.

Darius was not an Achaemenid, although he claimed otherwise. He restored the Achaemenid line by marrying Atossa. But not before he had disposed of two Kings in sucession.

The official palace account held that Cyrus's son, Cambyses, having peacefully succeeded to his father's throne, died accidentally, of a self-inflicted sword wound, while en route from Egypt to Persia. After Cambyses' death, a Magian was said to have seized the crown by impersonating Cambyses' brother, Bardiya, the next in line, whom he had murdered in furtherance of his plot. Darius, with the help of six compatriots, killed the Magian imposter, became an instant hero to his people and was crowned Great King.

Official stories often stray from simple truth. In the quest for a crown, the survivor's story prevails. Darius is a case in point. No Achaemenid King would so misuse his own sword as to kill himself. Cambyses was poisoned by his spearbearer, who happened to be the future King, Darius. It was he who applied poison to the King's blade. How he contrived to cause a wound no one knows.

When Cambyses was killed, his brother, Bardiya, took not only the crown that Cambyses had worn but, as custom allowed, Atossa, his wife. Bardiya lasted less than a month on the throne. He was killed by Darius, with the help of compatriots who had been convinced by their leader that the man sitting upon the throne was not a son of Cyrus and brother of Cambyses but an imposter who had killed Bardiya and taken Atossa, his wife, in marriage.

The story told by Darius, though rank with improbability, was accepted within the palace walls and beyond, throughout the Empire. Whatever doubts might have lingered in suspicious minds were put to rest by Atossa's apparent acceptance of Darius as her husband. How could such a formidable woman accept someone who had killed her two brothers, each at his moment of death her husband and Great King? Surely she would have known whether her husband was her brother, Bardiya, or the claimed imposter. If her husband was Bardiya, Darius would have had to kill her too, lest she proclaim the evil deed. Instead, she married Darius and they raised a family together, producing Xerxes, successor to the crown. The improbability of Darius' story would seem to be nicely offset by this equally improbable one. The truth requires deeper probing.

A man of Darius' daring and resourcefulness could have found a way to kill Atossa to prevent her from exposing Darius as a murderer of two Kings. Yet, she survived. That fact, alone, doesn't provide conclusive support for Darius' story. It took me much thought to reconcile Darius' evil acts with her silence and, to all appearance, the comfortable acceptance of Darius as her husband.

The path to survival for a woman is different than for a man. It must be, since women don't command armies or train in personal combat. Atossa knew that Darius, to become King, would have to eliminate Cambyses and Bardiya, the remaining male descendants of the royal family. But what of legitimacy, once the crown was his? He lacked dynastic ancestry. His proclamation on the Behistun cliff attributes his success to Ahura-Mazda. But when the deeds were done, and he prepared to confront the twice-widowed Atossa, sister to those he slew, wouldn't he have had doubts that merely an unprovable claim to Ahura-Mazda's support could grant legitimacy? Yes, killing Atossa would have been easy. But with the deaths of Cambyses and Bardiya, Atossa and her sister had become the only surviving descendants of Cyrus. If kept alive and wed, Atossa could enfold Darius in her legitimacy. He needed her to stamp him a royal, and, to stay alive, she needed to extend the royal hand. Their exchange proved to be propitious, both for themselves and for the Empire.

As it turned out, his first three wives were Atossa, her sister, and Bardiya's daughter. Here was a man who left little to chance or the fickle ways of God.

❧ ❧ ❧ ❧ ❧ ❧

Ochus knew his poisonous snakes. The viper and the cobra. The Empire had them in abundance. They were a popular subject at the children's table. Ochus was challenged in thinking of how to deploy them against one's enemies. Indeed, the idea of getting a snake to strike the intended victim challenged the collective imagination of the table. Staring at the blank faces around me, I threw up my hands in frustration, exclaiming "It can't be done. Snakes are every bit as independent as cats, and we all know what they're like."

"If the poison is so powerful and comes out of their mouths, why aren't they the first to die?" asked Ochus, beaming the self-confidence of one almost undone by his own intelligence.

I compared the snake's deadly bite to the sting of a worker bee, which, Noah had demonstrated, hurts the human but destroys the bee. "Perhaps, Ochus, the snake dies along with the victim, a fact seldom noted due to the distractions of the moment."

Bagopaios wondered whether one could "milk" a snake for its poison the way one milks a cow. Would the poison still be effective? Debate ensued over how one could successfully accomplish such a feat without getting bitten. Aristes, who had actually touched a cow's udder, wondered where its equivalent might be found on a snake.

I knew snakes. They stirred intense feelings. Fright for one. Attraction for another. I liked the feel of them against my skin. Despite crawling along the ground, their bodies were clean and dry, never sticky. Within, their muscles could be felt expanding and contracting. Those forked tongues, darting this way and that like the eyes of a great general, suggested a superior order of intelligence. I announced to the table my intention to find a poisonous snake and bring it to the group for milking.

"Suppose you have a victim but can't find a snake," asked Ochus, "what can you use?" He had directed his question to me.

"The garden. That's the place to go. Aconite is the best, I've heard." Blank expressions greeted my reference to this twilight blue beauty, a late bloomer in the perennial garden and a favorite of Noah, who had divulged its dangers to me. "One can use its roots, seeds, or leaves, and extract the poison by boiling them in water. The longer the water is boiled the more concentrated the poison becomes."

I had command of these tiny royals. And I experienced, for the first time, the power of knowing more than the rest. Of course, this can be a heady lesson, propelling one into danger on a wave of exuberant self-importance. Over a life-time I made more than my share of mistakes in showing off. It took many years to realize that even greater power lurked in the exercise of restraint. Wisdom, which I gained very slowly over time and through many mistakes, taught that, in palace matters, it was often better to appear a trifle dull-witted.

"Do you have to drink it?" Ochus asked.

"Of course, that works. But so does rubbing it on sensitive parts of the body. It's the quickest of all poisons. I saw a frog die within a minute of having his bottom rubbed with ointment containing only a few grains of aconite powder."

This was a lie; Noah had refused to let me even see the poison, although it was he who explained its properties. I was enthralled by knowing what those around me didn't. If exposing one's superior intelligence or knowledge can be stupid, even dangerous, at times, lying is likely to be worse. Yet, I was drawn to it as boys are drawn to weaponry. When mother confronted me about the aconite tale, as reported by more than one parent of the children who gave me rapt atten-tion that day, I realized how dangerous a lie can be. My boast had imperiled

Noah's life. Mortified and fearful, I confessed to Andia and persuaded her to accompany me to the beeyard, where, again, I humbled myself before them both. At the cost of becoming known throughout the palace as a budding braggart and liar, I was able to protect my friend from harm. Whether our friendship would be affected was then unclear, but I couldn't avoid imagining the worst, returning to this thought often, until I could visit the beeyard and find out.

❧ ❧ ❧ ❧ ❧ ❧

I soon saw Noah. It was mid-summer. I found him at work with cutting tools, which he was applying to an eight foot high tree trunk, rough cut just below the lowest branch and above the soil line. He was standing beside this project, half buried in wood chips, chucks and carvings. It was a chestnut, three feet or more in diameter. Emerging from this free-standing column, as excess wood was chiseled away, was a human figure with one arm raised, palm open, fingers outstretched, while the other hand held a sickle, arm extended at the waist, threatening.

Floating in guilt and unsure how to begin, I tried humor.

"What's this?" I asked with an accusatory tone to my voice, pretending to be the princess of our early days together, the one who would take offense at not being consulted.

He ignored me. I knew, once again, for the lesson had to be repeated over and over, that in his kingdom, he would never treat me as royalty. The only royalty he recognized was the hive. His respect for fellow human beings was deep and lasting. But his work always came first.

Putting down his tools, he held me with his dark eyes, his face hard at first, then melting into softness with a smile.

"The aconite matter is behind us."

I just nodded my head, blushing at the thought of that appalling incident.

"I like what's emerging, Noah. He looks eager to escape. Who is he?"

"Judging the age of this tree, a patient sort. He's been encased a long time. I hadn't thought to name him. Perhaps, with your help, we can come up with something. He's supposed to keep the swallows away. And other thieves. A practice of the Greeks. Their guardian's called 'Priapus.'"

I wondered how Noah knew of Greek ways. Before I could ask, he continued. "You wouldn't know this, but I came from Athens. Born there and learned beekeeping from my father. We lived in a small Jewish enclave. There was unpleasantness. As a youth I resolved to get away from Greece, if I got the chance. It came right after Xerxes burned Athens to the ground. A friend of my father offered him passage on an Aegean boat bound for Ephesus and the islands. Father gave it to me. I ended up here."

"Have you …"

"Never been back. If there's to be another journey for me it will be to Judah, to Jerusalem where my people are gathering strength. Thanks to your father."

I must have looked a total blank, because he said, "It's time you learned a few things about your father. Sit with me in the shade of the cypress. We will be near enough for Udusana to hear." He shot me a wry smile, as if to say "believe what you will, believe what will make you happy, for in the end it won't much matter."

The sun was hot, but where we sat, it was filtered by palm fronds and cypress leaves. Our skin was cooled by zephyrs, leaving us in that delicious state where one's body warmth is indistinguishable from the warmth around it, a condition even the royals can only command in the bath.

"The Great King has been kind to us. In his seventh year, he dispatched Ezra, a priest and scribe especially well versed in our God's commandments. Ezra went to Jerusalem with royal letters empowering him to command supplies as needed for the support of the Temple. It took my breath away."

"Why did he do it? You knew Ezra?"

"Of course. Your father was looking for peace and acceptance in Judah. Yes, and influence too. Ezra, with whom I spoke before he left, told me the Great King also wanted the sacrifices he was enabling to ensure divine protection for the Empire, for Artaxerxes himself and for his family.

"The Great King's power flows from Ahura-Mazda," I reminded him.

"So it's said. But if, as your father believed, our God is also filled with grace and might, why not bargain for his protection too?"

"Does my father accept your God, Yahweh?"

"You should know more about his beliefs than I. We believe in one God. 'Yahweh', the 'breath of life' as one knows from breathing, first out and then in, to say his name. A God who has chosen us. Your father, a man of many parts, elected to become the protector of Judah's beliefs and customs. Do we need to know why?"

There were vast regions of human activity, conducted by my father and the adults around him, of which I knew nothing. Growing up meant, somehow, becoming cognizant of, acquainted with, and, ultimately, as a royal, engaged in, the affairs of the Empire. This realization excited me and, even at twelve, made me impatient. Although I disliked my father, it was not through knowledge of the things he did outside the family. It had much to do with the many things he didn't do for his children.

"If Yahweh is your only God, and we Persians have many Gods, do they know each other and cooperate? Acknowledge each other's realms? Fight? How does it all fit together?"

I blurted out these questions in frustration, not really expecting Noah to have ready answers.

"What I know is the life of the hive. There is but one ruler. Pretenders are destroyed. What you ask is beyond my ken, unless I can reason by analogy. We were speaking of your father. I hadn't finished. There's another Jew, a friend of mine named Nehemiah, who is now in Judah on a mission similar to Ezra's, also sent by your father. He was your father's Cupbearer. You will meet him. But for now, my point is that your father has served my people well, like the Great Cyrus before him."

I left the beeyard consumed in conflict. I wanted to ask Noah whether his view of the Great King would change in the face of evidence, to me over-whelming, that he had in all important fatherly respects abandoned his daughter. How should a parent balance the needs of a child, who he was directly respon-sible for bringing into this world, with the needs of the Empire, which came before him and had many claimants to parentage. For all his wisdom, I doubt Noah could have answered this question. Of course, that's not why I never put it to him. It was embarrassment over my pathetic bout with self-pity.

Even now, with plenty of time to think, I find the answer elusive.

❧ ❧ ❧ ❧ ❧

It was mother's decision to celebrate my thirteenth birthday in the antechamber to her large bedroom. She wanted to bring together all the Great King's offspring. In the end she got five out of six. Was it an accident of planning that Xerxes, the only child by a woman formally his wife, failed to appear? Andia would not speculate, but the expression on her face, voluntary or not, sufficed. There was a tight bond among our concubine mothers, Andia, Cosmartidene, and Alogune, spun from common yarn. It existed side by side with the compet-itive fervor that touched all within the palace walls, the low and the high, even to the Great King, whose rivals included ghosts of past royals. I could sense both feelings at my celebration, as the mothers gathered together, well back of the birthday table, at which we had been helped to our assigned seats by the Magi, who hovered in their own cluster just behind the table as the food was served.

Oh, it was a feast fit for royals. There were three plain gold bowls on the table, one filled with pistachio nuts, another with dates and the third with figs. Pigeons and geese, each stuffed with honey-dipped capers and salt. The waiters carved the birds and served us on large silver plates. There were candied turnips and radishes. Also two bowls of sweet grape jelly.

For drink we had a choice: fresh milk from deep silver bowls or Chalybon wine from two silver rhytons. A waiter whispered to us that Chalybon was not a common wine. It was usually drunk only at the King's table.

We quickly named the two rhytons the "Griffin" and the "Bull," for their protome designs. The waiters had assured the adults that the wine was well diluted. It was my first time with the rhyton technique, and with wine as well. Except for Ochus and Arsites, the others were older and experienced. We consumed more wine than milk. The party grew jolly. I was seated between Ochus, he of the sandy hair, bushy brown eyebrows, and long lashes, and the moon-faced Sogdianus. Ochus paid more attention to me. Or was I paying more attention to him? I couldn't sort that out. But Ochus and I talked and talked, leaving Sogdianus to fend for himself. I spoke of Noah and the bee kingdom that had captured my imagination. He spoke of training for war, which for him was as natural as breathing, as certain of being mastered as puberty was of finishing its task any day now.

The meal ended with honey cakes of fine wheat flour and ground almonds. The waiters refilled the rhytons once and were about to do so again, when the Magi intervened. The party was over.

Mother invited me into her bedroom. "I was expecting your father. He promised, but something must have come up. Ours is a big empire, you know." She drew me to her for a big hug. "It's not worth crying over."

When she released me, I quickly lowered my eyes lest she discover I wasn't close to crying. My thoughts were with Noah, my only love, if I had thought enough to imagine where love resides.

"I have something for you. A birthday present for a princess. I was watching Ochus. He's taken with you. At twelve, it's beginning. I noticed you too. Never more animated."

She opened a drawer, the one she always went to for jewelry, and took out a small goatskin pouch. Handing it to me, she announced that its contents had been specially made. She hoped I would use it throughout my life.

I pulled loose the drawstrings and reached into the white pouch. What I felt, a smooth stone in the shape of a cylinder, gave nothing away. Despite not knowing what to hope for, my heart sank a little. I pulled the cylinder out, and saw that it was a seal, made from a beautiful chalcedony stone of grey-blue, an unusual color. Nice, but what did it have to do with me, I wondered. Mother, catching the question in my expression, said "Examine it closely."

What I saw in the depressions of the cylinder made my heart leap. There were two long-bodied bees facing each other, in design almost identical to the gold bee pendant that my mother wore, a gift of the Great King, fashioned centuries before in Crete. It was my favorite piece of jewelry. Beneath the bees on the cylinder was my name.

I was excited, insisting that we get some clay to try it out. Anticipating this, Mother produced wet clay from under a cover on the floor. I rolled the cylinder across the clay, pressing hard. The result, raised clay depicting in high relief the bees and my name, was thrilling.

"I don't need to tell you that these two are rulers of the honeybee world, facing each other in friendship."

"Yes. I mean no, you don't. I see what you mean. I will keep the seal safe. It will represent me to the world. You couldn't have given me anything better."

"And now, I go to attend your grandmother. You should return to your room, taking the seal with you. I suggest you lie down to assure a gentle decline to normal from this day's high, especially the effects of all that wine you drank." She swept out of the bedroom before I could obey, through the antechamber, sandals sliding over the marble flooring, and was gone.

I was pleased with myself. Delighted and reckless. I felt strange entitlement, as if I was free to do all that pleased me. On the table where my mother made herself up, I recognized a familiar bronze bottle with a metal rod on top. Sitting down, I dipped the rod into the bottle and applied the kohl to outline my eyes, trying to follow with my mind's eye the way I had seen Andia do it. Looking in the hand mirror, I liked what I saw. I rouged my cheeks and applied pomades of frankincense to my neck and arms and, then, very deliberately, to my chest, imagining a riot of growth. Emboldened, I raced to the dress closet, picked out a gauze-like floorlength gown and changed into it. And then, still held in the wine's novel embrace, I began opening drawers, mindlessly searching. I came upon the gold bee pendant, which had become detached from its necklace. I took it out of the drawer, thinking that by carrying it to my room, I could make it my own. When its loss was noticed, I reasoned, no one would guess I was the one. Quickly, I straightened up the mess I had created, changed clothes and hid the pendant under my dress. Only upon turning to face the anteroom through the door did I see Artoxares, standing tall, his scarred beauty now fearsomely etched by the strong shaft of daylight flooding the anteroom.

This man had a nose for mischief. It must be what made him so valued by Amestris, the Queen Mother. True, but as I discovered much later, there was more to his services than just enhanced insight. At her urging, he used his remarkably seductive charms to conquer wives and daughters of the most privileged and important men surrounding the King. For Amestris the purpose of this sport was not vicarious pleasure. Intelligence was the goal, and Artoxares succeeded brilliantly in bringing to his ladyship all manner of secret plans, plots, and accomplishments, from petty to profound.

I was the first to speak, my voice breaking against nerves despite efforts to beat back fear, to sound firm and accusatory.

"What are you doing here?"

Artoxares laughed. "Your mother sent me to be sure you got back safely. I don't need to ask what you're up to, my eyes and nose have the answer." His voice rising, he commanded: "Off to your room now. Be quick about it or my report will not be to your liking." As I passed by him at the doorway, he moved enough to let me pass, then caught me round the waist with one arm, searching for the pendant with the other. "I'll have that, my little thief. Show me where you found it." His hand came up, as if from nowhere, to grasp the pendant.

I felt numb with fear and humiliation. My skin grew wet with chilling sweat, which, mingling with the pomades and rouge, became a paste. I reeked of excess. I felt faint and close to sick with a churning stomach. I wanted to disappear.

Releasing me, he entered the bedroom, pendant in hand. Turning back, he saw me pointing at the drawer that housed the golden bees. I realized we had switched positions. It started me on the road to self control. I forced myself to speak. "You mustn't tell mother." He had finished putting the pendant away in the drawer.

He turned to face me as I continued in a voice quavering and contrite. "I beg you keep the pendant thing to yourself. No harm done and telling won't help you with your lady, Amestris." His face was a blank.

"You will only hurt me, and that's not a good idea …" Words raced ahead of thought. I stopped.

"Because?" he asked in a tone that sounded insolent.

"Because … Because I'm going to grow up and grow powerful in this palace, and because, when I do, I shall remember what happened today." The strength in my voice surprised me, as did the heavy thumping of my heart. Turning in the doorway, I walked quickly through the antechamber, hoping to escape with the last word.

※ ※ ※ ※ ※ ※

I must have been the last to learn of Nehemiah's return. It was early summer. Noah told me after he had been in the palace for a month, serving again as the Great King's Royal Cupbearer. I was helping Noah inspect the hives for dysentery, which can be devastating if not caught early. We were also inspecting the combs for mildew and infection from moths. The day was bright, the sun hot and the bees hard at work.

"I invited him to visit the beeyard this morning. Should be here soon. He's heard about you."

"From?" I asked in mock surprise, for I knew full well that Noah was the only one with any reason to speak of me to the Great King's Cupbearer.

"You'll have a chance for questions."

Noah knew why I was eager to meet this man. Partly to see my father through his eyes. Partly to see Noah's God. On both subjects, my mind was racked with uncertainties that I felt the need, almost as a test of becoming an adult, to resolve.

I watched Nehemiah closely as he entered the beeyard through the arch of roses Noah had recently established as what he liked to call the "door" to his "palace." He was a tall man with olive skin and a generous black beard that masked a lean, even gaunt, face on which the skin seemed shrunken wherever bone offered no resistance. His eyes were dots of movement, sunken deep under black bushy eyebrows that flaunted wayward curls. His nose was long and tapered to a narrowness suggestive of a knife's edge. Wayward hair sprouted like weeds from his ears and nostrils. He had a circular blotch of black skin on the right side of his face, which he was inclined to turn away, as if to hide, causing him to peer out of the left corners of his eyes. He greeted Noah with a kiss on each cheek. Then turning to me, he bowed slightly, extended his hand to take mine.

"Parysatis, I have heard many good things from Noah. Best of all, he says you show interest in us, like your father." His dark eyes twinkled as the lines of his taut skin etched an unmistakeably geniune smile.

It was time to eat. Pointing, Noah offered the shade of two tall date palms or a blooming chestnut, as wide as it was tall. Nehemiah tried to defer to me. I sent it back with the force of protocol, observing that he was the guest among us. With a nod towards the chestnut, Nehemiah led us to sit under its shade, where we could as easily hear as see the army of gleeful bees that covered its leaves, toiling with gentle motions and soft murmurings, fondling the flowers, becoming thick with nectar.

I never looked at date palms without seeing Udusana. She had once remarked on the wind passing through the great fronds of this tree, an invisible force bending them close to the point of breaking, allowing them to gather strength and spring back, only to be bent again, the cycle repeating over and over so long as the wind blew. She wanted to become that wind. Just for a day. To move unseen through fronds and leaves, to race across gardens and dunes, to climb mountain peaks, to dance across the sky. She bubbled with the joy of imagining and brought forth laughter from both of us. I thought of Udusana every time I heard wind in the fronds, recalling her wish and imagining it had been granted. And, for as long as it took to rehearse her remarks, I would be remote from those around me, alone with the wind and my memories, which ranged from the melancholy of loss to the mortification of guilt.

Fetching his basket from the lowest limb, where he had put it early that morning to stay cool, Noah offered us fresh milk in goblets, pease-porridge, lentils, and goat cheese, together with two kinds of bread, barley cakes with honey, and wheat biscuits sprinkled with poppyseed.

"Is Judah very beautiful?" I asked after we had sorted out the food and, reclining, begun to eat.

"No more than Persepolis. But you want to know why your father sent me there, to its capital. Or, since it was I who asked to go, why he let me go, and made me Governor.

"And so do I," said Noah. "You got away before I could hear your story."

"Jerusalem had been laid waste, its gates consumed with fire. This made me sad. I will compare it to having your palace destroyed. Or Noah's hives catching fire. All those of my faith are drawn to Jerusalem. My sadness turned to conviction; I felt summoned. But I did nothing. One day, as I was pouring the King's wine, your father asked if something was wrong. I responded. He released me for the assignment. What insight this King, your father, has when it comes to reading men's minds!"

Yes, quite right, I thought, but why is his skill exhausted whenever he turns to his children? In particular, those of my sex.

"So," said Noah, "tell us how you fared? My young friend must store up lessons in her small head as my bees distill honey."

"Like a flower, then, I shall unfold," he said, in a voice soft and inviting.

As Nehemiah warmed to his subject, perhaps stimulated by recollection, his voice rose, and he rose with it, getting to his feet and gesticulating like one of the more theatrical of our palace Magi, as if his audience numbered not two but two hundred.

When he had concluded, eyes flashing in remembrance, instead of bowing to the applause that his account generated, he turned to examine the insects at work on the chestnut flowers just above his head.

"I'm afraid they were too busy to hear a word I said."

"Come, Nehemiah, sit again," said Noah. "You're too tall to stand there, mingling with my bees, who, in truth, don't recognize you as a friend and may take offense. I'm sure Parysatis has a question or two. And I have a couple of ripe pomegranates to split open."

Nehemiah lowered himself to the ground, then crossed his legs and turned an open countenance towards me. Responding, I handed him a barley cake slathered with honey. "Here, try this. It's not the 'Governor's bread,' so you have no excuse," I said. Their laughter was rewarding. I knew how to amuse my contemporaries, and did so almost unconsciously. Here, for the first time, I was addressing adults. Beyond the pleasure of succeeding, I became aware of the disarming power that comes from making others laugh.

Noah had opened the pomegranates, which lay before us, bright scarlet sheathed in creamy white.

"Do you know what the pomegranate symbolizes, Parysatis?" Nehemiah said, popping a handful of seeds into his mouth.

"I could make up something having to do with its juicy sweetness, but better to hear what you have in mind." This man's a natural teacher, I thought.

"'Juicy sweetness,' you say. That's it precisely. It's God's gift, symbol of fertility and the very essence of life. Whenever we partake of the pomegranate, we should count our blessings."

Noah appealed to me again.

"I'm always asking Noah questions. He assumes I want to do the same to you. But it's not easy for me. I mean…talking about your God. But…was it really his doing? How did you know? What about the hard work of your people?"

Nehemiah looked deeply into my eyes, as if to probe beyond, to reach my soul. He spoke with quiet earnestness, seemingly bent on passing a secret that even Noah, seated as close to me as he was, couldn't hear. "There's something about the idea of God that makes one feel inadequate. The fear of appearing stupid. I saw it in your face. And I must tell you that everyone starts with that fear. It's as natural for us as gathering pollen is for your friends in the tree above."

I had dropped my eyes. Not because I couldn't hold his eyes with mine, although such would have been the case had he not looked upward at the bees to finish his thought. I had caught myself staring at the large circle of black abraded skin on the right side of his face, just above the eye line, a "rodent's ulcer" he had called it. It had begun to ooze and drip from the intense sunlight. Its ugliness, set against the qualities of this man, unsettled me.

"Yes, it was hand and will of my people. But there was much credit to pass around. Gladly did we share it with our God. And why not? Man's account can never adequately explain what happens in this world. Behind every answer lies another question. In the end, one is driven to believe. And there are practical aspects as well. To subdue one's enemies, it helps to have them believe that our God's finger tipped the scales.

"You Persians have Ahura-Mazda, creator of heaven and earth, and Mithra, God of light and eternal fire. At the celebrations honoring Mithra, I've watched the Great King receive 20,000 colts from the Satrap in Armenia for sacrifice. Can he prove benefits?

"Not really. In the end, it's just faith. His Gods are different from my God, but his faith and mine grow from the same root."

Nehemiah summoned a part of me that, in my youth, was free to heed the call with unalloyed faith. Perhaps it was my better part, but as the years passed, it never had a chance. In regard to decisions affecting the welfare of the Empire, faith in God's will was risky and took too much time to test. I preferred the idea that it was God's will to believe in oneself.

❧ ❧ ❧ ❧ ❧ ❧

I made a life-changing discovery soon after turning fourteen. It was an unused and forgotten corridor leading from an outer room in the palace kitchens to the drinking room adjoining the banquet hall. I had gone to one of those rooms to fetch a bowl of milk for my cat, Cyrus, who had just returned, dreadfully hungry, from a two-day absence, who knows where. I was handed the bowl and asked to step back against the wall so that a large wheeled tray of food could be taken to the banquet hall.

Stepping back while looking to see what food was being conveyed, I misjudged the distance, hit the tapestry-covered wall hard and dropped the bowl. Attendants quickly came to my rescue with rags to clean up the milk and a pail to deposit the broken pieces of the bowl.

As they did so, I bent down to join them, but not to help. I had felt something give as I hit the wall, something that gave ground and then returned to where it had been. The tapestry came to within an inch of the floor. Now on all fours, I was trying to examine the wall without calling attention to myself. It wasn't hard because the lighting was bad and the attendants were concentrating on the work at hand.

With my back to the wall, I moved one hand along the space between the tapestry and the floor, while with the other I fished around in the dark for pieces of pottery. I detected first one vertical crack and then, distant about the width of a narrow door, another. With growing excitement, I then sought and easily found a horizontal crack where floor joined wall, running between the two verticals. Against the tips of my fingers, a faint coolness came through the crack.

Rising with the attendants, I left the room atingle with excitement, forgetting the original purpose of my visit. Cyrus met me at the door to my apartment. Purr turned swiftly to whining complaint as he discovered I was empty-handed. His eyes seemed to burn through me in accusation. I was saved by a knock at the door. Opening it, I could hear the retreating steps of someone from the gracious kitchen staff, who had just deposited a bowl of milk on the floor. Before I could pick it up, Cyrus asserted control. The purring resumed.

Late that night, after all seemed quiet, I returned to the outer kitchen room, candleholder in hand. The candle was lighted and I brought an extra as well as a flint. Setting the holder on the floor, I pulled aside the tapestry and pushed against the outline of a door, gently at first until it budged, then harder until it opened wide. It was hinged from the inside, and mounted in such a way that it swung shut of its own accord.

Excitement merged with fear. The tapestry had fallen back in place, cutting off virtually all candlelight. I judged it possible to fetch the candleholder before the door shut. In fact, it had hardly started to move by the time I was back in the opening, candle in hand. I felt the side of the opening to see if there was some kind of locking device. Nothing. I reached around the door. There was a pull ring on the inside. Peering ahead, all I could make out was a corridor leading into perfect darkness. Looking down, I could see by the now flickering candlelight that the corridor's floor had a thin layer of dust, disturbed by my bare feet for the first time in who knows how many years.

With heart thumping loud enough, I imagined, to wake the dead, I allowed the door to swing back, testing the ring a couple of times as it moved to enclose me inside. I then turned to explore the corridor. It was straight and narrow, about the width of two adults. It ended at a wall with no door to exit. Two feet above me were fixed louvers, slanting down towards a room beyond, presumably for ventilation. That room was dark and silent. I caught the odor of haoma.

To be sure of my bearings, I would have to return with something to stand on. And I would have to do so when there was light in the room. The haoma, however, gave me a clue. That, together with my general sense of palace architecture, suggested that I had discovered a hidden corridor leading to the infamous drinking room adjoining the banquet hall, a room that, not being a concubine, I had never expected to enter.

On the way back, crouching at what I took to be the midpoint of the corridor, I drew my name in the dust with my index finger, then wiped it clean against my bed dress and returned the way I had come.

❧ ❧ ❧ ❧ ❧

The palace was electric with excitement over the arrival of Themistocles from the coastal city of Magnesia, bearing with him the stunning Greek statue of Penelope, promised to the King some twenty years ago, when this famous Greek general convinced my father to grant him sanctuary.

Themistocles was the genius behind the destruction of the Persian fleet at Salamis, in the seventh year of Xerxes' reign. It wasn't obvious why the Great King would want to extend a royal greeting to one who had defeated his father in this pivotal battle, a battle the Greeks called "the tomb of Persian power." It was the general's banishment from Athens, his home, that caught our interest. A man of this stature who is not wanted in Greece, indeed, who is being hunted by Greeks throughout the Aegean, could make a strong case, without more, for being welcomed in Persia. And so he was.

Themistocles got more than protection. He was granted land, a generous estate on which to live out his remaining years, and tribute collectable from coastal cities to prosper him and his family. In exchange, Themistocles promised to serve the Empire in regard to Greece, as events might demand. And he promised to bring from Athens, as soon as circumstances would allow, the white marble statue of Penelope, sorrowing over the absence of her husband, Odysseus. This sculpture was chief among the many gifts bestowed on the general by Athens, following his triumph at Salamis, when nothing but praise graced his ears. The subject had been picked by the general himself, and so too the particular sculptor, who was considered the best in Greece.

Penelope wore a Greek chiton. She was seated, her head resting on the palm of her right hand. The poignant beauty of this masterpiece had attracted the attention of delegates sent by the Great King to Athens. So effusive was their praise that my father began to covet it. When word came that Themistocles sought refuge in Persia, the Great King saw an opportunity to make the sculpture a central element of the bargain. I have no quibble with my father's handling of this project. I too was excited, but not by the general, of whom I knew nothing. It was the opportunity I saw when word spread of a great banquet for this aged Greek refugee.

My plan was to wait near the kitchen until the staff became occupied with clearing the banquet tables. No one would be in the outer room at that moment, a sure sign that the men were repairing to the drinking room. The banquet lasted a long time. Shouts of pleasure and applause mixed with periods of quiet, when I imagined a speaker addressing the gathering. These sounds reverberated down the four corridors that fanned out from the banquet hall, one of which passed close by the outer kitchen room, allowing me to catch a sense of the pleasures that grown-ups found in good company and the ballast of excellent food and wine. I looked to the day when I would be among them, not a minute after reaching full bloom as a woman.

Just when I had decided they'd all dropped off from too much haoma or been poisoned, the sound of things being moved over stone, of dishes being stacked, of ordering voices rising within the kitchen foretold the end of this phase of the evening. It was time to disappear behind the tapestry. With my heart leaping into my throat, I ducked under the weaving, pushing hard on the door, which opened as before, allowing me within a second or two to disappear in the darkness. I brought no candle, relying on memory to guide me down the straight corridor. Resting against the inside of the door, now tightly shut, I felt the intense pleasure of being hidden and alone, embraced by darkness. It was like being safely submerged in a perfectly drawn tub of hot water, only better because one didn't have to come up for air. So self-satisfied was I that it took some moments before I realized, from both light and sound emanating through the louvers at the end of the corridor, that men had gathered in the drinking room.

I tiptoed down the length of the corridor. Only then did I remember that the louvers started at a height above my head. I had forgotten to bring something to stand on. Dull light shown in horizontal stripes through the louvers, casting a faint pattern on the wall. I heard voices and conversation. I imagined these men, all favored by my father to be among the select retinue of royalty, reclining on their couches, being served Chalybon wine and haoma in goblets of gold.

"He was in fine form tonight, considering."

"He's looking very old. Old and tired. But what a mind. These Greeks must age from the bottom up."

"And sense of humor. Suggesting that our King must have been desperate for generals if the only reason he took me in was the fact that Athens had condemned him as a traitor."

"But the swollen conceits of the man. Hard to stomach. By the time one reaches his age, one should have exhausted the need to talk about oneself, and have run out of material to boot. He repeats himself. How many times in one evening did he compare himself in youth to a wild colt, claiming that the wildest colts make the best horses, if they get properly trained and broken in. I doubt he's even house-broken."

"True, true. All true, but we must give him credit for Penelope. A long wait, but he finally came through. It's a magnificent piece. The pathos of the scene, head upon hand, a face of great beauty, ambiguously at rest, and then the telltale eyes, downcast and sad—the saddest eyes I've ever seen."

"Greek artists must suffer. I'm sure of it. They regularly exceed the grasp of their audience."

A harp began. The player must have set up close by the louvers, for the sounds were much louder than the men's voices, which continued. A flute and lyre joined and then a woman's voice, rendering with great beauty a well-known melody in the Phrygian mode. Realizing the courtesans had arrived, I tried to picture them, just beyond the wall, facing the reclining drinkers. Had they been passing among the men, filling their goblets? I knew next to nothing of the courtesan, her ways and means. Among the Magi, the subject was beyond taboo. Their method of deflecting our questions was to ignore them. As if courtesans and concubines did not exist.

❧ ❧ ❧ ❧ ❧

The secret corridor competed with the beeyard for my attentions. I took risks to obtain accurate information about the drinking room. I had to know when to make the passage into darkness since, without activity on the other side of the louvers, the corridor was of no use. When the drinking room was filled, I was drawn to the louvers as powerfully as a bee to summer blossoms.

To listen unobserved, to learn the ways of men, their thoughts while at leisure, imbibing, to feel enclosed in darkness, immune from detection, to be alone and reaffirmed in one's belief of being exceptional, all these were products of the corridor, contributing to my happiness. At times, I wished I could purr.

My route to the outer kitchen room was not direct, for I enjoyed passing by the beautiful Penelope, which my father had placed in a vestibule of such size and shape as to lead one to suppose it had been designed solely to house this statue. I never tired of studying Penelope's ambiguities, of imagining the early years of solitude and watching, as they turned bit by bit, inexorably, into inconsolable loneliness. Was this statue, projecting as sorrowful a countenance as I have ever seen, intended to show Penelope before the return of Odysseus, or afterwards, when even a hero such as he must fail to meet the measure of the one embellished in her imagination, year over year. Gazing up at her face, I tried to imagine what it would take to put off so many suitors for so long. Surely Odysseus would have become a giant in her mind's eye.

I knew the secret would out sooner or later. Secrets are of two types. First, there is the kind one never wants to reveal. Here one thinks of terrible things one does that, if known to others, would be embarrassing, damaging to one's reputation, or threatening to one's safety or life. And then there is the kind one needs to reveal. This kind of secret can be empowering to one who passes it on to others. Sharing brings pleasure, to both the holder of the secret and to those with whom it's shared. Such was my secret of the corridor. The more consumed with it I became, the more desperately I searched for someone to tell, someone whom

I could tell with safety, who would share, vicariously, my pleasure. It wasn't just the fact of the corridor that I wanted to disclose, but the conversations. I thought of Udusana.

❦ ❦ ❦ ❦ ❦

The evening when talk turned revelatory, I had brought a footstool, allowing me, on tiptoe, to look downward into the drinking room. I could see the backs of two couches, with reclining drinkers in place. I could see the courtesans from their tight-cinched waists down, their translucent gowns suggestive of the limbs beneath, as they passed to and fro, filling the goblets of those closest to me. And there, on a table between the couches, were pomegrantes, cut in sections for eating, their deep red ooze glistening softly in the candlelight. That was all I could see. I could smell the courtesans. Their faces and arms must have been rubbed with myrrh, that most compelling of unguents. After exploring these very limited sight lines, I stepped down from the footstool and resumed my regular position on the floor, concentrating on the conversation.

An argument had broken out over the circumstances of my grandfather Xerxes' death. One of the men, whose voice I thought I recognized but couldn't fit to a face, one whom I named the "Skeptic," had challenged another, whose story was essentially the same as the one my mother had told me. The Skeptic's voice projected an arrogant confidence abetted by the consumption of much wine and the need to prove something to his companion.

"Ah, since we are alone, and you are a man of integrity, to be trusted with a secret that would have me killed were it to escape this room, I will share with you the truth. Your account fails because it leaves out Queen Amestris, Xerxes' wife. She believes in power, in its certain presence, and in her responsibility to see that it is taken up by the right person. As Great King Xerxes increased his daily dependence on the grape, Amestris acted on her belief by seizing what little power over the Empire she didn't already possess. That, of course, was the power still resting in the hands of her husband."

"Your lecturing tone is tiring. Get to the point."

"She had never approved of her son Darius' choice for a bride. The girl was simple-minded, a hopeless trait for one destined to become Queen. She was the daughter of Xerxes' brother, whose wife was a sly conniver intensely disliked by Amestris. A volatile situation, one that could not hold against two extraordinary events. First, Xerxes seduced the simple-minded girl shortly after Darius married

63

her. I doubt his well-stocked harem fell short of his normal appetites. But one wants what one doesn't have, even more so when what one doesn't have is forbidden. As King of Kings, Xerxes thought he could make up the rules. And for the most part, he could. But family rules, even for the royals, were different, especially with Queen Amestris as his dominant partner.

"Given his preference for wine, I doubt Xerxes' seduction was one of sensual prowess alone. It was the lopsided struggle of father against son. Amestris didn't blame Xerxes as much as the girl's mother, who, Amestris believed, had encouraged the match. Perhaps to the point of reversing the roles of seducer and seduced. She also blamed her son, Darius. She was heard to remark, 'He is, after all, the crown prince. If he can't keep his only wife out of his father's bed, how can he expect to rule the Empire?' It proved to be the turning point in her choice of successor.

"The second event involved the elegant robe woven for Xerxes by Amestris at an earlier stage in their marriage, when affections flowed in both directions. Darius' simple-minded wife took a liking to it and got Xerxes, in a moment of drunken weakness, to give it to her. This silly girl then appeared in the presence of Amestris, wearing the robe. She had to know on whose loom it had been woven. Think not of guile, however. Exceptional stupidity was the cause. Are these things new to you?"

My head began to ache. The pain grew as I tried to unravel the implications of what I was hearing.

The Skeptic, a natural story-teller, continued.

"At the new year's day celebrations that year, Great King Xerxes drew his wife, Amestris, and family around him, inviting them, as was the custom, to express their heart's desire. The Queen was last to choose. Her wish was a shock to Xerxes, who recoiled in horror. But, as an Achaemenid, he had no escape. She had asked for the sly, ambitious wife of Xerxes' brother, mother of Darius' dim-witted wife. Given how she felt about the girl, it was second best. But the girl was now in the royal line, and as such, untouchable.

"What happened next is not pretty, even at this remove. Even under the influence of what these girls keep brimming in our cups. Xerxes sent for his brother and tried valiantly to convince him to abandon his overzealous and conniving wife. To no avail. When the brother returned home, he found his wife lying on the floor, encircled by pooling blood. Severed beside her were her tongue and breasts, which, having been blinded, she could not see.

Feeling lightheaded, I let out a groan. The Skeptic stopped in mid-sentence. Could he have heard me? My heart was pounding like a drum. I heard a crash, followed by shuffling of feet.

"What a waste. Are you drunk or is my tale upsetting? Come girls, fetch rags. And show some common sense in whose goblet you top up."

I wanted both to escape and to hear more. The Skeptic had resumed.

"Behind the ambiguous smile of Queen Amestris, which she appeared to wear with carefree abandon, was uncommon foresight, granite-like resolve, and indefatigable grit. Although more estranged from Xerxes than before, her power waxed on waves of rumor that circulated within the palace.

"Xerxes' brother fled with his sons to Bactria, where he tried to rally a defensive force in revolt. Xerxes sent forth his army. The revolt was quickly sudued. Naturally, the rebels were put to death."

"Your tale is as horrible as it is hard to believe. But why don't you get to the point."

"And what was that, my clumsy friend?"

"You claimed my explanation of Xerxes' death was wrong. Impatiently I await yours."

By now I knew the Skeptic enjoyed the sound of his own voice. I suppose one must, to become a great spinner of yarns. I wanted the truth. Could it be that Amestris, who bubbled with gentle laughter as Queen Mother while bouncing me on her knee, could have done such things? How could I tell? Could I believe in this disembodied voice, reaching through the louvers?

"I come to that directly. It's absurd to imagine that the accepted villain in the slaying of Xerxes, his chief bodyguard, could have initiated the plot on his own. Xerxes' son, Darius, had been named crown prince and his other sons stood ready in the wings. This bodyguard had help, and before that, inspiration, from a woman of great power. The involvement of Aspamithres in the conspiracy and bedroom assassination provides the answer. Though it remained a private matter, this eunuch's long love affair with Queen Amestris was widely known. Known and respected, because she had taken no other lover, despite provocation and opportunity aplenty. After all, she was a beauty increasingly uncherished by her husband. This eunuch bore her message of approval to Xerxes' bodyguard, and together they completed the first step in the Queen's three-step plan to seat her youngest and most favored son, Artaxerxes, on the throne.

"Sheer fantasy, but go on."

The tunnel had become much warmer, the air heavy. I lowered my head to see if breathing was easier at ground level. My head came to rest on the honey cake I had brought with me and then forgotten as the tale began to unfold. Squeaks loud in my ear and movement against my hair brought me swiftly upright, carrying the sticky cake, now tangled in my honey-sweet hair. Mice had nibbled at the cake. I'm not fond of these creatures, but I was so riveted by the Skeptic's story that, unconsciously, I must have pushed fear into the dark recesses of the corridor, perhaps there to join the four-footed creatures supping at my feet.

"Fantasy as to what could happen becomes fact with the benefit of hindsight. Could Xerxes' youngest son, Artaxerxes, have killed his oldest brother, the crown prince Darius, just on the word of a bodyguard whom he hardly knew? Not likely, and yet we know he killed Darius. This was step two, with the strings again being pulled by his mother, Amestris.

"What's more, we know the first thing Artaxerxes did, upon seizing the throne, was to put the bodyguard to death. This, after declaring before all at the coronation that 'he owed the throne to the bodyguard's ardent zeal.' Finally, we know that he then put to death the Queen's eunuch, Aspamithres. Amestris could have saved her lover. Her resolve to have him killed was a matter of loyalty to the Empire, assuring safety for both her son, Artaxerxes, and herself. Literally, to bury the truth. These killings were Amestris' third step."

"In your tale, duty triumphs over love. Glorious."

This bit of sarcasm cut through the wall as if it were paper. I suddenly thought of the imposing Artoxares, the scarred beauty. Remembering palace rumors suggesting that he had replaced Aspamithres as Amestris' lover, I considered the possibility that, in regard to my formidable grandmother, duty and love went hand in glove, triumphing together.

❦ ❦ ❦ ❦ ❦

"How well do you know the Queen Mother?"

Noah was opening a hive. It was late fall. The pulsating sounds of the tawny workers were regular, like the beating of my heart. And, yet, their murmurings sounded an urgent note. Life in the hive is pitiless: work or die; work and die. Noah claimed they were making faster round trips now in an effort to capture as much pollen as they did in mid-summer, despite the shortening days.

"Well enough, from a distance." He applied the smoker, subduing activity at the top of the hive.

"Amestris stepped into the beeyard only once, praising my chestnut honey and then complaining that I produced too little. She had a way of looking at you that caused discomfort. Her eyes would concentrate their power on yours, but not just that; they penetrated, as if she could disrobe your mind. After that visit, I came easily to accept the palace rumors. I doubt she offers a simple compliment without balancing it with criticism or insult. No offense, but it runs in your family. Schooled in palace ways she is, and practiced too. Why do you ask? You have that mischievous look, prelude to trouble. Out with it, or my small friends will use force."

"I want to know the truth. She's one of those women in the palace who demands respect. Do you think she's deserving?"

Noah proved to be a disappointing listener as I revealed my secrets. He declined, even in imagination, to follow me into the corridor. When I tried to recount the Skeptic's story of Amestris' role in her husband Xerxes' assassination, he raised his hand, palm open, in protest, refusing even to listen. Frustrated, I seized his hand, pulling it down.

"What kind of a friend are you if you won't even try to understand? This is important." I tried to ignite a fire in my eyes.

Noah worked the bellows of the smoker again, forcing the bees deeper into the hive. Minutes passed. Sensing his firmness, I shifted tactics.

"What is it about smoke?" I asked, not sure if I had already heard, and forgotten, the explanation.

"The bees think there's a fire. They flee into the hive and gorge themselves on honey. They're preparing to abandon the hive."

"They're running away from a thief. Isn't that what you are? An honest thief, perhaps." I flashed him a smile.

"Or not a thief at all. Despite knowing what I'm up to, the bees stick around. Isn't that consent? Aren't they allowing me to take their honey?"

"How long has the honeybee been domesticated?"

Noah used a knife to extract comb that had not been used to lay eggs, placing each piece in a large clay bowl. Arrested by my question, he stopped what he was doing, put down his knife and turned to look at me with those probing, fawn-like eyes.

"Domesticated, you say. Like a dog or horse?"

"Like a cow or camel. Exactly." Playing around with words this way was always fun, but a flicker of sadness intruded. I glanced over Noah's shoulder at

67

the cypress anchoring one corner of the beeyard.

"You're mistaken. Don't worry. Many others, with more experience, have made the same assumption. The bees came to us wild. And they remain so. I'm their 'keeper,' not a 'trainer.' Huge difference. Under my care, they prosper, but not because they do my bidding. This is not enslavement. I simply facilitate what they would do without my help, in nature's wildness. And what they do is the miracle of miracles. They make honey out of pollen, nectar, and water. Alone among the animals, they make something of value to themselves, and to humans, out of elements that are all external to themselves."

"In contrast to…?"

"The cow, Parysatis. Consider. It makes milk, but where does that white fluid come from? Or, the sheep, providing wool, milk, and meat. All integral to the animal."

"Ah, Noah, my friend and guide. You never fail me on the subject of bees. There's no question you won't answer, and always with clarity. Why not treat palace questions the same?"

"I am your friend. A true one for certain. I am also Noah, Royal Beekeeper. And you, you are Parysatis, an Achaemenid royal. My tolerance for risk is different than yours. That you can't see that, at fourteen, is understandable. Your vision will change as you mature. In the meantime, find another royal to share your secrets."

❧ ❧ ❧ ❧ ❧

The Skeptic was telling the truth, as I discovered much later. His was the voice of that scarred beauty, Artoxares, the Queen Mother's arrogant servant, that devious eunuch who had upended my birthday celebration by accosting me in my mother's bedroom. I connected his voice to that of the Skeptic when my mother sent me with my two half-brothers, Ochus and Sogdianus, to sit at Artoxares' feet for lessons in Persian history. The more he talked the more certain of the match I became.

His account of my father's accession to the throne tracked my mother's precisely. I was dumbfounded and angry at being played for a gullible child. Frustrated, too, because I didn't dare tell my brothers and couldn't call Artoxares on his lies without revealing how I heard him convincingly advance an entirely different story. And what a story it was. As shocking as my discovery of how babies are made, it plunged my already complex feelings for my father into a dizzying dance of confusion. Clarity emerged only in regard to my grandmother, Amestris, whose triumphant manipulations in service to the Empire revealed possibilities beyond my ken.

◁ 4

COMPANY IN THE CORRIDOR

I HAD TURNED SIXTEEN before getting someone to join me in the corridor. As Noah had suggested, it was another royal. Among the Great King's offspring, the only one with whom I found rapport was the bushy-browed Ochus. A year my junior, he too was born of a concubine. Despite my eagerness to share the secret, it took months of maneuver to turn this idea into action.

Whether on account of an insecurity about my sexuality or something else, I found myself unexpectedly shy about inviting an emergent boy into this dark place. Had I considered the change in my attitude about nakedness, this reluctance wouldn't have come as a surprise. As a child I was happy to remove my clothes, regardless of who might be around. And with Udusana, I progressed well beyond the gawking stage.

When I started to develop breasts, however, I grew shy, unwilling to uncover myself. I felt humiliated by my body, which seemed impossibly slow to assume the features of what I imagined to be a royal's entitlement. At some point, things changed. The idea of being naked in front of males embarrassed me, but for reasons different than before, reasons I had difficulty cataloging. Although my body was no longer a source of humiliation, I feared it at the hands of others. Simultaneously, I desired to show myself off, a butterfly newly emerged from the pubescent cocoon.

Looking back, I can't claim now to know, or even then to have known, for sure, what I looked like. Whatever I thought was likely to have been an imagined account of what others saw when they looked me over. There were a few things I knew for sure.

I was of average height but appeared taller because, at sixteen, I was still skinny. The defining curves of a woman, so craved by men, were on their way, but much finishing work remained to be done over the next couple of years. I had admirable hands with well-tapered fingers. My legs showed muscle but, as yet, no distinct shape. My hair was soft and black as a raven's wing. I had let it grow, using braids or pins to keep it from flowing past my shoulders. Whereas my body was thinner than it would remain, my face was to migrate in the opposite direction. It was round and so full of adolescent flesh that my features were indistinct, save the eyes, which were uncommonly large. When no one was around, I would stare at them in the mirror, imagining a suitor whispering: "Ah, bright blue beacons floating in twin white seas."

Responding to a nervous habit formed in my early teenage years, my eyes seemed constantly on the prowl, darting left and right, ceaselessly in motion. In time my nose, cheekbones and chin would become sharply defined features. In combination they would not cause me to be considered a beauty, although it was widely agreed I was interesting to observe and even pleasing if one could catch me at ease. Rather, these features projected someone different, someone to ask about, hear her story, and get to know.

One fall day, Ochus was sent by his Magus to study the statue of Penelope, with an eye to discerning the greatness of Odysseus through the sculptor's rendering of his patient and faithful wife. He was to prepare a short talk on the subject, to be delivered to a palace audience that afternoon. The Magi had been subjected to withering criticism a couple of years earlier because their charges proved inadequate to adult eyes and ears in expressing themselves before a crowd. "Pathetic," one of the King's Eyes was heard to exclaim. Quick to respond to a change in the wind, the Magi became demons for declamation.

When I came upon Ochus, staring at the poignant figure, he appeared clueless, an object of excruciating torture. I had squirreled away many thoughts about this sculpture, waiting for the chance to share them. Without embarassment, he eagerly absorbed what I had to offer. By the end, he had peeled away the anxious look in favor of laughing brown eyes and soft smile.

I caught his ear.

At the appointed hour the next evening, as the last course of a royal dinner honoring the King's generals was being served, Ochus arrived in the half-lit anteroom that gave access to the secret corridor. I had come early. From the darkened wall we could see through the doorway to the well-lighted kitchens. Servants were scurrying back and forth between the kitchens and the banquet hall, clearing the tables of what remained of one course and bringing forward the next. Seizing Ochus' hand, I ducked behind the tapestry, pushed hard on the door, and led him forward into pitch black darkness. At our backs, what little light had entered the corridor with us was snuffed out first by the tapestry's return to place and then, more definitively, by the door's snapping shut.

"Didn't you bring a candle?" Ochus asked, clutching my hand harder.

"Come. The corridor is straight, and wide enough for us to walk side by side. You'll start to smell the haoma as we get close to the symposium."

Hand in hand we moved slowly forward. I caught an odor, but it wasn't haoma or the aromatics of the great beeswax candles that illuminated the drinking room. It was Ochus, who exuded, from parts unknown, a blend of sweat concocted from heat, fear, and excitement. A male odor, and, perhaps for that reason alone, not unpleasant. I could hear the fingers of his right hand sliding along the wall. I imagined how dependent on me he must have felt at that moment, but instead of being weighed down, I soared.

By the time we reached the louvered wall, conversation was well under way in the room beyond. I whispered to Ochus to sit down, which he did, back to the wall. I sat down facing him. Our legs interlaced.

There were many voices. We could hear the clink of goblets against marble, bowls being set down, the padding of concubine feet on the stone floor. Alas, more than an hour later, endless streams of banter and gossip had left Ochus disappointed and me embarrassed.

¶ ¶ ¶ ¶ ¶

We returned to the corridor a week later. Despite his first visit, Ochus was, again, on edge. I scolded him, forgetting how I had felt. Although he was only a year younger, I often treated him as a little boy I could easily control, despite ample evidence that he had emerged from puberty.

We had each arrived at the tapestry with a rolled up mat, obedient to my idea of how to avoid the layer of dust that stuck to one's bare legs, as they became dripping wet from the heat of this closed space.

It wasn't until we had reached the louvered wall that it became clear there was no activity in the drinking rooms. No candlelight, no movement, no voices. We laid out the mats and sat as before, facing each other across the narrow corridor, legs touching. In hushed whispers we began to talk.

"I saw that scarred servant flirting with you yesterday. I don't like him. Or trust him."

"He's a eunuch, Ochus. Flirting's all he can do." It was pitch black, making it impossible to read his expression. I felt deprived, reminded of how important eye contact was to my ability to converse.

"No, Parysatis. There, you're wrong. Artoxares can be a lover. All palace eunuchs can. My Magus explained it. They are castrated after puberty, not before. They can get erections and enjoy sex. They just can't get women pregnant."

I blushed, now thankful for the darkness. What Ochus said made sense. If all Artoxares could do was flirt, why had I heard repeated hints that he provided more than verbal comforts to the Queen Mother?

I tried to reassert myself. "They're entrusted with the harem because men know the women are safe in their hands."

"Yes, my Magus says that many of the women enjoy being in their hands, as you put it, and much more than that," Ochus whispered through a laugh, placing emphasis on the word "much."

Perhaps it was the topic. Or the lascivious lilt of his voice. Or the touch of his moist legs against mine. As the eldest, I began a harmless exploration, my fingers leading the way up his uncovered legs.

In the corridor, I could see no harm in visualizing what those sensitive fingers touched, as they mapped the covered regions of Ochus' young body. Waves of heat coursed the length of me. I tingled. Remembering my lessons, I planned to stay ahead of the playful game I had begun.

I had misjudged my younger half-brother. Ochus swung his body around and pulled me under him. I didn't dare shout. Frisson turned to fright. In whispers, I pleaded and cajoled, even threatened, remembering my success with the scarred eunuch. I scratched his face, pushed his chin, wriggled to escape the weight of him. His physical strength seemed twice mine or more. I would remember the helpless revulsion at being violated.

He got to his feet, then paused to stand over me. "If you speak of this, I will deny it. I will disclose how you led me into this corridor, asked me to bring a mat, then seduced me. No one will believe your story." Turning away from the louvered wall, he disappeared.

I got to my feet and ran, staggering through darkness, the length of the corridor. It wasn't until I got beyond the tapestry and saw the red stain on my white skirt that I realized it was not his semen I had felt on my thighs but my blood. Tears now coursed down my cheeks, conjured up by the thought that his seed was planted, irretrievably deep, in my virginal womb.

❧ ❧ ❧ ❧ ❧

Royals were taught the essentials about sex upon entering puberty, but not for the purpose of honing their skills. Intercourse with another royal was strictly prohibited before marriage. Not a serious hardship, since marriage could be arranged at almost any age, before or after reaching sexual maturity. Ignoring this injunction was perilous. At a minimum, one's position in the palace was destroyed. Depending on the facts, one's life was also at risk.

I kept picking at the failures and mortifications of that night in the corridor, like scabs that materialized again and again. Only years later did I discover one can ease the pain by coming out into the sunlight to share with another the torments locked in the darkness of one's mind. That was with Aspasia, of whom I will speak later.

I didn't misjudge Ochus, who was not inclined to reckless impulse. I had misjudged men. Ochus had behaved as any of his sex would under like circumstances. It didn't take me a lifetime to figure this out. However, more than that was needed for me to accept my own role in what happened. From the region of Shades, I could see plainly. I had toyed with feminine power, as a child might play with fire, and lost control.

Scurrying to my room from the corridor, head down, I had just begun to imagine the more obvious outcomes of my predicament, when I all but crashed into my scarred tormentor, the glamorous Artoxares. He had been drinking; indeed, at the moment we collided he was quaffing mead from a half-full goblet, which flew from his hand. I sensed his embarrassment and watched as it transformed into an anger fed on my own vulnerability and his suspicious nature. Feigning concern for my well-being, he seized my hand in one of his, swooped down to fetch the goblet with the other, and pulled me along, practically at a run, to my mother's apartments.

"Here, my lady, is your daughter. I found her sneaking about, guilt plastered across her face—see for yourself."

What was left of my composure collapsed with Artoxares' departure. Dropping to my knees, I threw my arms around Andia's legs and moaned. There are times when a mother's legs are a source of comfort. Even a mother in whom one has felt disappointment. Andia questioned me and I responded, weaving a story of uninvited attention and forced entry. Andia knew my period had passed ten days earlier, making pregnancy a risk. How big a risk she would leave to Apollonides, the Greek doctor who had become something of a palace ornament.

I had met this eminence once. Enough to take an immediate dislike to him. He had a lion's mane of curly hair, dyed a dingy yellow but with tell-tale white showing at the roots. Beyond being puffed up by his own importance, he treated me, and palace gossip held, all young women, in the same way: as mechanical toys to be played with for his own pleasure. How did this Greek rise so high in a Persian palace? His stature was first established by twin successes in setting the broken limbs of both my father, Great King Artaxerxes, and his charioteer after they were thrown to the ground during a lion chase.

It then soared, coming close to heights known only to the King of Kings and his deities, when Apollonides succeeded in driving away the frequent head pains that afflicted my father's wife, Damaspia. They could grow unbearable. When one descended, she would retreat into isolation, perhaps to avoid being seen in such misery, perhaps to avoid causing vicarious misery to others.

As a child of the sea, having grown up on the Aegean island of Cos, Apollonides was familiar with the black torpedo fish, or "sting ray" as it was known to the islanders. He was first to experiment with a live sting ray, using its strange jolting power to treat human ailments. When he sent for these fish to use on the Queen, many thought him mad. Indeed, but for the desperate straits Damaspia experienced when the pain split open her head, the Greek doctor, despite his successes, would have been treated as a fraud and expelled from court. She insisted he be given a chance.

Several fish were brought to the palace, alive. Apollonides instructed Damaspia to recline on a couch. He took one of the fish in gloved hands and placed it on the Queen's moistened forehead. Salt water ran off the fish into the Queen's eyes, causing them to smart. She welcomed the pain as a distraction. Using blocks of wood, the doctor held the fish in place for half an hour. Damaspia later said she felt a number of jolts to the head, like someone hitting her in a way that caused the impact to spread out before being felt. Suddenly, the Queen let out a cry. Her head felt release. Apollonides removed the fish. The Queen rubbed her forehead, discovering it was numb to the touch. "No matter," she declared, "I am rid of it. And you, Doctor, are a genius."

"Mother, I can't abide that man. I don't want him to lay a hand …."

Andia wasn't listening. She had a plan. Her resolve surprised me. "Your story must remain with me. I will handle things. And see to Apollonides. To bed now. Try to believe it never happened."

⟁ 5

GROWING UP:
THE MARRIAGE

 ON THE AUTUMNAL EQUINOX in my sixteenth year, amid
cloudbursts of sheeting rain wrung from dark foreboding skies,
Ochus and I were married. Ceremony and celebration were
held in the Apadana, whose immense size and limited windows turned mid-day
into night. Flickering torches around this audience hall wrapped the celebrants in
a warm glow that was intermittently etched in the ghostly white of lightning
bolts. In accord with palace custom, we were but one among many couples from
the royal house and among the families of the King's men who were being
married that day. Ours, however, had been the last to be announced, tacked on
to the long-settled list of engaged couples. Andia and Ochus' mother, the
Babylonian concubine, Cosmartidene, planned the marriage. Little more than a
week passed from the moment Andia learned of the incident to her announcement that we were to wed.

If I had feelings about my mother's plan, neither Andia nor the King of Kings
saw fit to inquire what they might be. The die was cast. My role was to conform
with as little fuss as possible.

Ochus and I saw nothing of each other until the ceremony, when we were
seated together in the first of several rows of armchairs for the future spouses,
placed to form a square in front of the offering table, a foot-thick slab of worn
marble supported by cypress posts. Originally a glistening white, the slab was
stained dark from years of sacrifice. Just behind the table was the holy fire,

79

burning briskly from a powerful draft created by a stone fireplace. It featured a firebox of enormous height and width but surprisingly shallow depth, giving one the impression of a fire dangerously close to escaping its confines. There were no seats for the guests, who were expected to mingle and move freely around the celebrants.

I was getting accustomed to the smell of my designated husband, which entered my nostrils in waves as he moved nervously in his chair, forcing my mind back to the corridor. Although the room was cool, sweat had soaked his tunic around the arms and chest and was gathering on his high cheek bones to form large drops that fell into his lap. His eyebrows, brown and bushy, met above the nose, making a spectacle of the frequent twitch he gave them when on edge. As if by prior agreement, neither of us showed interest in the other. We stared straight ahead, our eyes unfocused, our expressions determinedly calm, our minds like a churning ocean far beneath its placid surface.

❧ ❧ ❧ ❧ ❧ ❧

At the time, I was fearful, thinking only of how I wanted to relate, should relate and, in the end, would, in fact, relate to Ochus in the new guise of husband. Now, however, with the destruction of my Empire complete, I must acquaint you with the ceremony in which I was a participant. Its like will not be seen again.

A mighty blast from an ox horn held by a Magus at the main portal to the Apadana signaled the start. Guests had already gathered in the great hall, awaiting the procession in which we had been placed, last of the couples to be wed. We had formed at the bottom of the grand entrance to the palace, built by Darius I. It was a double reversing staircase 23 feet wide with graceful tread of only four inches for each of its 123 steps, making it easy for procession horses, as well as elders, to reach the broad landing at the top. From here, the procession would ascend another double reversing staircase and thence to the banquet hall. The centerpiece of the façade, which one faced before turning left or right to climb the stairs, was a large blank stone surface, intended by Darius I to be inscribed with the royal building record. To either side, four Immortals in relief salute the non-existent record, as if inscribed in all its glory. Darius I had died too soon to attend to this matter and Xerxes, his son, was too busy attending to his own glories to recall those of his father. What still surprises me, given what I know of my grandfather, Xerxes, was why he didn't simply use this beautifully sited blank to trumpet his own accomplishments.

The heraldic symbol of Persepolis, a lion tearing the hindquarters of a rearing bull, had been carved in relief on the outer sides of the two staircases, between another blank stone, three Immortals and rows of palm.

The procession was led by two Magi carrying bundles in their left hands, side by side. Three pairs of Magi followed, each carrying a live goat or ram. One more pair came behind, carrying containers filled with barley, flour, mead, wine, and beer. As customary, the Magi were clean shaven. They wore unadorned white turbans that extended across the mouth and nose, a custom intended to block pollution of the holy fire when they stood near, as the ceremony required them to do.

The Great King came next, richly robed in red robes with vertical pleats embroidered in cuneiform, expressing the leader's title in the three official languages of the Empire. A bejeweled dagger was stuck under his belt. Ample space ahead and behind made him appear alone, but, in truth, he was followed by four Immortals, as his personal bodyguard was known, at a distance that could be traversed by one or more of them in less than a second.

They were handsomely dressed in costume of ankle length, decorated in various shades of blue, brown, and black. Embroidered squares of sepals and stars covered their robes, with edging of shimmering dots dyed white. They wore a rope-twist headdress and carried not just a seven-foot spear but a bow slung over the left shoulder and a full quiver behind. Though abundant, their splendid beards were meticulously groomed, each hair combed out and cut to uniform length.

Finally, came the couples, the first five looking much too solemn for the occasion, the last shy and frightened, like colts about to be broken. On reaching the great hall, we proceeded to our chairs. The Great King sat in a throne chair placed to the side, between us and the ceremony table. The Magi gathered at the table and, at a signal from the King, lighted the large candles at either end of the table and commenced the sacrificial rites, the purpose of which was to propitiate Ahura-Mazda. Bleating and blood dominated the hall. Chanting by the Magi accompanied the butchery. The meat was roasted in fire consecrated for the occasion. The air filled with the complex odor of smoke from cypress logs, wax candles infused with frankincense, and the burning fat of ram and goat.

❧ ❧ ❧ ❧ ❧

When the rites were finished, I was amazed to see our father, Great King Artaxerxes, rise from his chair and turn to address the gathering. He looked solemn, enough so to satisfy the demands of a funeral. But there was more to discern, a desperate sense of discomfort, as if he wished he were elsewhere, as if he had been pulled into place despite kicks and screams by those strange powers on the distaff side that so often control even the life of a ruler.

I couldn't imagine what my father was going to tell us. His subject was marriage; his theme perfunctory: a brief homily on the special nature of marriage within the palace, the responsibilities of spouses whose marriages are thus sanctified, especially to Ahura-Mazda and through him to the people of the Empire, and the need for secrecy to protect and preserve the aura of mystery and power that emanates from the palace.

His delivery was a different matter. This King of Kings could summon a voice of the deepest resonance, as befitted his position. He used it with great skill, as if he were a great actor accomplished in rhetoric, varying both tempo and pitch to catch and hold the attention of everyone in the room. Marveling at him, I was distractedfor a moment. Could a King be endowed with such a defining feature of leadership from the outset? As my father's daughter, were these powers latent within me? But no, perhaps they emerge only upon being crowned, a gift of the gods to one chosen to represent them on earth.

Next came a reading of those to be married. As their names were announced, the groom took his bride's hands in his and kissed them. A servant brought forward a small loaf of bread, warm from the oven, handing it to the groom. He broke the loaf in two, gave one half to the bride and they both ate. A rousing cheer followed this ceremony, which signaled the moment of marriage. The couple was then invited to speak. The celebrants were likewise offered a chance for brief comment.

Ochus and I were last to be named. He declined to speak, and so, reluctantly, did I. Call it cowardice or prudence. Whatever stilled my voice at that moment overcame a well-rehearsed plot I had hatched to speak truth to those assembled in the Apadana that dark afternoon. I sometimes tremble at the thought of how my life would have been changed had I spoken. Or what life would have been like had I not spoken as I did later that night when Ochus and I were alone. Two forks in the road on the same day.

Only seconds separated ceremony from celebration. At a signal from the head Magus, lines of servants paraded into the hall, carrying tables and couches, at least 200 of them for the married couples and royal relatives. There followed more servants bearing silver cutlery, plates, cups and goblets, as well as platters and bowls of every size and shape, all fashioned of gold or silver. Swiftly, behind them, came another army of servants laden down with food and drink, which they distributed on the tables, each having been covered in fresh white linen, bordered in purple.

There followed musicians, prominent among them flute-girls, clad as Nymphs in skin tight tunics, sambuca-players and harpists. After playing a round, they were joined by a mixed chorus of one hundred, singing a wedding ode in the softly alluring and seductive Ionian mode. As the tables were made ready for feasting, the sounds of conversation grew, almost drowning out the music. Ochus and I did our duty in making conversation with the throng of celebrants eager to congratulate us. We spoke with them separately. Close enough to be seen as a pair, we stayed apart. Aware of each other's presence, we avoided contact.

The palace chefs lived up to their fame in the fare spread on tables that crossed the hall at either end. For appetizers, there were turnips done in vinegar and mustard, olives steeped in brine, sturgeon and tunny hearts, lentil soup, square-shaped loaves, freshly baked and seasoned with anise, cheese and oil, and flat pudding made of milt, meal-cakes, and honey. Other tables were heaped with chickens and ducks, ringdoves and geese, hares baked in curiously molded cakes and young goats, as well as pigeons, turtle-doves, partridges and other fowl. A roast pig lay on its back on a silver platter of amazing size, its belly open to reveal inside a bounty of roasted thrushes, ducks, warblers, and pease puree poured over eggs, oysters and scallops. Hot breads rushed from the ovens disappeared as fast as they could be brought forward. Rolls as white as milk. Voluptuous loaves, some sprinkled with poppyseed, others with honey and flaxseed, some shaped like mushrooms, others like sheep, horses, and goats.

The wines were from Cappadocia, Thasos, Lesbos, and other regions far and wide, including a limited ration of the famed Chalybon wine from Damascus. "Empty-handed I see." The words were addressed to me, I realized, as someone thrust forward a silver goblet of neat white wine. Thirsty from talking, I drank. Despite having eaten nothing since breakfast, I felt no hunger. Apprehension filled my stomach. I was having difficulty conversing. Someone nearby was comparing women who chatter to cicadas. Another, helping himself to the olives, was addressing a Magus. I could see him holding an olive aloft, directly in front of the Magus' face as he put the question: "Do you, Master Magus, love the ladies who are over-ripe, or the virginal ones with bodies firm as these olives, steeped in brine?"

The wine was assaulting a stomach depleted of all save fear. I wanted to retch, but there was nothing there to work with. The grape was clouding my mind. I felt hungry and began to eat. I consumed quantities that evening, all in the space of half an hour.

In the midst of this binge, Noah found me. I hadn't seen him since Ochus and I were last together in the passage. I could tell from his searching eyes that he was looking for clues to my state of mind. His hopeful demeanor quickly turned cloudy, even before we spoke.

"It's been too long. They miss you. So do I."

"I must get settled. Then…then…"

"There's much to tell…" His voice trailed off as he turned abruptly and moved away.

I didn't need a mirror to know that his swift departure was caused by the shame he saw in my eyes, the flush of embarrassment he read across my face. Looking back at this fateful day, I've often wondered how many of the guests were eagerly whispering to one another their dark suspicions of our misfortune and downfall, even as they stood in line feigning to partake of the joy we were pretending to express.

Ochus and I were the first wedding couple to leave the festivities. We were led by a Magus and servants to an apartment in the third house of the harem, often used for newlyweds. Alone, we separated to explore the quarters, an unspoken substitute for the more challenging prospect of exploring our future together. There were two dressing rooms, each with its own bathroom, flanking a large bedroom in the shape of a cube. The floors were of stone, edged with terracotta of black and white squares.

Brightly dyed wool and linen weavings covered the stone within each room. In the bedroom a large garden carpet dominated the space in front of the bed. Depicting water rills leading to a central pavilion of floral motifs, its geometric pattern was similar to that of the immense palace garden kept vibrant and green with the abundant waters of the Zagros, symbol of God's mercy, carried to the site by aqueduct.

Murals of wild animals, imaginary and real, covered two of the walls while the other two depicted the trees of the Zagros and others unique to the royal pleasure park. There were tall cypress, symbol of immortality, almonds, symbol of rejuvenation, white-stemmed poplar, favored as wind-breaks and the Asian plane, a refuge of shade.

Not a word had passed between us. After the Magus departed, what I most remember was the sound of silence. There was nothing in the world, myself included, that didn't disgust me in these moments.

I broke the silence with the speech I had planned to deliver at the ceremony. I recall trying to adorn my message with something like my father's oratorical flourishes.

"Hear me, celebrants. This marriage has been forced upon Ochus as it has upon me. There's nothing unusual about this. I am old enough to know. Within the palace, arranged marriages are the rule. Elders do the arranging, and the matches made by them are always based on what elders believe will best serve the palace. Sometimes this claim is worthy. Often it is not.

"What's different in our case is the cause of our being matched. Ochus took me in darkness and by force. Within the palace. What he did was a crime. A crime should have consequences. And yet, it's not that simple. For, as my mother put the matter, it's possible I am already with child. The interests of family and palace, which I'm told are the same, compel this marriage. That is why we now appear before you, in thrall to our elders. Not a propitious start for a man and woman expected to journey through life together; decidedly not a promising path to the marriage bed.

"In accepting your invitation to speak, I did what was natural; but to tell this story was not, unless one takes to heart the faith of our great founder, Cyrus, in commanding Persians always to speak the truth, regardless of consequences."

We had entered the bedroom and were sitting opposite one another, across a low marble table in the middle of the garden carpet.

I had risen from my couch to speak. Upon sitting, I could see that Ochus was shaking, his ashen face a mask of apprehension.

"Why didn't you?" He was more sad than angry.

"Fear and…like it or not, we have become a pair. The truth was more harmful than silence, even when it promotes a lie. But I had to tell you." Looking stern, I tried to catch his eye.

Lifting his face, he stared at me, then spoke with wary voice. "And still might? Your story leaves out some important facts. What I did came after you seduced me."

"What you did was to use force and violence."

"But you deliberately aroused me. Spread your legs, inviting me."

"Enough," I snapped. "Absurd. With that argument you'd become an object of palace ridicule. It's been a long day. I'm going to dress for the night. There's but one bed. We will use it for sleep."

A slight smile of surrender crossed his face, as if to seal a promise, warranting that Ochus was, at heart, a gentle boy. Later, after sleep had erroded the sharp edge of anxiety, I awoke to the need to discharge the food I had forced upon my nervous stomach.

I awoke again as dawn was breaking. I had been dreaming about Atossa and Darius, their marriage of convenience or, as I preferred to think of it, necessity. Atossa's dreadful knowledge of Darius' path to the throne was her path to power over him, power that would last a lifetime. Could the secret of how I lost my virginity be the key to our marriage, the defining feature of my relationship with the boy still asleep beside me? Not to even the scales, I comforted myself in believing, but as with Atossa, first, as personal shield, then for the welfare of the Achaemenid line, synonymous with that of the Empire.

⟅ 6

SATRAPY OF HYRCANIA

 OCHUS AND I were the first offspring of the Great King to marry. From a distance, I can now say it strikes me as strange that no one even noted, much less questioned, the pairing of two children of the same father. At the time, it didn't faze me in the slightest. I knew Atossa had been married, in succession, to two of her full brothers, first Cambyses, then Bardiya. The zeal to hold the royal standard tight within the Achaemenid family had always swept other considerations from the field.

Xerxes, three years my senior, was the only legitimate son to our father, being the sole son of Damaspia, his wife. As such, he was the designated heir. Palace gossip held that, thus far in his short life, his credentials for the post were sparse. He was tall and handsome of face, with a pronounced nose, high forehead and deep-set blue eyes. His ears were curiously turned outward, exaggerating the taper in a face that narrowed to a pointed chin. Xerxes took pains with his wardrobe. By outward appearances, he was divinely shaped to succeed his father.

But Xerxes had weaknesses that began to appear when he spoke and were confirmed when he engaged in debate or even lively conversation or banter. His mind was slow to work, the product of its labor thoroughly pedestrian. Early on, as a child, he came to realize this shortcoming. Encouraged by the Magi, his tutors, he believed it could be overcome through earnest endeavor. Whether they believed what they told him or not, it turned out to be a message of cruelty. For Xerxes was ambitious. He was propelled into paroxysms of heroic effort in an attempt to better himself. To no avail. There was only so much one could do with the raw material. Beyond his mental limitations, he lacked the eye-hand coordination so basic to horsemanship and hunting. Thus, as he grew to manhood, he found ingenious ways of excusing himself from these activities, not to mention the more challenging ones of combat with sword or spear.

Despite these blows to his self esteem, legitimacy and good looks attracted women of the palace. Many of them grew adept at ignoring his limitations and, by combining feminine instinct with well-honed skill, were able to preserve, and even enlarge, the young man's sense of being exceptionally important.

He moved about the palace as if enclosed in a royal coach designed for one. To his half-brothers, all bastards, he was haughty, often unapproachable. To me, however, perhaps because I was a girl, he behaved with charm, kissing me not on the cheek, as one would a person of lower status, but on the lips, a practice reserved for one equal in honor. As we passed through adolescence together, I first became aware of his disabilities and then, more slowly, his mighty ambition to overcome and cover up. A soft spot appeared one day in my heart. It grew over the years, as I saw his reach continuing to exceed his grasp.

I was my father's only child by Andia, a Babylonian. Apparently, the Great King's taste for concubines from that city was all-consuming. By the time of my marriage, they had given him seventeen sons. The eldest, Sogdianus, was born the same year as Xerxes. They had nothing else in common. Sogdianus was short and stout. He had a face like an almost perfectly formed pumpkin, round and vacant of feature, save for a nut-sized growth above his right eye that was hard to miss, with its three black hairs curling away from a pale white center as unruly eyebrow hairs sometimes do. He was careless of dress and slovenly of manner. But he could deploy his body with sure control. Likewise his mind, which danced with quickness, insight, and wit.

Not by dint of age alone did he become the informal leader of our bastard tribe. From a young age he was ambitious and worked assiduously to command. He would feign surprise whenever we turned to him for leadership; in fact, he did so frequently enough to expose the game. I didn't trust him.

Before the year ended, the King of Kings and his enormous retinue departed Persepolis for Susa, where, since Cyrus, custom required the court to settle for the winter. Ochus and I rose early to witness the procession, which set out at sunrise. For the first time in our lives, we were not participants.

Ochus, as a married man, was expected by his father to assume royal duties, and as his wife, so was I. Ochus was being put in command of Hyrcania, one of the upper satrapies on the Iranian Plateau, located north of Parthia on the southeast coast of the Caspian, an important outpost remote from the satrapies of Media, Susiana, and Persia, but not as remote as Bactria and Sogdiana, lying in mountains to the northeast of Hyrcania. Within a week of the court's departure, we would journey to Zadracarta, the well-fortified capital of Hyrcania, expecting to arrive before winter set in.

The signal to begin the migration to Susa was announced in the customary way by an ascending three-note blast from 50 horns held by as many Immortals. The long row of motionless humanity and horseflesh stretching away from the palace gates to the horizon was suddenly engulfed in rising dust as it came to life and began to move, a slumbering serpent awakened. Watching, I felt abandoned and alone. Beside me was Ochus, newly defined for me by the word "husband." Just a word, I thought, one that, at once, had changed everything and yet nothing. I dourly anticipated the bittersweet embrace of forced marriage and whatever else comes after childhood. At 16 was I really grown up? And how does one know? I would ask Noah, he who knew the answer to everything.

At the head of the procession came the 10,000 Immortals, followed by 4,000 lance-bearers and 200 superbly caparisoned Nisaean horses. Next came the sacred and eternal fire, carried on a silver altar by Magi. Close by was the holy chariot of Ahura-Mazda, drawn by eight white horses, with a charioteer on foot behind, holding the reins.

My father, Great King Artaxerxes, followed, riding in a two-wheel war chariot drawn by matched Nisaeans. He was covered in the royal robe of purple and held his bow and shield, insignia of power. His charioteer stood beside him. Without success, we tried to get his attention. More troops followed the King's chariot: 1,000 pike-bearers, 10,000 cavalry arranged in squares of 100, and 10,000 lancers dressed in gold and silver sashes. Next, riding on royal horses or borne on gilded chariots, came our relatives and friends, throngs of women from the Queen's household, the King's children, the Magi who served as their tutors, a herd of eunuchs and the 365 concubines of the King, regally dressed and adorned. Here had been our place in the parades of years past.

Xerxes and I exchanged warm glances and a wave of arms. Having passed by, he turned on his horse to throw me a mischievous wink, setting my mind to worry whether this was evidence that he knew, or didn't know, how I came to be married.

The King's bastards, led by Sogdianus, passed in a tight grouping, as if to call attention to their special status. They saluted us and we responded with a cheer that punctuated my sense of loneliness. It was more than just being left behind. It was being left alone with someone I hardly knew, someone who had physically attacked me, someone who, by the King's order, had become my spouse, with whom I would journey to Hyrcania and there make a home.

The sun was nearing its apex when troops of sutlers and batmen, covered in layers of dust, passed by us at the end of the procession.

Watching this migration from the sidelines, I was proud of the Empire and this royal court, its heart and soul. I felt close kinship to the procession and all that it represented. Not surprising, since I belonged, a part of it all, product of the Persepolian palace, whose flesh and blood, every bit of it, had just passed by. It was the kind of emotion that brings tears to one's eyes.

❦ ❦ ❦ ❦ ❦

"I've been expecting you. Word reached us: You're bound for Hyrcania."

Noah was standing at the entrance, beside the wooden statue of Priapus, garden deity and guardian.

"He seems to be holding up pretty well."

Noah laughed, then beamed me a mischievous smile. "Marriage has made you more observant," he whispered, full of mirth.

I blushed.

"You may not know it, but Priapus is a fertility god as well." Noah put his arm around my shoulders, held me close to his side and walked me into the beeyard, then steered over to the favored spot where Udusana was buried. We sat down beneath the aged cypress. I searched his face.

"Having children, the next step after marriage. A glorious one our faith calls duty. You've come to the right place for inspiration."

I felt vulnerable and indecisive. I was ashamed to tell him, yet afraid not to. If he later found out, the intimacy of our friendship, which meant so much, would seem a sham.

"Noah."

His expression said 'I'm open to anything.' As always.

"Noah."

He took my hands in his, just as the tears appeared, glistening my cheeks, salting my lips. I began.

Noah listened in silence to the end. "And what does Apollonides think?"

"He admitted finding no evidence." I stood up. "See," I said, rubbing my flat tummy, sucking breath to make it concave. "Yet, he's certain. 'You're pregnant,' he declared. Imagine. In front of my mother."

"And how do you feel?" He put the question gently, as one might ease an egg from under a sitting hen.

"How do I feel?" I sat beside him. "Is there anyone other than you who would ask? I'm going to miss you." I smiled, defying the emptiness that took hold at this thought.

"I wasn't prepared for what Ochus did to me, or for marriage. And certainly not for becoming a mother. Too much happening, too quickly. I feel like a cork bobbing in the Araxes. I thought royalty meant having choices. Wrong. It means assuming duties. No, worse, having them thrust down by seniors, who then blame the Gods."

"Hyrcania's an important post. The King thinks highly of you and Ochus. I hear he gave you property."

"Who told you that? Must have been your bees. The King's Eye claimed not another soul knew. I was given some villages in Babylonia, near Opis, and a foreman to govern them for me and collect the rents and tribute. 'Girdle money' he called it. I was surprised. I know the Queen gets property of her own. As the wife of a satrap, I didn't think I'd be entitled."

"One makes her own luck. It's something about you, something the King saw, something that makes people want to do things for you. I used to think that when you became an adult you'd grow into the person you were pretending to be when you were young, when first you came into the beeyard. Now, I wonder whether you've already become that person, and I just didn't see clearly enough to recognize it."

"I wish for the confidence you have in my future." I could feel tears welling up in my eyes.

"Hold on to the property. Treat it as your own and so it will be. It's your pass to independence."

"Noah, I can't bear the idea of not being able to visit you. People want to do things for me, you say. How about you? Come with us to Hyrcania. Bring your bees, or not. But come." I was crying freely now. I clutched his hands and, losing what dignity I had left, implored him.

He held my eyes until I turned them downward. With the gentleness of silence he was allowing me to gather my self-esteem.

"Parysatis, you will flourish in Hyrcania, of this I am absolutely sure. And in time you will return to Persepolis. Our friendship will abide."

I wince now in recalling how deliberate I was in omitting from my story any suggestion that I had encouraged Ochus' advances. Fear of losing that friendship drove me to paint a false picture, although at the time I didn't see it that way.

Much later, when palace suspicions of my motives tainted everything I did or was rumored to have done, some of those who knew about the corridor believed I had seduced Ochus to gain dominance over him. How swiftly the Greeks would have swallowed that one, had it escaped Persepolis.

❦ ❦ ❦ ❦ ❦ ❦

The Alborz range forms a great wall across the north of the Empire, merging east of the Caspian with mountain ranges running into Bactria and Sogdiana. Our journey led us up the south slope of the Alborz and down the north to reach the Caspian and our new home, Zadracarta, on its southern coast. We passed Mount Damavand, the highest peak of the Alborz, well to the west, using one of the lower passes that admit the traveler to the immensely fertile coastal plain that feathers down from the mountain tops to the humid hanging forest and thence to the lush coastal strip. The contrast between the beige mountainous desert with little vegetation on the south slope and the humid forest of indissoluble green on the north was unforgettable. So too was our discovery of an immaculately tended garden paradise hidden in the foothills of the southern Alborz in a well-watered valley near Damghan. Here, amidst the bland sun-bleached colors of the surrounding desert and dry forest of juniper, we passed the night in a hunting pavilion built beside a large pool of cold, pellucid waters bubbling up from an abundant natural spring. Surrounding the deep pool were towering plane trees whose roots exploited this oasis and whose reflections in the pool lent a peaceful quality to the surroundings.

By the time we reached Zadracarta, I knew Apollanides was right. So did Ochus, who was daunted by the prospect. His concern for my condition grew with the advance of my belly. Like an anxious mother hen, he scurried around the palace grounds, putting the satrapal staff on constant alert to meet my slightest need. And to report to the Satrap.

At first I took comfort in the fuss, thinking my husband had turned consid- erate. So zealous did some of the staff become, however, that my most private ablutions were attended by satrapal spies. Always with some pretext. "The flowers must be changed. They're drooping." "The vase needs water." "Excuse us. We're searching for spiders." Staff I thought loyal to me suddenly showed an indifference to my orders. My privacy was being sacrificed on the altar of protection. For a time I felt cosseted, rejoicing in the attention. That Ochus cared for me so much could open a new chapter in our relationship. With the arrival of kicks, however, the sole focus of the satrapal servants became my belly's bounty. As my eyes opened to exactly who was being protected, the possibility of this new chapter ended.

The staff we took to Hyrcania was selected by us, working together. So I thought. And so, in fact, it was. Having helped select them, I naively believed the staff would be loyal to each in equal measure. How Ochus garnered it all I never discovered. He may have bought it. Or it may simply have come from the title, for he, not I, was the Satrap. Upon delivery of the baby, I was still clinging to the idea that the staff served both of us. Abandonment followed hard on the heels of delivery, however, leading me to understand through the second bitter experience of my young life that the servants we had picked jointly were now directing their loyalties only to the Satrap.

The baby was a boy. They told me that much, after he let forth the infant's universal cry for recognition upon entering our world. He was swiftly removed from the birthing site by a wet nurse. My demands to see and hold him were ignored. Indeed, within minutes there was no one left in the room to listen. Whether all of this was Ochus' doing or merely the result of his servants' zeal I was never certain. He denied any part in my abandonment, calling it a terrible misunderstanding, something that wouldn't have happened had he been present. I tend now to believe him, although I didn't then.

Parts of my body felt bruised, other parts numb. My throat was parched, my mouth dry, my tongue coated with something akin to cotton. During labor, sweat had poured from my forehead and armpits, soaking the smock I wore until it was wringing wet, almost like a hot bath. Now the dampness had turned cold. Shivering, I began to cry out for blankets and water to drink, for I had developed a desperate thirst. No one came. I couldn't believe it possible. Hadn't I just delivered a royal son, first grandchild of the King of Kings. As labor progressed, I concocted the most generous view of myself, drawing on the opinions I imagined others would hold of me following such heroic accomplishments. Mine would be recognized as the selfless and courageous act of a woman for her husband, not merely for him, for the nation of Persia, for the Empire. As birthing this boy grew more difficult and painful, my daydreams grew more grandiose. I imagined myself the object of adulation, even worship, when word of my exceptional conduct reached Persepolis. Somehow, I had overlooked the banality of my accomplishment.

My fall from an epiphany of imagined grace to the reality of abandonment was harsh. More painful than childbirth, it seemed at the time, perhaps because I was so unprepared. I resolved never again to be without my own staff, loyalty undivided and zealous to the point of death.

Born of hurt, this decision became the elemental key to survival over a life-time of palace combat. Many saw it as the product of political acumen and vaulting ambition. I chose not to correct that impression.

The first of my own attendants, or "Parysatis' Immortals," as they came to be known, was Datis. He was a Sakai warrior from north of the Caspian who had been captured in battle with the Persians when his horse stepped into a ground squirrel hole, broke an ankle and tumbled to the ground. The fall injured his right hip, leaving him for life with a noticeable limp. I gave him the name Datis in honor of a highly regarded Median from Cyrus the Great's entourage.

Soon after the birth of our son, I asked Ochus for satrapal funds to hire my own staff. I argued that, overall, the expense would be slight, since mine would replace those assigned to me by the satrapy. He agreed, even offering to find candidates. "My Eyes know everyone; they will bring you the best," he said.

My husband could feign ingenuousness. He could also be earnest. I had yet to learn the difference. No matter. Instinctive caution ruled the day. "No. Thank you, Ochus, but no. I will find my own candidates."

His eyes, now downcast, turned innocent, like a dog appealing for a share of the roast. His voice, a plaint. "Why, Parysatis? It's not your strength. Let me help."

"Your Eyes might give me good choices, better in some ways than I could find on my own. But, in regard to loyalty, having been picked by you, they will always fall short. And in that, I place the most importance. You understand."

Ochus nodded, silent. The discussion was over.

I went outside, heading for the market to buy almonds, a favorite of mine that the palace never seemed to have enough of. There were a handful of slaves near the road, breaking stones for use in construction. One, a curious young man without beard, caught my eye. He was tall and markedly thin, too much so for his large bones, the outlines of which could be seen pushing against the taut, deeply tanned skin of his naked upper body. His hair was long, a riotous red. He wore pierced earrings of round silver balls the size of small nuts.

Again, on the way back to the palace, the same man arrested me, this time literally, for I stopped to stare at him. Here, I felt instinctively, was my first candidate.

"Sit down you dirty wretch. Do you know why I sent for you?" He was covered in stone dust cemented in layers to his still bare body by the sweat of hours swinging a mallet against stone. Despite the limp, he carried himself with quiet pride, rooted, I later understood, not just in the position he enjoyed among the Saka, but also in the pleasure of having mastered our tongue while protecting his own from our ken.

"No. I noticed you staring at me today. And wondered who you were."

"Now you know. You answer me like an equal. Here, have some." I pushed a bowl of shelled almonds across the mosaic table that separated us. My favorite, the bowl was fashioned of stone, a banded green chert that seemed to radiate light from a mysterious inner source.

"You treat me like an equal. We are alone. Aren't you afraid I might attack you on the way to freedom?" Instead of rising to threaten, he filled one hand with as many almonds as it could hold, and then some. Looking into my eyes with bittersweet expression, he smiled.

"I brought you here to offer a choice. Serve me until you die or return to the stone gang. If you choose me, it must be with unswerving loyalty. To prove the point, you will become a eunuch."

❧ ❧ ❧ ❧ ❧ ❧

He recovered in several weeks, with great pain but without complications. I visited him at bedside, immediately after the operation.

"Your name will be 'Datis'. Do you like it?"

"Not yet."

"Datis was a loyal servant to Cyrus the Great, the Empire's first King. A eunuch, handsome, courageous in war and the hunt. And devoted to his master."

Did this man have a family in Saka, a wife or children? I never asked; he never volunteered. The question occurred to me many times, but I didn't want to know. I didn't want to become connected to the life he had been forced to surrender. How would I have reacted had he opened the door to his past? I didn't let it happen, despite a relationship that grew closer, more interdependent, as our years together increased.

Some thought I was immune to emotions. Others accused me of using empathy to manipulate rather than care. They were wrong, but it was not that simple. In fact, my emotions made me so susceptible that I had to erect a wall to contain them. I learned protective arts to guard myself against the strains that came from other people's miseries. Constant vigilance against being drawn into another's life. It's easy to avoid the blatant appeals of the street beggar. But human appeals can be softly put with seductive subtlety or even camouflaged. I practiced restraint in posing questions, avoidance in answering them, and evasion of many invitations to share life's woes. Yes, selfish.

Datis was my chief of staff. With his help, I was able to gather others, a small band who owed their jobs solely to me. Datis grew rapidly in the position, demonstrating, with growing confidence, the ability to interpret my needs to the staff, even when I failed to express those needs; indeed, even when I didn't recognize their existence. He could anticipate and prepare, often looking far ahead, beyond my own capacity to think about the future. For too long I thought chiefly about loyalty, taking for granted his remarkable capacity for foresight.

❧ ❧ ❧ ❧ ❧ ❧

When we arrived, the satrapy had only a few retired concubines, whose loyal service was being rewarded by palace positions in the weaving center and as caregivers to royal children. Ochus, whose male spirits were undiminished by the change of scene, set about to restock the harem. Although he never connected this activity to our physical separation, he described what he was doing every step of the way. It was his technique for trying to put the burden of his nightly excursions on me, and he could tell I understood.

We slept in separate, unadjoining bedrooms whose doors opened to the same hallway. One evening, during our meal together, Ochus seemed agitated. He jumped at the servants over the food. Trivial things like not enough pomegranate sauce in the lamb stew; pease porridge that was too hot, cuttlefish fried in not enough oil. Generally, Ochus projected a calm, even placid mien. At table he was even-tempered and none too particular about food.

We weren't talking, an unusual occurrence since the day's events were normally a matter for discourse between us in the evening. His silence caused me to respond in kind. He wanted to say something but couldn't find the right path.

"I now have 14 concubines in the harem. My eunuch herds them like sheep. I'm their shepherd. You should visit some day. Take your eunuch, what's his name, with you. He's known to the harem. Well known. Eunuchs talk amongst themselves. Poor at keeping secrets. That's how I know. And soon the whole palace will. I demand that you stop this debauchery."

"Are you finished?"

As he nodded, I rose from the table and turned my back to him.

"Are you sure of what your eunuch claims? Have you considered how jealous of Datis he might be? Gather your wits, my husband, for you are being led by the nose. You have no proof. I know, since there is none to be had."

Just as I turned to sit down again, a servant came in with a pitcher of Chalybon wine, our customary post-supper drink. Ochus was slumped over the table, elbows akimbo, hands supporting a limp head. I heard convulsive sobbing. "Leave us now," I directed the servant, gesturing with my hand that he was to leave the pitcher on the table.

"Now, Ochus. Shed this fantasy and tell me what's really the matter." With my hand, I reached over to his, gently stroking it as the sobbing continued.

"This is the first time you have touched me, Parysatis. Voluntarily."

My husband, weeping in front of me, after accusing me of an affair with my new aide, was undone by something. Something beyond touching. I had no idea.

"We're married in name only. You care nothing for my concubines. They might as well not exist. And yet, I care that you care not. My eunuch is old enough to be my father. He alarms me. He believes you seduced me to force a marriage. He claims women of your age always find outlets. That you must have one. Nature's power, he says. If I'm not the one, it must be that eunuch. If he weren't, then you would be not just needy but jealous. He persuades me. But you deny it." The sobbing, which had ceased during this outburst, resumed. Finding him all too earnest and pitiful, I withdrew my hand.

"Don't talk to me of seduction. Don't even talk of love. Let us, instead, think about our role in the Empire. We have one child. We can have more. Our influence will grow in proportion to the number of offspring. I'm willing to try for more children if you'll do your part. Together we can lay claim to more, much more, than Hyrcania."

Ochus raised his head. Extending his arm he took my hand in his. His face showed shock and surprise. The tension around his eyes eased even as I studied him. A new bargain had been offered and accepted. We arose, in silence, and went to my bedroom for the first time, arm in arm. From that moment forward, we would apply both mind and body in service to the Empire. At the time, I had no sense of what a turning point it would be.

❧ ❧ ❧ ❧ ❧

He should have worried more about Noah than Datis. Since arriving in Hyrcania I had often dreamed of my beekeeper. We were outside, sometimes in a field of flowers, other times in a forest by a stream. He appeared as a long, lithe and sinewy man, bent at the waist, white unkempt beard, gnarled face and worn clothing, a shepherd's crook in one hand. He appeared not old but ageless. He had come to mentor me; I was there to learn. This recurring fragment was all I could remember until the night after Ochus' confession, when the scene expanded in time, texture, and action.

We were seated beside a still pool of water. I was examining my face in the pool's reflection, tracing it with fingers. I wore a beard. On one side of my face the beard was dark and covered with frost, white on black. On the other it was bright green, a dense and lush swath of new-grown grass. I began to cry, looking to Noah for help. He took a knife, sharpened it on a leather strap attached to his waistband and began to shave away the beard, starting with the dark side. I passed my fingers across the side of my face he had finished. It felt soft, as if the beard had never been there. The other side was different. As fast as he shaved away the glistening green growth, it grew back. After several tries, with a shrug of the shoulders, he put down the knife. The growth made me feel warm, snug and content. At the same time I was confused. I searched Noah's eyes for meaning. He said it might be necessary to divide me in half. I woke up in awe, convinced the dream was profound but lacking a sure guide to its meaning.

❧ ❧ ❧ ❧ ❧ ❧

Our lovemaking was infrequent and coarse, something I would be done with. Ochus felt differently. I appreciated the skills he had honed in the harem. He applied himself to the task of becoming my indispensable lover. It wasn't that I didn't feel throbs of desire, or even a moment of satisfaction. I felt no passion for the man. I never dreamed of his body next to mine, I had no hunger for his caress, only rote acceptance with the goal of offspring. Much later, I discovered that physical love was like an exotic sweet: if seldom tasted, desire for it all but disappeared; conversely, the more one had, the more one's hunger for it grew.

I dictated the timing of our efforts to create. What began as a marriage of necessity had become something more than convenience but less than love. We were partners in shared ambition.

For the second time I became pregnant, carrying to term, about the third week of May in my 18th year. Datis and the rest of my staff provided buoyant comfort to me, confirming the wisdom of creating my own. And Ochus, freed of the burdens of childbirth, crowded my birthing room with vases filled with tulips, iris, and poppies of bright red, orange, yellow and blue, refreshing colors that contrasted with the brown hills and umber-colored walls of sun-baked mud and straw that I could see through the window. Pushing them this way and that, he made room beside my bed for bowls of almonds, pistachios, pomegranates, and freshly picked sour cherries covered in Noah's honey, which I had arranged to have shipped to us in monthly batches.

The birth was quick and, if not painless, at least not enduringly so. Again, I produced a boy. With babe at breast, surrounded by husband and staff, my spirits tried to soar. But there was a problem. Like my first-born, the babe's skin had a yellow tinge that had become more noticeable during his first year. My eyes were blue. So were Ochus'. Yet his eyes were yellow, like my first-born. And there were other similarities: his cheek bones were unusually wide, giving his face a flattened appearance, at once more mature than the rest of his body, yet suggestive of future deformity. Instead of growing in size and energy, he followed exactly the path of my first-born, who had grown progressively weaker after birth, showing signs of shortness of breath and overall fatigue as his first birthday approached. We knew the symptoms for they were copies of those that ended our first son's life before he could turn two. With growing horror, we watched them grow with the passing days.

By the middle of our second-born's 15th month, he drew his last breath, expiring for no apparent reason other than to follow his brother into the grave. They both were buried in an alcove of willow, oleaster, alder, and ash, a fall setting of exquisite beauty where I had often lingered when the weather was fine in the latter months of pregnancy. The setting reminded me of the beeyard at Persepolis. Closing my eyes, I could imagine myself a little girl, watching Noah as he worked the hives. Sitting in this enclosure before it became a burial ground, I would feel both secure and homesick. Thereafter, recalling Udusana, those feelings intensified, driving me away despite my condition, or perhaps because of it. I was again pregnant and this time deeply distraught over the mystery of these successive births and deaths, which I feared might not be explained as accidents.

This time my baby was a girl. She had blue eyes, a fact that vanquished the clouds of doubt. She arrived in June. I was 19. I insisted on naming her Amestris, after the renowned Queen of the Empire, wife to Great King Xerxes and dark conniving champion of my father in securing the crown. Ochus didn't have to guess at my reasons.

My life became calm and uncomplicated. Mother of a healthy infant, I could at last rejoice. There were always demands, but they were the simple ones that a babe places upon her mother, and I was fortunate to have Datis and his staff at hand. I seemed to float from day to day in a placid sea, drifting far away from the hard realities of governing the Empire or even one of its satrapies.

Meeting the needs of my daughter was a self-indulgent pleasure, too much so for words easily to describe. Perhaps a youthful compound of a future filled with infinite possibilities, the power to pick, choose, and accomplish as one willed and the pleasure of being recognized as someone seized of this destiny. Oh, the glory of it, enabled by a mind numb to the pain of past tragedies and unaware of the agonies to come.

7

DEATH IN THE FAMILY

WITH ANOTHER PREGNANCY, contentment continued well into my 20th year with an easy birth occurring on my own birthday that resulted in a healthy boy, whom we named Arsaces. Soon after, our lives grew complicated. In the midst of the hottest summer any poor soul could recall, the scarred eunuch, Artoxares, appeared at our door. Despite the passage of years, he was still handsome. Yet he seemed less imposing in stature and affect than I recalled him at the Persepolis court, which could merely be the effects on my memory of growing up. But there were reasons. For the past five years he had lived in semi-isolation in Armenia, where our father, Great King Artaxerxes, had exiled him.

His arrival re-ignited suspicions etched in my childhood.

"So, tell us how you got yourself banished. It was a long time ago, and we were young," I said to Artoxares as Ochus and I sat down to dinner with this unexpected guest. "And then you can explain what brought you to us, here in Hyrcania, not exactly an easy trip, even from Armenia."

Artoxares eyed us both before speaking. He seemed to be searching our faces for something, an acknowledgement, perhaps, that we already knew the news he carried.

"I came not from Armenia but Persepolis, where I returned upon release. Megabyzus, who, you might recall, had been exiled to the island of Kyrta in the

Persian Gulf more than six years ago, escaped from the island last year, dressed as a leper, and returned to Persepolis, begging forgiveness. With the help of his wife, Amytis, and her formidable mother, Amestris—Xerxes' widow and now, I've learned, your daughter's namesake—the King relented, restoring Megabyzus to his former exalted position of tablemate. My exile had been the direct result of trying to intervene with the King on behalf of Megabyzus. His reconciliation led to my own."

While he spoke, servants had placed in front of us bowls of lentil and turnip soup, piping hot. In the center of the table were platters of different breads, some made of unbolted wheat and sesame, others flavored with oil, anise, and cheese, and still others sprinkled with poppy seed. For the breads, bowls of honey and olive oil were on offer. Pitchers of Chalybon wine and others from the region were put within reach. Three silver goblets, deeply scribed to depict griffins at play, completed the table.

Megabyzus was a prominent figure within the Empire. He was grandson of one of the Seven, the conspirators who delivered the crown to Darius I. A famous soldier, as well, who put down the Babylonian revolt against Xerxes.

"So, Artoxares, why exile?" I tried to smile as I threw him what sounded like a challenge. "And help yourself to the bread. You'll choke on the soup if you don't slow down."

"Your father can be gentle and forgiving. But there's another side. It's on display only when his entitlement to the crown, or his qualifications, are under attack. Megabyzus saw it during a lion hunt. I was there too. They were advancing on a lion. The beast had disappeared in some thickets. Suddenly, he appeared on a rock outcropping above your father, who was unaware. Being farther back from the rock, Megabyzus saw the beast immediately and, as he leapt, threw his javelin, bringing the lion down, literally at the feet of the King.

"There ensued two very different perceptions of what had just transpired. Megabyzus thought he had acted bravely in saving your father's life. With pride he assumed a reward.

"Your father thought Megabyzus had deprived him of the royal prerogative to hunt and kill lions. An act of disrespect. It wounded your father much more than I could have imagined. He took it as a challenge to his qualifications for the crown. His first instinct was to have Megabyzus put to death. Amestris, Amytis, and others prevailed to change the King's mind. He reduced the punishment to exile. As the only witness, I knew it was wrong to punish Megabyzus and said so, sure of my position and convinced that your father would come to his senses. I was naïve and over-confident."

"For all but the King, there's high art in the ability to see events as others see them," I said to no one in particular.

"Yes," replied Ochus, "and even for a King, but not this one, who seems oblivious to that possibility."

Having come from Persepolis, our guest would have tales to tell. I made sure the servants, who stood in waiting along the walls of our large dining room, kept Artoxares' goblet brimming. Although his tongue had never been reluctant to wag among friends, I hoped the wine might open doors to the less traveled paths of palace life.

"The two of you look hungry for more than these delicious breads. A veil of sadness has covered the palace many times since I arrived there about a year ago. Megabyzus died soon after being embraced again by your father. He was 76. His wife, Amytis, mourned but a week before resuming her licentious activities, for which she had grown famous during her husband's long exile. I'm sure you knew something of her reputation."

"Well earned. I know something of Xerxes. She takes after him," I said, smiling.

Ochus, whose diffidence in the presence of guests could result in an entire evening of silence, spoke. "But the palace isn't as forgiving of a woman, even one considered the most beautiful in the Empire."

"Amytis cared not a fig for forgiveness. She flaunted her attractions before any she chose. And there were many thus privileged. Some months after Megabyzus' death, she became ill. She consulted Apollonides, who removed her clothing, a privilege doctors consider necessary to their calling no matter what the aliment. He was quickly smitten. Tracing her illness to the womb, he prescribed congress with men to regain her health. To no one's surprise, he was the first and most frequent purveyor of his own prescription. She indulged herself to excess and forthwith died. Your father, at the insistence of Amestris, had Apollonides put in irons, tortured, then buried alive. Shortly thereafter, the remarkable Amestris died, suddenly, of a heart attack. Four deaths, in less than a year. I tell you they created a pall that even a team of palace fools could not dispel."

"The Queen Mother dead. We didn't know. How is our father doing? And what about you, who served her so well?"

The full range of Artoxares' services to the Queen Mother was a poorly kept secret. I'd never before alluded to it so directly. Amestris' death must have been as much of a shock to the palace as it was to me, an attack by stealth, coming with such swiftness to bring down the most powerful Achaemenid in our family. She was my model of what a royal woman could aspire to achieve. Not Aristotle's "good life" of virtue and moderation but a purposeful, calculating, sometimes sordid and compromised life in service to the Empire.

I had imagined myself, when the time was right, boldly visiting Amestris to confess and then to seek the central idea behind the life she had led. Now that door was shut.

Artoxares was uncommonly diffident in talking of Amestris. We learned only the bare essentials of the burial ceremony and nothing of the feelings expressed by those involved, including himself.

The service was cleared and sweets—a golden confection of honey and flaxseed, a pudding of milk, meal-cakes and honey and a basket of dates—were placed before us. Before withdrawing to the shadows of the room, the servants again filled our goblets.

"I had some dealings with Apollonides. Not the kind Amytis enjoyed. Or endured. Who knows? He was not my favorite. But didn't he save Megabyzus' life? I recall being told that Megabyzus was grievously wounded in the palace battle over Xerxes' successor and was treated by Apollonides."

"Indeed. This was the start of his exaggerated reputation."

"But why torture and that unimaginable killing? Was his crime anything more than a misdiagnosis?" I felt embarrassed. Deterrence as motive for cruel punishment and death I understood. In the main, I suspect, it worked. But where's the value in what befell Apollonides?"

I think we had all become rather tipsy with undiluted wine, which, unlike the custom in Persepolis, was standard fare in the remote and rugged edges of the Empire.

"Allow me, if you will, to come to the point."

We looked with amazement at Artoxares, having assumed we had just been given the main story.

"The palace air is poisonous. Rumors abound about the King's bastard sons…"

"Seventeen, one of whom sits before you," Ochus crowed, watching with devious pleasure the color rising in Artoxares' ears and the length of his scar, then spreading out to cover his fair, unbearded face. "What about those bastards?"

"It's the smell of patricide. The King's Eyes must have informed him, yet he feigns ignorance or disbelief. The Queen, ill equipped to feign anything, bears an increasingly worried countenance, yet does nothing. Xerxes, the sole legitimate heir and the King's designee, appears at times the picture of calm and patient anticipation, and at other times anxious and perplexed, as if he knew of the coming dangers but was too confused or conflicted to know how to behave."

"Or willing to give Fate a free hand," I suggested.

"I made a point of talking to Sogdianus, the eldest of the bastards, who wears high intelligence on the sleeve, encased in vaulting arrogance. He pronounced both King and Queen 'insufferable' in the collective mind of the people, claiming that this was just a report, not his opinion. He predicted that a corrective, already in motion, would solve the problem. When pressed, he would admit to knowing nothing beyond the promise of a solution. He talks, but I don't see him as a risk-taker."

"At last, we discover the cause of your visit. Do you really expect us to believe this tale? The King's never been stronger, or more loved. He's made the Empire more secure than it's been in years. Not even the Greeks threaten. And Damaspia, she too is loved. You speak of plots but can identify no plotters. Were you sent by anyone, or is this your idea?"

I looked across the table at Ochus. He was asleep. How could it be? If this story wasn't enough to keep a son of the King awake, what could? I wanted to criticize my poor husband for lacking backbone, but I knew it was in part the undiluted wine, whose dulling effects make no distinctions.

"Each of you commands respect in the palace. Together, you are the King's most important offspring. Our future may be in your hands. If so, I offer my help. You know how deeply I care for your father, for the Empire. If it comes, patricide will undo us. We've seen it before. No royal family can long endure against the unraveling effects of this crime."

It is good husbandry to store away grain in time of plenty for use when food grows scarce. Here, then, was my insight into the motive of our guest.

"And your advice?"

"There's nothing for you to do. Or that you can do. The danger is too nebulous, the hints too vague, to warrant a trip to Persepolis. Wait and see." His voice had dropped to a whisper, as if there were spies pressing against the outer walls to overhear. "Be suspicious. There could even be danger for you, here in Hycrania."

"In that case, we should conclude. Pardon me, I must wake my resting husband. You've frightened him to sleep." I ran my hand across Ochus' brow, then through his thick hair.

"Soon to bed. But first I challenge you to tell us about Amestris: the true story of her role in her husband's death and our father's accession."

And so he did, an account identical to that told by the Skeptic.

❧ ❧ ❧ ❧ ❧

Before falling asleep, I thought about the shift in relationship between Artoxares and myself, from the days when he had teased and tormented me. Our relative positions of power had virtually reversed, something we both felt and, by our behavior, acknowledged, without a word.

Artoxares set off for Persepolis the next morning. I avoided the subject of his visit over an ample breakfast, of which only the two of us partook. He spoke lovingly of the nightingale, whose insistent song drew him to the window in the middle of the night, as if her trills were designed to make him take note of the white climbing roses that sparkled in the silver path of a full moon. We talked of gardening, a subject he embraced more as poet than plantsman. Then, suddenly as he rose to leave, a cold edge intruded. I caught his glare, a blend of contempt and self-pity.

"Why that expression, my friend? It's not becoming."

"Forgive me. It's obvious you don't believe me. My life's been a series of predictions that no one believed. After a while, one feels powerless. It leads to anger." His glare had softened. He was still immensely handsome, with a taut face and sinewy physique projecting nimble athleticism and tight control over his appetites. The scar had become a mark of distinction, foil for aging beauty.

"But why? Haven't you been right?"

"Those who reject your predictions have even less use for you when events prove you right."

Artoxares moved close, near enough for me to recognize the frankincense he used on his face. Taking my hands in his, he kissed me gently, first on one cheek, then on the other, lingering enough with his lips to turn a moment of routine into one of pleasure. Wheeling on his heels, he departed as abruptly as he had arrived.

How complex, I thought. And pitiable.

❧ ❧ ❧ ❧ ❧ ❧

When word came, we were not totally surprised. I suppose to this limited extent, Artoxares' strange visit proved useful. Still there was shock. King and Queen found dead in the same hour, stretched out in their separate sleeping chambers. A cobra, blackish brown in color, with small eyes and round pupils, over three feet in length, found in a dark corner of the King's chamber. No snake occupied the Queen's chamber, but openings in the floor made escape a matter of choice. Two small punctures on the arm of the King. Similar ones on the Queen's leg.

Upon arrival at the palace, we were taken in hand by the Magus who led the investigation. He was consumed with self-importance, needing to recount every detail. Despite our obvious discomfort, he insisted on describing the cobra's way to death, calling it a matter of state.

He said the venom attacks not the blood but the nerves. Blurred vision, general paralysis, and difficulty in breathing follow. Then a brief period of dizziness, nausea and vomiting. The final phase begins with drowsiness, then unconsciousness and, within 30 minutes of the bite, death by suffocation. "An unpleasant way to die," he concluded.

Ochus grew ashen. I felt less alarm than fascination, which prompted me to ask questions. Ochus stood slightly apart, far enough to claim, if anyone cared, that he wasn't part of the conversation, which he considered indecent. I embarassed him.

Finally putting aside the technicalities, I put the looming question.

"It was a suicide pact. The dealer admitted supplying two snakes, on order of the King. The messenger who took them explained that they were to serve as props in a court play. Delivery occurred three days before the deaths. The King and Queen knew enough to starve them. Tragic."

"The official explanation?" I asked. The Magus nodded.

"No messages were found? What motive?"

As if bitten by a wasp, Ochus suddenly came alive. Before the Magus could answer, he put force behind my question.

"Her point is simple. In our experience, happily married couples in good health do not commit suicide. Particularly a couple at the pinnacle of power in an Empire stretching from Egypt to India."

"The facts speak for themselves. Finding no evidence of any other reason for death, recognizing that cobras lack easy access to the palace, determining that these snakes arrived in the hands of the King's servant, who showed us the King's written order, we are confident. There could be no other." His voice, rising to a crescendo, was emphatic in answering a question he'd heard many times before. "I see you're not convinced. There's more. Although undetected in our examination, many in the palace claimed both King and Queen were afflicted with a strange disease that caused increasing distress. Apparently believing they were going to die, they took matters into their own hands."

Nonplussed and fearful, we dismissed the Magus.

In the days it took us to reach Persepolis, the palace, as if directed by the deity whose earthly intermediary, King Artaxerxes, was lost, had organized itself with astounding precision to accomplish the two great tasks at hand. First, to crown Xerxes the new King of Kings. Second, to give fitting burial to the deceased King and Queen. If dangers lurked in the palace, we didn't detect them. At least not until visitors came to see us, beginning the afternoon of our arrival. After the Magus finished his report, we retreated to our apartment and latched the door, hoping to rest from the swift and arduous travel.

Sogdianus knocked first. "Are you alone?" he whispered, bending forward as the door opened to scan the breadth and length of the vestibule. Ochus stood at the door, ready to greet him. Watching from a distance, I imagined his head, so large and perfectly round, dropping to the ground from lack of neck and shoulder support. Ignoring Ochus' hand, he clasped my husband's shoulders with his upstretched hands and peered around him at me. "Dangerous times, these are," he announced. "Thanks to Ahura-Mazda for your safe travel."

He was covered in sweat, which beaded on his face and arms, running down his swarthy skin and dropping to the floor. He smelled. The odor, unpleasant. When I finally got a good look at his bobbing face, it appeared dirty and haggard, as if he'd neither bathed nor slept for days.

"Come, Sogdianus, sit with us and unwind. You're tighter than a bleached drum." In truth, he was consumed with impatience. His bullfrog eyes bulged. I guided him to a seat in our receiving room. Ochus poured wine. Over his head we caught each other's eye, sharing the same thought. But for the circumstances, a source of derision and mirth.

"We share a bond, don't we," he began, having quaffed the goblet and set it down beside the pitcher, a subtlety not lost on the host, who refilled the goblet and handed it to his elder brother. "Our mothers, Andia, Cosmartidene, and

Alogune, are Babylonian. It sets us apart. It must keep us together," his voice rising, his huge eyes locked to ours, "in this hour of peril."

"How so?" Ochus said. "We have just been briefed by the Magi. They are certain it was a suicide pact. They foresee no danger."

"I wanted to be the first to reach you. Too much to do, alas. Surely you don't accept that. A tale told by those in thrall to the legitimate heir, the impatient and scheming heir, who reeks of patricide. Oh, heinous villainy. We must not allow it to go unpunished. Time is short, for the crowning of Xerxes has already been scheduled, the bureaucracy set to work on what they do best. The burials occur tomorrow and will be quickly forgotten in the excitement of launching a new King. I want your help."

I detected a thinly veiled command.

"And the evidence? Have you told the Magi your theory?" I could see in the brightening colors of that moonscape of a face that he was losing what little patience he had brought with him.

"If crowned, you may be sure, the legitimate heir will eliminate us all. Such is the way with Kings."

I nodded, thinking "legitimate or not."

"Proof will out when I'm ready. For now, trust me. What I must have from you is a public demonstration of immediate and unwavering loyalty when I expose the villain." He rose to go. We said nothing more. Ochus escorted him to the door. We looked hard at each other, aware that nothing was clear except the arrogance and overweening ambition of Sogdianus, and the threat to our lives, a gift left behind.

"Suicide pact or impatient heir?" Ochus mused, staring into space.

"I don't like him. But the warning is apt. We are too naïve, too trusting. Consider the honeybees. Queens don't commit suicide. One survives by destroying the rest. We are faced with twin murders. But who?"

We had just settled down when another knock at the door brought Ochus to his feet. Before he could move, Datis, who had accompanied us on the trip, appeared in the hallway. With his customary limp, he moved to the door, opening it to admit our scarred friend. Although they missed each other in Hyrcania and had never met, recognition was instantaneous, as plain as a bitch in heat to a male dog. This much I could see from across the room.

Artoxares sat where Sogdianus had been, the seat still warm. Datis turned to leave.

"Stay," I called out, turning to Artoxares. "All that you have to say would be repeated anyway. Our trust is complete."

Artoxares sat facing us, a smirk covering layers of emotion.

"I've come again to warn you. Heirs like you are an endangered breed. What passes for order in the palace is a mask for chaos beneath. To survive you must have a plan."

"Wait." said Ochus, looking dubious. "We harbor no ambition for the crown, and no one would suspect us of that. Nor could anyone imagine us guilty of patricide. We won't scare so easily."

"Perhaps not, but at least you've got my husband's attention this time," I said softly, with a smile.

As if his own life depended on it, Artoxares was determined to make us appreciate our peril, to feel it, palpably, in the gut. By recounting what Great King Darius had done to the "liar-kings" who refused to accept his crown, he sought to paint as prologue our dynasty's dark past.

In truth, neither of us had visited Behistun. We had only the vaguest impression of what Darius had inscribed on its sheer rock face. Remarkably, Artoxares had much of it memorized. With prideful excitement bordering on malevolence, he quoted Darius on the fate of the Median leader: "I cut off his nose, ears, and tongue and plucked out an eye; he was chained under guard at the gate of my palace and everyone could see him there. Then I impaled him at Ecbatana. As for his trusted lieutenants, I hung their heads on the walls of the citadel."

In the back of our minds, we knew that torture was applied to rebels and usurpers, that often it involved the taking of nose and ears, that public displays, such as Darius' torture of the Median rebel, or the posting of heads on the tall bronze poles outside the Persepolis gates, served to deter. Still, the words carried shocking force.

"For a new king, still insecure beneath the crown, it is surpassingly simple to migrate from imagining every relative a risk, to enlarging that risk through worry until, swift and sure, it grows into a threat so imminent that preemptive action becomes urgent, and inevitable."

"I see, Artoxares." Leaning forward, I grasped his shoulders. "To protect the Empire, of course." I pushed him away, feeling angry, mostly with myself, for losing control, for allowing this visitor to increase my frightened state. I looked at Ochus. His face was pale, his brows tightly knit, his mouth open. Datis sat alert, expressionless, impossible to read.

"Your campaign succeeded. Now what?" I was still angry. Ochus asked Artoxares if he believed the suicide theory. He shook his head dismissively, then began to speak. I cut him off. "Look. We need to know whom to believe before we can have a plan. Stop the mystery and tell us what you know."

"Rumors swirl like sand in the heat storms of summer."

The man's pretensions were unstoppable.

"This is not the time, certainly not the place, to play the poet. Get to the point or I will ask Datis to throw you out on your tin ear." He looked aghast at my outburst, then resumed as if the interruption had not occurred.

"One story implicates both of your mothers in conspiracy with Alogune, Sogdianus' mother, who keeps snakes and is reported to cast spells over them. The hatred these women harbor against the King is as notorious as their ambition. They're suspected of planting the story that the King and Damaspia were afflicted with a withering disease."

"And what of Xerxes?" I asked.

"Of course. Among some, Sogdianus may be the prime source. And then, given the number of bastard heirs, there are plenty of other suspects, each with his own rumor."

I shot Ochus a glance of frustration. Was our visitor clueless? Trust in the man was growing thin, as anyone looking at my body language could read. He was recoiling even before I spoke.

"You describe a crisis, then lead us into it, totally blind. How many other 'puppets' dangle from your strings? By God, you won't play us for fools. Only loyalty begets trust. Show us or be gone." I glanced at Datis. His placid composure had cracked; lines of anxiety lurked in the corners of his eyes.

Artoxares was covered in sweat, his white tunic darkened from the arms down. His audience had turned hostile and it showed.

"I've told you what I know. You have friends in the palace. Menostanes, for one, whose vast properties in Bablyonia rest side by side with yours, Parysatis. Use them to discover the truth. You could be the first. I apologize, but only for pretense, never for disloyalty or lack of good will." He rose, bowed deeply and left before Ochus could escort him out.

As the door shut firmly, Ochus announced, to no one in particular, "We are in a mess."

Datis rose to leave. Again I asked him to stay. "Tell us what you make of all this."

He looked on edge, eyes flickering as they moved rapidly from one of us to the other, and back again, searching for some signal.

"Come, you have thoughts. You know I've always valued your opinions, which in this matter we pledge to hold in confidence. Ochus?"

"Absolute confidence. You must trust us, for your own safety as much as ours."

"The palace brims over with ambitions. The King is said to have designated Xerxes as his successor, but the Babylonian scribes do not recognize him. Nor does the powerful House of Murasu, which manages so much princely land around Nippur, including, as you well know, my lady, land belonging to you. Sogdianus is making the rounds, trying to line up key members of the court to his side. The crown's power floats like a butterfly, open to seizure by almost anyone. But it will only stay in the hands of one who knows how to use it. That person might not be Xerxes."

"Very good. But, for all your wisdom, or perhaps because of it, you avoid the cause of death. Solve that piece of the puzzle and the future path becomes clear." I stared hard at Datis.

"The Magus might be right. Wouldn't an assassin choose poison over cobras? A snake may or may not bite. Even if, uninvited, it bites, death doesn't necessarily result. As a path to suicide, however, the odds change. And, remember that cobras are holy, descendents of the Gods, whose bite purifies, assuring swift flight to the next world. The Magi aren't as stupid as your friend Artoxares would have it."

We debated, back and forth, testing one theory against another. In the end, recognizing that only through investigation could we stand a chance of knowing the truth, we composed a plan of action.

❧ ❧ ❧ ❧ ❧ ❧

Within days, Xerxes was crowned King of Kings in a ceremony of tradition designed to spread nostalgia for Achaemenid Kings of previous reigns. Sogdianus stood silent among the bastard princes gathered together to witness what should have been occasion for rejoicing but, instead, was weighed down with sorrow and dampened with the fog of fear. We guessed he had failed in his attempt to prove Xerxes guilty. For our part, we had little to show for our efforts, other than Ochus' account of his talks with Andia, Cosmartidene, and Alogune, which proved the vapidity of that rumor.

The crown fits differently on each King's head. On the royal head of Xerxes, it adopted a tentative tilt. So many questions still unanswered, so many rumors flying. All those with ambition kept their eyes down and their thoughts very much to themselves. Ochus, Datis, and I formed a tight cell, into which, try though he might, Artoxares could not penetrate. Datis, with access to the eunuch grapevine, reported that Artoxares was as attentive to Sogdianus as he was to us. And equally so to Ochus' brother, Arsites. His opportunistic hedging infuriated me, but we had never demanded, or even invited, the loyalty he proffered us, and this made his behavior somewhat more understandable.

We fanned out, searching for clues. I went to Noah. Ochus to the snake dealer, and Datis sought out the King's servant who had brought the snakes to the palace.

As the keeper of one of nature's wonders, it was to be expected that Noah would know the Empire's most prominent dealer in snakes. He vouched for the man's honesty. After meeting with him, Noah reported that the dealer's account of how his cobras came to be in the palace conformed to the story told by the Magus. The King's servant had told the dealer they were to serve as props in a play. Being cautious, particularly with a servant he had never seen before, the dealer demanded evidence. The servant produced a written order from the King, explaining the purpose and directing the servant to fetch the snakes and deliver them to the King. The dealer had never seen an order of the King before. To his eyes, it looked in good form, bearing both an official seal and the legible signature of Artaxerxes. Noah asked about the seal. "Oh," he said, "it was a cylinder seal to beat all seals. The winged disc was right there in the middle."

Datis could not find the servant. He was known in the palace to respond to the orders of many, including, in addition to the King, the harem, the Queen, Xerxes and a number of other princes. No one seemed to know where he had gone, although it was rumored that someone important had sent him with a message to the Satrap of Egypt.

A month passed. I was able to inquire of Xerxes whether he had sent the servant to Egypt. The answer was no. Then word came to the palace that this man had indeed been dispatched to Egypt and had been killed en route by bandits in the outskirts of Sardis. The messenger bearing these ill tidings had no idea at whose behest the servant was traveling. Our suspicions grew.

I went to see the Magus who had led the investigation. He greeted me warmly in his palace chamber, a place that had been strictly off limits to me growing up. Its large size and rich appointments took my breath away. Four

Death in the Family ❧

gorgeous tapestries hung on the walls from ornate moldings encircling the room; two huge carpets of thick pile and brilliant colors covered the stone floor. These weavings imparted a lush, ethereal warmth to the room, a palace within the palace, a place kept secret and sacred, as befitted its occupant.

We settled down on benches, facing each other above one of the magnificent carpets.

"Of course he was on an errand for the King. He showed me the order." His voice betrayed impatience.

"Did you keep the order?"

"Why, yes. I have it here somewhere, among our records." He dashed over to a large table piled high with scrolls and parchments. He began to rummage, casting things this way and that until, with a triumphant cry, he spun around, his outstretched hand grasping a parchment.

"Here. You may examine it, as we have done, most thoroughly."

My goodness, I thought, how disappointing this defensiveness. It took me but a minute to read through the order.

"So, you satisfied yourself that this came from the King?"

The Magus' impatience turned to anger. "Do you take me for an idiot. The paper's his, the signature's his. The script in the same hand. The seal's official. What more could you want?"

"Nothing, I suppose. I'm grateful for the help. And for inviting me into this space. It's a secret treasure. One I won't reveal."

❧ ❧ ❧ ❧ ❧ ❧

Ochus, Datis and I gathered together each evening to report, and compare notes. Six weeks had passed since Xerxes' crowning. I presented my findings.

"The Magus believed the order was in the King's hand. It wasn't. He believed the King had signed his name. He hadn't. He believed the seal was affixed by the King. Wrong again. How do I know? Because the King couldn't read or write. He never bothered to learn. Nothing purporting to be by his authority left the palace without his personal seal, a substitute for his signature. It was the sole source of his authority. The seal on that order was, indeed, official looking. Two hooded figures, each spearing a winged lion-griffin while Ahura-Mazda hovers overhead. It might have been his personal seal, for there were several he used in rotation. But whoever composed that order did so without his authority. The Magus should have known, but the King was embarrassed by his illiteracy and kept it a

114

state secret. In fact, those like Andia, who was my source, kept the secret because they shared the King's embarrassment."

Ochus announced the obvious. "If the order was a fake, the suicide story dissolves. If only we could trace the handwriting."

"Datis, you're deep in thought and quiet as a snake in winter. Out with it. Whatever it is."

"I think we have to bring the Magus around. Then enlist his help. He's the only one with the record. The risk is worth taking."

❧ ❧ ❧ ❧ ❧ ❧

Xerxes liked Chalybon wine. He was susceptible to its destructive charms when taken in quantity, undiluted. On the evening of the 45th day of his reign, his servants assisted him into bed, following an evening of male entertainment.

Sogdianus waited until morning to bring news of Xerxes' death. He explained the need to take matters into his own hands in a message posted just outside the entrance to the Apadana.

"I, Sogdianus, son of Great King Artaxeres and of Alogune, his beloved concubine, here record the death, by my hand, of the villainous Xerxes, of whose heinous murder of his parents I now possess proof beyond any doubt. In a deathbed confession, while en route to Egypt, Xerxes' perfidious servant described how Xerxes himself had written the order to procure the snakes, signed his father's name, and dispatched the servant to collect them. Thus did this servant return to the palace with two cobras, which he delivered not to the King, as reported to the Magi, but to Xerxes, who then deployed them with deadly effect to destroy our King and Queen. Last night, in his chamber, when confronted with these facts, King Xerxes acknowledged this unspeakable crime, a confession heard not only by me but by Pharnacyas and Menostanes, who accompanied me to his chamber to bear witness. Tomorrow, by Ahura-Mazda's grace, I will accept the crown and name Menostanes my Chiliarch."

I had returned to the Magus' chambers and was seated with him when word of the assassination spread like a driving wind throughout the palace. One of the Magus' servants rushed into the room, crying, arms outstretched.

"Quiet yourself, man. Speak, but slowly. There is time, for we have nowhere to go."

I could see the Magus thought the sound of his voice pleasing, and the ideas he expressed, clever. When one is constantly revered as a sage, a polymath, a man of mysteries and infinite knowledge, it brings on a fever of certitude, a spiraling adulation of self that knows no limit. My host was thus afflicted.

Still gasping, the servant spit out the words necessary to sketch the events posted by Sogdianus. The Magus was distraught, and so was I. He grew more so when I confronted him with our proof that the order was not what it purported to be.

"Sogdianus is right. Patricide, not suicide." The Magus began to weep. He bowed his head, clasping it in his delicate hands, elbows supported by knees. A sad sight.

"Patricide, perhaps. But not necessarily the story Sogdianus tells. The path to truth starts here. You can restore your reputation by uncovering the real author of the King's order. If it's Xerxes, so be it. But there are other possibilities. A mystery yet to be solved."

My voice had risen, becoming a command, something I did not plan. Over the years I grew to understand that, in times like this, much of what I did was instinctive. I have asked myself, again and again, with fear of the answer, whether my life's better moments were products of my design or a thing apart. Aware of the multitude of low points in my life, I drift away, never quite completing the analysis necessary to uncover the truth, which, of course, cuts in both directions.

The Magus lifted his head to stare at me. Streaks of salt covered his face. His expression turned from despair to hope as he imagined the route to redemption.

When we parted, the Magus was studying the order with the light of many candles. His memory for shapes, smells, and sounds was famous throughout the palace. More than his other talents, these exceptional skills defined the man. He was applying himself to each curled nuance of each letter found in the order. They would be parked in his brain in orderly fashion, easy to retrieve when comparisons were needed.

Reward for the Magus came rapidly. Upon leaving his chamber, he eased into the flow of people, all going to the entrance of the Apadana. There he read the proclamation. Not until he had finished a quick first reading did the lightning of recognition strike. Letter for letter he compared the imprints in his brain with the shapes on the proclamation. He then rushed to our chambers, knocking vigorously on the door. Datis admitted him, drawing away as he dashed through the vestibule, half-crazed with excitement.

"You have something to report?" I asked.

The Magus choked on his words. His face turned red, then blue.

"Catch your breath or it will be your last. You're as excitable as your servant." I shot Ochus a look, then gently slapped the Magus across the shoulders. Finally composed, he spoke.

"The hand that produced the King's order also wrote the proclamation. May the fist of Ahura-Mazda smite me this instant, should I be mistaken."

"That makes Sogdianus the author," Ochus said, his brow knitted, heavy with thought.

"Yes, but surely he was not so stupid as to think his writing at the Apadana wouldn't be compared with the King's order. Something's missing."

"You're right, Parysatis. I can explain. We interviewed the servant, of course, demanding proof of the King's command. At first he claimed the order to bring the cobras was oral. Only under duress, when we threatened to have him flayed, did he pull from his cloak the writing we showed you. He said he had been instructed by the King to destroy the order after it had served its purpose. Leave that to us, we told him, and sent him away.

"Enough. Ochus and I are in peril. And so are you, my friend, if he discovers that order, sitting on your table. Despite what we know, truth remains elusive, hard to explain, harder still to prove and withal, dangerous to the touch. He will be crowned. And he will seek to crush all who threaten his reign. What we must do will take time. Pray to the Gods for enough."

What started to enfold my heart in nervousness had suddenly, as if by a switch, changed. I felt confidence in my grasp of the situation and the path ahead, the ways and means of survival.

"What about me? To protect myself, I must destroy the order."

"Do that and sooner rather than later, you're a dead Magus. Your scrap of paper is the only evidence we have. Give it to us. If asked, you destroyed it, as you promised the servant. Either we work together and live, or we fall apart, dying separately. Bring us the order, now." Laying my hands on the Magus, whose stature seemed to shrink as the weight of discovery swelled in his head, I spun him around and pushed him none too gently toward the door, which Datis held open. Without a word, he was gone.

"Magus the mouse. No use exhorting that animal to be brave. Fear is our best tether."

"Our only," said Ochus.

❧ ❧ ❧ ❧ ❧ ❧

Sogdianus acceded to the crown three days after the proclamation. The date was January 21 in the 127th year of the Achaemenid Empire. In two months, if I lived that long, I would celebrate my twenty-first birthday, a notable landmark for Persians.

Sogdianus' rush for the crown did not allow for more than minimal observances of the triumphal customs that had evolved for coronations in the Achaemenid dynasty. He didn't even take the time to journey the short distance to Pasargadae, site of every coronation since Cyrus the Great. However, he did enter a small fire temple within the palace grounds, dressed, according to custom, as a simple warrior. The palace crowd stood outside. This ritual called for a trio of Magi to await the new King within the temple, where they would serve him a plain dish of sour milk, herbs, and dates. Presumably Sogdianus tasted this traditional fare before accepting the gold-embroidered Median cloak and war crown that had once belonged to Cyrus the Great. In any event, less than two minutes passed before he appeared at the door of the temple, crown upon his head, cloak across his shoulders, and proclaimed himself Great King Sogdianus. A cheer rose from the crowd. Ochus and I exchanged knowing glances, aware that the cheer was far from enthusiastic. Just then the chief Magus emerged from the temple, distraught, the lotus and scepter in his hands. So rushed was the ceremony that these ruling symbols had been left behind. A quiet gasp replaced the muted cheers as Sogdianus snatched the lotus and scepter from the Magus and lifted them high above his head. Tepid cheers resumed.

The newly crowned King did not choose to remain in the palace at Persepolis. Within days, he had organized the court to journey to the palace at Susa, a place I found too hot or too cold. To us his departure was an effort to rid himself of bloody hands.

We gathered just inside the great cedarwood gates of the palace to see the court's departure. Sogdianus caught sight of us, just as he was about to mount his large bay. He beckoned to Ochus, who obliged by elbowing through the crowd. They spoke briefly. Ochus returned to my side. "He's invited us to attend his court, once he gets settled. 'Won't be long,'" he promised.

Remaining in Persepolis, we worked feverishly against time.

❧ ❧ ❧ ❧ ❧ ❧

The lands around Nippur, on the plain between the Tigris and the Euphrates southeast of Babylon and southwest of Susa, were fertile and productive, having first by the hand of the mysterious Sumerians been redeemed from fen and desert through drainage and irrigation and then, century upon century, enriched with silt taken from these great rivers and cultivated with care and the expanding knowledge of agriculture, which no dynastic collapse or tribal war could arrest.

These lands hug the marshes, some six thousand square miles of astounding country around Qurna, where the Tigris and Euphrates join above Basra to form the Shatt al Arab. The marshes are the centuries-old result of the annual flooding of these rivers, caused by the melting of winter snows on the high mountains of Persia.

Cattle grazing shares the plain with farming. Vying for space are wheat, barley and rye, lentil and chickpea, flax, hemp and sesame, olive and pear, cherry and pistachio.

Much of this land was granted by my father to high court officials and many members of his family, including, in the case of a particularly large and valuable property, me. He said it would be important to me some day. All of these lands were managed by the Murasu company, experts in land use. Soldiers under control of the Babylonian satrap were given special rights to the bounty these lands produced, a security measure concocted by my father. It was this article of family diplomacy that gave us hope, for strangely enough, Sogdianus was the only surviving member of our family who had never owned land in the plain or showed any interest in the family holdings there.

When the summons came, Ochus was in Babylon, seeking the loyalty and support of the Babylonian army. Our plan depended upon his success, for Arbarius, commander of Sogdianus' cavalry, to whom we had disclosed the proof, and who declared himself convinced, and a patriot to the Empire, was, nonetheless, only prepared to stand aside, and even that, only if the Babylonians took to the field in support of our cause.

With the summons came a palace guard to escort us to Susa. Since Ochus was away, I thought I could postpone the visit, but the guard was instructed to bring whomever they found without delay.

I saw no way out. To Susa I went, packing for the trip the most alluring wardrobe I could muster, rich dresses gay with sea purple and gold embroidery, and my best jewelry. I added a bottle of kohl for the eyes. Also, rouge and perfumes of sandalwood, frankincense, and tuberose, the most enchanting ones I owned, those that often turned heads. What possessed me to pack these things? I had no definite idea at the time, but, with few exceptions, they represent a woman's armory, her weapons of choice.

Perhaps, it was the unconscious response to a favored passage from the *Iliad*, that transcendent poem that countless times had been presented to the court by bards skilled in the oral tradition. The palace boasted twenty-four papyrus rolls containing this epic in the Persian tongue, a treasure passed down from crown to crown. From first hearing, Hera's seduction of her husband had always been alive in my memory. I knew the lines:

> The breastband,
> pierced and alluring, with every kind of enchantment
> woven through it… There is the heat of Love,
> the pulsing rush of Longing, the lover's whisper,
> irresistible—madness to make the sanest man go mad.

I also packed the gold dagger that I had asked Datis to procure for me. Small, light in the hand, and very effective for piercing and cutting, its presence gave me comfort. The top of the blade was adorned with ibex heads. The handle ended in outward-looking lion heads. No small expense, this weapon of desperation. I had never used it in anger or fear.

The palace at Susa is sited southwest of the red sandstone hills that mark the end of that countryside. We reached its gate in late afternoon on a sweltering day. Dust surrounded our ankles as we moved through the well guarded entrance to the palace grounds. Ahead of us, dancing in the rays of a setting sun, clouds of mosquitoes hovered.

Upon arrival, I was whisked through the palace doors and there met by Menostanes, the King's Chiliarch, who accompanied me to chambers close by the suite of rooms occupied by the King. He was large and round, with an effeminate and flabby face that could once have been handsome. At first blush, I found it hard to imagine what Sogdianus saw in him. And, then, remembering that he had been witness to the alleged bedside confession of Xerxes, I knew. Nothing more nor less than loyalty.

Menostanes announced the King's wish that we dine together. I tried to determine my status. I despised sycophants. Something about this Chiliarch, his oily, self-satisfied and super-important manner, unleashed the reckless.

"Do I have a choice? Am I the King's guest or his prisoner?"

Menostanes recoiled, as if hit by a hammer. Stammering, he tried to reassure me. The more he said the less convincing he became. The man lacked the ability to lie, an essential skill for the head of the Great King's personal guard. It is the Chiliarch who receives the petitions of all seeking audience with the King, who decides their fate, and who then concocts the excuses and other stories.

Dinner proved to be a small gathering: Sogdianus and I, surrounded by a small army of servants, all smelling fresh from the bath and clothed from head to toe in white. They almost knocked one another over in their zeal to serve our culinary wants.

I had dressed to be noticed. My floor-length tunic was plain white, the background for my ornaments. Above, I wore a tall diadem. Below, my feet were clad in finely tooled leather sandals, inlaid with gold leaf. From my ears hung circular earrings of gold wire mesh, having three bars across the centre, from which hung pomegranates and discs fashioned of gold. From the bottom hung a larger pendant of lapis lazuli, contained in a mesh of gold wire. They were my parents' wedding gift. To set off the gold and attract attention to my long neck, I pinned snugly around it a black velvet ribbon, half an inch in width. A pair of gold bracelets with lion's head terminals completed my costume.

The aroma coming from the King's hair was close to overpowering. He was using labyzos, a perfume more costly than myrrh. A luxury favored by our father. Distinctly an acquired taste. As a child, I thought my father used it more to repel than to attract.

As an appetizer, turnips in vinegar and mustard were served. There followed fried cuttlefish and sturgeon, served with hot tawny-crusted rolls and relishes made of olives, dates, pears and pomegranates. A suckling pig came next, its roasted skin glowing in the candlelight. My host had spared nothing from the kitchen, it seemed, to please me.

At first conversation was strained. I was dreadfully hungry, which gave me plenty to do between the sparse pleasantries that passed for discourse. However, Thasian and Lesbian wines flowed in abundance. Sogdianus was partial to undiluted wines of quality, which he proudly described, each in turn, declaring them too fine to dilute. He then tricked himself into drinking more than even Xerxes, who, he claimed, had an enormous capacity.

Sweets consisted of fruits and flat cakes of many kinds, which were served in ivory baskets. By then the food and drink had erased all formality.

"These soft lights become you, Parysatis. Is this how you appeared to Ochus when he grew—how did they put it—overly familiar?" His lascivious laugh caused me to catch my breath. "The court knows of your married life, together and apart. Lonely for you, no doubt. I've arranged after-dinner entertainment. Without your husband, it will be easier to enjoy."

I stopped drinking. I had, in fact, consumed much less wine than I was accustomed to imbibe at dinner. I knew I would need all my wits to comprehend and anticipate the enemy's program.

At the snap of my host's fingers, a trio of Rhodian sambuca-players entered. They were followed by several ithyphallic dancers, a clown, and three naked female jugglers, their skin glistening with oil. They reminded me of the pig.

As the music grew more raucous and rhythmic, the dancers and jugglers were incited to faster, more furious steps, leading to a crescendo of sound and motion. At that the dancers and two of the jugglers departed, the musicians faded into dark recesses, the clown disrobed and he and the remaining juggler appeared to blend together in the flickering candle lights as they began slowly with foreplay, accompanied by the strings of the sambuca. The passion of the couple, feigned or not, proved highly contagious to my host. In contrast, from my seat on the couch beside him, my senses registered barely contained revulsion.

Of course, we royals knew this sort of display occurred from time to time in after-dinner symposia for males only. However cunning such performances may have appeared to those audiences, this one, before a mixed audience of two, was the very navel of vulgarity. I wished for Ochus, my thoughts turning to his mission, about the success or failure of which I knew nothing. I concentrated on the scene before me and what it was designed to accomplish. That was the easy part. What to do about it was much harder. What sort of exchange might be achieved? I was in too deep not to try.

Accompanied by grunts and moans, the two naked forms had just begun to couple when I got to my feet, leaned over almost within touch of his ear and whispered to my overheated King, "Your special dessert has achieved it purpose, even before the final scene. I repair to my chamber, where I trust you will honor me with a visit. Shall we say quarter of an hour?"

Spinning on my heels I departed before he could respond.

He entered without warning. A Great King's prerogative, I supposed, one among many. Save for the velvet ribbon and gold earrings, I had completely undressed and was reclining on my bed, under a flimsy cover, my head elevated by a large pillow. I had lighted one candle on the bureau beside the bed. A slight draft in the room caused it to flicker, casting shadows along the walls that moved, possibly in time with the beat of my heart, the sound of which seemed loud enough to attract guards.

Sogdianus rushed towards the bed, disrobing as he came, weaving from the wine's effect, then stumbling over his garment to fall to the bed, arms thrust forward for protection.

We embraced. He was wet with the heat of vicarious pleasure. His body's odor, unpleasantly pungent, crowded out the frankensense I had applied for the evening. With hope of controlling the action, I took his enormous pumpkin head in my two hands and kissed him with what I thought might pass for passion. He worked to implant his tongue in my mouth, pressing hard against my lips, which finally submitted. Unwanted sex with anyone is repulsive beyond civil words to capture, as I had discovered in the corridor. With this villain, it would be unimaginably horrible, impossible to endure. Unless, I kept telling myself, one's life depended on it.

"Sogdianus, I need something before we go further. I need your solemn promise, as an Achaemenid, as the Great King, that you will never seek to harm Ochus, my children, or me." Even this scoundrel knew the importance among royals of keeping one's word. As we all were taught, it was the defining feature of Persian culture and manhood. "Swear it, and I am yours."

Taking my hand in his, he said, "I won't harm what's mine. Nor her offspring. Have no concern for Ochus. He will soon be a minor part of the Achaemenid dynasty." Sogdianus had risen back on his haunches. He seemed to tower over me, his large moon of a head wobbling at the neck, a support far too impaired by the grape to last. He removed the cover. I could see the lusting glint in his eyes just before he crashed down on top of me, his head coming to rest beside mine on the large pillow, his breath heavy with partially digested wine.

My weapons of choice had succeeded in saving only one of us. For the other I would have to take bigger risks. I had imagined the scene imperfectly, hoping never to be put to the test.

There are situations in which we imagine ourselves, often when someone else experiences them, either successfully or not. The result doesn't matter, for the question is always the same, how would I have behaved? The drowning child, the burning home with one's infant within, the soldier about to hurl a javelin at one's unsuspecting husband, the charging boar about to strike one's hunting companion. Common to them all is the summons to greatness, an act of uncommon bravery to save another's life. One can rehearse these scenes repeatedly without knowing how one would handle them if destiny called.

What I had begun was described by some wag as the equalivent of holding a wolf by the ears. I couldn't shake this image.

For a moment or two, as he paused beside me to catch his breath, I thought he might pass out. Oh, wishful one. He was merely gathering strength for the assault he thought I craved, the conquest he imagined I would beg him to repeat.

Before he came through the door I had resolved to deny him. The thought of it contaminated my brain. Couldn't what I now had to do be done as well before as after, although, if he slept post orgasm, as so many do, the task might prove easier. On the other hand, I reasoned, if he were quick to leave the scene, delay had its risks too.

With effort, he positioned himself directly above me.

"Parysatis, the moment has come. Royalty knocks. Open in the name of the King."

Here, but for grim circumstance, was low humor beyond imagining, ready source of ridicule and parody.

I spread my legs, feeling his lower body slip down. My hands were resting under my head, not for the provocative pose they produced in that position but to assure they were free to move. Slipping my right hand under the pillow, I seized the dagger by its handle and carefully moved it down along my right side and then up above his now undulating back.

"What progress, my King?" Reaching above his back with my left hand I clasped my hands together and pulled the blade down, hilt-deep into his lower back. Then, as instructed by Datis, I moved the dagger up and to the left, hoping to assure a mortal wound.

Hot blood drenched my hands. I felt it pouring down the side of my body. He stammered, found voice and screamed, at first loud, high-pitched and defiant, then soft and low, a doleful cry. I released the dagger to shake the blood from my hands. Just then he rolled away from me, falling to the floor on his back, the dagger now held in place by his weight. Coughing replaced the cries as blood came to his mouth, suffocating him. Moments later, the Great King was dead.

The palace retinue had no idea what to do with me. Fearful and uncertain, they turned servile, according me space and every comfort I requested. Even Menostanes, whose unctuous tendencies vanished with the life of his master. I knew this treatment wouldn't last.

Before I arrived in Susa, Sogdianus had sent an armed party to Babylon to bring Ochus to the palace, willing or not. Three days after my night with the King, the party returned, itself escorted by a large contingent of elite members of the Babylonian army, who had formed a protective shield around Ochus. Their commander was Hydarnes, a royal who traced his ancestry to Vidarna, one of the seven conspirators who brought the first Darius to power. On the other side of my husband rode Arbarius, commander of Sogdianus' cavalry.

Each of us, in our separate ways, without knowledge of the other, had been successful. Although we always professed having never sought it, the path to the crown lay open.

Despite much time to relive these moments, I still have trouble untangling motives. An instinct for survival, yes indeed. But there had to be more, otherwise why not take the far less risky path of accepting the Great King's offer? There was loyalty to Ochus, my partner in an enterprise that, however edgy at the start, had grown wings. And loyalty to the Empire, although I won't wallow much in that. Far more important was simple stubbornness: a voice telling me to "just see it through."

❧ 8

OCHUS BECOMES
GREAT KING DARIUS II

 SOGDIANUS HAD REIGNED for six months and fifteen days. To gain the crown he had murdered two Kings and a Queen. First, patricide; then, fratricide. Now, a third King had died, by the hand of his half-sister, adding another fratricide to the Achaemenid record.

Word of the Great King's death swept across the Empire, leaving in its wake restlessness and alarm. A royal palace creates its own atmosphere and is often, if unwisely, content to drive away unsettling odors that come from beyond its walls. Thus, the royals within the palaces of Susa and Persepolis were unaware that, from this news alone, anxieties had begun to gnaw away at the health of the people. We thought it possible to hide the truth. Naively, I assumed that, even within the palace, very few knew how the King died, and those who did would be so loyal to the Empire, and to me as the heroine of the moment, that they wouldn't breathe a word to others. We would publicly announce his death but avoid spelling out the circumstances.

Looking back, I find it a remarkable misjudgment to have seriously believed the truth could be contained. But I've learned that any human being can turn wishes built on hopes into arguments built on facts. The more clever one is, the more easily one can achieve this alchemy. And, alas, the more facile one becomes at this game, the more tempting it is to play the sophist, deceiving not just others but oneself as well.

During the three-day interlude before Ochus arrived in Susa with power sufficient to command those left in the palace, versions of the truth had escaped the palace to travel, like sand in a turbulent summer's storm, in every direction, spread by a thousand mouths and more. If the first wave of news was like a hard punch in the stomach, the second was a sharp blow to the now exposed chin. Persians recoiled at what seemed to be the royal house gone mad.

Word filtered back through the palace walls, albeit at a much slower pace than outbound news. This is the way of the world, where so often a tribe's leaders, despite their power and access, are insulated from the attitudes of those they are trying to lead.

When we finally realized the extent of our daydream, we tried to react with decisiveness. But we were lonely and isolated. Palace fear swept the floors, pushed under closed doors, circulated throughout the restive royals, who without exception averted their eyes from us. What power we possessed, and, with hindsight, it was awesome, seemed slight, our position in the palace insecure, the loyalty we could command uncertain.

Ochus summoned the scarred beauty. There were not many in the palace we could trust at this moment. Artoxares was the best among a handful, despite the questions we had about his loyalty. We mainly wanted someone with an ear to the ground. He lived for gossip and thrived on it, his stock in trade.

Ochus proposed that the palace correct the rumors by explaining that he, Ochus, had killed Sogdianus in self-defense. To admit that Parysatis was the murderer, he argued, would taint the effort to justify the killing on the basis of villainy. The circumstances were too sordid, bespeaking entrapment, the killer a woman using deceitful wiles instead of manly force to achieve her ends. Who seduced whom would become a question to be answered. Justification would be lost in the course of imagining how the murder occurred.

Artoxares said, "I understand your point, and it seems to have merit. But first, tell me the truth, firsthand, for I know only the rumors that swirl about the palace. How did Sogdianus die?"

Distrustful, I held my tongue. Ochus pushed ahead, answering in full. Whereupon Artoxares said, "The risk of proclaiming the truth is too great. Death of a prone King by the hand of a woman will beget many plausible explanations, none of which gets at the truth of this villainy. If Parysatis is cast, even by a few, as a seductress, sympathy for Sogdianus will spread like weeds wet with Tigris silt." Ever the poet.

I was proud of what I had done. Immensely so. It took planning and bravery.

At the time I believed I had done it for love of country. The easy route would have been to ingratiate myself. Marriage to Ochus was not based on a deep or profound love, although our lives together had begun to breed more than infants. We were forging a team with shared understandings and goals. I could have succumbed to the King's drunken urge. I could have easily convinced myself that he would spare Ochus in exchange for future nights of love. Instead, in my own eyes, I had become the Empire's heroine. Shouldn't the public, my public, understand what I did and why?

Looking back, I recognize the tricks my mind was playing. For one as eager as I was to have a starring role, it was easy not only to believe one's exploits were heroic but to imagine that others would see them that way; indeed, that they would become magnified in the eyes of our people. My first childbirth involved the same misjudgment, the same fantasy dashed on the hard rocks of reality.

The response of Ochus and Artoxares to my plaint was the same. Slowly, I began to understand their point of view, and, while not agreeing, to accept it as a better reading of our audience than my own. We would announce that Ochus had dethroned Sogdianus. We would publish a story of the King's death that gave dignity to Ochus, his reluctant slayer, who found himself with no alternative but to act in self-defense against the King's determined efforts to eliminate him. We would then offer proof of the late King's villainy.

It's easy now to imagine how the Greek historians would have twisted the story of Sogdianus's death to their one-dimensional account of me, had they but known the truth. Remarkably, they never found out, leaving the historical account at best uncertain.

With even more haste than Sogdianus had exhibited, Ochus was crowned in simple ceremony on August 10 of the 127th year of Achaemenid rule. After long debate, in which I engaged him and his inner circle of advisers, he picked the name Darius II. The choice came down to Darius or Cyrus, the two most widely known and beloved Kings to rule the Empire. We thought that Ochus' destiny was more likely to be that of a consolidator. This suggested Darius.

More compelling, however, was the historical parallel, assuming one looked only at the publicly accepted version of history. Darius had emerged a leader from deep ferment and uncertainty within the Empire caused by the sudden death of King Cambyses. Except by those, like Artoxares, whose cynicism could now and then overcome his pride of Empire, what I now know to be the real story would not be accepted as truth. That story is simply told: the crowning of Bardiya, who, like Cambyses, was the son of Cyrus, and his murder by Darius and the other six conspirators, famously called "the Seven," who convinced the country that Bardiya was an imposter named Gaumata, who had killed Bardiya, the rightful heir, and occupied the throne. In fact, there was no Gaumata.

Darius' imposter story had become firmly embedded in Persian minds. Of course, the whole nation knew that, once having seized the crown, Darius ruled with immense distinction.

Ochus believed that picking the name Darius would carry the similarity forward, bringing good luck to his reign. I hoped he was right.

The other parallel, one that brought wry smiles as we conspired with Artoxares to keep it secret, was the fact that just as there was no real Gaumata for the first Darius to kill, so there was no Sogdianus alive for Ochus to kill.

Even before the crowning, we sent forth to the four winds of the Empire the King's Eyes and many other specially deputized agents of the King, each armed with proof of the vile acts that justified our assumption of authority and a careful explanation of how the King met his death. There would be time for inclusive celebrations, but we both had finally recognized the urgent need for stability. This required a settled crown, which in turn depended upon a convincing explanation of how Sogdianus died.

Many royals quickly appeared before us in support. Only three declared our ascension to the throne illegitimate. These rebels were Arsites, Ochus' younger brother, and two colleagues from prominent families.

Surprisingly, Menostanes, the conspirator whom Sogdianus had named his Chiliarch, who was first to discover the slain King in my bedroom, was not among them. He became paralyzed by uncertainty. Shortly after the crowning, to which he was invited but failed to appear, he was found hanging by the neck from a rafter. A finely woven woolen scarf had served as the instrument of death. A letter was found in his tunic. It contained a deed conveying all of his Babylonian properties to Artoxares. In flowery words, the letter described Artoxares as both lover and bosom companion, to whom he owed much, "more than anyone could imagine." Menostanes closed with two apologies: one for ignoring Artoxares' strong advice to back Ochus rather than Sogdianus in the battle for succession; the other for ending their relationship in this cowardly fashion.

The reach of our friend, Artoxares, never ceased to surprise. As with an onion, one got to know him one layer at a time, with no idea how many other layers must be peeled away to take full measure of the man. Of course, we had long worried about his loyalty. For the first time I understood that our concern, while well founded, came not from actual disloyalty on his part but from the large number of those to whom his loyalty was promised. He was, at bottom, a self-effacing man given to loyal attachments. He defined himself absolutely by the opinions that others held of him. Our problem grew out of his effort to be loyal to so many.

To deal with the three rebels, Darius summoned the two generals whose loyalty enabled our success: Arbarius, commander of the King's cavalry, and Hydarnes, commander of the Babylonian army. Seated on the throne in Persepolis, staff in his right hand, lotus blossom in his left, he looked to me as my father had appeared on the one or two occasions when I was called before him. There was the attendant, fly-whisk in hand, standing behind the throne. The canopy above, as in generations past, displayed rows of bulls and lions, together with representations of the winged disc. Above the canopy, I could imagine the hovering presence of Ahura-Mazda, protector of the earth, the springs, the rivers, and the streams, investing my husband with the legitimacy, the power and, with my help, the energy and wisdom to govern the Empire. Circular like the seasons, I thought, this scene would be eternal, renewing the Empire from generation to generation.

The commanders appeared at the entrance to the throne room. They dropped to the floor, resting their heads on the carpet, arms outstretched, until Darius summoned them forward. They obeyed, getting within ten feet of the immense throne, as close as one would comfortably go for an audience. I stood watching, enthralled with my new station and that of my husband. How splendid the commanders appeared, all polish in tight-fitting tan trousers under flowing white robes with elegant border decoration in bright-colored patterns of fringe, rosette, and lozenge. Their meticulously cut and combed beards of glistening black hair concealed the bottom half of their faces, contrasting with the white skin above. Adorning their heads were ribbed tiaras shaped to stay in place despite the extreme bowing expected in the presence of the Great King.

Though dressed as one, they were otherwise a study in contrasts. Arbarius was in his 50s, of medium height with a wiry frame and legs, though partially hidden by the robe, that were bowed enough to prove a lifetime spent in the saddle. Born a royal, he scorned the aristocratic ways of his family and their friends. His style with the cavalry was open and guileless. He led not by exhortation but by example. He was quick to anger and quick to forgive and forget. The troops loved him as one of their own.

Hydarnes was not yet 40. Tall and tapered from shoulders to waist, he carried good looks with a regal bearing that seemed to say "It's the breeding. I can't help myself." In fact, his style was his own highly self-conscious creation, as so often is the case among the military, and it set him inexorably apart from his troops. He was clever and brave, traits that earned him loyalty but no love. In fact, his theory of control and command was to make his soldiers more afraid of him than of the enemy. At this, he proved successful.

"Come closer," my husband commanded. Until that moment, I hadn't fully appreciated how extremely nearsighted he was. It explained many of his short-comings over the years. His eyesight prevented him from gauging the reaction of those around him. It was a language he lacked, a handicap that often made him profoundly ignorant. Combined with a natural reserve and lack of humor, his myopia was the cause of some uneasy relationships with others. Even a King, to be effective, must be able to empathize, inspire, and persuade as well as command. My role, which defined itself as we bound together our strengths in common enterprise, was to furnish the facial teachings he was bound to miss.

Although the Queen's position in the Empire lacked definition, that I would generally have leave to occupy the throne room and participate jointly with the King in matters of state had been established by quiet assertion and uncom-plaining acceptance. We had, indeed, become a team.

My husband was about to give his first order as Great King. I moved closer.

"All within the palace have honored me with obeisance, offering earth and water. All except the three rebels, who, the King's Eyes have reported, are even now spreading lies in their effort to assemble armies. You will bring them to me."

Arbarius said, "Great King, do you condemn them to die by our hands, or do you want them returned alive to be judged by your tribunal?"

"What do you say to that, Hydarnes?"

"The decision of the King is paramount. You can issue an edict calling for their death and we will obey. You can appoint esteemed Persians to judge them. But, in the past, judges have themselves been condemned to death by your pred-ecessors for handing down iniquitous judgments, often in exchange for money. I recall one instance where judges were flayed alive and their skins stretched tight on judicial benches, a gruesome reminder for future judges. Here, evidence of treason is overwhelming. There's nothing left to judge."

"My orders are simple. Hunt them. Kill them. And bring me ears and nose."

132

The audience was over. The commanders backed out of the hall, bowing.

Within two weeks, the rebels had been eliminated. Darius now rested comfortably on the throne, and I with him. Prospects for the Empire, and for our rule, seemed equally bright.

¶ 9
A QUEEN IN THE PALACE

I BECAME THE EMPIRE'S QUEEN in my twenty-first year, and Queen I would remain for the next 19 years, until my husband's death at the young age of 39.

My compact with Ochus had one simple focus: to assure family succession by creating a pool of royals. They would all be legitimate heirs, unlike ourselves. To allow for choice and "accidents," our word for the mysterious deaths of our first two sons, we would try for a goodly number. Amestris and Arsaces had been born in Hyrcania. We would try for more.

Our marriage rested on far less ambitious foundations than most newly-weds proclaim at the start. Its goal, however, was unattainable without occasional coupling. I was the vessel for his seed, the purpose solely to assure the future. We were copulating not out of passion for each other but for love of family. All that the word "passion" comprehends we retained in privacy, each to and for ourself, to be shared with others as we wished. The burden we put on our marriage was light, easy to bear. In the bargain, our respect for each other grew with the passage of years, evolving into a dependent affection for one another too important and complex to be explained by saying "we loved one another."

As Queen, I bore only two healthy children, Cyrus when I was 22 and Ostanes much later. Between the births of these two, I carried to term in nine pregnancies, each time giving birth to a sickly infant who died before reaching the age of two, much as my first and second born. At a distance, it's an effort to recall the hideous cycle of pregnancy, birth, and death, repeated so many times over the span of 19 years, with each cycle building on the last, so that fear of failure and then failure itself became more and more painful to anticipate and endure. I look back at this persistence in amazement. And yet, we reasoned time and time again, Amestris had survived and so too had Arsaces and Cyrus. Indeed, they flourished. For ten rounds of pregnancy, hope rose up from the ground to drive fear and experience from the field.

❧ ❧ ❧ ❧ ❧ ❧

If Noah aged, it was imperceptible. A man who retains his hair has big advantages in trying to arrest time's effects. Even more so if his hair remains mostly color-fast past middle age. My beekeeper had all this and more. His was an ennobling profession for the fittest. Physically demanding, mentally challenging, spiritually inspiring, the keeping of bees was designed for men of practical optimism, men who took life into their own hands, as if it was all they would ever have, as if it could be shaped to suit their desires. Beekeepers were nature's best precisely because they understood, and therefore revered, nature.

When the turmoil of Sogdianus' brief reign ended, we settled down to rule primarily from Persepolis. It was, after all, our childhood home. The climb to the throne entailed many changes, some good, others bad. The most distressing one of all was the unnatural isolation that came with the possibility that some, perhaps many, around you were sycophants. A purgatory of doubt. With Noah, I knew before visiting him for the first time after becoming Queen, nothing would have changed.

I had often missed his company during my time in Hyrcania. Upon seeing an insect or just sitting alone in the gardens, my thoughts would return to the beeyard and our times together. Slowly, like a plum blossom unfolding to the sun, my mental wanderings took me on a migration from recalling Noah as my mentor to imagining him as my lover. At first the thought surprised me. Laughable. In time, however, I began to see this journey as an easy and natural outgrowth of our friendship. The more I imagined it the more likely it became until it seemed fixed in my mind, ineluctable. The idea became a wide path of escape from the demands of motherhood and service as wife of a Satrap. It was a source of pleasure that grew in intensity with my skill at imagining the details of our love. In the playground of my mind, anything was possible; everything gave pleasure. I grew addicted to these retreats, which I could summon in the blink of an eye, often to pick up the imaginary thread where I had left it and resume weaving a narrative of my own design.

"I've come to see the slaughter," I said, closing the gate behind me and touching, like an old friend, the huge sculpture of Priapus that Noah had carved during my childhood. He looked up from a hive he had just smoked. A smile broadened across his darkly tanned face. I could see an abundance of bees resting from their labors on various parts of his black beard, now streaked with curly white plumes, barely visible. Unwinding his jackknifed frame, he stood straight and arched his back, a brief grimace crossed his face before he strode towards me. His embrace was untamed and wild: a bearlike grasp; an indescribable mix of strong odors, some his own, some from the hives, some from vibrant forms of flora within the beeyard, each vying for dominance. How sharp the contrast from the domesticated hugs that prevailed in the palace.

Was this man the Noah of my youth, who treated me, first, last, and always, as a fellow human being, one for whom he evinced gruff affection, but never more than he lavished on the bees? Or, as surely as my daydreams had changed me, had he changed too? Expectations, grown rampant from repeated imaginings, filled my head.

"You're late. Been north for more than two years, I would say." He had pushed me out the distance of his long arms, his hands holding my shoulders, examining me top to bottom. "Queen becomes you," he announced, as much to the bees, now restless on his beard, as to me.

"Why's that?"

"Because it hasn't changed you at all." He paused, exchanging his professorial look for a smile. "Don't let it," he intoned, for the moment, serious.

I wriggled free, threw my arms around him and tried to kiss him on the lips, just as I had rehearsed this moment over and over again. He evaded my lips, which landed on his cheek. In doing so, he spared me only a tiny bit of the embarrassment that hovered above my yearnings, ready to descend into the reality of the beeyard. In that instant, I realized the impossibility of taking Noah as my lover. Suddenly, I knew he had already considered the idea, rejected it, and prepared to repulse it if necessary. We exchanged not a word, but I knew, as surely as if he had spoken, that the rewards of our relationship for the future depended not on change but continuity. From that tiny movement of his face, I understood that the possibility of "Noah the lover," so amply elaborated in the fertile world of my imaginings, had been stranded far to the north, in Hyrcania.

I pointed over his shoulder, to Priapus. "Didn't Moses descend from the Mountain bearing Yahweh's order to stop worshipping carved images?"

"Come now. You know this image promotes fertility in bees, not humans. It works, without offending Yahweh. As for the massacre, it won't start for another six weeks. Remember? I let you watch from the front row many years ago."

As he studied me, I examined him. What a fine specimen of man. Large, well-formed head set upon a frame of Herculean proportions. Eyes of brilliancy, flashing splendor. And yet there was something I hadn't noticed before. A drop of his right eye lid, creating an arresting duality, as if two men, rather than one, looked out upon the world. Had this flaw always been there? Probably. Human perfection exists only through the eyes of children, storytellers, and fanatics.

"Let's sit near Udusana," I said. "Within earshot, as you used to say."

We walked to the spot under the large cypress. How long it's been, I thought.

"I hear you lost a baby in Hyrcania."

"Two actually. Each died after birth. Until Amestris came along, I felt cursed." My eyes welled up. I turned away, as if to attend to something beside me. How pathetic I was at that moment, afraid to show my feelings to the only human being within the palace walls who, without doubt, would handle them with understanding and kindness.

"Do you mind telling me? The similarities? And look here. Don't wipe away the tears. Only one capable of loving strongly can also suffer great sorrow. But that person's capacity to love will counteract the grief and heal her. Let the tears be confirmation of your grief." Gently, he placed my hand in the palms of his, one, strikingly small and white, enfolded in two, worn dark and scruffy.

"Each infant was tinged with yellow, a pallor that grew more noticeable as the days passed. Dark urine. Swollen stomach. Irregular heartbeat. Irritability that neither feeding, bathing, or playful contact could ease. Finally, massive infection, heart failure, death. Too much alike to be anything but a curse."

Tears poured forth, streaking my face, wetting my hands. I sobbed.

"Against these, you have two healthy children, one a boy with high promise to be successor to the Great King. Why not stop?"

"While I live, there's no other woman who can create legitimate heirs to the throne. I expect to be here a long time. With the deaths of our mother and father, then of Xerxes and Sogdianus, Darius and I know up close the fragility of palace life. He wants many children. It's all he asks. At times I think as you do. When that happens, the memory of those swift killings overwhelms the logic." I tried to end the conversation, but Noah had one more point to make.

"You mentioned the possibility of a curse. Beekeepers are, in general, non-believers. We tend many hives. In each we watch for the waning and waxing of signs: numbers, health and sickness, strength and energy, the pulse of life. In all we measure the life force of each hive. They differ, sometimes greatly. When we detect a trend, we try to understand cause and effect, the better to preserve and enhance our bees. Curses are the invention of those lacking answers. And those lacking belief in their capacity to find answers. In this beeyard, some hives flourish while others die. In neither case is the cause a result of blessing or curse. In this much I am a believer."

I got to my feet while he was carrying on, a lecture without purpose. I was impatient.

"Allow me one minute more. From generation to generation, queen bees pass their traits on to their offspring. There is reason to assume humans do too. Indeed, that's the point of your wanting to carry forward the family's greatness. You have placed it well in two of your children. But the other two suggest to this beekeeper that there are other, dangerous, traits that can emerge from your congress with Darius. The risks are not in balance with the rewards, for childbirth itself is life-threatening. I hope you will weigh my words."

I glared at him. "I don't recall seeking this advice." Turning, I flew from the beeyard, his words following inescapably behind.

❧ ❧ ❧ ❧ ❧

Arsaces was the first of my sons to survive infancy. He was born on my 20th birthday, shortly after noon. This date was the vernal equinox, the day we celebrated the beginning of a new year. But I remember the exact time of Arsaces' birth, because it was the beginning of a new lunar month and just minutes before Arsaces began to emerge from my womb, the sun began to darken. By the time Arsaces was born, brightening the room with his cries, the sun had assumed the shape of a slim crescent and stars had begun to appear in the sky. Minutes later the sun emerged from behind a shadow. The Empire was transfixed by this omen. People turned to the Magi for interpretation. At first they were unsure, wishing to be positive but troubled by an event that blocked the sun's nourishing rays. When they learned it was my birthday and that, while the eclipse was in process, I had delivered a baby boy, they saw the need to find a basis for rejoicing. "There is no possible doubt," they declared. "A royal son has emerged from the shadow of the sun, renewing both the sun and the Empire on which it daily shines forth. He is blessed by the eclipse."

Without the Magi's forceful vision, I might easily have reasoned my way to a darker interpretation.

Arsaces assumed the throne upon Darius' death. He called himself Artaxerxes II, after my father. Among the people he came to be known as the "Mindful." Much did it mask.

Without him I might not have been Queen Mother. Might not, but probably would. Of our children who survived past early childhood, there was my daughter, Amestris, born in Hyrcania when I was 19, and Arsaces when I was 20. Despite Noah's warnings there were two more healthy sons. Cyrus was born in the 128th year of Achaemenid rule, when I was 22, and Ostanes was born, remarkably, in the 141st year of the Empire, when I was 35. Either could have worn the crown. Cyrus came very close to doing so, a subject on which I will speak shortly. His was my easiest birth, his cry the most insistent affirmation of life, his suck the most tender and rewarding. I knew he would be my golden apple. I named him Cyrus, sun of my life and future leader of the Empire, as was his namesake, the mighty Cyrus, Cyrus the Great.

❦ ❦ ❦ ❦ ❦ ❦

My husband was clever in handling relations throughout the Empire. And for that matter, among the Peloponnesians as well. He was not naturally inclined to make war. Our father, Artaxerxes, just before his death, had made peace with the Athenians, who had dispatched an envoy to Ephesus to open talks with the Great King. We tried to build on this truce and the budding friendship with the Athenians that followed. Of course, this was a decade before the Athenians were demolished in Sicily during our Empire's 137th year. Their complete downfall occurred over two years after the Sicilian expedition was launched to "order Sicilian affairs to suit Athens' interests." Command of that expedition was placed in the hands of Alcibiades, Nicias, and Lamachus after intense debate in the Athenian assembly. Alcibiades, leader of the Athenian hotbloods, favored extending Athenian control by a quick attack that he averred would be painless. Nicias advanced powerfully argued warnings that were as prophetic and ineffectual as those of Cassandra centuries before.

Darius was not ignorant of the fact that neither he nor his Satraps had a navy to sally forth around the Aegean in pursuit of booty. Better to consolidate control of the Asia Minor shoreline, urge his generals Tissaphernes and Pharnabazus, whom he had appointed as Satraps in Sardis and Dascylium, to seek revenue instead of conquest, and strive throughout the kingdom for peace at tolerable cost.

We deliberately underfunded the armies maintained by these Satraps, pushing them to carry on, at their own expense, the business of gathering tribute from the cities within their purview. We looked to Tissaphrenes and Pharnabazus to seek to outdo one another in collections. Each of these men was supremely confident of his own abilities and privately contemptuous of the other's. Darius played on their jealousies. Like an experienced captain, he caught the mighty wind of competition that blew between them and sailed before it.

Not only were these generals ruthless in amassing tribute from the Persian cities within their control, they were effective in using the Lacedaemonian contingents within their armies to gather collections from cities still under Athenian control.

In the winter of our 139th year, Darius summoned to Persepolis all of his Satraps with a view to honoring Tissaphernes and Pharnabazus for their successes in Asia Minor. I thought it a risky idea, given the competitive fervor that flowed between them, until now always expressed at a distance. Darius was derisive in spurning my concern. In fact, for entertainment at the celebration, he invited each of them to put forth his most distinguished warrior to do battle in single combat.

I accused Darius of mischief that could lead to no good end. Battle between soldiers in a serious army, I argued, ought not to be treated as spectacle. He grew immensely proud of his idea, so much so that, stepping out of character, he attacked on the ground that, as a woman, I knew little of men's nature as warriors. He answered me with the claim that this battle by proxy, regardless of outcome, would spur each of his generals to greater heights of achievement in their Satrapies. With that, his ear turned deaf.

Here was a lesson in the futility of taking Darius on, head to head, in matters military. To get my way, only a much earlier and more subtle approach would answer.

The palace was aglow with torches on the night the Satraps gathered. There must have been 5,000 in attendance. In the center of the Apadana was a large empty circle, with soldiers seated to form a protective circumference. The Great

King's long table was close by. Darius sat at the end, facing the circle, wearing his cloak of dazzling purple, and close to him on either side were Tissaphernes and Pharnabazus. They were encased in the same remarkable bubble of sparkling energy, a personal force that made one's blood tingle to the fingertips. Yet, there were differences.

Tissaphernes was tall, with a thin flint-like face full of angles, deeply set eyes of cornflower blue that blinked every other second, sharp brows lightly covered with tan and white hair, and a long narrow nose extending so far out from his cheeks that one wondered if it might impair his vision. His mouth was small, his lips well formed, the lines on his face etched more from frowns than smiles. His teeth, those that were still in place, gleamed white when one saw them, which was not often because in this gathering he had become self-conscious about those missing from the middle of his lower jaw. A sharp protruding chin, rival to his nose, completed the picture. He wasn't much of a wit or orator. He took himself and those around him seriously. I guessed him incapable of banter. But ask him a question and one always received a thoughtful response, often from an unexpected angle.

Pharnabazus was broad where Tissaphernes was narrow. He exuded compressed strength, summoning forth the image of a bull, potent, rampant, and in rut. One imagined him, as a child, immovable, an implacable force in boxing or wrestling, capable of crushing his mates. His arms were noticeable for their length, in contrast to his short frame. Hair on his arms spilled out of his jacket, covering his wrists, extending almost up to the knuckles of his hands. His face was marked with deep lines depicting worry and laughter in equal parts. This was a man who took on his shoulders the weight of the world and could still laugh about the human condition. He had hair of raven's black, despite his age. His eyebrows were robust, black, white and curly. His dark eyes were constantly in motion. His mouth seemed enormous against the modest proportions of nose and chin. His teeth, like his wit, had survived the challenges of a lifetime spent in battle.

When the time for combat arrived, Darius set the rules and introduced the men picked by his generals to engage one another. The Macedonian had been selected by Tissaphernes, the Lacedaemonian by Pharnabazus. I mused over the choices, wondering—just for a moment—whether the generals had chosen to spare Persians or whether, in fact, these men were the best they had.

The Macedonian advanced into the circle, clad in expensive armor and

142

bearing a javelin, lance, and sword. He was large in all directions. What could be seen of his muscles was enough to project well-developed hardness across his entire frame.

The Lacedaemonian then appeared, his wiry body naked and oiled, carrying only a well-balanced club. Where the Macadonian's strength might allow him to hurl thunderbolts farther than other men, the Lacedaemonian's quickness would combine eye and hand to catch them in midair. Both men were magnificent to look upon, not only their physiques but their overflowing ardor for combat.

Darius gave the signal to begin. They advanced towards one another. The Macedonian flung his javelin, well aimed to connect. The Lacedaemonian, antic-ipating the oncoming weapon, inclined his body slightly, enough to avoid contact. Tissaphernes' champion poised his long lance, threatening his naked opponent; then charged. Pharnabazus' champion waited, his body tense like a bent sapling, and when his opponent came in range, struck the lance with his club, shattering it. The Macedonian tried to continue the battle with his sword, but as he reached for it, the Lacedaemonian dashed forward, leapt upon him to seize the swordhand with his left hand and with his right, upset the Macedonian's balance. As he fell to the floor, the Lacedaemonian placed a foot upon his neck, and, holding the club aloft, looked to the Great King for guidance.

The audience was in an uproar due to the stunning quickness and superiority of the Lacedaemonian's skill. Tissaphernes stood still, frozen in place, his sharp features expressing the shock he obviously felt from his cornflower eyes right down to his toes. Pharnabazus stood opposite, exultant. Darius signaled to let the vanquished soldier live. Among the audience, the reaction was divided. Raucous shouting increased, turning nasty in tone.

To Pharnabazus, the King's decision violated the rules by which contests of single combat are decided. He considered it a personal offense as well. He protested with unbecoming vigor and the backing of half the audience, which I sensed was at the edge of violence. Darius seemed unaware, handicapped, I real-ized, by his nearsightedness. I began slowly to clap my hands, making as much sound as possible so as to be noticed amidst the turmoil. Others joined in. The contestants were escorted out of the circle. The threat drained away as Darius sat, others followed his lead, and the banquet's final course was served. Darius flashed me a smile. It was an evening to remember.

❧ ❧ ❧ ❧ ❧ ❧

Artoxares didn't change when we ascended the throne. He was a shameless sycophant before and remained one after. Less so, however, because he had become noticeably rich with lands in Nippur, inherited from Sogdianus' despicable Chiliarch, whose sole act of bravery, so far as I know, was to take his own life when Ochus donned the crown.

Artoxares came frequently to call on me in my ample quarters at the rear of the harem. I always summoned my "Chiliarch," Datis, to join us. His presence seemed to wring out of Artoxares any evidence of sycophancy. I found joy in sharing these hours with "my boys" as I began to call them. We had no agenda. Conversation would break forth and start to sparkle by the time the customary baskets of fruit had been served, accompanied by the first jug of mead or wine. I had this odd idea that eunuchs have more energy to expend on verbal intercourse because they have lost the energy-consuming equipment that males are born with. By the end of these gatherings I felt both challenged and fed intellectually, so much so that I was physically exhausted as well.

I used a silver amphora to serve the refreshment. It had two gilded silver handles in the form of a leaping ibex. By flexing the forelegs under the body and tucking the head down against the beast's hairy collar, the artist had succeeded in making the ibex both dignified and playful. I loved this vessel, despite its aged condition. It had two serving spouts at the base which often leaked because the plugs were worn.

Gradually, the frequency of Artoxares' visits increased. His attentions were flattering to me. On one memorable occasion, he arrived with a newly turned gold jug. Its proportions were exquisite. "Burnished splendor," I said.

"A gift," he announced, insisting I take it. He expected to see it used to serve the drink that had become central to the pleasure of our time together.

Conversation turned to the epic of Gilgamesh, the legendary king of Uruk, a city on the Euphrates near Nippur and even closer to the lands that Artoxares and I owned on the great fertile plain between those two cities. All Persians knew the story well. Many studied it, trying to understand its mysteries. Most failed. The few successful ones loved the epic with such passion that they came to know it by heart. Although Artoxares and I had studied Gilgamesh, neither of us would boast of having unraveled the yarn.

"Why did Gilgamesh spurn Ishtar's overtures?" I asked. "That was the consuming question among us, growing up. We didn't accept the Magus' explanation."

Looking back on that afternoon, I find it odd, even comical, that I was the one to introduce this subject. I hadn't spoken of the epic in years.

"Remind me," said Artoxares. I could see that Datis was about to speak. I cut him off, thinking that as a Saka, he knew little if anything of the story.

"Ishtar, goddess of love and war, invites Gilgamesh to become her lover and husband. He declines, alleging that Ishtar has had many mates, all of whom were eventually disposed of. The Magus claimed Gilgamesh was afraid of being treated the same. We had doubts."

"Where's Enkidu in all this?" asked Artoxares, looking pleased with himself. "If Gilgamesh married the goddess, what would happen to their friendship?"

"That's it precisely. Bravo, Artoxares." I clapped my hands, then took a sip of wine and rummaged in the basket for dates, which always seem to sink to the bottom. Datis wore a puzzled expression, eager to speak.

"Datis, our apologies. We've been talking over your head. Allow me to start at the beginning of this tale. It will spark your interest."

"The beginning?" Datis replied. "Listen," he whispered, rising from his couch to stand before us, transformed into actor and guide.

> See its wall, which is like a copper band,
> Survey its battlements, which nobody else can match,
> Take the threshold, which is from time immemorial,
> Approach Eanna, the home of Ishtar,
> Which no future king nor man will ever match!

His voice had become deeper, resonant with rhythms he had shaped and refined through childhood to enliven words descriptive of ancient Uruk. His gestures had turned words into pictures, vivid to our eyes. In stunned silence we stared at this Sakan, become balladeer.

Seating himself again, he said "You deserve an explanation. How, you wonder, could one born north of the Caspian have learned the Gilgamesh epic? Pure chance. An accident brought to our village a grand master of the tale, who taught in the oral tradition. His passion instilled a lasting love in those who sat in a circle around him, listening for hours at a time, enthralled. Committing the epic to memory became unavoidable."

I replenished our minstrel's cup. "There's much left to learn about you, my Chiliarch," I said. "Wasn't I wise to have selected such a scholar?"

Artoxares couldn't restrain himself. "Wisdom comes with hindsight, when success is certain. Only then will a decision based on God's choice or chance be tossed out. But come Parysatis, join me in toasting the learned Datis. Let us raise our goblets and drink the hive-stored toil of murmuring bees."

Again the prancing poet. He's improving, I thought.

Datis looked embarrassed.

"So, Datis, what's the answer?"

"Perhaps you're right. It could have been his friendship for Enkidu. Some believe they were lovers as well, and if so, that would add weight to your argument. However, I take a different tack. At the time, Gilgamesh was seeking eternal life. Ishtar was hinting that by marrying her, a goddess, he would live forever. The fact that none of her previous mates had lived beyond a human span of years taught him caution."

"Interesting. But how do you explain the fact that Ishtar, having been spurned by Gilgamesh, took Enkidu's life? I see signs of a jealous woman."

"Again you make a plausible point. But I doubt Ishtar was jealous of Enkidu. No, she knew her man and wanted to hurt him. Death wouldn't achieve that goal. Only the living weep. The way to punish Gilgamesh was to destroy his best friend."

"That's good. Very good."

"I'm persuaded," Artoxares declared. "It reminds me of the way Yahweh, god of the Israelites, punished King David by taking the life of his wayward yet beloved son, Absalom. You know the story? The King is undone upon learning that his guard had killed his beloved son in battle, brought on by Absalom, who sought to usurp his father's kingship. 'Oh Absalom my son, my son,' King David cries, heavy with inconsolable grief. 'Would God I had died for thee.'"

"These tales build on one another," I said. "Little that's worth remembering turns out, on inspection, to be new."

By the time we concluded, we had drunk more than the accustomed ration of mead. Datis showed Artoxares out. It was my custom to slumber until supper, some three hours later. It was Datis' habit to do likewise, napping for at least an hour before resuming his daily chores.

After sleeping briefly that afternoon, I awoke from a discomforting dream. I was in a vast room dominated by large ceramic vats, which were throwing off steam. There were shelves along the walls, crowded with small jars marked with lozenges and triangles. Netting hung just above head level across the room. Dangling from the netting were dried flowers of many types and hanks of wool, spun and dyed as many colors as could be found among the flower heads. An imposing man in charge was serving me hot water in a goblet of pure gold. He assured me the water was pure, collected from rain. Just as I began to feel pampered and important, he urged me to finish the water as the time had come for me to be gilded. "That vat over there, you see it don't you, contains liquid gold. It's cooling. In a few more minutes it will be ready for you. But first, you must remove your clothes." I awoke in a sweat, feeling deeply afraid but unable to recall why. I had a powerful desire to examine the gold jug, something that I didn't do when Artoxares handed it to me, since we were all eager to put it to use. I knew something of the new "lost wax" technique, a process of using a solid wax model of the object to be made, in my case the jug, to create a clay mold for casting the object in gold. As I set off to find Datis, who would know where the jug was kept, the dream returned, frightening me a second time.

Coming to his room, I decided not to knock, lest I awaken him. If he were asleep, I would go to the kitchen in search of the jug myself. The room was unlighted save for the shafts of an almost sunken sun entering from the window at dusk. I made no sound upon entering, and thus did not disturb the astonishing activity etched in the fast-fading light of day. I saw naked before me the two eunuchs of my salon. Datis was kneeling on his bed, facing the window. Artoxares was behind him, also facing the window and moving forward and back as if to rhythmic music only he could hear. His groans conveyed a sense of urgency.

I screamed out, demanding to know what I already knew at first glance. Without waiting for the answer, I rushed Artoxares, put my arms around his waist and pulled him towards me. Prepared for resistance, when there was none, I toppled backwards to the floor, carrying with me the naked intruder. Before I could get to my feet, Artoxares had leapt up, run to his clothes and started to put them on. Datis had found his cloak, tied the belt around it and was standing beside his bed, mumbling what I took to be an apology.

"Out. Get out," I yelled, my arm extended, finger pointed at Artoxares. Time seemed to stop as I waited for him to clothe himself. How could it take so long. He moved swiftly past us, his sandaled feet slapping hard against the stone floor. He was gone.

I took the few steps necessary to get close to my Chiliarch. He was emitting an almost overwhelming smell of frankincense. I stared at him. His eyes sparkled unnaturally in their dark setting. They had been etched with kohl, exquisitely applied. He began nervously to smile. I brought up my right hand to slap his face.

Misjudging the distance, I hit nose, not cheek. A flow erupted, pouring down from his nostrils, wetting the white cloak with bright red blood. I directed him to lie down on the bed, head up as high as it would go.

"Careful not to choke on the blood," I said, realizing as I did so how unnecessary this advice was. Finding a piece of cloth in the adjoining room, I wet it and began to wipe away the blood that had dried on his face.

Eunuchs, I was slow to discover, have a special way of communicating, much of it unspoken and not easy for others even to discern, much less comprehend. At some point, as Artoxares' visits increased, I should have realized that they had become lovers. It didn't happen. Not for the first time nor the last, I had flattered myself into believing that his increasing attentions had something to do with me.

I couldn't have cataloged my emotions at that moment, had life itself depended on it. I sorted them out later, in the course of reliving that afternoon. I did so many times. Anger and revulsion, yes. Pangs of jealousy, yes. But there was more. What I had previously taken to be dependency-driven affection for Datis suddenly revealed itself in that darkening room to be a shockingly powerful longing for him, a need so great that it ripped away all roots of restraint.

I untied the belt. He raised his hands in objection.

"Don't," I said. As he returned his hands to the bed, I gently opened his cloak, letting it gather along the sides of his body. I could see that his turn with Artoxares hadn't begun. What followed was an ecstatic union.

Whereas I was a vessel for the Great King to plant his seed, a function that was no less a duty for being not wholly unpleasant, with Datis I cast off duty to become a torch in his hands, eager to be ignited, to burn with an intensity theretofore unimagined. Thus began a new phase in my life, one that allowed me to look through a window different from all the others requiring my attention.

I resolved to keep my affair with Datis secret. Queen Amestris, Great King Xerxes' wife, enjoyed a widely known affair with the eunuch Aspamithres, now deceased, followed by a less notorious one with the ubiquitous Artoxares, leading palace gossips to conclude that it was her way to strike back at her husband's debauchery. My love had no ulterior motive.

All of this I told myself at the time. But, in fact, I consist of layers upon layers. As do others. The instant I first saw Datis, across the carriage way in Hyrcania, breaking stone with other slaves, I imagined touching that sun-browned skin. It was the body, bright with sweat and stone dust, that singled him out and drew me to him, although I would never acknowledge it. What I did with Datis the afternoon was bound to happen, and in some remote corner of my mind I knew perfectly well that it would, despite my pretense of surprise at being swept away. My mind was ample enough to house contradictions, to know and not to know, to believe and to deny belief, to pretend, confuse, and lie not only to others but to myself.

❦ ❦ ❦ ❦ ❦ ❦

The more I had of Datis, the more I wanted. He became an obsession. A recurring fulfillment. But, then, one day a problem emerged. It dawned on me that availability and physical skills at lovemaking were not enough. I was ratcheting the game up a notch. He should want me as much as I wanted him. I now know that if he had faked it, and he could easily have done so, I would never have known. His talents were so refined, his sense of duty so complete, that had he simply lied, I would have believed every word. I should have known that his integrity, which in theory I found attractive, would cause him to respond with honesty. What's more, I should have known that, if he were forced to respond, the truth would hurt.

What is it about love that causes so much self-inflicted pain? In intercourse, social or political, by demanding answers, seeking certainty, insisting that ambiguities be resolved, holding out for pledges, probing for more precision, more promises, more of everything, one ends up with less, sometimes much less, than where one began. It's often better to repress one's emotional needs, just as in negotiations, it can be more effective to put a lid on one's brilliance.

On the night of August 27 in the 137th year of our family's reign, while the Athenians were eviscerating themselves in Syracuse, as Tissaphernes had predicted they would, I met Datis for an evening of indulgence on the ample balcony of my quarters. The couch I had commissioned for this space, with Datis in mind, was long and wide. Except for its fabricator, no one other than my Chiliarch had seen it. Just as well, for its generous size would have raised eyebrows.

We would try it out that night, under the watchful gaze of a full moon. We would see it rise in the East and, with luck, watch it set, although that would depend on how Datis responded to the plaint I planned to confront him with that night.

As the moon ascended, we embarked on what by now had become well established ritual.

Thus engaged, with one eye on my partner and the other on the moon, I watched in amazement as there appeared on the moon's perfectly round face a curved shadow. It moved across the ivory white surface of the moon, darkening it until not even the circle's outline could be detected. Then, as deliberately as it had blanketed the moon, it withdrew, leaving that pale white orb more radiant than before the eclipse began.

I directed Datis' attention to this extraordinary sight. Immediately, we unwound ourselves to watch what was happening in the distant night sky. Datis had never seen an eclipse before. I had just missed the eclipse of the sun on the day Arsaces was born and had never seen another. Of course, I immediately connected this eclipse to the eclipse of the sun that marked my son's birth.

In our search for meaning, it proved easy to imagine a God pulling the strings to make the shadow come and go. For what purpose? The next step was easier still. It had to be God's personal message to us. All we had to do was interpret it correctly.

It didn't immediately occur to us that multitudes of humankind were watching the same eclipse at the same moment, each believing it to be God's personal communication. Much later that evening, rather than present my plaint about the missing element of love, I tried to understand the eclipse. Datis started us thinking by asking whether Darius was watching. I guessed no, that he had been at a palace dinner and probably was unaware.

"He wouldn't have missed it if God had intended it as a personal message," Datis reasoned.

"That's right. If Ahura-Mazda could cause an eclipse, surely he could cause those he intended to receive it as a divine message to be on hand. If it's seen by all, and comes from Ahura-Mazda, it must be a message to mankind. What is it about us humans that makes us always see God as personal to us. We claim to serve him, but our attitude suggests that, underneath all the sacrifice and show, we really expect him to serve us."

We tossed and turned over this matter until the warm fingers of a rising sun crept into my balcony, warning us of the hot day ahead. By that time neither of us was prepared to accept the night's eclipse as a message from or to anyone we knew.

Two months later, I learned from Tissaphernes that the eclipse had not escaped the notice of Athenian warriors gathered in the Sicilian harbor of Syracuse. His detailed account carried lessons to ponder.

The invasion of Sicily, commenced two years before, had proved to be far more difficult than imagined by the overweening Athenians. So difficult, in fact, that now, after two years of fighting, the Athenian generals had issued an order to their land and sea forces to abandon the fight and sail home.

By nightfall on August 27, all was ready. When the full moon was high, lighting the harbor like a silvery torch, the landing boats were filled, ready to carry the Athenians to their ships. At that moment the dark shadow of the eclipse, the very same shadow Datis and I had observed, began to pass across the moon's face. Immediately, it was claimed by the Athenians to be God's omen to them alone.

The generals, perhaps overaddicted to divination, consulted their soothsayers to fathom the meaning of this heavenly sign. The answer was inconvenient: an ill omen, they declared, requiring the Athenian forces to remain in place for 27 days.

Thus condemned to remain in weakened condition in a hostile country, the Athenians were attacked by land and by sea, beaten at all points and destroyed, their fleet, their army—all was destroyed. So much for omens and the infallibility of those who interpret them.

The Sicilian expedition had become the bitter harvest of hubris predicted by the great Athenian general, Nicias, who, by a twist of irony, was himself among those destroyed.

Here was a lesson that I took to heart, being aware that hubris brought calamities of almost equal size to Darius I and Xerxes. I resolved then and there to see that nothing of this kind would happen again in my Empire. Nor did it while I was alive. Tragically, by the time Alexander entered the Empire, hubris had returned to feed my royal house.

❦ ❦ ❦ ❦ ❦

In the 15th year of our reign, we celebrated the weddings of our two eldest children, Amestris and Arsaces. The aristocrat Hydarnes still commanded the Babylonian army, which he had steadily enlarged with Darius' approval since using it to secure my husband's kingship. He had produced two children, Teritushmes, who was the age of Amestris, and Statereia, the age of Arsaces. Both were frisky, headstrong, and imperially arrogant, a condition that descendants of the Seven wore as naturally as an everyday cloak. One day, without warning, Hydarnes appeared before us with a proposal. He called it "divine inspiration."

"These children are growing up. They will want to marry soon. Good parents stay ahead of their children's wishes, the better to channel them. I propose that we unite our families, not by one marriage but by two. The unions should occur on the same day, the celebrations being combined into one glorious event. My lineage will reinforce yours, preparing the way for the next generation of Achaemenids." Hydarnes smiled expectantly, radiating confidence, his mouth curving upwards at the corners in an unnatural expression that I found repulsive.

"There's efficiency to your idea," I said, deadpan.

Darius said "My friend, you have served us well for many years. Your appeal... Intriguing. Give us time. And, now..." Darius rose.

"My King, if you will allow me, this is not meant to be an appeal. My proposal seeks no charity from you. It needs no argument, and but modest thought. Never has the Empire seen such an event. It will amaze and delight the palace and the people. You know Statereia and Teritushmes well. So do your children. Their lineage and breeding, their education and training, second to none. No other match could rival these. Give me your hand."

While he was speaking, I rose to stand beside my husband, awaiting the fool's discovery that the meeting was over.

"We will consider all that you have said, Hydarnes. Now, kindly leave us."

My voice was hard. Hydarnes shot me the fierce glance of one not accustomed to be at the receiving end of an insult; then, registering where he was, he quickly dropped to his knees and bowed to the ground. Still jackknifed when he got to his feet, he backed out of the room and was gone, without another word.

"He wants the exceptional power these matches will bring," Darius explained.

I summoned Datis. "We need some wine. Fruit too." Turning to Darius, I said, "Yes, but to what effect? He minces words, prances around with insufferable pride, making arguments he claims are unnecessary, appropriates airs fit only for a Great King. I despise him. And, yet..."

Darius poured the wine, handing me a goblet and passing the bowl of fruit. "What more, Parysatis?"

"I ache all over from imagining the triumphal uses he will make of these matches. But... Always a 'but' in matters of state. I can survive if this proposal makes sense for the crown. I see how it might. Do you trust Hydarnes?"

"As much as anyone who commands a large army. His is a force vital to our interests. His two children are talented and ambitious, excellent matches for anyone. No less so because of his obnoxious boasts. If we don't bring them into

RETURN OF THE SHADE

the family, they will make other alliances, which in time could cause us harm. As for the father, I trust him more with his children within our tent than beyond it."

Darius was persuaded.

"They can make mischief inside as well. But you're right, it will be easier to keep an eye on them. And on the father. I loathed the idea, as you know, because of its source. But you're good, Darius. Calm reason floating above the muck of my personal disgust for the man. We should proceed."

Weeks later, I would recall, Noah questioned me about the proposed union. As I explained our reasoning, a flash of disgust crossed his face, though he tried to conceal it.

"Something's missing," he said. "How do you feel about your children? How do they feel?"

I had no answer. Yet, at the time, I did not flinch from guilt. Nor did I digest the end note to this conversation: "You have amassed great power, Parysatis. Take care. Take great care in how you use it."

☙ ☙ ☙ ☙ ☙ ☙

And so two of our children were joined in marriage to the children of Hydarnes. What took less than an hour of glorious pomp and ceremony to effect proved a twin disaster that unfolded over more than a decade. What could have prevented us from making this mistake? Did we exercise bad judgment? For years afterwards, as one misery led to another, I blamed Darius for being a bully, for using logic to separate me from my instinct, which I recalled as being strongly against the matches. He claimed I had a highly selective memory, especially when it came to my instincts, which I believed were never wrong.

We fought frequently over words: "logic" and "reason" were to Darius what "instinct" and "experience" were to me the key to good judgment. He claimed "experience" was a weak reed, because no two cases were alike and using the experience of one as a guide to the other would often lead to disaster. What I called "instinct" he claimed was pure emotion, a frailty no less destructive because it was commonly relied upon.

I agreed that logic and reason were weapons of opportunity for the cleverest among us but claimed they were often used to annihilate better judgments through an intelligent facade of plausibility.

Darius went to the grave defending himself from my attacks. Quite correctly, I'm willing now to admit. He had argued that we made the fatal decision jointly,

153

persuaded by a number of arguments that appeared sound at the time.

I've spent a lifetime making difficult decisions, some based on reason, some on instinct; some rooted in principle, some in pragmatism; some successful, some disastrous. What's troubling in all this is my inability, looking back, to say much about what works and what doesn't. Conclusions are slippery, elusive. I know spinning lies to oneself doesn't work. It can be worse than spinning lies to others, as without any doubt, the Greek historians did in their treatment of us. Without honesty in examining the whys of one's behavior, one can't hope to profit from one's bad judgments, errors of fact and other mistakes. Yet, even without deceiving myself about the past, I'm at a loss.

Tossing dice is pure chance. Perhaps, despite my efforts to choose rationally, whether by reason, instinct, or a combination of the two, all my outcomes were like playing at dice. If God interests himself in our affairs, we must put the dice aside. If God is God, he wouldn't play at dice for any purpose.

When I was very young, I appealed to Ahura-Mazda. I thought he would speak to me, showing the way. He never did. If he was responsible for my outcomes, but never claimed responsibility, to me it was the same as rolling the dice. I accept the idea that the Great King was his appointed agent. Yet, even Darius never claimed the voice of God spoke to him. Ahura-Mazda hovered over the Empire, watching his anointed but staying out of the way. We all have free will, even the Great King: both the freedom to make mistakes and the misery of not being able to learn from them. Noah called it "the human condition."

❧ ❧ ❧ ❧ ❧ ❧

Our son, Cyrus, was 15 when Amestris and Arsaces wed Hydarnes' offspring. The next year, Darius sent him to Asia Minor as the Satrap, with orders bearing the King's seal to his generals, Pharnabazus and Tissaphernes, directing them to serve Cyrus as their lord. Given Cyrus' age, not an easy assignment for grizzled soldiers hardened through years of combat.

I concurred in this assignment. In truth, I planted the idea in Darius' head. With the passage of puberty, the rivalry between Arsaces and Cyrus grew. Arsaces' marriage to Stateira only served to intensify it, due to rumors that the Great King had already designated Arsaces to be his successor. I traced these rumors, not surprisingly, to Hydarnes.

Cyrus was my favorite. The Greeks got that right. Is a mother entitled to a favorite? In a perfect world, perhaps not. Is a Queen entitled to her opinion regarding succession? Without question, yes. Cyrus was a natural leader. Self-confident to the point of rashness, ambitious as any hero must be, headstrong as every youth who achieved greatness must have been. I loved Arsaces for what he was, the opposite of Cyrus in all traits, but I became consumed with the need to place Cyrus on the throne. I was convinced the Empire would rise or fall with this decision. But on this matter, this matter alone, Darius rebuffed me. While assuring me he had not selected a successor, he refused my entreaties to name Cyrus. There was time to spare in changing his mind.

Amestris had been married to Teritushmes for only two years when the first tragedy struck. In that year, Hydarnes became ill. The Magi were unable to reverse his decline, which within less than 12 months led to death. The following year, the 18th of our reign, brought another calamity, one even more devastating. Teritushmes had fallen in love with his younger sister, Roxanne. He became consumed with unseemly passion and afflicted in equal degree with regal arrogance, the curse of the Seven. Deeming himself untouchable, he decided to make room for Roxanne by killing his wife. To us, a loving daughter; to him, disposable trash. His plan was to have her die by mistake at the hands of an assassin charged with murdering another woman. The assassin was supposed to leave a note at the murder scene to suggest that the writer was this other woman's unrequited lover. Sadly for Teritushmes, the assassin got the women's names mixed up. The note left with Amestris, the assassin's victim, was addressed to Roxanne, not the other woman. When asked for an explanation, Teritushmes assumed we knew more than we did and bolted, affirming his guilt.

Our response was swift. Darius directed the commander of the palace guard to find Teritushmes and eliminate him. There ensued a small battle, for Teritushmes had fled with a score of loyal soldiers. The palace guard gave chase. Confrontation ensued. Teritushmes fell from a dart to the head. Resistance ceased.

Darius ordered that Hydarnes' family be gathered up and brought to the palace. I had convinced him that vicarious punishment was justifiable and served the Empire. In fact, I had argued, there was responsibility across a clan, if one looked hard enough for it. And, of course, punishment, vicarious or not, was a deterrent. My zeal sprang from personal bitterness as well. My mistake in allowing this union stung, pushed deeper against the heroic role I had armed myself with to deflect Noah's penetrating questions.

Roxanne, her mother, two brothers, and two sisters appeared prostrate before the Great King. They were reluctant to look at him, so much so that he had to repeat the command to stand. Looking each of them over, top to bottom, he noted the ashen faces and trembling limbs, which had replaced the haughty look that ran through the whole family, despite the fact that none of them, save Hydarnes himself, had ever seen the purple.

Darius was not a cruel man. He could act in anger, but this occurred infrequently. The pain of awaiting his decision, which he prolonged, was purposefully inflicted, but not with evil intent. Rather, it prepared them for what was to come. His sentence was torture until death intervened, as it regularly did. Not that this case was in any way routine. Darius could think of no other where a sitting King's child had been murdered. It called for an especially taxing punishment. Yet, being human, Darius found it difficult to imagine anything more severe than torture and death.

For my part, having lost so many infants over the years and, now, having lost my only healthy daughter to a vicious and clumsy murder, my rage knew no bounds. In seeking my concurrence, he was inviting me to join in designing a punishment worthy of my pain. So tasked, I suggested a refinement.

The family would be tortured, one by one, beginning with the youngest. Those remaining would be compelled to watch until their turns came.

The family group being sentenced included Stateira, the wife of Arsaces. She had become beautiful, turning heads within the palace. To outward appearances, the marriage was a success. They were an intensely private couple, making it difficult to discern the truth.

Arsaces entered the throne room as his father was issuing the edict. "Spare her, Great King. Spare my wife, who had no knowledge of her brother's villainy."

Darius ignored his son's pleading, acting as if he hadn't heard it. Indeed, since Arsaces spoke from the entranceway, I thought it possible, given his nearsightedness, that Darius couldn't tell who was speaking. Whatever the reason, the Great King brusquely dismissed all from his presence, then repaired to his chambers. I went to mine, followed closely by Arsaces, who had begged to see me.

I tried to prepare. Giving something for nothing, in my experience, never serves the giver well. Arsaces pleaded with me to save his wife's life. "Why?"

"Because I love her; and need her. We make a good team, she's more like you than I am. She thinks ahead, for both of us, and helps me decide and act. If I should succeed the Great King, I want her by my side. For the sake of the Empire, I will need her. Finally, because she's blameless. She's been estranged from her brother for years. You must change father's mind."

He dropped to his knees, resting his head on my legs, an older version of the needy child he had been long ago. I had to push away memories crowding for attention.

"I will try, but only if you promise me something." He looked up and nodded. My eyes locked onto his. They had always been beautiful and brown; they were still so, but now had become large and wet with tears that coursed down taut skin covering his sharp chin bones.

"Promise me you will give your brother, Cyrus, the crown when the time comes. He's my first born to the Great King. I want him to succeed Darius." Putting my hands to either side of his face, I held him in place. His eyes remained locked on mine, which now burned with intensity.

"I promise, mother," he whispered.

"This is our pact, a secret between us. I will do my part. But there's an obstacle. Remember the Achaemenid rule: Once given, an order of the King may not be changed. Help me design a way to spare Stateira while honoring the rule."

Arsaces looked befuddled and newly frightened.

"There are ways around it," I continued. "One needn't be a scribe to figure something out. Remember the story of how Xerxes reversed his thoughtless decree empowering Haman and his followers to kill all Jews within the Empire. At Queen Esther's request, he issued a decree empowering the Jews to defend themselves against any who might act under his first decree. Not a perfect solution, but it worked."

"I know the story. Where's the parallel?" he said, looking even more puzzled.

"I think I have it. The sentence was imposed on Hydarnes' family. Darius couldn't have intended to sweep in Stateira, because, when she married you, she left her family to become part of ours. It was a mistake to place her in the family group. I think he'll support this reading of the edict. Now, leave. I will ready myself for your project."

I found Darius in a troubled state.

"I've ordered the destruction of an entire family. One of the Seven. Vicarious guilt appeals more to you than to me. I think of those little girls, and the young boy. Doesn't it shake you?"

"Darius, we've been over this before. You make a hard decision and then try to blame its harshness on old stories of my childhood. How I cultivated an immunity from human feeling by pulling the wings from flies, decapitating chickens, drowning cats, and other crude behavior. As you well know, none of this is true. Yet you accept palace garbage when it suits. These fantasies all derive from one unfortunate incident years ago, my youthful experiment with a cat.

"You and I are different. Humankind embraces many different types: some faint at the sight of blood, some weep at the sound of a flute, others at the reading of a poem. I never faint and seldom weep. I see what you do, what you must do, as the discharge of a Great King's duty to the Empire. No more, no less. If you allow personal feelings to intrude on decisions like the one you made today, your capacity to make the right decisions will atrophy and eventually die. Trying to shift blame to me only makes things worse. Just as commanders in battle can't linger over the human cost of their decisions, so you must not dwell on the human cost of what you are duty-bound to direct. But here, listen to me; for I know how to save you from wiping out the entire family."

"First, you harden me; then turn soft. You've come to plead our son's case. I don't understand. You've never liked Stateira. Before the wedding, you predicted she would be trouble, and you've repeated that warning ever since. Of all the family, I would think you'd pick her first, then order her to be the last to go."

"He needs her. I'm urging you to spare her for his sake. He thrives on her energy. He even compared her to me."

"Perhaps you should reconsider your opinion."

We continued the discussion in what would surely have appeared to others a shockingly lighthearted way, as one would sort sheep for slaughter.

Darius seemed willing. I offered the interpretative solution. He took it. Before sending an Eye to address the matter, he pushed me one last time.

"If I do this, Parysatis, mark my words. In years to come you will regret it."

He was right, this time on pure instinct, which he was so accustomed to deplore when used by me against him. And I, being young and consumed with hubris, allowed cleverness to drive instinct from the field.

❧ ❧ ❧ ❧ ❧

The final year of our reign was dreadful. Not just because Darius was swept away at his prime. That came after our fight, which, who knows, might have contributed to the arrest of his heart. Darius decided to put an end to the rivalry between Arsaces and Cyrus. In truth, the competitive fervor blew only from the West, its source Sardis, where Cyrus had taken up residence as the Satrap of Lydia and the coastal regions. Some claimed I was directing his every move. False, but

I now see that by doing nothing to discourage him, I gave rise to this belief.

That he was my favorite, everyone knew. In denying any role in Cyrus' efforts to garner support, I thought I was being honest. After all, my covenant with Arsaces made advocacy unnecessary. As best I could tell, Arsaces was abiding by his secret promise. And there was no urgency, since we couldn't foresee the looming tragedy. Once the issue surfaced, it took on a life of its own, abetted by those within the palace having a stake in the outcome. A multitude, to be sure.

Darius summoned me to his chambers to discuss the matter. Until that moment, we had avoided the subject of succession, as if it were either too big or too little an issue to touch, a contagious, death-dealing disease or a triviality so banal as to be unworthy of a minute's time together. There are many subjects that husbands and wives will do anything to avoid. Like sailing by dead-reckoning when far better tools of navigation could be deployed, these unmentionables erect a conspiracy of silence around them, with the conspiracy itself being hatched without a word.

"You won't like this," he began, addressing my back as I was arranging cushions on the couch where I always sat. "There is tension in the palace over my choice of successor. It grows by the day and is becoming unhealthy: Cyrus' wooing from afar, the promises he's making, his claims of superiority over his brother in all things, the overreach for the loyalty of Tissaphernes and Pharnabazus, couched more in the language of demand than appeal. I can no longer tolerate this behavior. Before the week is out I will announce that my choice is Arsaces. From now on we groom him to the purple."

I could see in the taut lines of my husband's face that he had girded himself for battle. His voice fairly sang with determination. In the big battles of our marriage, my record was unblemished. This vigorous assault had to be the bluster of one afraid of suffering another defeat. Best keep it simple, lighthearted.

"Darius, I've never seen you so exercised. You exaggerate in calling this a rivalry. Arsaces does not compete. Have you sounded him? Not only does he not seek the throne, but if asked, he would decline it. He knows himself far better than you know him. But beyond that, my main point is that any announcement is premature. Of course, if you would substitute Cyrus for Arsaces, I could live with an early decision." I tossed him an ingratiating smile.

Darius rose from his couch and came to where I was seated. He stood over me. I felt the heat of physical threat. In an instant it brought to mind the only other time I had experienced this sensation, some 24 years earlier in the dark corridor where our relationship began. A shiver scurried up and down my back.

"It belongs to me. I know your preference, as do all in the palace, and many far beyond its walls. I know, too, that your thirst for power admits no bounds. I have shared the King's prerogatives with you. More than any before me, I'm told. But in this matter, my mind is settled. I will brook no obstacle."

The bowstring of my will was taut, but having no winning arrow to release, I rose to leave, deciding it best to relax and cede him a little victory in the war I was determined to win.

"Before you go, one other thing. I know about the bargain you extracted from Arsaces. He's performed his part, despite the whole thing being thoroughly dishonorable. Forcing him to choose between the life of one he loved and the crown? Despicable. Unworthy of an Achaemenid Queen."

I looked into his eyes, then quickly away. He was coiled, tight to trembling, a snake ready to strike at its foe, now frozen in fright.

Play for time. I sat down.

"Did he tell you that story?"

"Indeed. I had to drag it out of him. He wasn't going to lie to me, as you apparently do with ease. He's afraid of you. Even the Gods cower in the face of a mother's vengeance. I assured him I would contain you."

Deny and attack.

"Our son lies. Of course, he knows my preference. But his passivity comes not from a promise to me. It's a measure of his ambition, or lack of it, a forecast of his failings as a leader. He must not succeed you. Announce what you will, nothing will deter me from working to change your mind. I have many years to accomplish this. You've never gotten over the Magi's interpretation of that eclipse, when Arsaces was born. Together, we've experienced enough Magian logic to make us ill. Cyrus is the rightful heir, not only because, unlike Arsaces, he was born to the purple, but by dint of his mental and physical gifts, his personality and his capacity for leadership. I know he's a braggart. But in truth, what he claims is true. Credit me, now that we have finally spoken, for being direct."

I rose to face him. Little space separated us, despite our being oceans apart on this issue. There was nothing more to say. I took his hand, gave it a soft squeeze as combatants respectful of each other might do, and departed.

On the next day he made public his decision, which would be sent to Cyrus by regular courier the following week. On the day after that he left on a fateful hunting expedition.

160

❧ ❧ ❧ ❧ ❧ ❧

Why did I care so much? This question often came to mind when, alone before the dressing mirror, I would comb my hair, a deeply etched habit that never failed to open doors of introspection. I would count the long white hairs, which, being wiry, separated from the rest in response to the comb. Advance scouts of encroaching age.

I always cared. From earliest days. But that's not an answer. Was it the thrill of winning? Or because I knew I was right? Or because it was an important issue? To me? The Empire? Or because it was 'baked in the bread' when I was born? In the warp and woof of who I was? My comb couldn't tease apart these strands.

With hardly a wayward hair in sight, I would continue combing. The world is filled with leaders and followers. How is it that a flock of geese stays in formation, a school of fish turn and turn again, always at the same moment, a pack of wolves hunts in silence, yet with military precision? Each beehive has but one leader, the queen, with wings of glistening gold, long body, and jet black face. She presides over endless toil by her army of tawny worker bees, murmuring as one in the astoundingly complex process of making food and drink fit for the Gods. She directs the swarm, which moves in one body on her signal and follows her every command until a new home is found. Could nature offer a better example of leadership?

By the time I was ten, I had discovered that in most things, and especially in affairs of state, there will always be a leader. I also learned that the one who led was not necessarily best qualified for the task. And so I began to put the question: why not me? Why not follow the path of Atossa, wife of Darius, and Amestris, wife of Xerxes. Anyone familiar with palace life knew these women were leaders, formidable and effective. They were women. They thought like women, but not only like women.

"Yes" became my answer, voiced tentatively at first, but over time with growing conviction.

◁ 10

A QUEEN MOTHER
IN THE PALACE

 MY LAST SIGHT OF DARIUS was standing beside the driver of his two-horse chariot as it departed for a lion hunt. He appeared to be in perfect health. Raising his bow above his head, he waved confidently to me, a boy again, grinning from ear to ear in anticipation of the day's adventure. The smile was insouciant, amused, an "I've been here before and done it all but why not pretend" sort of look on his tanned face, which was already wet from the gathering heat of what I would recall as a searingly hot day.

As the sun climbed through a clear blue sky, he felt pain in his chest. Apparently believing it caused by the meat he was quickly consuming as the chariot raced to its destination, he said nothing. The sun had just reached the zenith of its arc across the Great King's Empire when Darius' heart skipped its rhythmic beat, then briefly resumed only to skip again and stop for good.

So carefree a smile had my husband served me on the day he died that, as his chariot disappeared in clouds of dust, I had marveled at our success in so managing the routine affairs of state over this 19 year space that excursions of pleasure could occur at will. With the kind of luck that we had fashioned for ourselves continuing, even without the favor of Ahura-Mazda, I thought we could count on many more years of the same.

I've rehearsed for you the landmarks of importance to me over my long reign as Queen. My most rewarding years? When that question was put as I lay dying,

163

with reference to the royal span of all my years, first as Queen for those 19 and then as Queen Mother for 12 more, I found it easy to account. My best years came after my husband died. Why? Not just because, in his absence, I became more important. It was often the case with Achaemenids that the Queen Mother was more powerful than the Queen. Of course, the thread of one's life is continuous, one part connected to all the others. What made those years more fulfilling was a sense that I was making a growing and, ultimately, large contribution to the Empire while my son was on the throne. At the time I believed this story. Now I know. Any fair assessment of my role would reach this conclusion, although it was far from the minds of Greek historians.

Word of my husband's death didn't reach me ahead of his bodily form, which elite members of the Immortals carried on a stretcher into the anteroom of my palace quarters and there, having removed the cloth cover, set down before my disbelieving eyes.

Datis had admitted them, not realizing the burden they bore. His face, torn in agony, came into focus as I looked up, searching for an explanation. Without a word, the Immortals had vanished. Apparently no one thought it necessary to brief the newly widowed Queen. Plain ignorance or the more sophisticated kind that might have considered me too hardened to need a breaking-in session? I never knew.

Can one be too shocked to grieve for the loss of one's husband? Grief in full needs time to incubate. Only if one anticipates a loss time and again, holding it up for examination, front, back, and sideways, from odd angles as well, can one be prepared for the grief to follow.

With no time to prepare, instead of grief, I turned to feverish activity in service, or disservice, as many suspected, to the question of succession. I decided to use the King's couriers to summon Cyrus from his satrapy in Sardis. Since the founding of the Empire, posting stations have existed along the royal road, each a hard day's ride from the next. The stations were equipped with fresh horses and couriers supported by grooms and overseen by station chiefs. This system enabled royal mail to travel across the Empire more swiftly than the crane can fly.

I chose speed over privacy. No message in the hands of the King's service could be presumed to remain private. Were I to write about the decision Darius had made, a decision Cyrus was not yet aware of, I would have to say much more in explanation, and it would not be suitable reading for anyone other than my son. All I could safely tell Cyrus was: "Come quickly; your father is dead."

With Darius' choice of successor freshly planted in everyone's head, it was impossible for me to stop Arsaces from assuming the mantle of crown prince, who, Achaemenid tradition demanded, would be in charge of funeral rites. What I hadn't expected was to see Artoxares, sycophant and one-time lover of my Chiliarch, emerge at my elder son's side, obviously having insinuated himself into an important advisory position.

With unseemly haste, and, remarkably, no deference to me, Arsaces pushed forward the funeral. By his order, all sacred fires were quenched. In keeping with Achaemenid custom, they would remain out until the funeral was finished, conveying the idea that "life" for Persians, being dependent on their King for all things, was suspended until a new King was crowned. Men shaved their heads to signal affliction and mourning. My son put Artoxares in charge of guiding the sumptuously ornamented funeral chariot to Darius' royal tomb, which with foresight befitting a Great King, had been excavated near the tomb of his father on the cliff at Naqs-I Rustan.

In the midst of preparations, Arsaces paused to visit me in my chambers.

He brushed past Datis to stand before me. I rested on my sitting room couch.

"My son, the crown prince, come to apologize. Sit. You've been at it night and day. Why such haste?"

"The sudden loss has shocked our people. They mourn for your husband and worry greatly for the future. Only a royal investiture will calm them. The funeral must come first."

"Your brother won't be here for several more days." Without much success, I tried to project the worried mother's look. Out of practice.

"There's nothing to apologize for. The announcement shattered my promise, which until that moment I had kept. The issue is resolved."

With that, he rose to go. "Come, mother, give me a hug and a promise of support. I'm going to need help." We embraced. I felt trapped. That and a deep pang of anguish over my lost husband, whom, suddenly I desperately missed. My grieving had begun.

Cyrus missed the funeral. Upon arrival at Persepolis, he came straight to me.

I flew towards the door, meeting him halfway. Before he could wrap me in his arms, I saw through the dust that covered him head to foot how handsome he was. His face had narrowed and lengthened. Gone was any remnant of the teenage fat that had rounded his face, infusing each expression of emotion with the pastel of adolescence. Now, grief and anger played across that face.

I started to speak. He cut me off.

"I've heard. Funeral over. Investiture three days hence. How could this be?" He spit out the words, one by one, pausing between them. His dark eyes, deep-set under thick eyebrows, darted from side to side, making his head appear to be moving, though in truth it was motionless. Even when he locked his eyes on mine, it was only for an instant.

I did my best to explain. Listening had never been his strength. As children, Arsaces could languish with patience and passivity over detail, while Cyrus burned with impetuosity, a fiery meteor always moving, bound somewhere with no time to linger over directions. Nothing much had changed in the process of growing up. To outward appearances, they sometimes were taken for twins. Both tall and muscular. Equally handsome in the Persian way, with extended forehead turning down at a right angle to a slightly rounded head, nose distinct and slightly hooked, eyes deeply recessed below black eyebrows, chin sharply chiseled beneath a pointed beard that rounded the cheek bones to join a neatly tied bun of hair behind the ears.

Beneath the surface they were different. Arsaces had always been the easy one to handle. His brother, now almost crazy with frustration and despair, paced back and forth before me.

"Cyrus, stop a minute. You are young. The Empire won't vanish just because your brother takes the crown. His time is now. Yours, in the future. Remember, our talk of your succeeding your father was based on his living at least 20 more years. A long life awaits you and it will include the throne. Listen to your mother. She counsels patience."

"I can't share your confidence. The Great King betrayed me, his only royal heir. But for vengeance, my heart is empty. He took destiny out of my hands and laid it in the feeble hands of my brother. Even if Arsaces hates me only half as much as I hate him, I am a ruined man. Goodbye, mother." He wheeled on his heels and was gone, leaving me with the image of a tortured face hot with angry desperation.

The investiture ceremony was planned for noon at the temple of Anahita, the warrior goddess, in holy Pasargadae. We had made the twenty-five-mile journey there the preceding day. Early the next morning, Noah appeared at my door, looking drained. My friendship with him was as strong as it had ever been, but always, when we were together it was in his home at the beeyard. Now for the first time, my calm mentor had come to me, appearing at my door in Pasargadae in a highly excited state.

"Noah, my friend. This is a surprise. The day moves on and I have an investiture to attend. But sit down. Briefly, what news?" Fear bridged my shoulder blades.

"Yes. I know. A Magus who helped to raise your younger son told me he had been enlisted by Cyrus to aid in killing his brother. Cyrus plans to lie in wait for Arsaces in the temple at Pasargadae and there to assassinate him after he has entered according to ritual and taken off his robe to put on the ancient garment of Cyrus. He will seize the crown."

"Do you believe this Magus?" I asked, having already concluded that the tale was true.

"I do. You see, he loves Cyrus. Knowing of our closeness, he came to me, hoping to find a way to save Cyrus from self-destruction."

I summoned Datis.

"You must find Cyrus. Go to the temple and search from there. Noah will go with you. Say that he must come to me immediately. That his life depends on it. If that doesn't work, subdue him."

Within the hour they returned with Cyrus. I asked both Noah and Datis to attend the audience. Cyrus appeared distraught. Noah repeated the story. As he began to respond, I interrupted.

"My son, don't speak. I didn't summon you here to question. What the Magus claimed you intended to do will not happen. Intention, real or imagined, is therefore beside the point. Charges against you will be made. I will deal with them. There's nothing more to say. It's time to attend the investiture."

The day was fine: a clear blue sky and light zephyrs to wick away moisture from the sun's heat, making one's skin tingle with coolness. Perhaps the horses felt especially happy to be alive, for they could hardly be controlled in the short chariot ride to the temple.

The crowd assembled to witness the investiture of Arsaces was small and select, if one ignored the King's bodyguard of five hundred, picked for their rank from the infantry troop of ten thousand called the "Immortals." They stood at attention in a ring three deep beyond the audience, which had positioned itself just outside the temple. The bodyguards were notable for their splendid white uniforms festooned with red sashes and their sparkling spears, unique in having golden pomegranates instead of spikes on their butt-ends.

Arsaces had decided to use his grandfather's name. I was never absolutely certain as to his reasons, since he refused to say. But Artaxerxes had earned a reputation for gentleness, and Arsaces, being considered gentle and kind, compared to his brother Cyrus, sought to have these traits reckoned as strengths rather than weaknesses. Calling himself Artaxerxes II would help.

Announced by six blasts from a band of horn players and led by three Magi, Arsaces moved deliberately toward the temple. The crowd opened a corridor for them to pass. Their faces shone with a yellowish tinge in the sunlight, having been made up for the occasion, as was the custom, with an ointment combining a rare Cilician plant with saffron and lion fat. One Magus carried the ancient garment, threadbare in places, which Arsaces would put on in the temple as symbol of dynastic continuity and transmission of the founder's power. Another Magus carried the newly woven robe of purple, which Arsaces would wear upon emerging from the temple. The third bore a newly fashioned shield for the Great King. Although none but the Magi could observe the ritual, everyone in the audience knew what was happening. It was the presence of the Magi that would convey the mantle of divinity to Arsaces, changing him from heir-designate to Great King. Garbed in the robe of Cyrus the Great, Arsaces would eat a cake of figs, then chew a piece of turpentine wood and, finally, drink a cup of sour milk. These tokens of humility were offered through the Magi to Ahura-Mazda, from whom the Great King's power was believed to flow.

It was Tissaphernes, the general hungering for the satrapy that Cyrus ruled, who broke the news to the new King. He fingered the Magus, who had told one too many people of Cyrus' plotting for the story not to get around. By the time Tissaphernes heard the scheme, and confronted the Magus, I had dealt with my son. The Magus denied having ever made such a statement, assuring Tissaphernes that the whole thing was a false alarm. The general, however, seeing huge opportunity for himself, took the story to the freshly anointed King.

Cyrus was brought before his brother, now seated on the throne. The Magus had been sent for, but was not yet present.

"We will await the arrival of the Magus to discuss what you have to report about him. You said there was another piece of evidence. Bring it forth."

Tissaphernes took from his cloak pocket two coins, one silver, the other gold, handing them to the King.

"Here your majesty, examine these coins, both struck in Sardis by order of your brother. On one side, they are identical: the Athenian owl with olive spray and crescent. On the other, the silver coin displays a portrait of the late King Darius, while the gold coin displays one of your brother. This coin is proof of Cyrus' overweening ambition for the crown. A coin of soaring arrogance and revolt."

"Will you answer to this charge, Cyrus?" the Great King said.

Cyrus rummaged around in his pockets, finally producing a number of coins. Examining them, he found the one he was looking for and handed it to the Great King.

He then extended his long arm, hand limp. Slowly, he raised his hand, using only the index finger to point at the general, standing less than ten feet away. Many seconds passed before he spoke.

"This silver coin was struck in Sardis by my predecessor, Tissaphernes, the opportunist who now presents himself as my accuser."

Dropping his arm, Cyrus continued. "Look carefully. See on one side the Athenian owl, with olive spray and crescent. Now look on the other side. You will see the unmistakable face of a former Satrap, this faithless general who bears false witness against me, hoping to reclaim his satrapy. If the coin I struck bespeaks revolution, doesn't the general's coin do likewise?"

The King held his tongue, looking at Tissaphernes for some response. Crimson colors appeared here and there under the general's unruly beard, a blend of black, gray, and white. He stammered, uttering nothing comprehensible. Finally, something must have popped into his clouded brain. "It's gold, a gold coin, your majesty. The Darius one's only silver."

Just then the Magus appeared, saving the general from further embarrassment.

"Now, Tissaphernes, bring us to the main point of this audience, which, till now, has proved a disappointment."

The general led off with the story he had heard. The Magus spoke next, denying everything, claiming he had been misunderstood. The King asked Cyrus to respond to the general's charge. He refused, creating a cloud of doubt that, so long as he remained silent, would hang about him. The only reasonable explanation for his silence, I knew, was his unwillingness to break the royal Achaemenid code of truth-telling. The King would surely have reached the same conclusion, adding weight to the inference. I was determined to save Cyrus. I knew the only opportunity was now, before sentence was rendered. I sought a way to intervene that wouldn't cause the King to lose face or Cyrus to lose self-control. Before I could devise a scheme, the window had shut.

Artaxerxes II ordered that Cyrus be stoned to death forthwith. He was taken to the amphitheatre reserved for carrying out such verdicts. We were forced to remain in the throne room until the King had departed, a matter of ten or more minutes. I rushed outdoors and ran to the site. Palace guards had just finished binding Cyrus hand and foot. They now encircled him, a large stone's throw away. Here they were busy selecting from several piles of stones those to be used in the first round.

"Stop," I cried, dashing through the ring of guards to wrap myself around my son, clasping him in my arms, allowing the tresses of my long hair to cover his head. "Hear me, the Queen Mother. To carry out this order you will have to slay me first."

They could easily have pulled me away. My bet was that first, they would seek guidance, turning this fraught scene into a battle between Artaxerxes II and his mother, a battle I thought I could win.

My hair still hid Cyrus' face when Artaxerxes II appeared before us.

"How can you protect this traitor?" His voice wobbled slightly, resonant with frustration and anger.

"Like you, he's my son. Like you, he's no traitor. The claim is intent, and that is unproven. Like you, he's needed by an Empire short of Achaemenid leaders. Send him back to Sardis, so he can continue to do the job your father directed him to do, the job we all know he has done exceedingly well. Orders within our family, being personal to us, can be altered without shame. Your father did it at your request, and so can you, at mine."

Looking hard at the Great King, I could see his spirit for battle ebb away. Cyrus was released with orders to resume his western post. Switching sons, I humbled myself at the King's feet, both in gratitude for his order and out of concern lest this incident diminish his stature.

In years to come I would savor this victory, which was not of the moment alone; it established a pattern of behavior that stretched into the future, shaping events to come.

❧ 11
FRATRICIDE

BEFORE NAMING ARSACES SUCCESSOR TO THE THRONE, Darius had anointed Cyrus with unprecedented powers as Satrap of Lydia, Greater Phrygia, and Cappadocia and commander-in-chief of all forces mustered in the Plain of Kastolos. By so doing, he intended to avoid strife between his sons. He died believing the plan would work. He based it on the assumption, safe when made, that he would rule for many years and, thus, have plenty of time, and ample power, to insist on peace within the family. He had tried hard to assure me.

"I know Cyrus hungers for the crown. But the sharp edge of this youthful ambition will inexorably dull with age, as surely as man's erotic desires erode."

I lacked first-hand experience in these matters. That didn't stop me from disputing his claims. Who's to know in a given case, I asked him? From one as exceptional as Cyrus things could turn out differently.

And, so, I always took the opposite position, arguing that only by naming Cyrus his successor would strife be averted. With enough time, I think I could have brought Darius around, but his life was cut short. Was Ahura-Mazda the cause, he who the Magi claim is our constant protector? If so, he could not be our protector; if our protector, far from being the cause, he could not have allowed Darius to die.

Grief often turned to anger in my early days as a lonely Queen Mother, when

I kept searching vainly for someone to blame for taking my husband from me. And from the Empire. Until he was gone, I hadn't realized how much we leaned on each other. In managing affairs of state, I knew we performed as a team but didn't appreciate our mutual dependence. At times we imagined ourselves an arch, supporting the Empire. Darius viewed himself as the keystone of our arch, a conceit I readily accepted, all the while telling myself that, in fact, I served that function, and did so very well.

Now, at great distance, I blush at my conceit as well as his. For, in truth, if an arch, we were its two sides, equal weaknesses leaning in to create the strength necessary to support the whole edifice. His death left more than a void. The depth of one's grief varies in proportion to one's grasp of the loss. If I had comprehended what made us a good team, my grief would have been many times greater.

After returning to Sardis, Cyrus kept up a steady stream of correspondence with the Great King, reporting on all manner of things relating to management of his territories. To me he wrote nothing, entrusting his thoughts to the memory of Mithradata, a talented and loyal eunuch who had served him from the day he first entered Sardis. I had several visits from Mithradata. What he had to say in that first visit started a storm of conflict in my head that grew more turbulent with each subsequent visit.

Cyrus was convincing himself that duty to the Empire compelled him to dislodge his brother from the throne. He had concluded that I wanted him to strike, even though I repeatedly told Mithradata the opposite. I'm afraid my frequent talk of Achaemenid destiny and duty laid the groundwork for his misapplication of these noble principles.

Everyone has selective hearing about something. I can see, now, that it might have been easy for him to imagine me winking with a wan smile as I spoke sternly to Mithradata. I can even consider the possibility that Mithradata imagined he saw me behaving this way. What I will never accept is the idea that I encouraged or enabled such thoughts.

Cyrus was assisted in shaping his self-serving opinion by the disgruntled few among palace royals who were never satisfied with the status quo. Prominent among them was Artoxares, who, while continuing to profess loyalty to Artaxerxes, secretly traveled to Sardis to fawn over Cyrus and stoke the fires of ambition growing hot within him.

Since adolescence, Cyrus had believed himself in every way superior to his older brother. One could sense it from being around him, although he never had asserted this belief to others. At least not until recently. For several weeks, now, reports filtered in from Sardis that Cyrus had begun publicly to heap praise on himself, like a fighter just before entering the ring. Artoxares returned to Persepolis convinced that Cyrus had resolved to snatch the mantle of power away from his brother. For the first time since I had found him in bed with Datis, he came to my apartments. He was armed with a weapon to which he knew I would submit.

"I have just returned from Sardis, pushing my horses hard to cover the 1,500 mile trip in just over two weeks.

"Artoxares, come here. Sit on this couch and give us your news. Look at you, caked with dust. Fetch a wet cloth, Datis."

"I bring good tidings from your son. He asked me to see you immediately."

"Use this on your eyes first." The water on the cloth served mainly to darken the dust and move it in smudges here and there on his still handsome face. I couldn't restrain a laugh when he said, "How's that?"

"A mud pie. No matter. Speak."

"What I have to say is for your ears alone." He lowered his voice to a whisper.

"Since you were last here, and I assume you remember, there have been no secrets between my Chiliarch and me. Speak to us as one."

"There are a number of us, as you know, who believe the times demand a Cyrus. I journeyed to Sardis to convey our feelings and take his measure. Your son's a bold and enterprising prince. With enough encouragement, he will take up arms. I am convinced of it."

"You're always at the center when it comes to palace plots, imagined or real. The one you now predict pops out from an overactive dream world. Artaxerxes is settled on the throne. You supported him in this and claim still to be a loyal friend. Cyrus is well established as Satrap of the western territories. How, in the name of Empire, can you think civil war will serve our interests? What has the Great King done, or left undone, that makes the pain, sacrifice, bloodshed, and, above all, the uncertainty of a war preferable to his steady rule? Is the value you attach to loyalty and trust as shredded as it would appear?"

"We should have the best. Artaxerxes is a coward."

"Who told you that? Do you have even a scrap of evidence?" Artoxares looked as if he wished he hadn't embarked on this subject and longed to escape.

From the look I threw him, he knew he could not avoid a response.

"Cyrus himself told me. He said his brother could neither sit his horse in hunting nor his throne in time of danger."

"And so you believe that nonsense, which comes from one obsessed, near to drowning in a sea of self-interest. And worse, you goad him on, instead of using your eyes to observe how the Great King handles himself. I give you fair warning, Artoxares: if you and your troublemakers cause what should be nothing more than a remnant of boyish competition to migrate into war, I will have your head."

"But how can you say...I mean he's your favorite, we all know that. You're too harsh, I'm here only because Cyrus wanted me to tell you." He had lost composure. Great beads of sweat rolled down his cheeks, wetting the floor.

"Be precise. What did Cyrus direct you to say?"

"He wanted me to send you his warmest greetings."

"As I thought. You walk in peril. Turn back before it's too late." The visit was over. Datis showed him out.

Artoxares' report disturbed me much more than I had shown. On learning of Cyrus' leanings, I felt paralyzed, my loyalties divided among the obvious claimants: my two sons and the Empire.

Through Mithradata I had offered Cyrus financial support should he need it for his work in the west. He accepted the offer, taking substantial sums. I didn't realize I was feeding his growing appetite for the crown, that my unconditional financial support spoke louder than the words of caution I sent to him via Mithradata. Cyrus had transformed my well-known opinion of him as "pick of the litter" into a loyalty so complete that he assumed he could command my support, even against King and Empire. There is a kind of madness that over-weening ambition unleashes: first, it puts the desired result ahead of the analysis required to deliberate and judge impartially; then it misuses those tools to justify what was preordained.

Should I have known? This question haunts me now as it did in my years as Queen Mother. So, too, the markedly similar question applied to Ochus' behavior in the corridor.

Beyond knowing how Cyrus was reading his mother, should I have accepted some responsibility for the forces gathering within him to lift high his ambition and carry it forward with reckless speed? As the threat grew, from time to time I would consider this question, always rejecting the possibility out of hand. And, yet, the question would return, begging, I finally realized, to be answered by recognizing my own powers, the very powers I reveled in exercising for the Empire's benefit. It was hard to consider oneself the cause of a looming threat to all that one loved.

❧ ❧ ❧ ❧ ❧ ❧

Following investiture of Artaxerxes II, three years passed without incident. Cyrus sent his brother detailed reports of successful campaigns against Aegean towns, accompanied by tribute he had collected on behalf of the Great King. He reported on growing difficulties with Tissaphernes, suggesting in a message delivered early in the 148th year of our family's reign, that he would have to assemble an army and march to Cilicia to subdue him.

My visits with Cyrus' courier, Mithradata, continued. His messages from Cyrus were warnings of intent. On each occasion, I responded with alarm, in strongest terms advising him not to raise a hand against the Great King. Mithradata, I thought, would convey my message precisely. Whether he did, in fact, I never knew. Alas, even if he did, he couldn't have corrected his master's selective hearing.

In the fall of the 148th year, palace rumors that Cyrus was assembling an army began to circulate. Around the turn of the year, the Great King summoned me. A King's Eye had uncovered the fact that one of Cyrus' envoys had enjoyed private audiences with me during his frequent trips to Persepolis.

"Come now, my Great King, do you find that strange?" I answered, voice steady and relaxed, after he had pounced on me with this charge. "Sardis is a long distance from us. When Mithradata arrives, he has many people to see, including your ministers. I don't pry into what he tells them and, until now, they haven't pried into what he, as proxy for a son, and I, as that son's mother, discuss."

"I'm sure you've heard the rumor that he's gathering an army. You're my mother too, and loyal to the Empire, although, of that I am less sure now that I learn, for the first time, of these secret meetings. What can you tell me?" His soft lamb's eyes blinked a few times, making him look not just hurt, but vulnerable. He knew I hated signs of weakness in those I loved and would do all within my power to erase the cause.

"I have no information about an army. I know your brother's ambition, but so do you. When, through Mithradata, he tells me the Empire needs him, I reply that he must abandon that goal if it involves force because the Empire would suffer, regardless of outcome. I also tell him that, for now, he is needed in Sardis and best suited to that post, but that in time and continued success, when you

175

have finished your rule, he may be summoned by the family to accept the crown. I believe my message has been heard and accepted."

Did I believe what I just said? Not entirely. Change "believe" to "hope," add a dash or two of doubt and the truth be told. I saw no advantage to laying out my fears.

On March 21 of the next year, in the midst of a quiet family gathering to celebrate my 43rd birthday, a handful of Immortals interrupted our party to inform the Great King that Tissaphernes had just arrived from Cilicia with a personal force of many soldiers.

Artaxerxes and Stateira withdrew, accompanied by the Immortals. The audience they were about to have with the general was one I wanted to see. Begging the celebratory eating and drinking to continue, I followed the Great King and his wife into the throne room, arriving just as he was arranging himself to receive Tissaphernes.

Stateira glowered at me from across the carpeted corridor as I slipped silently into my customary position on the King's right side. Precedent for my attendance had been set early in my son's rule, beginning with his first audience with Cyrus and the general. So established had the practice become that the Great King expected me to attend important audiences, occasionally sought my opinion and even expressed publicly his disappointment when I didn't appear.

It could easily have been different. There was no tradition of Queen Mothers having easy access to the Great King's court. Had I not asserted, at the beginning of his reign, the right to be present, objections could easily have been laid before the King by those who saw me as a threat. Stateira, for example. And the King could easily have ruled against me.

Like one's physical or mental capacity, one's power over others expands with use, diminishes with disuse. In palace politics, I found that the trick was to push one's authority to and even a bit beyond the threshold of acceptability. Going too far could result in setbacks from which it took time to recover. Not going far enough could cause power to atrophy, making recovery even more difficult. From the early days of childhood, it had been my bent to deploy power zealously, even at the risk of overshooting, a misfortune I experienced more than once.

Tissaphernes entered in his traveling clothes. His nose was caked with sand, dried by the sun. His lips were broken and raw with cracks. He emitted a strong blend of stable odors.

How odd, I thought, recalling Noah's lecture to me on the desert. It's odorless. The wind howls, with warbles and whistles, making music, without which the desert would be lifeless as well.

Tissaphernes' obeisance to the Great King was hurried and perfunctory, as was uniformly the case with our most exalted generals. He got immediately to the point.

"Your brother, with an army of 15,000, left Sardis at the beginning of March, moving east towards Cilicia. He claims his purpose is to subdue me and extend his reach to my satrapy. In truth, he marches to seize your crown. I have come to place myself under your authority."

"What a moment to launch this adventure. We've had reports that he was planning this almost from the day I ordered his return to Sardis three years ago. He knows we are presently engaged in putting down the insurrection of King Amyrtaeus in the Delta. We will need your help, general, both in assembling a second army and leading it."

The general bowed low, less perfunctory this time.

"Speak of the army."

"He assembled mercenaries at Sardis. Mainly from the Peloponnesus. Arranged through hospitality pacts with a handful of Greeks. He gathered up the exiles, attracting Chearchus, who was exiled from Lacedaemon, to be his general-in-chief. As he marched toward Cilicia, others from Asian cities joined. I suspect he has called for a general mobilization throughout Asia Minor, planning to gather forces as he moves toward Babylonia. His army's ultimate size is hard to predict. He will need plenty of money to hold the Greeks." The general shot me a glance. Stateira saw it and exploded.

Advancing toward me, she stopped directly below the throne and pointed at me, arm extended, face beautiful despite being flushed with anger. "Is this what you saved Cyrus' life for? To conspire against his brother? To launch a civil war? You speak of peace, but finance his army of mercenaries. That you sought to put Cyrus on the throne is well known. That, as a mother, you love him more, that too. Less known, or talked about, is the unmotherly, incestuous love that you once enjoyed with him and wish to resume." Her eyes burned with the fires of long-repressed hate, a look that effaced all remnants of charm.

I struggled to contain my growing rage despite knowing that, to get the upper hand, I had to retain self-control.

"I have no need to defend myself against these baseless charges. I take my cue from the Great King, with whom I have been exchanging private thoughts on

Cyrus' activities for three years. It appears you were not aware.

"I've never sought gratitude for saving your life, when it hung from Darius' hand by a thread, but this savage, implacable hatred comes as a shock. I've heard that among certain tribes, for example, the Greeks, it's not uncommon for the weak to despise those among the strong who come to their aid. I shouldn't have been surprised."

I smiled as a cat might upon eating a precious caged bird, looking first up at the throne, as if in search of applause, and then across to Stateira, seeking satisfaction. What I saw was a woman in the process of falling apart. Tears were forming in the corners of her eyes, causing her make-up to dissolve in descending streaks. She became suffused with tears, then burst forth in cries. Another minute and she was gone. The Great King appeared to be unruffled.

"Family matters do not belong in the throne room. I regret this incident, which I trust all within earshot will cease to remember. Tissaphernes, we must send a message to Abrocomas, in Egypt, urging him to finish the campaign as soon as possible and return, perhaps doing harm to Cyrus on the way."

"Yes, if he could get past Cilicia without being detected by Cyrus, he might burn the bridges at Thapsacus to slow your brother's advance. I will look into this matter, if it please your majesty."

I couldn't help but admire this tactician's skills, which seemed as honed for use in the halls of power as they were in the line of battle.

❦ ❦ ❦ ❦ ❦

I had been expecting Artaxerxes to send for me. We met in the exquisite library connected to the throne room by a passage reserved for the Great King alone.

I knew this room, every inch of it, from much time spent here with Darius, planning its redecoration, top to bottom. The floor was marble, without design. The walls were of polychrome glazed brick in brown, yellow, white, green and black. They depicted eight Immortals in procession around the room, each in richly decorated costume with a bow, quiver, and spear, facing right. The design of each costume, using stars, rosettes, fortresses, circles and triangles, differed from all the others. Against the wall opposite the entrance, centered between two Immortals, was a magnificent statue of Darius I which his son, Great King Xerxes, had commissioned in Egypt. Originally installed at the palace in Susa, I had it brought to Persepolis and installed in the library, site of the Great King's most intimate meetings on matters of state. Carved from grey granite, it depicts an all-powerful yet dignified king bearing the look of father to his people. He stands tall and straight, one arm at his side, the other at right angle across his front, just above a dagger stuck into his belt. The superbly rendered pleats of his robe descend almost to the rectangular base on which he stands. It was a symbol of Achaemenid continuity and strength during my husband's reign, and now that of his son. Being in its presence always filled me with pride.

Would Artaxerxes begin with apology or accusation, I wondered, as he beckoned me to sit opposite him. On the table between us were bowls filled with dates and almonds. Two silver drinking bowls and a double-handled amphora filled with wine completed the setting.

"Since my investiture, I have trusted you. Done your bidding. Accepted your excuses. Believed your motives. And yet he's on the march, something you claimed to stand in the way of. Have you played me for the fool, mother?"

"Do you mind?" I filled both of our drinking bowls and took a fistful of almonds.

"There's nothing I can do to stop him. My efforts to help him excel in Sardis, to discourage him from violent pursuit of the crown, both have failed. I haven't seen Mithradata for three months. I have no means of reaching him or his leader, even if I had something new and persuasive to say. The impending battle is unprecedented in our history. We are threatened at the heart of our Empire by a single man at the head of a large army bent on seizing power. He happens to be my son, your brother. This is precisely the nightmarish debacle I have long feared. For the past three years I was sure I could prevent it."

"The money. What about the money?"

I looked closely at my son, then at the face of Darius against the wall behind him. A study in contrasts.

"Rather than averting a battlefield catastrophe for, regardless of who prevails, this is what it will be, the money I sent to Cyrus as fuel for his western ambitions served only to whet his appetite for the throne. My motives were good; the ways and means fell short."

"We know you fought Darius to name my brother rather than me. Doesn't that taint your motive?"

I looked across the table at this man, in one sense a child of mine whom I had known from birth, in another sense a total stranger whose mind I could no sooner penetrate than the Egyptian granite behind him. Nor could he plumb the contents of my mind. We knew essentially the same facts surrounding Cyrus, but we experienced them differently, in ways known only to ourselves. Perhaps not even known in the true sense, but received as fleeting and imprecise, even inconsistent, impressions.

"All that I did was done to preserve peace within the family. Service to our family is indistinguishable from service to the Empire. My sole motive. You look skeptical. Are these motives too lofty for you to accept? Then try survival. Were I to pick one son over the other and lose, in short order my power would be gone, followed, in all likelihood, by my life. Not a safe bet, my son, wouldn't you agree?"

"You intervened with me to save Cyrus. Why, if not to encourage him to fight another day?"

"Stale news. Past time to forget it. I intervened to save Stateira too, and for the same reason. You have heard it many times: the Empire." Artaxerxes had risen from his couch and moved to stand beside the statue of his father's namesake.

"You keep glancing over my shoulder at Darius. He's not questioning you, I am. And I'm not convinced."

"Stand if you must. But hear me on a matter too sensitive for either of us to brook. Why do you think Darius and I tried, again and again, to have children? We did so against the wisdom of the Gods, conveyed through mounting evidence that something fatal was hidden within the bodies of our infant offspring. Eleven died within two years of birth, a fact of which you are aware. Early on, after the second death, Noah, wisest of the wise, cautioned me against continuing. He argued that, however whole and healthy Darius and I were, as individuals, mixing us together to create offspring was dangerous. He pointed to oil and water, each pure, each valuable to humankind, but when brought together, impossible to blend, difficult to restore. His advice was driven not just by the dim prospects for our offspring, but by the grave risks to me. I ignored him, not because I enjoyed the nine months of pregnancy, or the delivery, or losing one after another of those I carried to term and bore through the pain of birthing. I did it for the Achaemenid line, to create a margin of safety."

"And, for the same reason, you saved Cyrus?"

I nodded, my taut face relaxing.

"And this other business, about loving him more than me, I mean loving him more than a mother should ..."

180

"I hoped you knew me enough to blot out that abomidable thought. She's an embarrassment to us both. But even your wife couldn't dream up that libel. Before I answer, tell me this: out of whose filthy fly-filled mouth did it come?"

Artaxerxes moved back to the couch, leaned forward, and whispered the name.

"I doubt anyone is trying to listen, or could through these thick doors. When did he first publish this calumny?"

"After you intervened to protect Cyrus. He begged an audience, saying he had intelligence that could help me understand."

"And you believed him?" I asked, my voice rising in anger.

Beneath heavy black eyebrows, his eyes flickered.

"No, at first I didn't. I tried to ignore what he had said. But I made the mistake of telling Stateira, who inhaled deeply. She kept me aware. It gnawed at her, and she wanted me to wallow with her in this agony of belief."

His face was flushed with embarrassment, his legs crossed, posture tight, body pulling away from me as if in fear of being hit.

"You're aware, aren't you, that the scarred beauty has long been sycophant-in-chief of the palace. He shifts loyalty as the wind shifts direction. He's as nimble and indifferent as a cat. And prodigiously ambitious. He professed love for Darius and me when we were in Hyrcania, came to see us, to warn us, with prescience as it turned out. But he professed love for many others as well. Recently, I know he has courted you. But, here's something that may be news to you. He has courted your brother as well, making the long trip to Sardis for the purpose, then returning to test my loyalties, which proved disappointing. I had to throw him out of my apartments. For the second time.

"Five years ago I made a discovery that turned him against me with a hatred that endures. I caught him naked in my quarters, in the act with my Chiliarch, Datis. I sent him packing, with an injunction never to touch Datis again. Artoxares was so smitten by this lovely man that my order inflicted severe pain. Eunuchs harbor grudges. Artoxares is no exception. His hatred knows no bounds, as the hideous falsehood he has circulated proves."

Artaxerxes looked startled. He rose, moved around the table separating us and took my hands, lifting me up.

"You've helped me understand many things. I shouldn't have put you to the test. Is that what you're thinking? No matter. You've defended your reputation with patience and grace. Will you attend our councils as we prepare for battle? I want you there."

Cyrus isn't the only one who hears what he wants to hear. Each of us deals with facts in unique ways known, if at all, to ourselves alone. Did I need further evidence of this?

"Dear Artaxerxes, my son, I am not going to join your council of war any more than I would join Cyrus'. Do I want to be informed? Of course, and I will be grateful to you for keeping me so. I will travel with you to Babylon. There, within its palace walls, so high and thick, others will think me safe from harm. Yet, I will feel exposed and insecure. There, I will await the outcome, which perforce will cause me great loss.

"The tragedy of the Greeks is upon us. Hugely superior I believed us to be, as the Peloponnesian War dragged on, destroying those puny, prideful states, whose successes against our Empire seemed ephemeral, mirages from the past. Hubris consumed me. It consumed us all. Just as it did in the time of Darius and Xerxes.

"If some way to avert this looming disaster appears on the horizon, let me know and I will pursue it with all my heart."

I squeezed his hands hard, then again, before turning from the Great King to exit a room filled with memories of happier days as Queen.

❦ ❦ ❦ ❦ ❦

Reports of Cyrus' advance became as regular as the rise of the sun and circulated as freely through our Babylonian palace as the daily winds warmed by its rays.

From Cilicia came one of the sons of its tyrant, Syennesis, who had been dispatched in secret to profess loyalty to the Great King. He told of his father's forced assistance to Cyrus in the form of large sums of money and a strong contingent of Cilicians for his army, to be led by the tyrant's other son. He conveyed his father's continuing loyalty to the Great King, claiming that, as soon as opportunity allowed, he would desert Cyrus to join the army of Artaxerxes.

From Abrocomas, whom the Great King had dispatched to lead the expedition to Egypt and then, upon learning that Cyrus was on the march, had recalled, came word that Cyrus had tried through many lures to gain his loyalty without success. Further, that he had returned from Egypt to the Euphrates, crossing at

Thapsacus and burning the bridges behind his army to slow the rebel's advance.

"Burning bridges" is what I was unwilling to do. Thinking about the behavior of Syennesis, I began to imagine the whole countryside between Sardis and Persepolis torn, as if a mother, between loyalty to one son or the other. Very few, I suspected, would voluntarily bet their worldly goods, their lives, and the lives of their families on one or the other. They would see this conflict as beyond the orbit of their daily lives. A conflict of siblings, rivalry carried to an extreme, but not an external threat to the Empire. If possible, like me, they would avoid choosing sides. If forced, they would cooperate, but reluctantly, and if possible, like Syennesis, try to balance the promise of loyalty to one with similar promises to the other. A difficult and risky business, as the estimable Orontas discovered.

Orontas was first cousin to the King, a noble Persian of immense prestige. He was reckoned second to none in matters of war. With subtle flattery Cyrus had won Orontas to his side, giving him a corps of horsemen to render service to the rebel cause. On the march, Orontas began to have second thoughts, and upon entering Babylonia, he secretly switched allegiance, dispatching a messenger to the Great King with a letter expressing newly minted loyalty to the crown.

The messenger was a thinking man, one whose loyalties Orontas had not been careful to test. When directed to deliver a letter to the enemy's leader, he became suspicious, and upon commencing his journey, opened the letter. He delivered it not to the Great King, but to his rebel brother, who had Orontas arrested.

Cyrus assembled a tribunal to try Orontas. It consisted of the seven most distinguished Persians in his army, plus Clearchus, his Greek general. Relatives of Orontas had been forced to attend the trial. They were able to provide us with eyewitness accounts and did so, as Cyrus, intent on deterring others, had hoped they would. The eight members of the tribunal, upon hearing the evidence, rose as one, encircled Orontas and grasped him by his belt, signaling the verdict of death. The relatives reported that he was swiftly taken to the tent of Artabates, Cyrus' most faithful chamberlain, and there put to death. No one knew how this was accomplished. The body of Orontas was never seen again.

In vain I waited for some sign that a nonmilitary solution could be pursued. Much of the news that came to the palace bore the stamp of a brilliant effort by Cyrus to create in the minds of the Persian people an aura of invincibility, a latent and deserving ownership of the crown, a rendezvous with the inevitable, the inescapable certainty. We were told, for example, that Cyrus, upon arriving at Thapsacus to find the bridges burned, was able to lead his soldiers across the Euphrates without wetting them above the shoulders. The people of Thapsacus, it was said, saw divine intervention in this feat, declaring that the river had retired before the one destined to be king.

One of the King's Eyes reported that Cyrus had entered Babylonia. He seemed able to move his army with the swiftness of wind-driven sand. Only later did we understand why. After crossing the Euphrates, he had embarked on forced marches along the east bank of the Euphrates, a much shorter but far more difficult route towards Babylon than the Royal Road, which followed the west bank of the Tigris.

After destroying the bridges at Thapsacus, Abrocomas proceeded some 270 miles northeast along a minor branch of the Royal Road leading to a junction with its main branch at the Tigris. His large army, and he thought Cyrus' as well, would have to stick to the Royal Road because only along its developed path could one be sure of re-supply for an army on the move. Upon learning that Abrocomas was only a day ahead, Cyrus saw a way of engaging his brother before Abrocomas could join the fray. He would go overland, without a road and with nothing in the way of forage for man or beast, straight towards Babylon. As surely as the hypotenuse is shorter than the sum of the right-angled sides that connect it, this painful route would cover a much shorter distance than Abrocomas would travel.

That night I had a riveting dream. I had summoned Artaxerxes and Cyrus to my quarters, where now they stood before me. My brilliantly cunning purpose was to propose an alternative to the battle that loomed, now but a few days away. They sat down beside one another on a couch. I stood over them, thinking of myself as a mother hen guarding her chicks.

I told them we must avoid civil war. Their armies must remain loyal to the Empire. Anyone who would lead them into this battle was a criminal and could not call himself an Achaemenid. The fight is between the two of you. You alone. Therefore, I said, the right thing to do is for you to settle the issue alone, by single combat.

At that moment, Datis, who had been in the room listening to the exchange, claimed an even better idea.

The Empire needs you both, he said, and so too does the Achaemenid line. Instead of fighting to the death, you should draw barley straws from your mother's hand. He who picks the longer straw wears the crown."

I awoke from this dream in a state of euphoria, convinced I had untied the knot that held opposing armies in place. This condition lasted only for the minute or two necessary to realize I had been dreaming. An ache lodged in my heart, as if I had just lost my dearest friend. I tumbled into the world of hard reality, where there wasn't the slimmest possibility of achieving either Datis' solution or my own.

Towards the end of October, word came that Cyrus' army was within 100 miles of Babylon, now traveling swiftly along the east side of the Euphrates. Artaxerxes mustered the diverse elements of his army and prepared to march north against his brother. He had hoped to await the return of Abrocomas in order to add his troops, some 300,000 strong, to the enterprise. Cyrus' advance made further delay impossible.

I paid a visit to the Great King on the eve of his departure.

He was in an elegantly appointed welcoming chamber, seated on a throne. He hailed me cheerfully as I was ushered in.

"Welcome, mother. Most welcome. How are you bearing up?"

"At times like these, my son, it's not easy to be a woman. Wishing, waiting, watching, listening, wailing, these are the passive arts men expect us to practice. With a fury I hate them. But look at you. Positively glowing."

"I've been waiting too. Six months and more. The time has come. We are prepared. I lead an army of more than 800,000. We outnumber him; he is exhausted from the march; and his army consists mainly of mercenaries, who lack the zeal of Persians fighting on their own soil for their King. I am confident."

"Which makes you happy. There's a way you could make me happy too."

"Speak of it, mother, and it will be done." He leapt up from the throne, picked up a pitcher and two goblets that were on a side table and came to sit beside me on a couch. Handing me the two goblets, he poured wine in each, set the pitcher down, took one goblet and held it high, saying "Drink to our victory, and then speak."

I put down my goblet as he quaffed the contents of his. "Allow me to speak first, drink afterwards. I want an escort to take me to your brother's tent. I'm going to ask him to lay down his arms and pledge obeisance to you. In exchange, you will restore him to his satrapy and agree to turn over the crown to him on the tenth anniversary of this day." A hot flush crossed my face, by-product of a mind intoxicated with the rapture of engagement.

185

"You're mad. Do you think the Great King bargains with a traitor? Do you want me to become the object of ridicule? Suspected of cowardice? Trade a crown for a life? Achaemenids, past, present, and future, would hang their heads in shame. I should be damned in time and through eternity."

"This battle will most certainly take the life of one Achaemenid. It could easily take the life of two. It is without precedent and harbors vast uncertainties. It is civil war, hurling Persian against Persian. It could end our line and destroy the Empire, as the Peloponnesian War did to Athens and Sparta. In any event, it is civil war. Against this mighty ocean of looming risks, the risk of having to explain and justify the lofty bargain I propose to escape the evils of this war is but a puddle in the sand. We can credit you with the idea or say it was forced upon you by the pleadings of a heartsick mother. Your choice."

This one, among all my children, was best at listening. I watched as with one small part of his mind, he took in my every word, as if a member of the audience watching a difficult play. The bulk of him wished to be off on the campaign. Frustration showed across his face as he got to his feet and began to gather his things.

"We are at floodtide. The coming rush of waters is beyond any earthly power, even that of an exceptional Queen Mother, to restrain." He spun around and was gone.

I was diminished. And furious. I returned to my chambers in search of Datis. I ordered him to gather an escort to take me to Cyrus' tent. He resisted, asking me to explain. The more I elaborated my goal and argued the logic behind it, the more assertive he became.

"You failed to persuade Artaxerxes. That means you have nothing to offer Cyrus. Knowing the character of each, isn't it obvious that you had the easier one to convince? Consider that Cyrus has spent almost three months traveling over 1,500 miles to engage his brother in battle. Is it conceivable that he will surrender his goal at your request just hours before the victory he believes will be his?"

Datis was right. I couldn't admit it, however, until my anger and hurt feelings had ebbed.

"I am back to playing battlefield mother. We will wait, because that is all we can do. Come, Datis, make love to me. I need distraction, something strong. The feelings you summon are far more pleasurable than getting tipsy, even from our best wine."

❧ ❧ ❧ ❧ ❧ ❧

In my presence, Tissaphernes had described to the Great King the most fearsome element of the rebel's army. It was the 14,000 Greek mercenaries, of whom more than 11,000 were hoplites, the heavily armed infantrymen whose name derived from the huge circular shields they carried. They wore helmets, body armor, and greaves. Their main weapon was a spear of over six feet, used for thrusting at close quarters. They also carried a slashing sword, slung over the shoulder. Battle prowess came from collective might and individual discipline. In formation they presented a tight phalanx of fifty men across and eight deep, protected almost completely by the enormous shields. Moving inexorably forward as a unit, if discipline held they could withstand attacks from almost anything, including cavalry.

The battle-hardened spirit of the Greeks was well known to us. It was said that a Greek would die before abandoning his shield. Anything to avoid the implication that in his haste to run away from battle, he had cast it aside. Across the years, their reputation as fighters had escaped the human dimension to take on mythic qualities.

Considering the size of the Great King's army, some 800,000, it was hard for me to accept the idea that these mercenaries could pose a serious threat. I hoped Artaxerxes and his senior military staff would recall that the Greek reputation was shaped by a tiny state defending itself from Persian invasions. Whether a mercenary in the middle of a foreign country will fight as one would in defense of one's homeland was open to serious question. I had doubts.

Messengers returned to Babylon almost hourly with reports. We heard that battle lines were drawn up in Cunaxa, some 62 miles from Babylon, with the mighty hoplites from Greece, led by Chearchus, anchoring the west flank of Cyrus' army, beside the east bank of the Euphrates.

Cyrus had placed himself in the middle of his line of battle, and so too had Artaxerxes, just behind his highly favored chariots, which were equipped with scythes, some of which were mounted on the axles and extended sideways while others were set on the bodies of the chariots, pointing downward.

We next heard the battle was joined with such sound and fury, enshrouded in dust, that even the closest observers had no way of evaluating the scene. They did report the disquieting news that the Great King's chariots were the first to reach Cyrus' front line and disappeared within his advancing army as the line parted to let them pass without contact. There was also an ominous report of the feared Greek mercenaries, in phalanx ahead of the main line, advancing swiftly in silence and cadenced step on the right flank, to the beat of an incongruously mellifluous flute.

Three hours passed without news. Then a messenger arrived to announce Cyrus dead and the battle over. My marriage had lasted 23 years, during which I had tried to flood the Empire with Achaemenids, giving birth to fifteen children. I shouldn't have tried so hard. Noah was right. Only four survived infancy. Three were males, but only two had the necessary qualities of leadership. And, now, one of them, the headstrong Cyrus, was gone.

What had I done to deserve this? Coming so soon after Darius was taken from me, it seemed, at the time, more than I could bear. I hated self-pity in others, and judged them with intolerance. Now, being soaked with it, I was forgiving, forced to it by my own indulgence. I asked myself, are we no more civilized than the honeybee, whose queen must kill all other would-be queens before establishing control over the hive? I was 43 years old, a widow with narrowing purpose to life. The death of Cyrus hurt, as would the death of Artaxerxes. I admit to believing this loss hurt more. Odd, since I wielded much greater power over Artaxerxes than I ever could wield over Cyrus. Perhaps not. Being untamed made him all the more attractive to me. Physically, yes, of course, physically. Every which way. But Stateira was wrong to think we had ever become intimate.

I grieved for my son. I knew then I would grieve for him the rest of my life, or at least so long as memory served to recall vivid images of him growing up, his loud laughter, his insouciance, his arrogance, sometimes insufferable, his argumentative spirit, which soared when he caught a compelling idea and threw his soul into it, his vulnerability, which explained most of the bluster.

From his earliest days, he embraced risk. Whether in riding, hunting, or fighting, he was always the one who went to the edge, to the extreme, where the odds of success narrow as the rewards for beating the odds grow. In assembling an army and marching across the Empire to attack the Great King and what he knew would be a much larger army, he gambled on a scale few could imagine, much less undertake. I admired the zeal and boldness, even as I despaired over the damage that would be done to the Empire, regardless of outcome.

Often, since leaving the Persian world, I have imagined how history would have treated Cyrus had he won the battle of Cunaxa, a battle today none but dusty scholars have even heard of. Had Clearchus obliged his paymaster by turning inward, away from the Euphrates, to attack the center, where Artaxerxes and his six thousand cavalry were positioned, the outcome might well have been different. Hoplites carry their shields on the left arm, making the right flank of any phalanx its weakest point. Clearchus used the river's edge to protect that flank as he drove back the Great King's left in a completely successful, yet utterly useless, deployment. He missed the main chance of his engagement. It's enough to make even Spartans weep.

Were the Gods in charge? The workings of fate? The lightning bolt of chance? Or did the better army prevail? I had no opinion. It mattered not.

❧ ❧ ❧ ❧ ❧

Truth becomes battle's first victim. All that is known for certain is that on the field of battle Cyrus was killed and Artaxerxes was wounded, later to be attended by the Greek doctor and historian, Ctesias.

Word of Cyrus' death reached the King swiftly. He was led to his brother's body. The King's eunuch, Masabates, cut off the right hand and head of Cyrus, this being a Persian custom when engaged in warfare with other nations. With the aid of torches, Artaxerxes displayed these remnants to the Persian army, which was now, with speed equal to the outward-spreading word of Cyrus' demise, pressing inward in growing numbers around him.

Artaxerxes didn't return to the palace for two days following the battle. We heard that Cyrus' retinue of noblemen had rendered "earth and water" in swift submission to the Great King. We also heard many battlefield tales, often conflicting, as palace-bound rumors about Artaxerxes raced far ahead of him.

I saw my son the morning after his triumphant entrance through the massive gates of Babylon. As I was ushered into his bedchamber, Stateira exited, sweeping by me with haughty mien. I could see that she had awaited my arrival before departing, lest I imagine the Great King had summoned me first. I detested her for trying to dilute my influence. But there were so many other reasons. Like counting grains of sand in an hourglass. With sorrow, I reflected on my husband's prediction at the time I salvaged her life.

Artaxerxes was propped up with pillows. Despite the warmth of the room, he wore linen bedclothes and had a wool blanket pulled up around him. His expression, set in deathly pale skin, was radiant.

"I am the victor. Does that surprise you, mother?"

I bent to kiss him. "You're white as a snowcap. Show me the wound." I took

189

his hand in one of mine, while using the other gently to pull away blanket and clothing. There it was, stuffed with a clutch of herbs. The skin beyond the opening was red and swollen, on its way, I thought, to becoming much worse.

"How do you feel?" I asked. "Hold still while I try to find your pulse." My index finger caught the faint beat on his wrist. Too slow.

"Are you better or worse?" I knew the answer before he confessed.

"Who put those herbs in your wound? Just nod if it was Stateira's Magus, that clown, Pharandates,"

He nodded.

"For how long?"

"He rode out to meet me two days ago. Not my idea. I was being cared for by Ctesias. I know what you're thinking."

"We both want you to recover. It comes down to trust. And, in this matter, it's life or death. I have what I need to treat you." My eyes searched his, eager to find consent.

"I'm in your hands, mother."

"Mine and Noah's. I've brought honey from his hives to feed you, as the gods are fed. Noah tells of two famous Greeks, Pythagoras and Democritus, who attributed their long lives to eating much honey. Here, it will extend your life too." I spooned several helpings of honey into his mouth.

"Good. Next, let's replace that herbal stuffing with a cloth dressing drenched in honey. Time and again, Noah has proven this to be effective. Why? Perhaps, he says, because it's the food of the Gods, and as such, can ward off the spirits of infection and other evils that enter open wounds. Honey never dries, so changing dressings will not hurt your healing flesh. Hold still." When I had finished, I took away the extra pillows, directing him to sleep.

I returned the next morning. His attendants reported he had slept much of the night, an improvement over the night before and the one before that.

"I've heard that it was you who slew Cyrus. Conflicting accounts circulate. I need the truth."

Artaxerxes looked at me as child to mother, searching for a sign of sympathy, weighing the risks of truth-telling.

"Until I heard he was dead, I thought only of the course of battle and my own wound. So soon after my throw did his lance strike me that I had no idea what damage mine had done to him. It might have struck him dead. And so,

190

when I heard, and knew I should be the one, I decided, with the support of those around me, to make it so."

"I was prepared to hear from one son that he had slain the other. I was not prepared to learn that you ordered the head and hand of your brother. A Greek, yes. A Persian Achaemenid, your own blood, no."

"Masabates lies when he claims I directed him. I intend to punish him. At that moment, on the battlefield, when he brought these things to me, uninvited, a delirious army was swelling around, cheering, demanding to see the head of my brother. I had no choice. They were beyond control. You are right to cry shame."

Our eyes locked on each other, bright, brimming, wet. I took his hand. Together, we wept.

I knew we had to head off, in particular, two battlefield tales being told by scoundrels, each claiming to have killed Cyrus. The Great King must act swiftly.

To Mithradates, who was claiming to have hit Cyrus in the temple with a dart that proved fatal, the Great King sent lavish gifts in thanks, as the special envoys publicly announced, for finding and bringing to the Great King the bloodied horsetrappings of Cyrus. Nothing more was mentioned.

To the Carian who claimed to have killed Cyrus with a dart to his thigh, the Great King sent a reward, taking care to explain publicly that it was in token of the King's appreciation for the Carian's eye-witness report that Cyrus had fallen dead.

The aftermath of Cunaxa was proving difficult for me. That Artaxerxes was alive, and on the mend, was cause for rejoicing. But Cyrus' death weighed heavily on my heart and soul, so much so that I couldn't abide the battlefield tales that continued to circulate. Neither the Carian nor Mithradates had caught the unstated premise of the Great King's message. Dealing harshly with them was something I could do to express my pain; indeed, it was all I could do other than to grieve, which had already proved too passive to meet my needs.

So carried away was the Carian by his claimed prowess on the battlefield that he spurned the King's gifts, protesting that he alone had killed Cyrus. I became maddened with hatred for this man. With sly argument, I helped the Great King devise an enduring public death with high deterrence value.

Mithradates proved himself another fool at a palace feast for eunuchs of the royal family. After drinking beyond his power to remain discreet, he began to complain about the gaudy rich clothes he was wearing, gift from the Great King.

He claimed to deserve far greater gifts, because, as he put it to one of my eunuchs in attendance, "I tell you plainly that this hand was the death of Cyrus."

When the eunuch told me the story, I went straight to my son. Together, we decided to condemn Mithradates to death in boats, a particularly gruesome way slowly to part from this world in public view. With the passage of time I've come to regret having promoted these cruel punishments. Beyond being unnecessarily harsh, they fell short as remedies for my sorrow.

I insisted on a funeral for Cyrus befitting an Achaemenid prince second in line for the crown. Despite intense protestations by Stateira, about which he would only hint to me after being pushed hard—I couldn't leave it alone— Artaxerxes agreed. I personally supervised the Magi's treatment of my son's remains, including the parts detached by Masabates, and then accompanied their passage from Babylon to Persepolis. They would be placed in an empty sarcophagus within Darius' tomb at Pasargadae.

Present throughout the ceremonies was Aspasia, Cyrus' transcendent jewel, a concubine of exquisite beauty and careful breeding and education. She was by birth a Phocaean from Ionia, born of free parents but brought up by her father in poverty, her mother having died in childbirth. She had the apparent misfortune to be one of a group of four young Greek girls taken from a ship by a boarding party of Persians under Cyrus' command.

The group was brought before Cyrus one evening, as he was finishing dinner with many companions and about to commence the wine-drinking that customarily followed. As Cyrus told the story, the other three girls were splendidly turned out, their hair meticulously groomed and their faces made up with cosmetics, powders and perfumes. Though young, they had been superbly trained to trade in beauty by flattery and coquettish flirtation.

Aspasia was also made up and dressed in seductive finery, but Cyrus later discovered she had to be beaten before submitting to such costume. She had fought every effort to be presented as a courtesan, invoking the Greek gods to protect her or let her die. She viewed these trappings of beauty as not only unnatural but sure signs of slavery.

As the Satrap dallied with the other girls, who gave way freely to his casual advances, Aspasia stood apart, looking ashamed, her downcast eyes full of tears, her face covered with fiery blushes, a contrast to her milk-white skin. He beckoned to her, but she refused to approach. His chamberlains lifted her up and brought her over, seating her forcibly beside him. When he touched her, she spoke with firmness. "Whosoever lays hands on me shall rue it." He then put his hand on her breast, as he had done with the others, to their apparent pleasure. Instantly, she swept his hand away and got up to leave. The chamberlains restrained her. All those in the room except Cyrus thought her sullen and rude. Cyrus instructed his attendants to let her go, declaring her the only woman among the group who was truly noble.

In time he came to love her above all others, calling her "the Wise." Cyrus treated her as an equal and she responded with affection. He had brought her with him in the campaign, and she had been taken among the other spoils of his camp. Now she belonged to Artaxerxes.

My mind can become aimless at ceremonies, especially those designed for the dead. Like a grappling hook on a flat stone surface, it slips off the familiar rituals. From experience, I know that, in these circumstances, unless I can quickly find something meaty to dig into, my mind goes as numb as an unused limb.

At Cyrus' funeral, without any plan, my mind formed a tight grip around Aspasia, who stood across the room, statuesque with long black hair unbound in mourning. I stared, struck by her unstudied beauty, her natural reserve, the grace and dignity she projected. I compared her to Stateira, who stood but a few feet away. The contrast in names foretells the rest. How did Aspasia come by such a mellifluous name, invoking precisely the qualities of mind and body one sees in the flesh. Did her parents know when they named her? Did the name shape the character? Sometimes couples grow more alike as they age. Sometimes they come to resemble each other, sometimes even their dogs. Do they pick pets that resemble them? What about my dreadful name? Before drifting further, I snapped back to Aspasia.

I imagined her in the arms of Cyrus or sitting, naked and cross-legged, on his bed, deep in discussion. She was both distraction from and channel to my deceased son. What did they share besides physical attraction, desire, arousal, and release, that age-old cycle, enjoyed with more or less intensity over and over again? Did she share his love for gardening? His strict, often severe, approach to justice and its rewards and punishments? His sharp sense of fairness? His consuming ambition for the throne? He often sought her counsel on matters of state. What made her "wise" to him?

Now, it was said, she had a new owner. Surely, Aspasia was beyond "owner-ship." But where would she find a place in the royal landscape? There was Stateira, a strong presence beside the throne, loved by Artaxerxes more for her unquestioning support and her role as confidante than for her performance in bed. Her flaw was jealousy. So powerful was her resentment of my influence over her husband that she burned with hatred. She would be jealous of Aspasia, fearing her power to gain influence over one brother as she had over the other.

The Great King maintained a harem of many concubines, one for each day of the year. Symbolic. Trappings signaling power rather than potency. Artaxerxes was fond of his eunuchs, with whom he spent far more recreational time than he did with the harem. Particularly with Tiridates, widely considered the most handsome and attractive man in the Empire. As far as I could tell, my son's sexual preferences were not the subject of palace gossip. Nor did he discuss them with his mother. I knew because I was part of the harem, and every eunuch of stature owed me loyalty for favors given over the years.

I couldn't imagine Aspasia and the Great King bedding together. How could her love for Cyrus be transferable to his brother? As a mother, I loved them both, but in different ways, ways that were by no means fungible. Her love, far more than a mother's, had to be specific to the man.

How could Artaxeres make love to her, knowing he was the cause of Cyrus' death, the man she loved beyond measure, knowing he would be compared, caress by caress, in every detail, to his brother, who had projected a superior instinct, skill and passion for the art of making love to the opposite sex. I imagined the scene as he led her to his bed, his mind darting off the mark, becoming unmanageable, creating all manner of difficulty, even for a body in need just inches away from an obliging, highly skilled woman.

I resolved to answer this question myself. I would go to the Great King and persuade him to consecrate her a priestess to Diana of Ecbatana. Placing her beyond connubial chores was my goal. A fitting conclusion to the love she freely exchanged with Cyrus.

❧ ❧ ❧ ❧ ❧

The Great King's wound had healed. For each of 45 days, I had supervised the process. First, his dressing was removed and the wound examined for signs, rose to red for healing, pale white for infection. Then, a fresh dressing, lathered with honey, was placed over the wound and secured. Progress was steady, the wound closing from within as the days passed until fresh scar tissue covered the opening. Stateira did not interfere. In fact, I never saw her at the Great King's bedside. To note the day on which the wound was sealed, Artaxerxes invited me to stay with him through the afternoon and evening and to play at dice.

From his childhood, games of chance with dice had been the most pleasant way we had found to be together. Once he passed the age of finding it inconsolable to lose, Artaxerxes combined what, given his placid disposition, was an uncommon passion for wagering with a graceful acceptance of the results, no matter how disappointing. I cared more than he about winning. He had a quicker mind for reckoning the odds. Our games were always serious but lighthearted.

Seated on a black stone floor, we cast the dice on a low table of black-and-white-veined stone, polished silky smooth to a bright lustre. Artaxerxes had planned a special dinner in my honor. The theme, he informed me when I arrived at his private receiving room, would be honey.

We started out with an herbal drink made with leaves of chamomile, served hot in green glass cups. Beside them the attendant placed a matching glass bowl with flared rim that was filled with honey. It contained a silver ladle with beaded stem and calf-head terminal.

"I hope you've plenty of gold, my son. I'm feeling lucky."

The attendant returned to place around the edge of the dicing table a number of small glass bowls, each filled with a different condiment. There were figs, chestnuts, onions pickled in honey-seasoned vinegar, candied turnip, radishes prepared with salt, and an exotic dish of quince and pear compote covered in a sauce of finely chopped pistachio nuts and honey.

"So you singled out Tissaphernes for rich gifts, including your daughter's hand, all without consulting me." I tried to sound the scold.

"You're baiting me; the smile gives all away. I try to limit my consultations to those with a chance of proving useful. Look at the facts. He assumed command of the army when I was wounded. He turned our right flank inward and swept all before him to reach the rebel's tents, even before word of Cyrus' death had circulated. He's preparing to deal with the Greek mercenaries, who camp among us like an unnatural growth in the stomach. It's his loyalty that makes you dislike him. He's the best I have."

"Perhaps you'll consult with me regarding your eunuch, Masabates."

"I'd intended to do exactly that, even before you asked. We will consider that matter tonight. Later. Let's begin. I have 500 darics on the first game of 36. Here, roll for position."

He handed me a die. We each rolled. Five for him and six for me. "You go first," I said, handing him back the die.

He rolled ten, then nine, then four, then seven, a total of 30. He hesitated before throwing the dice once more, then decided to hold at 30, handing the dice to me. As he explained later, the probabilities of throwing six or less were slightly less than throwing seven or more, which would put him out of the game.

I rolled three, then ten, then nine, then eight, a total of 30. I had a choice. I could declare a tie, in which case we would start over. Or I could roll the dice again. The odds of rolling six or less to me seemed pretty good, so I plunged ahead. The dice came up three and four, putting me over the limit by one. I paid my son in gold.

"I may have told you this, but as a child, when I first played at dice, we used sheep anklebones without much sculpting. They were four-sided, of course, and rather rough. We didn't know the word 'dice.' The game was called 'Knucklebones.' These cubes are a big improvement. The Lydians claim they invented dice, but I doubt it. They're hopeless braggarts, claiming many firsts, like the coinage of pure gold and silver, and the dyeing of wool. I don't believe them for a minute. Why, the Egyptians used dice before anyone had even heard of a Lydian."

We switched to mead, with absinthe added for flavor. After a few more throws of the dice, the winnings had more or less evened out. Dinner was served. Artaxerxes couldn't contain his enthusiasm for the casserole prepared at his detailed instruction. I knew Cyrus was a gardener of wide repute around Sardis, but I had somehow missed the devotion of his older brother to food and the infinite possibilities for combining and preparing it. Before we began, he insisted on disclosing the ingredients. The meat was hare. It was layered between honey cakes, made with fine wheat flour and eggs. Combined with the hare were Phrygian cheese, dill and fatty broth, to which pomegranate seeds and juice had been added. We suspended play to address our hunger.

The mead was starting to go to my head. It works with more stealth than wine, advancing gently by tiptoe until positioned to jump down upon one's head. It could turn an otherwise pleasant evening into a nightmare. I returned to chamomile and honey.

We had finished the main course when Artaxerxes asked, "How do you suggest I deal with Masabates?"

"Before we come to that eunuch, I must toast the magnificent stew. Indeed, the whole meal has been a surprising delight. Is there more?"

"A light course. Compote of dates and figs, apples and raisins, a sprinkling of almonds, stewed in terebinth oil and saffron." Responding to the ring of his bell, attendants brought forth the dish.

"You agreed he must be punished. It's only a question of how and by whom." I smiled as serenely as I knew how. Word had reached me that the passage of time was erroding the Great King's resolve to punish his eunuch. Whenever he recalled the value of having irrefutable proof to show the doubtful throng of troops swelling around him, he weakened. After all, the Great King believed that Masabates, one of his most favored attendants, had acted out of loyalty, thinking only of service to the Great King.

"I have given this matter much thought, mother, and..."

I cut him off, trying to prevent the issuance of an edict.

"Listen. I have the solution. We will play at dice for him. It's that simple. It's my turn to go first. Hand over the dice."

He looked at me hard, trying to measure my resolve. A quizzical expression melted into a smile. He placed the dice before me on the table.

"To 36?"

I nodded, then rolled a ten, followed by a six, a seven, and another six, putting me at 29. Even I knew the odds of hitting seven or less to be high. Not a sure thing though. I handed him the dice.

"Not bad," he said, looking surprised. "You're going to hold there, eh."

He rolled a three, followed by a ten, a four, a six and another six, totaling 29. I held my breath as he paused but an instant before rolling again. Each die came up four. Masabates was mine.

Nervousness intruded to hang over us, as neither wanted to continue the evening or knew how gracefully to end it.

Artaxerxes rang for the servants to clear the table.

"I suppose you've had enough for one evening," he said. "What plans for Masabates?" Through the haze of one glass too many, he was trying, unsuccess-fully, to appear the idly curious innocent.

"Come now, my son, isn't that my business, having won him in a fair fight? It's gotten late. What a perfect evening you've given me. Absolutely beguiling." He ushered me out without another word.

With swiftness driven by my fear that the Great King would renege, Datis and his staff carried out my orders the following day. The King's eunuch was flayed alive and then his body was set on three stakes for public display with his skin nearby, stretched taut on three other stakes. They posted a sign nearby:

"Here is Masabates, who mutilated the body of Cyrus."

I was driven to it. But why? Was it a sacrifice to the memory of my son? That's what Stateira claimed. Retribution for disgracing his body? A warning to those who might think the Achaemenid strain was growing weak? Or to those who might think of taking my other son's life?

Over my remaining years as Queen Mother, I developed a convenient theory to evade the true answer to this question. While each of these explanations had the ring of truth, I resolved that all were afterthoughts. None hit the mark, I told myself, because what I did to Masabates, and the others in whose punishment I had a major role, I was compelled to do, without thought, as the wild boar attacks when cornered, as the queen bee kills upon emerging from her cell.

Not until I had settled in Hades' realm did this gross abdication of responsibility for my acts become clear. For a thinking human being, to excuse her behavior by attributing it to instinct was a contradiction in terms, a denial of one's humanity. Of course, no one can claim a life of perfection. But mine was badly askew: Overweighted in the pursuit and use of power; underweighted in the practice of tolerance, compassion, and kindness. Now, it was too late to try for balance. My only solace came from honest self-knowledge and deep regret.

❧ 12
DEMANDS OF THE EMPIRE

 ASPASIA CAME TO SEE ME soon after Cyrus' funeral. She was inquiring about Artapates, the most faithful and beloved of Cyrus' scepter-bearers. What had become of him, she wanted to know. It was the first time we had met, although my knowledge of her from Cyrus and from observation since she came to the palace had made me feel I had known her for a long time.

"I am overjoyed to see you, Aspasia. We have much in common, most recently much woe. Sit with me over a glass. What do you prefer, mead or wine? I'll tell you all I know."

She wore no make-up, yet appeared before me a radiant beauty. My eyes locked on her, leaving nothing unnoticed: the black hair in gentle waves, the smooth, tender skin, the complexion, pale as alabaster but with the subtle warmth of an incipient rosebud, the pierced ears, one hole slightly larger than the other, neither adorned, the voluptuous mouth, wide and inviting, bounded by lips more refined than one might expect, the chiseled nose, tapered to a point with a slight turn up at the end, suggesting a ball balanced there to enthrall the close observer, the long, delicate neck in no rush to join head to shoulders, a stand-alone object of stylish beauty.

"I came because of what I know about you from Cyrus. He was an exceptional man. But you know that. Perhaps, however, you don't know the loyalty he commanded. Just being able to assemble such an army and march it from Sardis to Cunaxa bespeaks loyalty on a grand scale. Artapates was the best of the best around him. Cyrus rewarded him with all manner of personal gifts, from gold bracelets and a necklace to a magnificent gold dagger that Cyrus had made to his own specification. Its handle ended in lion's heads. Its hilt at the top of the blade was decorated with ibex heads. I know you will want to find him, if he survived."

Her voice was soft, pleasing and persuasive. To conjure it, imagine oneself enthralled by the voice of a Siren. I saw my son becoming bewitched, as vivid a picture as if I were there with them both at the moment it happened.

I knew the story of Artapates. It was at once tragic and noble.

"Alas, this Artapates died with Cyrus on the field of battle. When his master sprang forward on horseback, getting ahead of his followers, Artapates stayed where he was, awaiting Cyrus' return. When word came that Cyrus had fallen, Artapates ran forward in search of his master. We don't know if Cyrus was dying or dead when Artapates reached his prone body. All we know is that when the retinue of soldiers came with the Great King to identify Cyrus, Artapates was stretched out across the body of this prince, dead from the very same dagger you described, which he had used to take his own life. I believe the Great King took the dagger, which he found embedded in Artapates' chest."

Aspasia grew tearful at the news.

"So much pain from this war. To live is to grieve, but I ask you why must it be so?"

I had no response, but before I was forced to admit it, Datis came before us with terrible news. The Great King's most beloved eunuch, Tiridates, had just died.

He was only 15, a beautiful boy with piercing blue eyes, a pearl white body with just a hint of musculature and long blond hair that covered head and shoulders, everywhere in curls like ripples dancing across a sandy beach. Disease, swift and sure, had cut him down.

Aspasia didn't know him personally although she knew of his connection to the Great King. She excused herself, observing that we would obviously have matters to discuss and would want to grieve in private.

Datis and I knew Tiridates well enough to sense the void his death would create for the Great King. In the year since Cunaxa, Artaxerxes had turned more and more to Tiridates for physical pleasure and release. He continued to rely on his wife for counsel, as he did me. Our competition for preeminence continued, often with ambiguous results, perhaps a product of his design.

At the same time he grew increasingly attracted to Aspasia, but not in the ways of his brother. He was drawn to her for the taste and skill she brought to playing the flute. At first he summoned her to perform before guests. This evolved into the practice of asking her to perform weekly for him alone. And, then, for what turned out to be the last two months of Tiridates' life, he had her play in the antechamber to his bedroom, while he and this young eunuch made love behind an opaque curtain drawn discreetly across the open doorway.

Artaxerxes had in his harem what other men could only fantasize about. It could furnish the Great King variety every night of the year. And, yet, he chose Tiridates, the one over the many, night after night. This harem was a serious drain on the palace purse, one I considered silly, given that its only role was to sustain a fiction.

In a far less dramatic way, one devoid of fictions, I had done the same thing as my son. Was this a family trait? A human one? Should it be called loyal affection and praised or lazy lack of adventure and condemned? I was never sure.

While Datis and I were trying to think through the implications of Tiridates' death, Stateira appeared at my chambers, seeking audience. I could not recall a single instance of her having come to see me. Datis showed her in and turned to go. I beckoned for him to remain with us, my customary practice, given the now established prominence of his role as counselor. Stateira objected strenuously. Worry spread across her carefully made-up face.

"May I get you some wine? Datis will serve us and then depart." We sat opposite one another, across a low table of blue-gray stone, fidgeting in silence.

The eunuch brought in a tray with a jug of wine, two goblets, and a small bowl mounded high with pistachios and olives. After filling our goblets, he turned in silence and was gone.

I was struggling to remain friendly and welcoming when she broke the silence.

"I will come directly to the point. With the death of Tiridates, Aspasia will become his favorite. He's already started treating her like a senior wife. Of course, he denies being reliant on her for the kinds of opinion he used to seek from me. But I can feel it happening. You're the only person who might be able to stop it. I've never asked your help before. We've often had our differences. I know you dislike me. Never mind. I've come, swallowing my pride. I thought it possible you might have a similar concern."

She was wringing her hands between gulps of wine. I refreshed her goblet, deciding to turn the knife a bit.

"That he loved Tiridates was no secret. Nor is it unknown that his harem bulges with women of talent, well trained to give pleasure and available to him at all times. If you weren't bothered by them, what is it about Aspasia?"

"She's more than a boy; much more than a concubine. She could replace them all. And me too." Her hands trembled as she held out the goblet for me to refill. "Both of us," she added emphatically, staring at me with hopeless look.

"Your concern is different from mine. I don't think Artaxerxes will ever lay a finger on Aspasia. However, as long as she remains in the harem, she will be thought of as a concubine and, therefore, exposed to the risks these women face. Here's how I will help you. I am going to ask the Great King to consecrate her a priestess to Diana of Ecbatana, that she may live out her days in chastity, free from the burdens of serving men. I assure you he will do it."

Her downcast expression changed to wonder, as if a miracle had occurred. She had entered my chambers in desperation, seeing virtually no prospect for success. Would she discover that I had already made this demand on her husband? I weighed the possibility as remote.

❧ ❧ ❧ ❧ ❧ ❧

Tiridates was buried with pomp befitting one who had attracted the Great King's love. Throughout the Empire the King's subjects mourned his loss, which seemed profoundly tragic given the eunuch's tender age, a nipping of the apple bud just when its tip had emerged, pale green with promise.

On a daily basis I tried to visit my son. He was inconsolable, turning me away three times. On the fourth day following Tiridates' burial, I was admitted. He was not himself. His clothes were soiled. His beard, always well tended, was a riot of disarray, like an abandoned garden after much rain.

"Please sit down, mother. I need your help. Yesterday, I went to the baths. On the way, I passed Aspasia. She had put on mourning black and stood motionless as I approached. Seeing me, she started to weep, her gaze fixed firmly on the ground. 'What brings you here?' I asked. She said she had come to console me in my grief and pain. She would meet me in the anteroom to my chambers with her flute. There she stood upon my return. She piped three mournful tunes. Her playing infused my grief with the beauty of her music, transforming it. The room shimmered. When she had finished, she spoke softly, saying that she would come to my bedroom. I had wanted to ask her; something held me back. You can probably explain that better than I. She didn't inquire. She acted, as if the matter were free of doubt, as if she knew my mind.

Once there, she saw Tiridates' cloak on my bed. Picking it up, she threw it over her black dress and stretched out on my bed, her ravishing hair spread across the pillow like a bird's wing. In the candlelight, the flush of her pale skin shone like an ember. Last night, for the first time, I slept soundly. On awakening, I felt it possible to recover from my grief. She had promised me that time alone would heal. Here, she was wrong. I knew that, without her, time would not suffice. She said she would return daily in this attire until the process was complete. The certainty with which she guided me last night was beyond the most profound Magian mystery."

"The Gods who shaped Aspasia broke the mold. Why do you tell me this story?"

"You asked me to protect her and I agreed. Since then much has happened. I seek your approval," his voice beseeching. "Here's what she told me last night, just before she left me to sleep. 'My King, understand this: every pleasure performed with art is chaste.'"

Perhaps for the first time, I could intellectually appreciate the tight connection between physical needs and those of the mind. Loss of a loved one like Tiridates creates havoc in the brain. Physical release can resolve that havoc or at least ameliorate it. With Datis I behaved as if I understood the nexus, when in fact I was acting through instinct. How often had I turned to him for physical pleasure and release, driven to it by needs originating in the head.

"I support this process. With all my heart, I do." I rose and walked over to him, standing there. He stood to meet me. I hugged him tight.

"For the cure to take hold, you must attend to your beard and change to clean clothes. This is your mother speaking."

I laughed softly, inducing a smile in his pale, unkempt face.

"I trust the arrangement will not last beyond recovery."

Aspasia didn't return to my chambers for several weeks. When she finally appeared, I had already heard from the Great King that the enabling process had ended. He needn't have told me of its success, for a glance at his careful dress and confident manner spoke of a cure well done.

"Come in, Aspasia. Join me for fruit and wine. Datis will serve."

She followed me into the sitting room. We sat on couches beside a low square table, which Darius had ordered to be made for me following delivery of my last baby, the end of a long and mostly sad road.

"I have some things for you. They belonged to your friend, Artapates. Come, Datis, lay them out on the table."

With doleful eyes, blankly, Aspasia stared down at the gold dagger, the necklace, and the bracelets that he was wearing when he took his life, all gifts of Cyrus. To me they were ornaments of a life I hadn't known. To her, I could see, they brought to life the man who wore them, compounding the pain that news of his end had already caused. Life to death, a one-way route, can happen in the blink of an eye, more quickly than it takes to say the words. Suddenly, what was is no more and everything is changed. As she thought of Artapates, I was thinking of Darius.

"I can imagine that you were very close to Artapates."

"The only part of this story that I can feel good about is that Cyrus died without knowing. I must do the grieving for us both. He was a zealous man, to be sure. Even so, he would have considered this act of devotion beyond all reason. This gold wraps my mind in painful grip. Forgive me."

Her face was streaked with tears, glistening in the candlelight. She sobbed quietly, even soothingly, although that couldn't have been a goal.

"I want you to have his belongings. They carry much meaning." Her sobs continued.

"I have more. Would you mind if we changed subjects?"

As she shook her head, teardrops angled off her high cheek bones, dropping silently to the table and floor.

"I want to read you something from Cyrus, a letter he sent me some years ago."

Then I read this letter aloud:

> *Mother, my dearest,*
>
> *This letter explains the necklace contained in the accompanying box. A gift to you. It came to me from Scopas the Younger of Thessaly, who had acquired it from Sicily, where it was produced and ornamented with what, to my eye, was amazing skill. I showed it to Aspasia, observing that it was fit for a king to bestow upon a loved one. She agreed. Thereupon, I tried to give it to her, asking*

her to show me how it looked around her neck. Gleaning my
purpose, she deflected this effort, saying "How can I make so bold as
to wear a gift worthy of your mother Parysatis? Instead, you should
send it to her. To you I will continue to display the beauty of my
neck, unadorned."

I was greatly charmed by her response, which was both
amusing and wise. As I do so often, I obliged her request by writing
you this letter and forwarding the necklace with it.

Your son,

Cyrus

Aspasia had stopped crying. Her face began to dry. She was smiling. Only the salt remained, in streaks, ineluctable clue to recent sorrow.

"Here. I'm returning it to you."

The necklace gleamed softly in the candlelight. Gold rings strung tight, from which gold pendants cast in four animal forms alternated around the string. I tried to hand it to her, but she would not extend her hand to take it. I placed it on the table, apart from the gold of Artapates.

"Why?" she asked, as if I were about to hurt her. "How can you know what memories are set astir, what pain accompanies them. Even if you had nursed me through childhood and been my companion ever since, you could not burrow into my head. We are islands, all of us, lapped by surrounding waters, but penetrated not at all." Sadness suffused her voice; despair etched barely visible lines across her face. "Why?" she implored.

"I too know sadness. We share the loss of Cyrus. Of course, the size and shape of my loss is unknowable to you as yours is to me. What I now understand, however, is your essential humanity. It filled your time with Cyrus. Over the past few weeks, it rescued Artaxerxes from the ditch of despond.

"The sun rises and sets only for the living. You are restless and brimming with life and have much left to do. My goal is not only to protect you, but to enable you to serve the Achaemenid family in the future as you have in the past. Today, the gold spread out on my table inflicts pain. But in time, I promise you, these objects will unleash the joy of remembrance. Take them."

❧ ❧ ❧ ❧ ❧ ❧

After Cunaxa, the Great King began to include me in his military councils. I didn't know why. At the first one I attended, Stateira wasn't present. In fact, as a woman, I was one of only two. The other was Aspasia. I concluded it was she who advised Artaxerxes to include me.

I thought better than to ask my son why Stateira wasn't present. His silence in regard to his wife on occasions when it would have been natural to speak conveyed clearly enough the message that he did not welcome questions or comment about his wife. His thoughts about her were kept private to a remarkable degree. He never committed the gross error of complaining about her to me, or even the more subtle error of excusing or praising her.

This meeting was called upon the return of Tissaphernes from the north, where he had been, at times leading, and at times scouting, Clearchus and his 14,000 Greeks. At the Great King's direction, Tissaphernes had made a truce with them right after the battle of Cunaxa, then led them to nearby villages where they were allowed to reprovision with grain, palm crowns, and dates, now deep amber with ripeness. They also stocked up on the wretched palm wine, inescapable cause of hangover and headache. From these villages, the Greeks had moved north along the east side of the Tigris, shadowed by Tissaphernes and his army.

I had already learned from a scout returning ahead of Tissaphernes that the general had led the Greeks to my Median villages, which he gave over to them for plunder. He was a friend of Datis, whom he happened to see upon arriving at the palace. The scout told Datis how upset he was by this crude effort to insult the memory of Cyrus through me.

My revulsion for this general, fed by past encounters, was absolute even before I heard of this new outrage. The prospect of participating with him at the Great King's council set me on edge.

Artaxerxes was on his throne, surrounded by various army personnel. Tissaphernes stood in the middle, facing the throne. Aspasia was close to the Great King. Having no assigned place, I positioned myself as far away from Tissaphernes as possible. On seeing me, his face registered minor shock, then chagrin. I looked over, around and through him, anywhere to avoid acknowledging his presence. Childish behavior, but on occasions like this, irresistible.

The Great King asked the general to report. As usual, Tissaphernes was caked with dust. It was an essential aspect of who he was. Even at my distance he smelled of horseflesh, sweat, and dung. It was hard not to acknowledge his command presence, the sheer force of him, the only one among us who wore the weather across his face and the weight of military decisions in his brain, who could turn physical hardship into joyful play, whose ordinary work was life-threatening, day in, day out. Even now I wonder at my ability to respect the object of my hate.

"Clearchus and I met just before I returned for this meeting. He doubted our trustworthiness. I informed him that we doubted his, particularly because senior officers within his army have warned us. He offered to serve the Great King. His arrogance knows no bounds. He boasted of a unique ability to subdue any tribe, mentioning by way of example, the Pisidians and Egyptians, implying that without his aid, we would fail. He claimed a willingness to do these things not only for the sake of pay, but out of gratitude for our sparing them. An unusual type, this Clearchus. He grovels while he struts, whining and boasting from one moment to the next."

"The Greeks are like a plague of locusts, cutting a swath through our country," the Great King declared. "Since Cyrus the Great, we Achaemenids have been lions at home and foxes abroad. And yet, attacking them now would strain us. The King's Eyes have learned that Sparta is astir, with possible plans to land an expeditionary force on the coast to defend the Ionian cities. To protect them from you, Tissaphernes, now that you have demanded that those cities bow to your suzerainty. Besides that, conditions in Egypt require that we send back an army to secure the region. What, then, should we do about the Greeks?"

Only silence followed the Great King's question. I assumed the general would have been ready with an answer. Perhaps he wasn't because his personal interest in returning to his satrapy and the pleasures of power that came with his position, now enhanced by having been granted all of Cyrus' domain as well as his own, conflicted with the Great King's interest in having him scourge the Greek plague.

At last a voice was heard. It was Aspasia, whose tranquil face softened even the hide-hard heart of this grizzled general.

"Kill the head and the body will destroy itself," she said, the words a jarring mismatch with their source.

"Good plan, Aspasia," said the Great King. "Now tell us how to achieve it."

Tissaphrenes emerged from his shell to offer an answer.

"She's right. I think it can readily be accomplished. Clearchus is eager to have me identify those within his ranks who plot against him. He has offered to bring five generals and twenty captains to meet with me if I promise to expose those who seek his ruin. I will accept this proposal. None will return to the Greek army.

The 'head,' as she put it, will have been destroyed. If we succeed in this, the army can be left to straggle homeward as best it can. Annihilation at the hands of fierce northern tribes will await the Greeks before they get close to the Black Sea. That or starvation. "

This council was not the forum for me to register my bitterness over Tissaphernes' treatment of my villages. The meeting ended. Tissaphrenes left by horse, with relays spaced along the route to speed him back to Media as fast as possible.

Not many days later, a messenger returned with news. Clearchus had delivered. Five generals and twenty captains. He allowed them to be disarmed. Tissaphernes led the generals to a separate room. The captains were detained under guard elsewhere. At a signal the generals were seized for delivery to the Great King and the captains were cut down where they stood. A triumphant Tissaphernes turned west to the coast at the head of his army, leaving the Greek "body" to self-destruct.

Within days the generals arrived at Persepolis. The Great King gave them brief audience before having them beheaded. Clearchus blurted out his terrible anger at having been duped by Tissaphernes. He claimed Greek honor would never allow the practice of such deceit on even the most despicable enemy. The Great King reminded him of the Greek horse used by Agamemnon to gain entrance to the gates of Troy and, more recently, of the lies practiced by Themistocles on the Persians under Xerxes.

"Speaking of honor, Clearchus, you are each soon to be beheaded, an event lacking in honor. Before you go, I think you will be interested in learning that the strategy Tissaphernes used to bring you here and destroy your captains was designed by Aspasia, a Greek woman with whom most of you are undoubtedly acquainted. The audience is over."

Word of the Great King's triumph over the Greek mercenaries swept through the palace, and with it the remarkable fact that he credited Aspasia with designing the winning strategy. When Stateira heard, she became mad with rage. She accosted the Great King, accusing him of having replaced her in both his heart and his head with what she called "your brother's slut." I took the measure of my son's anguish from the fact that he told me the story. She was out of control, screaming as loud as she could, even at one point flying across the room, flailing with her arms, then pounding on Artaxerxes' chest with clenched fists.

Her jealousy made Artaxerxes sad, for he thought he still loved Stateira as his wife of many years. His love had never been fired by physical attraction, but her support and counsel had bred closeness and affection. He even claimed to me that she had often provided sensible judgment on delicate matters of state, although when challenged, he couldn't recall one instance.

Now all that seemed broken. Perhaps beyond repair. He admitted that, as his reliance on Aspasia increased, his need to lean on Stateira declined. Alas, he said, her perception of a diminishing role was accurate. He didn't have a solution. Nor did I.

❧ ❧ ❧ ❧ ❧ ❧

I expected her visit. She swept past Datis as if he were a stone figure. She appeared imperious, dressed to perfection and made up with care. If her purpose was to impress me, it worked. She looked the role of a great Queen.

"Do sit down, Stateira," I said, "and have some wine."

It was early in the day for wine, but I thought it worth a try to ease her sharp edge.

She sat, but not before hovering over me to announce her purpose, a predatory bird.

"You know why I'm here. Your commitment isn't worth even one of the figs that eunuch lover of yours just put in front of us." Leaning over, she took a ripe fig and threw it hard against the wall. Somewhere, along the way, she had acquired a man's skill at throwing, including a wrist snap that propelled the fig, splashing it upon contact. I tried to ignore her provocations.

"I told you I spoke to Artaxerxes. And that he accepted my advice. It's only a matter of the timing." I poured the wine. She sat but didn't drink. Talons taut, ready to pounce.

"That's not good enough. She's bewitched my husband. He's in thrall to her. She's an enemy of the Empire, a Greek worm, working from within. I've watched her; I know. I see what the Great King cannot. I want her returned to Phocaea. Now."

Her voice rose as she hurled the words at me, one by one. I thought of the fig. She stared hard, sitting up straight, back arched, breasts sharply etched by a white linen bodice kept tight by a wide pale green belt cinched around her body. A full-throated imperious Queen.

I took up my cup of wine. "Try this," I urged, taking a long slow sip. "I will speak directly. Your solution doesn't appeal to me. Though born a Greek, in the eyes of Achaemenids she's one of us. She has served each of my sons with intelligent devotion and a kindness rarely found in one endowed with such physical beauty. In good time she will serve the Empire as priestess to Diana of Ecbatana. There are few among us her equal. Aspasia will remain here as long as she lives."

I lowered my voice, uttering the words slowly. It helped to control my anger, which I could feel in my chest, pressing to be heard.

"So be it. If you won't help me send her off, I will find another solution. We differ, you and I, about the influence she wields over the Great King. You think it's beneficial. I think it's deadly. As his wife, I have the right to protect him from danger, to save him from himself, even from you if necessary. As Queen, not just the right, but the duty."

She rose, turned on her heels and walked rapidly to the door. Before leaving, she twisted her head around to shoot me another imperious glance. "If you should decide to help, you know where to find me."

Stateira was 24 years old; she'd been Queen for four years. I was two decades older. At her age I'd been Queen for almost as long. Had I been like that? I can't recall feeling jealous. Ever. He had his concubines; I had Datis. We met in bed out of duty to the line. Neither of us was physically possessive of the other. As King, Darius treated me as a confidante. In fact I was his closest adviser. On matters of state, I usually had my way with him. I never felt threatened by others.

Stateira was losing Artaxerxes two ways, and in both the cause was Aspasia. That was her problem, and given her nature, it was enormous. I understood but could not find a place in my heart for forgiveness. In truth, as I thought over her visit, it became clear to me that in seeking to remove Aspasia, she posed the greatest risk to her husband. Consumed by the canker of power, she was driven to preserve power for herself. Even with my instinct for skepticism, however, I didn't imagine the lengths to which she was prepared to go.

❧ ❧ ❧ ❧ ❧ ❧

Several weeks after her visit, Noah summoned me to the beeyard for what he told Datis was an urgent visit. It was a fine spring morning when I entered his domain, past the weathering statue of Priapus to search for him among the hives, which were alive with the comings and goings of worker bees newly imbued with the spirit of their shared purpose. I found him peering into a smoke-filled hive in search of its queen. Just after I spoke his name, he announced success, beckoning me with his arm, without taking his eye off the scene. "Here, Parysatis, you'll want to see this."

Noah had thoroughly subdued the bees, making my approach without covering not particularly risky. I looked into the hive as Noah explained what to look for. Under his guidance, I caught sight of last year's queen systematically opening a queen cell and killing the incipient queen in her pupa stage, just before she was due to emerge by eating through the cell cap.

"Watch, she's opening the third cell. Three more to go. Considering her age, she's perky. Going about her business with energy."

"Years ago you showed me this ritual. I've never forgotten. Is it just instinct, or does she have some awareness; does she know?"

"I'd have to be a queen to answer that. I think there's something beyond instinct, call it judgment if you like, or life force. When a queen is too old to preside, she'll just vacate the hive, sometimes escorted out by workers. How does she know, why does she chose to give up the hive to an unborn queen rather than destroy that queen's cell? It's part of the hive's glorious spirit, which informs every aspect of life among the 40,000 or so occupants, a life of service, adaptation, and sacrifice in the present to assure the future."

We watched until the queen had finished her work, a matter of minutes. Then we walked to Udusana's burial site and sat.

"Here's why I asked you here. An acquaintance of mine is an attendant to the Queen. She asked a favor of me yesterday. She wanted me to get her a quantity of leaves and roots of aconite, the beautiful deep blue flower I grow here in abundance. You know the one. I asked her why, and..." I cut him off.

"Acquaintance? Come, now, Noah. I know this woman. 'The rapturous Timosa' as she's known. Palace gossip holds that, when she's not serving Stateira, she's with you, for what purpose no one knows."

I had never spoken to Noah of love before. But all within the palace inhaled the same aura of mystery about this man, who was kept young by his bees, unmarried except to them, and at 68 years old, seemingly able to hold the attention of this young and attractive servant to the Queen. Timosa was known to her peers to be ferociously loyal to Stateira and secretive about her service. Timosa had been a noted courtesan in Egypt until she was sent by the Egyptian King as a present to Stateira.

"I don't intend to recount how I got her to explain. Suffice it to say I did. As you will recall from childhood, the only purpose in gathering leaves and roots of aconite is to make aconitine, queen of poisons. She admitted to this, but told me not to worry. The poison is intended for an enemy, a Greek. There are few secrets within the palace. Aspasia's many roles reached the beeyard long ago, as did the story of your efforts to protect her. I fear she is this 'Greek enemy.' I had to pass along this story."

His face bore the marks of stress, something new to me, even though I had studied him closely over many years. Receiving this information must have produced some lines in my face as well. I shuddered.

"Two questions: Did you give her what she sought? Second, is it possible she will disclose what she told you to the Queen?"

"Yes and no. For the first, I had no choice but to respond, as not to do so would have endangered her for having disclosed the purpose behind her request. For the second, I'm sure you can see that her life depends on keeping that conversation a secret."

"Noah, I will be sending my attendant, Gigis, to see you. I think you know her, the one who would have been a great Magus had she been born a male. In the same spirit that caused you to send for me today, give her what she seeks."

I rose and started to walk towards the gate. He quickly joined me, putting his arm firmly around my waist. We spoke no more, the silence a testament to all that we shared.

Returning to my chambers, I summoned Datis. Talking a difficult issue through with him seemed to help me resolve it. He was not the quickest, smartest, or wisest man in the palace. He was just a careful and patient listener who had the ability to ask the right questions, to make certain that everything relevant to a decision was before me. From more than one painful experience, I knew that, acting alone, I often didn't get there.

After briefing him, I said, "So Datis, what's the right thing, the smart thing, to do?"

"Not necessarily the same. Let's put all options on the table. Your goal comes first."

"That's easy. To protect Aspasia from harm." He searched me, looking for more.

"All right. Without sending her out of the Empire. Here are the possible measures: Get the Great King to consecrate her a priestess now. Talk Stateira out of this malevolence. Tell the story to the Great King and get him to intervene." I saw that Datis was, again, searching for more. I issued a soft laugh because, of course, there was another option that I had quite deliberately withheld.

"I could render Stateira incapable of executing her plan. Is that what you're waiting for?" He nodded.

"There are variations to each of these ideas," Datis added. "For example, there are many ways the Great King could protect Aspasia. How do you see it now."

I stared out the window, my left hand fingering a certain curl that covered my ear. Again and again. This was a habit I had first developed in childhood when alone and summoned to hard thinking. As I aged, the habit deepened. I fell prey unconsciously, even in the company of others.

"Essentially two of the four involve getting the Great King to do something. I'm afraid he's not going to send her to Diana any time soon, precisely for the reasons that have brought Stateira to the brink."

Datis nodded.

"So I'd have to tell him what his wife is about. Here's the danger. He can be very soft in dealing with people close to him. By telling, I turn over the problem, and with it the solution, to him. If his approach isn't good enough, we'll awake some morning to find Aspasia dead."

"That leaves trying to deal with it yourself. What could you say to turn her?"

"Not much. Perhaps mention the old idea of destroying one's life in an effort to save it. Perhaps point out that the passage of time will leech away from her heart the barnacles that now afflict her as surely as it allows the tide to rise and fall and rise again. I can try without disclosing anything to the Great King. I can judge the results. And, if unsuccessful, I can pursue a different way."

"You should be prepared. We don't know Stateira's schedule. Time works against you."

The next day I set Gigis to work on the aconite she had brought from Noah. I also sent Datis to Stateira to invite her to dinner the following night.

She came. From the outset, our conversation focused on Aspasia. Stateira was no less upset than she had been at our last meeting. I tried every argument I could think of to dissuade her from the compulsion, as she put it, "to do something." In begging me, again, to join her project, she dropped the personal to emphasize the needs of the Empire, a theme she had told her husband was my conceit.

I found her somewhat less hostile than before, but highly suspicious. When I poured wine from two jugs, using one for myself, just to finish it up, and the other for her, she objected, claiming an old superstition had always prompted her to share everything offered with her hostess.

"I know it's silly, and you mustn't take offense, but it's the rule I live by."

213

I poured half of my cup into hers and then filled them both from the other jug. This incident set the standard for treating each item served. Later I realized I had never hosted a meal for her before. Whether her rule was newly developed out of suspicion or long rooted in ancient superstition I couldn't tell.

Later, in the middle of a sentence, she stopped to sniff, obviously alarmed.

"There's an odor here I don't recognize. What is it?" she demanded. "Where is it coming from?"

"Oh, I hoped you'd notice. See those large bowls on the table over there," I said, pointing with my hand. "They are made from the scented woods of Ophir. I had ordered them long ago. They just came this week. Nice, don't you think?"

Without commenting, she picked up exactly where she had left off. Wooden objects held little interest. It was taste and smell that mattered. We concluded the evening with each promising to consider all that the other had said. She would return a week hence.

The days passed swiftly. Datis tried to speak to Timosa. To no avail. I sent him to see Noah in hopes of discovering what Stateira was doing. Something was amiss, Noah informed us. Timosa had not responded to him for over a week. When he last was with her, in the beeyard, it was to cut fresh aconite, which she had carried off.

Stateira was, again, superbly made up and attired when she arrived at my door. I'd never seen her looking better. She swept into my chambers, exultant. I remarked on this. She credited the weather, bright sun, cooling zephyrs. When I looked askance, she croaked about her winning game at dice against the Great King himself, over the midday meal.

"That's worthy of a toast," I said, handing her a cup of wine and taking up my own from the table.

She laughed loudly, handing me her cup. "How easily you forget my eccentricity. Honor me by sharing."

My ears must have reddened, for I felt the heat of embarrassment. "Of course. How foolish." I divided the wine and we resumed the toast. "I'm delighted you spent some happy time with your husband."

We sat, eyeing each other while sipping wine, two suspicious lionesses bent on dominance. We began to consume, with carefully monitored mutuality, the various condiments that had been set before us. I repeatedly introduced the subject of Aspasia. As often, she rebuffed me, shrugging off the subject as a duck repels water. She wanted to discuss the campaign in Egypt, the looming dangers from the city of Sparta, the problems facing Tissaphernes, even the condition of the Great King's harem, anything it seemed but Aspasia. I became uneasy.

At first I took this to be a signal that her alarm had grown so large that she couldn't face the subject at all. Slowly I dropped that reading of the situation in favor of one more frightening: she had finished with Aspasia. How could that be I wondered? Could she have put plans in motion to erase the problem? The more I considered the facts, the more convinced I became. Either it was too late, or there was little, if any, time left.

On the way to the dining room, I excused myself. Finding Datis, I sent him to find Aspasia alive, to warn her of the possibility of poison, to trust no one, to avoid any food or drink not tested first by others. Finding Gigis, I ordered that she implement our contingent plan, which would serve, whatever had brought my guest to her present state of mind. Only a matter of minutes, and I was back at table with Stateira.

"I hope you're hungry, for my kitchen labored long today to produce this dinner. Come," I said, beckoning to the attendants, "serve us."

They brought in bread piled high on a silver platter, bowls of candied capers and turnips, sweet grape jelly and radishes prepared with salt. Small bowls were presented to each of us with raisins piled high. We each had a large silver plate from which to eat and a goblet of gold for wine. A silver-handled iron knife and silver duck-headed spoon completed the table setting. An attendant brought in a silver tray on which a small well-roasted guinea hen sat, surrounded by spiced quince and pear. The air became infused with the complex aroma emanating from this bird, just taken from the oven. It would be our meat course. Stateira commented. I answered, identifying oils of saffron, terebinth, and pomegranate.

My guest invoked her rule to cause a rearrangement of the raisins, the only item served in individual dishes. "I know you'll forgive me this silly indulgence," she said. "Nothing personal, believe me."

One attendant divided each portion of raisins in half and exchanged those halves. Two of them proceeded to serve us from the bowls. Carefully, in equal measure. Then one handed me a large knife.

"I like to do the carving at table." Holding the hen with a three pronged serving fork, I cut it down the middle from head to tail. The well cooked bird easily yielded to the sharp blade, falling away to either side in two nearly equal portions. Putting the knife to the side, I used the fork to take the slightly smaller half to my own plate first; then served the other half to Stateira.

"To your health," Stateira said, raising her goblet. I responded in kind. We began. She was hungry, or so it seemed considering the speed with which she consumed the turnips and guinea hen. Within minutes she pronounced her throat parched. An attendant brought water. It didn't help. She described a burning sensation, extending from throat to stomach. From this she said her whole body was tingling, then that her arms and legs felt as if they were being flayed.

Not that you've ever been flayed, I thought.

"My vision is dimming," she said. Then, she let forth a long scream, unnatural, contorted, and altogether hideous.

"You've poisoned me. I must get help."

She tried to stand. Her legs failed to respond. I watched as she tried to speak. Without success. Her facial muscles twitched. She turned white. Convulsions followed. And then her system for breathing collapsed. In less than fifteen minutes, it was over.

Datis had the idea of smearing aconite paste on one side of the carving knife. Gigis made the paste. Only those two knew directly how Stateira met her death. Noah knew by inference. I would protect them all, with my life if necessary.

❧ ❧ ❧ ❧ ❧ ❧

If not quite commonplace, poisoning was a frequent occurrence in the Empire, especially among the upper classes. So easy was it to accomplish, and so horrible the death, that a particular punishment had been assigned to those found guilty. Within the palace grounds there was a large flat stone on which the poisoner's head was placed. The executioner then used another stone, large yet capable of being handled, to crush the poisoner's head and, with repeated blows, pound it to pieces. I didn't expect my son to inflict this punishment upon his mother. Datis thought me reckless of my own welfare when I refused even to consider a defense.

Soon after the Queen's attendants took away her body, the Great King summoned me. He looked more alarmed than severe, more my grown-up child than my King. We sat facing one another across an alabaster table bare of condiments or wine.

He looked at me through sheep's eyes, heavy with sadness. He waited. I wanted him to start. Finally, he did.

"Even the crown can make a mistake. May the Gods protect me from one as serious as what you have allowed to happen under your roof. Who's responsible? Datis was involved, no doubt. They must all be punished."

"My son, please listen carefully. No one helped me. No one knew. The initiative was mine alone, as was the execution. Other than me, there's no one to punish."

"Oh, mother, pitiless heart of a mother. I can't accept this. You put me in an impossible position. What do I say? 'With cunning and aconite, the Queen Mother took the life of the Queen, my wife. She admits to the crime. The King grieves for his fallen mate but reminds his people that time cures all. He will recover. In the meantime he will forgive his mother and direct his people to do likewise.' No. I need victims."

"What I did was no mistake. Not yesterday. Not today. What's more, it won't be viewed that way tomorrow or next year. It will be seen as it was, as I saw it, an awful deed done because it had to be done. Do you think for an instant that my dislike for your wife caused me to kill her? My feelings have changed little from the time, many years ago, when I intervened to save her life. Hear me. Listen carefully, for this is the crux of it. Your wife was going to kill Aspasia. Within hours of my taking her life. Ironically, she planned to use the same poison on Aspasia as I used on her. Fortune called and I acted. To save Aspasia's life; to protect your reputation and that of our family. I deserve no prize. In truth, as the eldest in our line, I acted in self-defense, although not everyone beyond this room would be capable of understanding that."

Artaxerxes pressed me on Stateira's intentions. He knew she had lost control but couldn't imagine her desperate enough to do such a thing. "She's not the brave one, you know," he said, with a nervous chuckle. He looked fatigued. Lines of sweat followed the creases of his robe. His face was wet. Perspiration pearled above his upper lip. Despite ample use of royal powders, he stank. A look of resigned acceptance formed across his face.

"I'm beginning to understand some of this." Summoning an attendant, he ordered wine. "Still, we know of no more heinous crime. You preach protection of our family, the Empire. Now, I'm the one who needs protection. You must sacrifice someone."

"I'm not prepared to do that. If you must have a victim, take me. Let me remind you, though, that the last time I killed within the clan, it was Sogdianus, a predecessor of yours. Darius and I didn't apologize. We offered no sacrifice, nor was any sought by others."

"There are differences. They are large. Don't pretend you can't see them," his voice rising. Then, soft, imploring, "Let's not fight over this. Please. I need a plan."

He was right. I had pushed him too far, bent on winning the argument, protecting my own at any cost, challenging him, almost mockingly, to stone me to death. Tears had joined the sweat around his eyes, brimming over to run down his cheeks.

"Here's what you can do. Publicly identify me as the poisoner. Declare I acted alone. Explain my motive. Banish me to Babylon. I will gladly live in the palace there for so long as it takes for wounds to heal and public acceptance of our reconciliation to become assured."

"That will serve. Mother, you keep surprising me."

A minute earlier, seeing no way out, the Great King had been a spent man, exhausted and forlorn. Now, through the magic of hope, the prospect of a solution, however difficult, a metamorphosis occurred, invigorating him with optimism and energy.

He filled two goblets, handing me one. "I will also announce that I will not visit Babylon so long as you are there. I salute your idea."

Our goblets touched. His smile was relaxed and confident, expressing not just his own feelings but mine as well.

❡ ❡ ❡ ❡ ❡

In the 156th year of the Achaemenid Empire, I turned 50. One and a half years had passed since my banishment to Babylon. Although couriers kept me in touch with my son and developments across the Empire, I was not able to participate in matters of state.

There was ample time for reflection. Especially about my son's accusation: "Oh, pitiless heart of a mother." Was my heart pitiless? I couldn't toss off this characterization, which had tunneled into my mind, to rest by day and stalk my thoughts by night. I was endowed, as most humans are, with power both to create life and destroy it. I was born to the purple and, therefore, laden with duties in the exercise of these endowments.

From my Babylonian perch in exile, I fashioned what at the time seemed to be a watertight argument to justify my acts. Being challenged only by myself, I waded deep into duty's currents, immersing myself in its rips and eddies until soaked in self-righteousness.

I well knew that during my years as Queen, with Darius on the throne, palace chatter called me "the woman in charge." In fact we were a team. Strong-willed Queens, like Atossa and Amestris, were encased in an aura of heartless invincibility, just because they were strong-willed partners of the King. I am victim of the same simplistic reputation, which had even seeped into the mind of my son.

Except for one childish experiment, I had never been cruel to living things either wantonly or for pleasure or personal advantage. Torturing? Killing or causing to be killed? Yes, several times, but only, I told myself time and again, to serve the Empire. Sogdianus, because he was a tyrant who had killed two Kings and a Queen. Masabates, because he mutilated the body of a prince, my son Cyrus. As for Mithridates and the Carian who each claimed to have killed Cyrus, yes, I helped design hideous public tortures, but only to serve as deterrent. And finally, Stateira, for reasons I've made clear.

I argued to myself that there's nothing inherently evil or even inhuman in taking a life. When Darius and Xerxes led their armies against Athens, when Athens invaded Sicily, when Sparta and Athens set out to destroy one another, countless lives were going to be taken, a certainty known to those in command of those campaigns. Yet, never had I heard those leaders described as evil, inhuman, or pitiless. Does it matter if death comes by stealth, through the use of poison?

For me, the crux of the matter was not how it was done but why. Killing one or more for a worthy cause was justifiable. Killing for unworthy reasons was not. What's worthy remained a matter of judgment, to be weighed over and over again through the course of history, often with different outcomes.

In the midst of my restless Babylonian nights, I could easily convince myself that I did not remove wings from butterflies. With equal facility I could wallow in the all-encompassing sense of royal duty. However, I could not entirely shake off the charge that Artaxerxes had leveled against me. I didn't sleep well until I was able to turn my defensiveness into a shield by the sudden insight that a truly pitiless heart feels not even an inkling of guilt.

If exile afforded time to reflect, it was but a blink of an eye compared to time spent in the region of the Shades. And, yet, even now, were I to speak truth, as I've tried to do in proving the Greeks' accounts false, I could not easily rest my case on duty alone. What I've learned is how flickering truth is, how hard to pin down. Motives layer one on top of another, each affecting the others in ways too deep to plumb. Having returned to fight the Greeks, I see now that this battle is easily won but gives way to a far more difficult battle to close the gap between my life as I saw it from day to living day and my life as I now perceive it.

If my heart was not pitiless as some claimed, I now realize it lacked that measure of kindness that made Noah and Aspasia, each in his or her own way, such remarkable human beings.

❧ ❧ ❧ ❧ ❧ ❧

My staff and I found much to do in the villages I owned in Babylonia. So much that I marveled at how well they seemed to have survived, indeed, flourished, over the decades when I had almost nothing to do with them except pay my overseers and answer infrequently-posed questions. I would never know the amount of revenue that slipped through my careless fingers into someone else's well-placed hands.

I believe in the deep corruptibility of humankind. It's bad enough for those in responsible positions serving the Empire to give way to corruption, a common occurrence in Persia. It becomes tragic when mendacity and greatness coexist in a single human being. This, too, is all too common.

Take a simple virtue like honesty. It's a relative value, honored in varying degrees by different actors on the human stage. If one discards the thorough-going saints and sinners at either end of the spectrum, the practice of honesty becomes an act of self-interest. It will cease the instant its weight on the scales of self-interest is exceeded by that of dishonesty. Reputation being a weight all its own, one's self-interest tends to be served by honesty so long as one's actions are observable by others. Stated differently, when the risk of being caught in a dishonest act is high, one tends towards honesty. The converse is also true. What makes it hard to judge in individual cases is the fact that every human being weighs the value of reputation differently.

I tried to evaluate my overseers for honesty and thought I had picked well. They assured me they would maximize my revenue and act solely in my best interests. I now realize it was naïve to think they would be true to their word. Without close monitoring, I had no way to detect cheating, and they had no fear of detection.

❧ ❧ ❧ ❧ ❧ ❧

I hadn't seen Aspasia since leaving Persepolis. I often heard of her continuing importance as adviser to my son. I also heard that her role as the source of physical comfort to him had ceased even before I was banished. Visualizing her one day made me realize how much I missed her. As my birthday approached, I wrote a letter to Aspasia, inviting her to represent the palace at this celebration. For the first time in what seemed years, I used the elegant queen-bee seal that Andia had given me to authenticate my signature. I had put it away when, upon Artaxerxes' accession, I ceased to be the Queen. Symbolic gesture, I suppose. No one had asked me to do it or even noticed. With Stateira gone, I would resume using it.

Datis and his staff were in charge of the celebration, which I decided to make a public affair, inviting several hundred royals resident in Babylon and the environs. Datis consulted me on every detail.

Day by day, as the event came closer, I grew increasingly morose. Looking at myself in the mirror as the last day of my fifth decade grew near, I saw only the remains of what beauty I had possessed, the remnants of a face formerly fetching. How had I become thus? My daily routine involved making myself up before a mirror. Could years pass without my seeing what was there to see? In spring, the daily swelling of a pear tree's winter bud is impossible to miss. The blind eye works best when turned on one's self.

Awareness arrived with a rush, like a desert storm, tearing off the mask that for so long had blinded me to the true effects of aging. Turning 50 was the catalyst, concentrating my mind, forcing my eyes to accept the truth.

I didn't hate myself or indulge in self-pity. Acceptance brought sadness and doubt. At 50, what was there to celebrate? My interest in the remembered delights of bedding down with Datis had waned. At first, it had been lust. In time that gave way to desire, a happy platform for devising many routes to satisfaction. Of late, even desire has vanished. In its place, alas, has come those mysterious physical changes known to all women who survive to their sixth decade. I ceased to have my monthly period. At the same time I became afflicted with heat, particularly at night. Emanating from no identifiable source, tumultuous heat suffused my body, creating a desire to remove all that touched my skin, sheets, clothing, hair, everything. I would often awaken in the middle of the night drenched in sweat.

The heat would recede as mysteriously as it advanced, lasting no more than five minutes but in perception much longer. Sometimes these hot waves or pulses would attack during the day, when I was in the company of others. I would feel my face flush with heat and know it had become noticeably red. Embarrassment would follow as the heat spread across my skin and penetrated deep within me. It demanded release, a route of escape. Driven to find a way to eliminate my clothing, I would flee the room.

Lack of sleep made me grumpy. Lack of desire made me sad and kept Datis wondering. At some point, I realized that as my interest in lovemaking declined, his grew, although he never whispered a word.

In the end, Datis overcame what, on analysis, proved to be a simple case of self-pity. I had spent a lifetime searching it out in others and despising them for what I considered the ultimate indulgence. Practiced scorn made it hard to realize the disease had infected me. He lifted me out of the miasma by playing on the joy I found in good food, a desire undimmed by age. He drew me into his plans for the celebratory feast. He promised my favorites: a sublime marmalade of fresh figs steeped in honey; roasted lamb and goat, marinated in olive oil, garlic, and pomegranate concentrate; and mersum, a God-like porridge combining dates, sesame oil, terebinth, garlic, and coriander. He offered to perfume the wine and beer with myrtle and scented reed. And, considering the season, he proposed a specialty of Babylonia, fresh locusts, fried in oil after removal of legs and wings. There would, of course, be fish: carp, crawfish, and eel.

"It's still the season for fruit, Datis. We must have plenty."

"Pretty late here, actually. I've made arrangements with merchants from the north who come by boat, sailing down the Euphrates and Tigris. They're still bringing ripe fruit to market. We'll have enough."

"And spices? The young can get along without them, but when one reaches my age, they become necessities. Cumin, saffron, terebinth oil, our bakers and cooks must use them all."

My enthusiasm for the party ebbed and flowed with the approach of March 21st. After word came that Aspasia had accepted my invitation to represent the palace at Persepolis, I turned joyful and stayed that way well past the event. We ransacked Babylon to assemble the finest platters, bowls, flagons, goblets, cups, and other tableware, and the most luxurious and ornate furniture within reach. I knew we couldn't approximate the magnificence of Persepolis, but all that could be done, Datis assured me, he would do.

In the end, the treasure on display in the reception hall and dining room was all that even my son, the King of Kings, could have wished for. As befitted this sumptuous celebration, everyone, myself included, dressed in their finest evening clothes and had painted and perfumed themselves to excess, as if this were their last chance for display. Not quite. True to her beginnings with Cyrus, Aspasia stood out for beauty of face ungilded, elegance of dress sparsely adorned. She lacked the accouterments that the rest of us, indistinguishable within the crowd, considered vital.

When the celebration ended, Aspasia whispered that she had brought a birthday gift from Artaxerxes that, for obvious reasons, could not be presented in public. She had promised the Great King to deliver it on his mother's birthday. Would Parysatis receive her in chambers?

It was close to midnight when Aspasia arrived at my door carrying a tightly woven cloth sack of varying shades of red, with embroidered bands of lotus and bud in blue, alternating with honey bees in gold. The sack was cinched at the top with wool thread of red and blue strands, braided with strands of gold. We sat beside one another on my couch. I admired the design and artwork.

"He was determined that I place this in your hands. I think he conceived the whole idea many months ago and commissioned artists to complete the work in time. Have a look."

I opened the sack and removed the object, a gold rhyton. They are normally made of silver. I had never seen its like before. It was horn-shaped, terminating in the foreparts of a winged lioness. Just beneath the ample rim of the vessel was a frieze of lotus, bud, and bee, reflective of the sack's design. The lion's head extended more than half-way up the length of the horn. There was no pouring hole. Wine or mead would be drunk from the horn's wide rim.

"How it glows in the candlelight. A gift fit for the Gods. Shall we give it a try? There's good wine over there." I fetched the jug and poured its contents into the rhyton, then offered it to Aspasia. She shook her head, pointing to me. One hand on the horn, the other tucked under the beast's chin, I raised the vessel to my lips and drank. The wine was undiluted. It was not the first taste of the grape I'd enjoyed that evening. I handed the rhyton to Aspasia and watched her drink.

"Was that a philter you gave me? I feel a surge of warmth."

"I feel it too. But, my dear Aspasia, I need no potion to love you. As I have from the day I watched you at Cyrus' service. As I do now."

"The seal you used on your letter to me. Two large bees facing one another. I've never seen anything similar. Are they about to attack?"

"Queen bees. I prefer to think they find each other attractive."

In silence we passed the Great King's gift back and forth until it was empty. Our hands touched with each exchange, the contact lasting longer each time, as if controlled by a force beyond ourselves. I rose and put the jug back on the table, and with it the rhyton. Without a sound, Aspasia followed me and, when I turned to face the couch, she wrapped me in her snowy arms, pressing her body hard against mine, as if trying to still the slight trembling that I felt at first touch. For a long time she held me tight. Then, unconsciously, we swapped roles, just as we had exchanged the rhyton, her body relaxing in my firm grip.

"Are you wearing frankincense?" she asked, her voice a whisper at my ear. She gave me the soft radiance of her eyes. "It works."

I felt desire. It coursed through my body, mocking the pulse of heat that over the past year and more had all but replaced it. Was this real, I wondered? Would it last?

Later that night, just before falling asleep, I had a bittersweet moment, recalling my first experience with desire, shared with my friend, Udusana.

❧ ❧ ❧ ❧ ❧ ❧

In September of my 50th year, the Great King made public the tightly scripted text of a message sent to Babylon, forgiving his mother and recalling her to Persepolis. By intention, news of this reconciliation circulated widely, gaining approval.

My son had been heavily engaged in matters of state during my absence, as I discovered upon homecoming. His western ambition extended not only to the Aegean coastal cities, over which he sought to regain control from the Greeks, but to all the islands graced by those bright blue waters. The point of his lance was Tissaphernes, so serious a threat to Sparta that its King, Agesilaus, had been sent to the east coast of the Aegean at the head of a 12,000-man expeditionary force. Occupying Ephesus that spring, his mission was to assure the autonomy of coastal cities. After a brief truce, agreed to by Tissaphernes to allow the gathering of his own forces, the opposing armies clashed near Dascylium on the south coast of the Bosporus. Tissaphernes carried the battle to Agesilaus, led by a vibrant trumpet that sang defiance, bloodshed, and defeat. The result was indecisive. Agesilaus returned to Ephesus, turning this city of culture into a workshop of war.

Tissaphernes again informed the Spartan leader of the Great King's demand that the coastal cities retain their independence and render him the ancient tribute of earth and water. With spring came a battle on the banks of the Pactolus River near Sardis. The Spartans were victorious. The Persian leaders in Sardis, who witnessed the event, indicted Tissaphernes for gross failures of leadership. Upon reviewing the record, Artaxerxes condemned his principal general to death, a painful decision given the long service rendered by Tissaphernes and the Great King's belief that he had been steadfast in loyalty. Swift execution by beheading ensued and Tissaphernes' abundant possessions were confiscated to provide funds with which to pay his soldiers.

I had known nothing of these matters. To my surprise, I heard through palace gossip that I was credited by some, and criticized by others, for having been instrumental in persuading the Great King to destroy his favorite general. This sort of calumny, along with many others, was so devoid of weighty fact that it could be carried by the east wind to the coast and beyond, across the Aegean to settle in the vacant minds of Greek historians.

I confess that news of the general's downfall was pure pleasure. His lust for fame was robust, an outsized phenomenon. His betrayal of Cyrus had stuck in my throat.

About the time of my return to Persepolis, the Great King was pressing his advantage among the islands through the efforts of Pharnabazus and the brilliant Athenian admiral, Conon. Together they drove the Spartans from the islands of Cos and Nisyros, and later from Cythera and the Cyclades, as well as the coastal cities of Ephesus and Erythrae.

We learned from Pharnabazus that the Spartan King had tempted him, offering support if he would declare himself independent of the Great King. Watching this general dramatize the attempted "seduction," as he called the Spartan King's blandishments, keeping us dangling in suspense until the end, I saw the extent to which a warrior, to be great, must be a great actor. Before the curtain opened we knew he would remain loyal. How else to account for his presence? And, yet, his tale compelled us to abandon that logic. He made it seem as if, in service to the Great King, he had survived the most hideous torture of Greek devising.

Atossa and Amestris were great warriors too, and as such, had proved themselves accomplished actors on the royal stage. I, too, knew something about role-playing and used it with skill. Looking back, I now find it hard to distinguish between reality and performance.

The truth of the matter could be found in my son's calculated promise to

Pharnabazus, made several years earlier, to give him a daughter in marriage. Watching Artaxerxes as he listened to the general's elaborate story of resisting the irresistible, and observing the general as well, I could see that the daughter's hand (exactly which daughter wasn't clear nor was it clarified) became a grip tight enough to hold the general's loyalty in place. Perhaps the Great King hadn't really expected to honor this promise of years past, but by the meeting's end it was obvious he would have to, and that gladly.

❧ ❧ ❧ ❧ ❧

Following my return to Persepolis, Aspasia and I were together more than apart. Although she had produced no offspring who could claim the Achaemenid line, in fact no offspring at all, I considered her part of our family. With each of my sons, and now with me, she had come in kindness and with quiet wisdom to undertake the task of providing whatever was needed to make us whole. A volunteer, doing her part as if assigned by an unseen guardian. If I was mother to the Achaemenid line, she was its wet nurse.

How much the palace knew of my relationship with Aspasia didn't concern us. That we were close friends, even intimate ones, was obvious to any observer. What we did in my chambers we assumed was known only to us. A not unreasonable belief, given the observed value of privacy among royals and the dire consequences of leakage by servants. Of course, all within the palace were free to imagine, even to conjure, so long as they didn't turn thoughts into gossip. Among humankind, experience teaches, the practice of this mundane sin is as unstoppable as envy, greed, or theft. But the palace set a very high price on those caught out, replacing whatever good reputation there was with that of a public liar. Nice touch, since, true or not, tales told by palace gossips were tainted and suspect.

Throughout his reign, with my support, Darius had sharply distinguished between morals and decency. Artaxerxes had continued the practice. Morals were matters to be settled by private agreement among those involved. Decency was a matter of public concern. Thus, whatever one did with whomever in the privacy of one's home was beyond the bounds of public rule-making or gossip. What one did in public, on the other hand, affecting as it must the beliefs, sensitivities, and attitudes of others, called for ordering to serve the public interest. In practice, this meant rules reflecting the Great King's sense of decency.

For the first year and a half after my return, I experienced renewed purpose, both in my public life as Queen Mother to an unmarried King who relied on me, and in my private life with Aspasia. Sometime in the summer of the 158th year of Achaemenid rule, Artaxerxes summoned me for a private meeting. It was a dark morning, overcast with hurrying clouds driven by huge winds blowing erratically down from the mountains far to the north. The air was moist with humidity and filled with the threat of driving rain to come. But for his call, I wouldn't have ventured out.

When we met, I could see, as could any mother of her son, that he was agitated. I decided to play offense, my normal reaction.

"Artaxerxes, you look uncomfortable, as if you have an awkward duty to perform. If you want my approval of your love for your daughter, you need only ask. I'm not alone in knowing you're smitten by the young Atossa and how hard you've tried to conceal it. And to check your passion. But, alas, it peeks out from the shadows. Word passes like wind through the palms. The Greeks frown on this sort of thing. I know that's what disturbs you. Superstitions, that's all. Among animals, strength comes from preserving the line. Honeybees recreate themselves within each hive. I'm sure you recall that your daughter's namesake, the first and mighty Atossa, Cyrus' daughter, wed both of her brothers, one after the other.

"Atossa's a noble beauty, a daughter of virtue and majestic bearing. Why permit her to marry outside the family if there's good reason to keep her with us. Looking at her hips, I'd say she'll prove fecund. If you're not thinking of marriage, you should be. My blessing's there when you want it."

Sadly, I could see in his flickering dark eyes tht my generous outburst did nothing to relieve the anxiety.

"You surprise me with this. We will pursue it later. I asked you here because of rumors. Ugly rumors about you and Aspasia. Do you know what I mean?"

I shook my head, trying to appear as I felt, open and quizzical. What rumors could there be that would call for an audience? Among Achaemenid royals, sexual mores were flexible, taboos unknown. The extent of my relationship with Aspasia, if uncovered, would carry little shock value. I had no reason to be defensive.

"The story being circulated, by whom I haven't discovered, is that long ago, before Stateira's death, you used magic potions and spells to bewitch Aspasia, turning her away from me to become your love slave, that you killed Stateira not, as you had me proclaim, to protect my reputation and our family's honor, but to preserve your ability to misuse Aspasia, and that in all this you were aided by your obscure beekeeping friend, Noah."

The wind whined and howled outside, pelting sand against the palace walls.

227

The Great King had prepared carefully. He had raised his voice to be sure I couldn't miss what he was saying. He spoke with solemnity and sadness, laying out the case against me as if it were the final argument in a rhetoric contest. I sensed he believed every word. Absurdly, I remembered my husband's favorite expression, "the winds of destiny are either with us or against us."

"If there's anything more dangerous than falsity, I can't imagine it. Combined with the power of a ruler, it's a sure path to heart-wrenching tragedy. This fantasy of yours disturbs me. Perhaps it's the weather, but I'm feeling worn down. I've lived a long time. Enough to experience the power of lies to change lives. Enough to have learned the lessons of others: The great horse packed with Greeks, their parting gift to Priam, bringing down his realm; the message from Themistocles to Xerxes, causing the catastrophic defeat of our navy in the Bay of Salamis; the soothsayers' divination regarding the moon's eclipse at Syracuse, denying the Athenians the escape planned for that night, sowing seeds of utter destruction. Whether a product of deliberate lies or reckless claims, the result is the same. Of all those who know Aspasia, you are the least likely to think ill of her or imagine her doing anything she doesn't chose to do. As for Noah, he's blameless. And, need I say it, I'm no witch. What more can I tell you?"

"If the story's false, who's responsible?"

"I have enemies. More than I know; more than you can imagine. Queen Mothers attract them, like flowers do bees. If she doesn't conform to what Persian women are expected to do and not do, the list of enemies grows. The great Atossa had her share, and Amestris, Xerxes' wife, had hers. Now, I have mine. I don't mind praise or blame for the things I actually do, but seldom do the rumormongers get it right. Who's responsible? If you hadn't dispatched the scarred one, Artaxares, to Egypt, I would suspect him. I have no idea."

I could see his dark eyes go soft, his mouth the shape of forgiveness. He would doubt me no more. He would question me about Aspasia not at all. Even Great Kings recognize boundaries. I dropped my eyes. Seconds later I returned my gaze, to behold my son in a more regal guise.

"The danger is we revive the poisoning story. The rumor must be nipped in the bud. Unless we can discover the source, I see only one way. What about your servants? Could they be responsible?"

"You know Datis. Loyalty unquestioned over decades. Runs the staff with a grip of iron. You could check Aspasia's people. What's the other angle?"

"In fact, I have. Carefully. I wanted to see what I could find out before meeting with you. Nothing there. A test of blood is the sure way out. The chief Magus will take your blood and Aspasia's to test in the usual way. He will then publicly declare the rumor to be false. That will be the end of it."

"Sure? What if we fail the test? My confidence in the ways of our Magi vanished long ago with their claim that your grandfather and his wife had used vipers to kill themselves."

"Have no concern. You've told the truth; the test will confirm it."

"Another issue. Humiliation. I don't want to be directed by you to submit. Aspasia and I, upon learning of this gossip, could demand the test to prove it false. I will discuss this with her. Enough for one day. I'm exhausted."

I rose. Artaxerxes rose too and took me in his arms for an extended hug. "Once we stamp out this little fire, I will take you up on that offer," he whispered.

❧ ❧ ❧ ❧ ❧

Magi were widely believed to possess supernatural powers. Like the majesty of kings and queens, infallibility among the Magi attached to the office rather than its occupant. Thus, faith in their mysterious powers survives even the most obvious human failures, those that, except for this magical sleight of hand, would have planted strong seeds of doubt long ago.

The Great King announced that Aspasia and I had demanded blood tests to challenge the rumors, now rampant throughout the palace. As he had predicted, we passed the trial, our drops of blood having risen to the surface of the Magi's bottle of fluid and remained there. What would have happened if either of our blood samples had sunk to the bottom, an apparent sign of lying, was anyone's guess. The test was unobserved. We were sure the Magi knew well the outcome desired by Artaxerxes. Measuring the risk of failure caused us to exchange wry smiles.

The results announced by the Great King crushed the rumors, which swiftly faded away. What wasn't forgotten, at least by me, was the evil spirit that invaded my body through the Magi's incision, a cut in my right index finger that failed to heal. Within days, it had caused streaks of red from wrist to elbow. I developed a fever and collapsed into bed, where I began to be attended by the very same men whose practices had put me there.

I kept thinking how insane it had been for the Queen Mother to submit to the pretense of a test for truth, an unnecessary fiction designed to offset the equally fictional account of her motives. How ironical for her to fall prey to the reality of an illness caused by indulging a fantasy. The more I thought about the cause of my illness, the absurdity of it, the angrier I became. I sent the Magi away, asking instead that Noah come to my bedside.

I couldn't stop reliving that meeting with my son, when I agreed to be tested. As a child, I would have insisted on going back to that moment, and changing the outcome, as adults can sometimes do in dreams, when they swerve off in unwanted directions. It takes some growing up before one accepts the notion that a human command cannot redirect the tide, that bobbing along in the stream of life isn't like being in a boat on the Tigris, where you can row back upstream to pick up something you left on shore or start over in discussion with someone you left there, having mishandled it badly the first time. The stream of life carries one forward without any possibility of passing the same point twice. Working through these thoughts was painful, but the process caused my anger to ebb, leaving only the detritus of sad regret and irony by the time Noah appeared. I knew he would have a cure.

An inferno blazed within me. Combined with the extreme heat of that summer, I found the conditions unbearable. I asked to be moved to a bedroom on the ground floor that opened to a courtyard in which a fountain of water rose many feet in the air, pushed out of the mouths of playfully sculpted dolphins. In relays through night and day, two servants with large, long-handled fans kept a steady flow of water-cooled air coming into my room.

When Noah arrived, he brought honey to apply to my wound, a tiny crack in my 52 year-old hull, a crack that, as we both recognized, if not sealed, could admit enough water to sink the vessel.

"Parysatis, the bees send greeting. They've missed you. So have I. This breeze is luxurious. Let's have a peek."

"When a luxury becomes life saving, it ceases to be a luxury. Noah, you look older." I smiled at the platitudes, his and mine, substitutes for feelings too deep to utter, lest they credit the circumstances with the frisson of danger that I knew he could smell in the room.

"My dear young lady, you must remember I am 25 years your senior, an old man looking very much his age."

He took my right hand. He examined the swelling around the wound, then followed the red streaks up to the elbow and beyond to the shoulder, where the trail grew faint. He felt my skin, his eyes registering the heat. He put his head to my chest and listened to my heart. He held my wrist, seeking out my pulse, then tapped his foot in time with the beat, as if to master the rhythm. He tested the temperature of my forehead.

"I want you to promise me something. The truth. Nothing but." He nodded.

"Tell me how you feel from day to day. What's the direction? Strength, energy, fever, headache, pain. Getting better or getting worse?"

"If that's the measure, things haven't gone well. None of them. Aren't you going to feed me some honey?"

Nodding, with incongruous gentleness, given his rough clothes, leather-tough skin and craggy face, he applied honey to the wound and then poured more in a cup for me to drink.

"Could we mix in some chamomile leaves and hot water?" I asked. My appetite for solids was gone, but something held me back from telling him.

"Of course. While the water heats, I will try to answer you. The wound has let some bad things in under the skin. They are spreading through your body, which gives battle. All your strength is being thrown into the fight, which is why you feel weak on the outside. There's nothing we can do except ask the Gods for help. But in truth, the cure, if cure there be, will be found mainly within yourself."

"Here's something, Noah. The Achaemenids lack a queen. Perhaps, as you've taught me, the hive never fails for lack of a queen. The workers create one. In this Empire, it's not that simple. I have some work left to do. I'm going to be all right. But I need your help. Come often."

"It will take many visits even to begin reciprocating for yours to the beeyard. I'll start tomorrow."

❦ ❦ ❦ ❦ ❦

Noah came every day, tracking the progress of my engagement with the forces of death. In addition to honey, he brought haoma, sap from the highlands plant drunk by Magi and others during sacrifice. He said it was deified, with powerful healing properties. I was dubious, but took it anyway because it made me comfortable, producing an almost trancelike state.

I had other visitors: some, like Artaxerxes and Atossa, whom I summoned; others, like Aspasia and Datis, who came of their own accord.

I had little energy to spend on convincing my son to take his daughter in matrimony. That was good, because little was needed. They honored my request to perform the ceremony in a small gathering at my bedside. Perhaps others beside Noah guessed my need to see the thing through, although I never hinted at what might be considered a lack of trust. I'd lived long enough to grasp the truth that, frequently among humans, the most well-laid plans fall apart, the most convincing promises dissolve, the staunchest resolves fade away.

Noah monitored my fever, which seemed to be gathering force from day to day. He felt my feet and hands, which were for a time hot and then turned cool, pale, even bluish. He nursed me through the days, and not by chance Aspasia took a turn with me through the evenings, spooning herself in my bed until morning to pass her warmth the length of my chilled body.

By the time Datis came to see me, my breathing had become shallow and rapid. My heartbeat had speeded up too. He asked Noah, who was attending me, to allow him a moment with me alone. I said we had no secrets that Noah couldn't hear. He was insistent.

"Well, Datis?" I said, my voice a faint echo of its healthy self.

"I've come to tell you something. It's as difficult for me as it's important for you. I was the source of those rumors."

"Oh, Datis." I moved lower in the bed, pulling the sheet up around my neck, too late to ward off the shock that had already penetrated.

"Aspasia had supplanted me. I couldn't stand it."

He stood looking down at me, tears rolling off his sharp cheeks, a face of misery. I closed my eyes and tried to clear my mind of the tempest this news had wrought. What seemed like minutes passed. I opened my eyes to see Datis' wet face above.

"Life's a puzzle. For years I wanted your love without the use of my power to demand it. Yet, so needy was I that I couldn't avoid making demands, and you, wrapped in these coils, could never feel free to love me as I dreamed of being loved. When Aspasia came to my bed, the deep grooves of our shared life eroded, releasing you to love me as long ago I had hoped you would. Too late. You know what awaits you when this story passes beyond that door?"

"I set out to ruin Aspasia. Looking at what I've done fills me with self-loathing. Nothing remains except to die with whatever small honor I can achieve through confession. That, and my apology." He sank to his knees, putting his head at bed level, face tilted up to stare, hollow-eyed, at me, like a dog riddled with guilt. I thought of Stateira. And the disparate emotions Aspasia could summon. My heart quickened. I extended my hand to rest on his head and pull it towards me. I couldn't bear the sight of his forlorn eyes.

"I have a plan. Listen carefully for my strength is ebbing. You will serve Aspasia until her death. You will also watch over and protect Noah. They are the crowning gems in my necklace. Upon Aspasia's death you will become a free man. As for what you did, I forgive you here and now. Your tale will not leave this room." I lifted my hand. Datis stood up. His face spoke to me, the message beyond the measure of words to convey. Our eyes locked for what seemed a lifetime. He smiled, then spun on his heels and was gone.

Noah returned, remaining with me until evening. Aspasia arrived to spend the night. While they were there, together, I summoned enough energy to broach the unspeakable subject on everyone's mind.

"I'm dying." They nodded.

"For weeks I've fought the idea of ceasing to be, of not being here to enjoy the rhythms of the seasons, the changes in the weather, the foods and flowers, the bees and other insects, the birds, the air, the breath of life, and, of course, the company of friends. I compared my age to that of others who have lived much longer. You, Noah, for example, but many others besides. Where's the fairness, I kept asking. I began to notice everything about me, big and little. Doing so made me fight the reality even more. For a time I found myself hoping that, when I ceased to be, whatever I became would possess a detailed memory of all the sweetness of my life here. It proved too much. I abandoned that hope as carrying the possibility of eternal torture. And, then, I stopped fighting altogether.

"Is it so terrible a thing to die? With your indulgence and my own, I skip over mistakes and disappointments. Never mind the measurements, for it's the striving that matters, and never mind the opinions of others, for when the last page is turned, it's one's own sense of things that counts."

Neither friend spoke. Neither departed. Aspasia joined me in bed, curling close, emitting a warmth I could no longer feel.

❧ EPILOGUE

THE SHADE DEPARTS

GREEK HISTORIANS WROTE FOR GREEK AUDIENCES and were guided by ambition and desire for praise from the universe they served. I don't begrudge their motives; indeed, I applaud them as eminently human. That universe, Greece as we know it, was to them the center of all things, the place around which the sun daily revolved. All else, including the Persian Empire, had significance only as it supported their Greco-centric world view.

In their day, the Greeks invented the field of history and then occupied it completely. I have returned to level the field, at least as it pertains to my brief lifespan and the Empire at that time. Every human life has value, its story worth telling. Historians record the stories of only a few while ignoring multitudes. It has always been thus. Moreover, the stories told by historians contain distortions of the truth, not only because truth, like quicksilver, is hard to hold in the palm of one's hand, but because historians, being alive and ambitious for praise, are themselves, consciously and unconsciously, affected by all that surrounds them, including, the needs of their immediate audience.

My account has been honest, insofar as any account by humans about humans can be honest. This is the story of my life, told from my perspective. Whether I was conflicted, a victim of self-interest, is for the reader to decide. As a Shade, I have no chance for earthly praise and glory, those being the brief rewards that the living gain from telling a wonderful story about themselves and having it believed. It is far too late to bask in the praise of others.

My purpose has been to set the record straight. This task was much more difficult than changing black to white. The "record" of a life as complex as mine doesn't lend itself to simple, declarative sentences. As the reader knows by now, my life was imperfectly lived. I pursued power at cost, justifying my behavior as necessary to meet the needs of Empire, to fulfill my destiny as Queen and Queen Mother.

When death came, and my earthly power ended, I retained pride in an Empire I thought would continue forever. With Alexander's destruction of that Empire, and Hades' insinuations about my role, even from the region of the Shades, in bringing it to an end, there was nothing left for me to salvage, except the story of my life. It remains for the reader to decide whether mine was a life worthy of my effort to explain and of the reader's to comprehend; whether, in the end, it was a life important enough to be remembered.

❧ PRINCIPAL CHARACTERS

FROM THE BIRTH OF PARYSATIS, MARCH 21, 444 BCE

Those marked * are recorded in history.

* Abrocomas, general under Artaxerxes II

* Alogune, concubine of Artaxerxes I, mother of Sogdianus

* Andia, concubine of Artaxerxes I, mother of Parysatis

* Amestris I, wife of Xerxes I

* Amestris II, daughter Darius II and Parysatis, wife of Teritouchmes

* Amestris III, daughter Artaxerxes II and Stateira

* Amorges, Persian rebel sought by Darius II

* Amyrtaeus, King of Egypt

* Amytis, daughter of Xerxes I and Amestris I

* Apollonides, a Greek from Cos, court physcian to Artaxerxes I

* Arbarius, commander of Sogdianus' cavalry

* Arsaces, son of Darius II and Parysatis, became Artaxerxes II

* Arsames, satrap of Egypt

* Arsites, brother of Ochus

* Artabanus, chief bodyguard to Xerxes I

* Artabates, chamberlain and scepter-bearer to Cyrus the Younger

* Artagerses, leader of Cadusians in army of Artaxerxes II

* Artapates, lover of Artaxerxes II and eunuch in his court

* Artaxerxes I, Great King from the 85th year of the Achaemenid Empire to its 126th year

* Artaxerxes II, Great King from the 146th year of the Achaemenid Empire to its 191st year

Artoxares, servant of Damaspia, and wife of Artaxerxes I

* Aspamithres, eunuch and lover of Queen Amestris I

* Aspasia, concubine and adviser to Cyrus the Younger

* Atossa I, daughter of Cyrus the Great, wife of Cambyses, Bardiya and Darius I, mother of Xerxes I

* Atossa II, daughter of Artaxerxes II and Stateira, wife of Artaxerxes II

* Bagopaios, son of Artaxerxes I and Andia, brother of Parysatis

* Bardiya, son of Cyrus the Great, Great King upon the death of Cambyses

* Cosmartidene, concubine of Artaxerxes I, mother of Ochus and Arsites

* Ctesias, a Greek from Cnidus, court physician to Artaxerxes II

* Cyrus the Younger, son of Darius II and Parysatis

* Damaspia, wife of Artaxerxes I, mother of Xerxes II

* Darius I, Great King from the 28th year of the Achaemenid Empire to its 64th year

* Darius II, Great King from the 127th year of the Achaemenid Empire to its 146th year

Datis, servant of Parysatis

* Fravartis, leader of rebel force in Media opposed to Darius I

Gigis, servant of Parysatis

* Hydarnes, commander of the Babylonian army, father of Stateira, Roxanne, and Teritushmes

* Macrochir, son of Xerxes I and Amestris, became Artaxerxes I

* Masabates, servant of Artaxerxes II

* Megabyzus, nobleman who married Amytis, the daughter of Xerxes I and sister of Artaxerxes I

* Menostanes, Chiliarch to Sogdianus

* Mithradata, servant of Cyrus the Younger

* Mithradates, soldier in army of Artaxerxes II

Noah, royal beekeeper at Persepolis

* Ochus, son of Artaxerxes I and Cosmartidene, became Darius II

* Orantas, first cousin of Artaxerxes II and Cyrus the Younger

* Ostanes, youngest son of Darius II and Parysatis

* Parysatis, daughter of Artaxerxes I and Andia

* Pharnabazus, satrap of Dascylium, general under Darius II and Artaxerxes II

* Pharnacyas, lieutenant and confidante of Sogdianus

* Roxanne, daughter of Hydarnes, sister of Stateira and Teritushmes

* Sogdianus, son of Artaxerxes I and Alogune, became Great King in the 127th year of the Achaemenid Empire

* Stateira, daughter of Hydarnes, wife of Artaxerxes II

* Syennesis, tyrant of Cilicia

* Teritushmes, son of Hydarnes, brother of Stateira and Roxanne, husband of Amestris II

* Themistocles, Greek general exiled from Athens and granted sanctuary in Persia by Artaxerxes I

* Timosa, servant of Stateira

* Tiradates, servant of Artaxerxes II

* Tissaphernes, satrap of Sardis, general under Darius II and Artaxerxes II

  Udusana, childhood friend of Parysatis

* Vidarna, one of seven conspirators bringing Darius I to power

* Xerxes I, Great King from the 64th year of the Achaemenid Empire to its 85th year

* Xerxes II, Great King for 45 days in the 127th year of the Achaemenid Empire

SELECTED BRANCHES OF THE ACHAEMENID EMPIRE'S FAMILY TREE

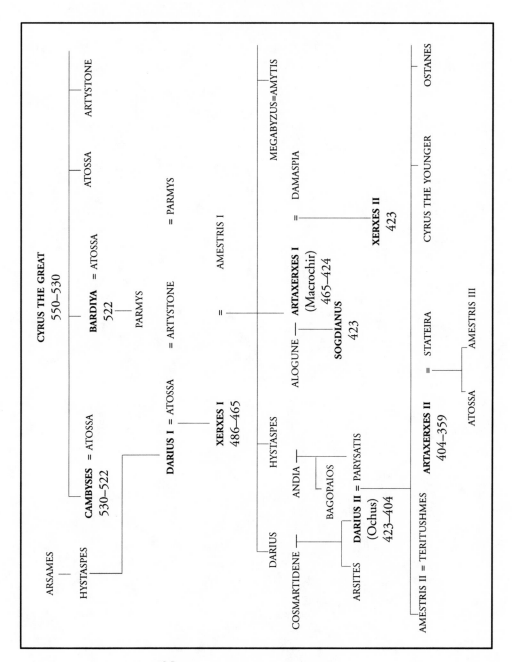

Notes:
1. Formal marriage designated by =
2. Concubine designated by —
3. King designated by bold type
4. Dates of reign Before Common Era

❧ SELECTED BIBLIOGRAPHY

 Parysatis: Return of the Shade is a work of imagination. However, it was written within a framework of knowledge about the time, place, and people involved in the story. It accepts the events of Parysatis' life asserted by the historians of the time to weave an interpretative account that is at once plausible and true to the character of this great Queen and Queen Mother of the Persian Empire. The listing below includes, in alphabetical order, the most important historical and other references relied upon to align the narrative with the large body of relevant scholarship.

Aeschylus, *The Persians*, trans. Vellacott, P. 1961. Penquin Books.

Aelian, *Historical Miscellany,* trans. Wilson, N.G. 1997. Loeb Classical Library, Harvard University Press.

Athenaeus, *The Deipnosophists,* trans. Gulick, C. B. 2002. Loeb Classical Library, Harvard University Press.

Briant, P., *From Cyrus to Alexander: A History of the Persian Empire*, trans. Daniels, P.T. 2002. Eisenbrauns.

Brosius, M., *Women in Ancient Persia.* 1996. Oxford (Clarendon Paperbacks).

Curtis, J. and Tallis, N., *Forgotten Empire: The World of Ancient Persia.* 2005. The British Museum Press.

Diodorus Siculus: Library of History, Volume VI, Books 14-15.19, trans. Welles, C.B. 1954. Loeb Classical Library, Harvard University Press.

Fraser, H. M., *Beekeeping in Antiquity.* 1931. University of London Press Ltd.

Grottanelli, C. and Milano, L., *Food and Identity in the Ancient World* (*History of the Ancient Near East/Studies–Vol. IX*). 2004. S.A.R.G.O.N.

Herodotus, (John Marincola). *The Histories,* trans. De Selincourt, A. 1996. Penguin Books.

Hobhouse, P., *Gardens of Persia.* 2003. Kales Press.

Hubbell, S., *A Book of Bees.* 1988. Houghton Mifflin Company (Mariner).

Maeterlinck, M., *The Life of the Bee,* trans. Alfred Sutro. 1903. Dodd, Mead & Company.

Olmstead, A.T., *History of the Persian Empire.* 1948. The University of Chicago Press.

Pliny the Elder, *Natural History: A Selection,* trans. Healy, J.F. 2004. Penguin Books.

Plutarch, *Lives of Illlustrious Men,* Vol. III, trans. Dryden, J. 1895. Lovell, Coryell & Company, New York.

Preston, C., *Bee.* 2006. Reaktion Books.

Teale, E.W., *The Golden Throng, A Book About Bee.* 1943. Museum Press Ltd.

Thucydides, *The Peloponnesian War.* 1996. The Landmark Thucydides, ed. Strassler, R. B., trans. Crawley, R., Free Press.

Vidal, G., *Creation.* 2002. Vintage International.

Xenophon, *Anabasis,* trans. Brownson. 1998. C.L., Loeb Classical Library, Harvard University Press.

ABOUT THE AUTHOR

Bevis Longstreth is a graduate of Princeton University and the Harvard Law School. From 1981–84, he served as a Commissioner of the Securities and Exchange Commission. In 1993, he retired as a senior partner in the New York City law firm of Debevoise & Plimpton, where he had practiced since graduating from law school. Since retiring, he has taught at Columbia Law School and pursued other interests, among which was writing.

Over his professional career he has often spoken, and written many articles. His books include two on finance, corporate behavior, and the law. His first novel, *Spindle and Bow*, was inspired by the Pazyryk, the world's oldest known pile carpet. Discovered in a Siberian tomb in 1949, this textile dates to the 5th century BCE. It now hangs in the Hermitage in St. Petersburg, Russia.

Mr. Longstreth's imagined biography of Parysatis, *Return of the Shade*, is his second novel. In it, this exceptional Queen and Queen Mother of ancient Persia speaks of her life and times, refuting the Greek historians in the course of revealing a compelling story of a formidable woman worth knowing.